I0822803

DEATH UNEXPECTED

DEATH UNEXPECTED

Galen Barbour

ARPress
45 Dan Road Suite 5
Canton MA 02021

Hotline:1(888) 821-0229
Fax:1(508) 545-7580

Ordering Information:
Quantity sales. Special discounts are available on quantity purchases by corporations, associations, and others. For details, contact the publisher at the address above.

Printed in the United States of America.

ISBN-13:	Paperback	979-8-89356-512-6
	eBook	979-8-89356-514-0
	Hardback	979-8-89356-513-3

Library of Congress Control Number: 2024902395

Other Books by G. L. Barbour

Academic

Quality in the Veterans Health Administration
Redefining a Public Health System

Fiction

The Ron Looney Series

One, Two, Three Times a Murder
A Twisted Death
A Researched Death
Naked Death
Alibi for Death

Other

Montana in the Rearview Mirror

Contents

Prologue

Monday, March 8

The rain was steady but not hard and in the early morning darkness the streaks of water were illuminated in flashes by the lights from the Emergency Room entrance. The shadowy figure in the long coat and large hat standing in the dark just outside the lighted area was almost opaque. As a group of people started to enter the Emergency entrance together, the shadow joined and slipped to the rear of the waiting area and into the toilet at the far end of the room. Minutes later, minus the long coat and full brimmed hat, the figure slipped through a rear door into the old hospital and entered a stairwell.

After gaining the third floor landing, the shadow quietly entered into the far end of the ward and stood quietly, watching the nursing station at the other end of the hall. Satisfied there was no one in the hall or observing from the station, the shadow eased into one of the rooms on the left side, staying away from the windows on the right side of the hall.

Three minutes later the shadow reappeared and silently moved back down the hall and down the stairs, slipping into the Emergency waiting area and again entering the toilet. Moments later a figure in a long coat wearing a large brimmed hat exited the toilet and left the Emergency Room. The clerk was busy with people at the front desk. The large clock on the wall over the Reception area read 0548 on Monday, March 8.

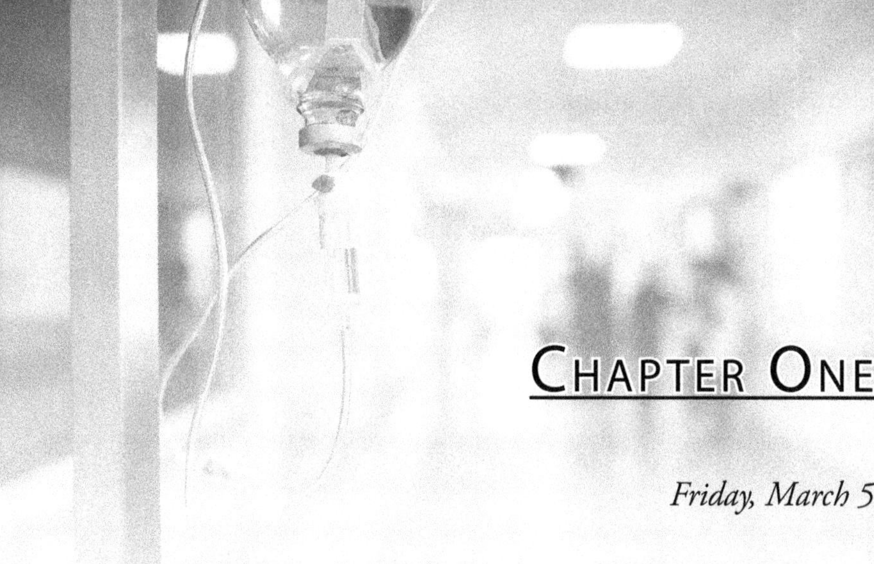

Chapter One

Friday, March 5

"Ms. Harding?"

"Yes sir?"

"Would you take these files on the Geterman merger and organize them?"

"Yes sir."

Patricia Harding took the files to her desk in the cubicle just past the junior partner's office and put them on the left hand corner. Left hand corner is the 'in' box and she intended to work the files from left to right. She sat in her Herman Miller chair and thought, briefly, how lucky she was to have this paralegal job. She had been working here at Tillson and Martin for nearly three years and she felt respected and highly thought of by the partners. Of course, that couldn't be said of all the other paralegals. But there's just no accounting for some people; at least that's what her mother used to say.

Further, this would really fit in well with her long-range plans. As that thought crossed her mind, she smiled and looked at the screen saver on her computer. It showed a panorama of the desert near Four Corners – a place of quietude, still air and low humidity. Being there would also fit in with her long-range plans.

The lawyers in the firm trust her work. She had been given some of the more 'desirable' cases to work on several times – especially by that one associate. And at least one of the partners has been supportive of her newfound desire to go to law school herself. Things were working out for her here at the firm.

Patricia had actually discussed this with her friend Elaine, at lunch. "I'm really thinking about law school," she said after the first bite of her salad.

"Good for you. When?"

"Well, that's the thing. I don't think we have the money right now."

"Can't you get a loan?"

"Sure, if we want to be in debt for the rest of our lives."

"What about your folks?"

"They might help but Benjie is another issue."

"Because?"

"Well, he isn't working and we're living entirely on my income."

"But, he's looking isn't he?"

"Sure. But you and I both know that market has passed him by. He would have to go get a degree himself to get back in the game."

"Why isn't he doing that?"

"Still the money, Elaine. Even at the Cincy State campus here, the cost is over our head." In her head she briefly thought of the many different times she and her husband had come to that topic over the past few months.

"So, what are you gonna do?" Elaine pressed.

"I'm actually working on something. But the safer and better way would be to get Benjie back in the ranks of the employed – even if it's not the programming job he wants right now.

"So, doesn't he grasp that?"

"Well, we can't really talk about it. He keeps bringing up having kids, too."

"Is he not paying attention?"

"Really."

"I mean, unless he can get a job, there's no way you guys can afford kids right?"

Patricia thought of the last conversation she had had with Benjie on that topic. They had been finishing breakfast just that morning and he was excited about a plan for a baby crib he had seen on the Internet the night before. Benjie was convinced that he could make the crib by himself and save considerable money. Patricia had tried to talk him out of the project because their finances were too cramped to take on the unneeded crib construction and Benjie had looked like she had hit him in the face.

"Unneeded! How can you say 'unneeded'? Do you expect me to allow our baby to sleep on the floor?" Patricia had seen how irrational he was and tried to walk the conversation back by saying, 'Really, Honey, there will be plenty of time for you to do that when I am actually pregnant. We just don't have the money right now."

Benjie responded, "That just keeps coming up, doesn't it? We don't have the money for this or that – and it's because I don't have a job, right?" And he slammed his fist on the tabletop and stormed out of the room shouting, "I'm looking every day. Every damn day! It's gonna happen. But in the meantime, I just wanted to do something for us, you know?" He was still closed in the bathroom when she left for work.

"I have tried to tell him that but he just says, 'I'm gonna get a job pretty soon, I know it.' And then we're back at square one," Patricia said to Elaine. They fell silent and worked on their food for a few moments.

"Have you talked with the partners?" Elaine asked.

"Yes. Well, with Mr. Hall. He thinks I should do it – go to law school – but he doesn't know about our finances."

"Do you think the firm would help you?"

"I don't know why. It's not like I could pay them back or anything soon." Another period of silence.

"You going to eat that?" asked Elaine.

"You know I never eat the pickle. Take it."

Patricia had been just picking at her pasta salad and Elaine knew that meant she didn't want to continue this line of conversation, so she asked about whether they should get into the office pool on March Madness. Patricia had actually won a little money last year and maybe she could do that again.

They lingered over dessert, splitting an apple turnover with ice cream. Then they walked back to the Starbucks across the street from the office and Patricia ordered a macchiato to take back to her desk.

And now she was just back from lunch – the pasta salad was really quite good – and would like to put her feet up on the desk for a brief spell but she knows that would not be a good example of the type of employee she wants to be. So she sips at her macchiato and reaches for the first file. Before opening the file, Patricia looks again at the screen saver and smiles to herself about her plans involving the Four Corners.

About thirty minutes later, Elaine Johnson in the next cubicle heard a brief cry and the sound of something hitting the floor as files went tumbling around. She stood, peeked over the cubicle wall and saw Patricia lying on the floor beside her desk with files scattered all around over and under her.

"Help, something's happened," she hollered to the room as she scurried around the to enter Patricia's cubicle but when she got there all she did was stand and stare.

Other people came running and started bending over Patricia and calling her name, "Pat! Pat! Can you hear me?"

"Call 911!" someone yelled and three people grabbed at their phones.

Patricia lay still and unmoving with short gasps of breath and her co-workers stood around and watched while one of them bent over and lifted her head and put his jacket underneath for support. Two of the women crouched nearby and rubbed her hands and someone else started picking up all the files and straightening them on the desktop and knocked over the cup of macchiato. That led to several cries of dismay and more scrambling around, this time for towels to mop up the mess.

The legal staff were helpless in the face of a medical emergency. They had some minimal knowledge of the Heimlich maneuver but each of them felt this was obviously not a situation that called for such intervention.

They were feeling more and more agitated as they stood around doing nothing; the two women tried again to rouse Patricia with hand rubbing and calling her name but there was no response. The women looked up and around at the coworkers hoping someone had a better idea.

And then the EMTs arrived and began their assessment. They easily moved everyone back and began checking Patricia's vital signs.

"Anyone know her medical history?" asked one.

No one answered.

"Is she diabetic?" asked the lead EMT, looking up and making eye contact with each pf the people standing around their fallen coworker.

"I don't think so," someone said.

"Has she eaten recently?" the Tech asked, zeroing in on the speaker.

"Yes, we were at lunch together." Elaine volunteered.

"Does she take any medications?" The EMT shifted his attention to the new source of information.

No one knew.

"Is she epileptic?"

No one knew. They had all worked together for three years, had lunch and coffee together and no one knew anything about her medical history - or really anything about her outside of work. They looked at each other, expecting one of them to know the answers to these questions. But no one did. Elaine slumped back against the desk feeling like she had betrayed her friend. She remembered times she had asked Patricia about her earlier life and Patricia had dodged the issue but Elaine had not pushed in follow-up. Now she thought, "I don't know how to help her!"

The EMTs pushed the observers back some more and slipped a couple of ECG leads on her chest and arms and legs.

"Looks like VT" said one, looking at the monitor.

"I'm ready to shock," said the other.

They shocked her. Twice, and then one said, "OK. Back to normal sinus. Let's get her to New City." And they pulled out their gurney, unfolded it and lifted her up on it, quickly strapping her small body on the frame and then, almost without looking, picked up all their gear and equipment and headed for the door.

The space around Patricia's desk was littered with pages from some of the files and with wet and dry towels. The workers stood around for another minute just staring at the now empty space before someone said, "Anyone know how to call her husband?"

Chapter Two

Friday, March 5

They came through the door calling out information to the ED staff that sprang up to assist. "Twenty-eight year old white female. Passed out at work. V Tach on first exam. Shocked twice to NSR. BP 100 palp, pulse 80."

Together the Staff and EMTs wheeled the gurney into an empty treatment room and began moving Patricia to the examining table.

"What else do we know?" asked the resident.

"Nothing else. She's apparently not diabetic." The resident noted the intravenous line in the left forearm. "Any seizure activity?"

"Nope. And no incontinence."

"OK. Any family?"

"No one came with us."

"What's her name?"

"Patricia . . .ah, Harding it says here. She's never spoken to us."

"Patricia. Patricia! Can you hear me?" ask one of the residents, leaning over her face and speaking more loudly than needed. He pulled up her eyelid and said, "Rolled up. Can't see pupils."

"Check corneal reflex," said someone."

"OK. Give me a Q-tip. . . . reflex OK. And now I can see pupils. Mid and reactive."

"Doll's eye?"

"Negative."

Meanwhile the nurses quickly stripped off Patricia's clothes, covered her with a warm blanket and put cardiac electrodes on her chest and arms and a blood pressure cuff on her right arm.

"I got a weak systolic at 90." Called one of the nurses.

"Turn that fluid up" said the resident.

"She's back in V Tach," said another resident looking at the monitor.

"She's unstable. Let's shock."

"We shocked her twice at the site" said one of EMTs, as they were packing to leave.

"Ready."

"Clear." The shock arched Patricia's back.

"She's back."

"What does that trace look like? Why's she jumping in and out of tach?" asked one doctor.

"This doesn't look right. Look at that QT." said another one.

"Do we have labs yet?" The Chief Resident spoke this to the room in general.

"Drawn and sent." Answered one of the medical students.

"Can I have some magnesium sulfate?" asked the physician.

"How much do you want, doctor?" asked the medication nurse as she opened the drawer on the crash cart.

"Put two amps in 250 of normal saline and start it running at 5 milliliters a minute for 10 minutes. Tell me when that's in."

"Two amps mag sulfate in 250 saline at 10 per minute. Coming."

Two minutes later the magnesium was running and over the next 15 minutes Patricia's heart rate slowed and her blood pressure rose but she did not awaken.

"What's the deal on her being out?" asked the Chief Resident.

"No clue. You heard the same thing I did."

"Check her again."

No abnormal neurological signs were noted.

"Did she hit her head?"

"No bruises or bumps. They said she went down from a chair."

"At least she's stable now. Leave that Mag running and chase it with a banana bag. Let's get her down to CT."

Everyone recognized that the immediate crisis had passed; the patient now seemed stable as far as the heart issues and the most important question was centered on the question of why she was still comatose. The nurses surrounded her and lifted her to a gurney for transport. One secured her to the gurney with a chest strap and another strap across the thighs. Another one placed another warm blanket on her and the two of them started for the rear door into the service hall pushing the gurney.

"Hey, my wife was sent here." The speaker was a young man, about 30, dressed in khakis and a short-sleeved sport shirt. He was wearing loafers with no socks.

"What's her name, sir?" asked the receptionist at the desk

"Patty. Patty Harding. They said she passed out at work."

"Oh, yes. She came through the Emergency entrance. The doctors are in with her now."

"Where? I gotta be there." Having said that, he began moving toward the doors behind the receptionist desk that led in the treatment areas. "Is she back here?"

"Sir, just wait right here."

"No. I gotta be there!" But he stopped at the door and only peered through the glass window.

"Sir, I will get Security if you don't wait right here. I'll go see what's happening."

"I just want to know what's going on."

"I understand, sir. Now stay right here in the waiting area. I'll be right back." The man hesitated and then backed away from the door and walked to one of the empty chairs and sat down.

The receptionist pushed through the doors and was only gone for a minute; she returned with one of the nurses from the ED and pointed at the man.

The nurse came over to him and placed her hand on his shoulder. "Mr. Harding?" she asked with sympathy in her voice.

"Huh? Oh, yeah. I'm Benjie."

"We have your wife in the back and we are working on her right now. She's stable for right now."

"What do you mean, 'right now'?"

"Well, we aren't sure what happened and we're still running some tests."

"Omigod. What happened? Is she alright?" this came as he suddenly stood up and looked toward the doorway into the ED.

"As I said, she's stable and we're running some more tests. If you'll just sit here I can get one of the doctors to talk to you. Would you like that?"

"Yeah. Sure. Anything." And Benjie slowly resumed his seat.

The nurse nodded to him and walked back to the receptionist desk and said something to the woman behind the desk. They both turned and looked at Mr. Harding and then the nurse went through the doors into the treatment area.

The next 10 minutes passed very slowly for Benjie Harding. He was 30 years old but doesn't have the look of a mature individual. His clothes were a little baggy on him and the shirt is rumpled. He clearly had trouble sitting quietly; his feet were moving constantly and every minute or so he shifted around in the chair. He didn't appear to know what to do with his hands – sometimes they were in his pockets, sometimes on top of his head and other times tapping on the arms of the chair. After about eight minutes he got up suddenly and started toward the reception desk. The receptionist raised her head and looked directly at him without a smile and he stopped walking, then turned and walked quickly toward the back of the room where he started to examine a piece of art work on the wall.

Then the nurse returned with one of the resident physicians who introduced himself, and asked, "Has your wife been sick lately?"

"What? No, she's been fine."

"Has she ever passed out like this before?"

"Passed out? Is that what happened? No, she's always healthy. She eats right."

"Do you know what happened today at work?"

"No. I wasn't there. I mean I was at home."

"We think she may have a head injury."

"Omigod, that's bad, isn't it? Is that bad?"

'We're going to get a CAT scan on her head right now. I'll let you know in a few minutes."

"Can I see her?"

"She's already on the way to the scan. Just wait out here and I'll let you know when we get the results."

"OK."

Benjie paced all around the waiting area. He tried to get a soda from the vending machine but it took his money without dispensing a can. He kicked the machine and the receptionist looked up sharply at him and pointed to the chairs. He resumed his original seat and put his head in his hands. And his feet and hands kept moving.

Thirty minutes later the resident returned to the waiting area and walked over to Benjie. "Mr. Harding? I have some news about your wife."

The CT scan of her head was normal; no bleeding and no obvious cause for the stupor. She continued to be stable with a good blood pressure and pulse and the tachycardia had not returned. The resident now had some of the initial laboratory results and tells Benjie that Patricia had a low potassium level when she came in. Benjie was puzzled by this because "she always eats well and is always after me to eat better." Nonetheless, she would be admitted to the hospital, Ward 3-C, and would be on monitors for her heart and blood pressure. The resident explained to Benjie that the medical plan was to wait and see when she would wake up. He also explained why Patricia was still in the Emergency Department by saying, "We're just holding her here until a bed clears out."

"Is she gonna be alright?" asks Benjie

"She certainly should," said the resident. "I imagine she'll wake up tomorrow and everything will be all right."

"Thanks, doc. Can I see her now?"

"Sure, you can go sit with her until they move her upstairs."

"Thanks."

Chapter Three

Friday, March 5

Jimmie Harper was really tired. He had been at the hospital since early that morning making his intern rounds, following up on patients with the attending, running down some radiology and laboratory results – and skipping lunch. He knew he was in the 'downhill' part of the internship but that was of little encouragement to him when he heard of still another admission to his service – at 7:35 that night. He had two other admissions to see already, that heart attack guy and the fellow with pneumonia. Now they give him this young one who passed out at work.

Really not fair, he thought. Some of these people could probably be treated just as well at home – certainly the pneumonia guy, probably. Well, he hadn't seen him yet but that was sure possible.

Jimmie made a couple of notes on the index cards he held. Those cards held all the necessary information on the people admitted to his service. He had jotted down some particulars when he got the call from the Emergency Department resident notifying him of the admissions. Age, diagnosis, status of their vital signs and brief information about the treatment already delivered. All noted on the card. Now all he had to do was a complete history and physical on each of them and write up their orders for the night. He figured that was going to take him a little more than an hour on each of them – "that'll be close to 11:00 PM by then", he thought. And he knew that's only if he doesn't get called for anything else.

The man with the heart attack was in the Coronary Care Unit and Jimmie went there first. Tired as he was, being in the CCU usually made him perk up. The lights and the activity and the nurses moving around gave the Unit a feeling of suppressed urgency and efficiency. Jimmie liked that feeling. He thought of it like a military ship moving quietly on its mission with all hands alert.

He finished his history and physical in less than an hour. Surprisingly, the man didn't have much in the way of medical history. As he wrote orders for the night, Jimmie thought he just might get through it all early.

But the man with the pneumonia ate up all the extra time and then some. He was not so old in years but he certainly was in 'cell cycles' – he appeared much older than his stated 60 years and he was so short of breath that every answer to Jimmie's questions took twice as long as they should. Pneumonia as a friend of the elderly, indeed. These two weren't getting along at all. Every other breath brought a cough and every third cough became a spasm of mucus producing rattling – Jimmie drew some blood cultures and started an i.v. in order to give some antibiotics. He was tired and only semi-efficient.

And then, after a quick PowerBar, he stood at Patricia's bedside and realized he wouldn't be taking an elaborate history after all. She lay there quietly with very little response when he called her name or shook her. She was young and likely had no serious medical history anyway, he thought. Banged her head and tomorrow will be all "what happened?" and "How did I get here?". He checked her monitors and then noted the sticky note pinned on the front of the monitor: "Lab called" it read, "K is 2.6"

What? Nobody mentioned this. She was passed to him from the ED as a young woman who fainted at work. Now he looked more closely at the ED record.

"What? V. Tach? And shocked twice at work?"

Jimmie stepped out to the Nurses' station and called the lab – it was almost 11:00 and he knew the shift might be changing. But he got someone on the third ring. When was the potassium level drawn? The phone was put down and he waited another two minutes before the technician came back and said, "Looks like they drew it in the ED."

Cripes, that was hours ago, Jimmie thought as he pulled out his Washington Manual and sat down to calculate her deficit.

Thirty minutes later, his calculations done twice and checked, he pulled out the Doctor's Order Sheet and began writing. At least he had seven hours to get some potassium in her and make some repairs before the morning blood draw. He made sure that the morning potassium level he ordered was STAT and then he dragged himself off to the call rooms.

And he had missed supper, too.

Chapter Four

Saturday, March 6

On Saturday morning Patricia did not appear to have changed clinically. She might have been rousable but even that was a very minimal change and she didn't talk or add any history to her present illness. Her husband, Benjie, had been at the bedside all night – except when he was pestering the nursing staff about one or another question or minutia of change in the readings on her monitors.

Jimmie Harper came around about 0900 and noted in her chart the lack of change. He came back again when the morning laboratory results were reported – Patricia's serum potassium level is 'critically low' at 3.2.

Jimmie wondered, in passing, where all the potassium has gone that had already been given to her and decided he would just give her some more. He looked at the heart tracing on the monitor and then went to the nursing station and ordered that her potassium infusion be continued at 10 milliequivalents per hour. "That ought to do it," he thought and actually got all the way to the elevators before considering that he might do something else. He went back to the nurse's station and ordered another potassium measurement at 4:00PM and added a note to call the intern on call with the results.

Then he went back to the elevator and went hunting for the Saturday intern to check out. He found her up on one of the medical wards.

"Hey, Sally, I'm getting ready to leave. You got a second for check-out?"

"Sure. Jose just finished."

"There's really only three to think about. One's in the CCU, documented STEMI. Pressure is stable, pain free and ate his breakfast. And there's an old guy with bad pneumonia, big infiltrate, on three antibiotics but gases are stable."

"The other?"

"This girl on 3C with V tach and torsade with hypokalemia."

"On replacement, right?"

"Right . . . but it was still only 3.2 this morning. I'm giving her additional K and ordered a repeat lab at 4 to be called to you. Check on that will you?

"Sure."

They exchanged names and some cards and Jimmie headed back to the elevators. His interest was no longer on the finer points of medical diagnosis and treatment; he was focused on getting a Big Breakfast and into his own bed.

Meantime Benjie Harding was making a name – or at least a reputation – for himself on 3C. He had a permanent chair next to Patricia's bed. The chair was padded and could recline down to almost horizontal if he wanted it to. A nice place to rest and relax and even take a nap. But, of course, Benjie spent little time actually in the chair. He walked the floor of the room and up and down the hall like he was in training for a walk-a-thon. Even when he confined himself to the room, he was restless and almost constantly in motion. Sitting in the chair his feet and legs were either pumping up and down or flapping from side to side. And his hands were always busy with something, fiddling with one of the intravenous lines, tapping on the arms of the chair or rubbing his face. The nurses said they got nervous by just being around him.

But what most annoyed the nursing staff were Benjie's questions. He would appear at the nursing station several times an hour to ask about something regarding her care – what were the medications she was receiving, was the intravenous running at the right rate, what was the meaning of the variation in her heart rate on the monitor? Would any of this affect their plans to have children? Initially the nurses tried to be understanding and give him answers that would calm him down and let him return to the room. Too often, though, giving answers seemed only to draw more questions until one or another of them would have to say, "I have to go take care of other patients now" and just walk away from him.

Nursing staff slowly became evasive, both in their answers and in their willingness to make eye contact with him as he approached the Nurses Station. By suppertime, no one was willing to talk to him and a quiet conversation in the lounge came to the obvious conclusion that someone needed to 'send the boy home.' Thereafter, the focus of discussion was on who would draw that short straw.

Sally Pedersen got the call about Patricia's potassium level just before 6:00 PM. She was sitting in her call room with her shoes off, reading the previous week's *New England Journal of Medicine*. She had put the idea of the low potassium in the back of her head – she did not need to put it on her 'reminder list' because she knew the laboratory would call her with the results. Nonetheless, when the call came she was momentarily lost as to why she was being notified. Who was this patient? But it all quickly came back and she remembered the conversation with Jimmie: "young woman, hypokalemia, v. tach, getting replacement" and the potassium at 4:00 PM was? What? Only 3.3?

She said thanks to the technician for calling and then she sat up at the small desk in the call room and pulled out her notes and began to do a little figuring. And it did not take her long before she looked up and asked, of no one in particular, "Where did it all go?"

After looking at the wall in the room for a short while and getting no answer, Sally pulled out her phone. Her most recent attending had given her his cell number to call if she ever had questions and the question in her head was right up his alley. He answered on the third ring.

"Dr. Donaldson."

"Sir, it's Sally Pedersen."

"Hey, Sally, what's going on?"

"I've got a patient here with funny electrolytes and I need a little guidance."

"OK. Tell me what you have."

"It's a 28 year old female who presented Friday evening with v. tach after passing out at work. She went into torsade and converted after getting some magnesium but then we found out she was hypokalemic, too."

"How low?"

"Well, it appears that she was at 2.6 in the ED but nobody saw that until she got to the ward. She got about 70 milliequivalents overnight and was 3.2 this morning.

"How much does she weigh?"

"112 pounds . . . 51 kilos."

"What else?

"Well, now she's gotten another 70 and only got up 3.3"

"Is she alkalemic?"

"No, gases and bicarb are normal."

"What did you calculate her deficit to be?

"Problem is I don't know if this is acute or chronic."

"So . . .?"

"Well, if it's acute her deficit may be less than 100."

"But . . .?"

"But if this is chronic, she may be down 400 or more."

"Have you just answered your own question, Sally?"

"Now don't go all Socrates on me, Dr. Donaldson. I need to understand whether I should be pumping more potassium into her tonight."

"Look, Sally. I've got six burgers on the grill and it looks like it's going to start raining here pretty soon. Let's get to your bottom line."

"OK. What do I do?"

"Wrong question. Ask instead, 'why didn't her serum potassium rise more than it did with 140 milliequivalents going in?"

"That's what I thought I was asking you."

"You know this." Long pause. "Think of the bathtub."

"OK. So, more in than out and the level rises . . . or . . . wait! You mean there may be more going out?"

"Do you have a urine potassium?"

"No. At least I didn't see it."

"Does she take diuretics?"

"I don't know. It wasn't mentioned. I'll ask the husband."

"Does she eat a lot of licorice?"

"What? I don't know that either. What's that got to do with it?"

"Look it up. Is she bulimic?"

"I don't know that, either."

"So, you need more information but you have an idea what needs to be done."

“I guess so. If she’s really losing it, I need to be giving her even more.”

“Right. Now check your idea with a urine potassium level.”

“OK. Thanks.”

“Good luck. And let me know what you find.”

“Sure.”

As she hung up the phone, Sally smiled to herself. Donaldson had dragged the answer out of her instead of just brushing her off or ‘simply’ telling her what to do. She actually knew all that information - except for the thing about the licorice. Feeling much better about herself, and with far less self-doubt than she experienced a half-hour before, she left the Call Room and headed for the ward to see Patricia’s husband, promising herself to read up on the licorice very soon.

Chapter Five

Saturday, March 6

Benjie was siting bedside Patricia's bed. He had held her hand for quite some time but after realizing that she did not respond to him calling her name or squeezing her hand he just sat with his hands in his lap. He would watch her breathing for several minutes and then would turn and watch the squiggly lines of the monitors run across the screen – wondering what they were conveying and whether they indicated his wife would soon be better – or not.

There was a knock on the door and someone called, "Mr. Harding?"

"Yes."

The door pushed open and Sally entered wearing the ubiquitous scrub suit that interns wore on call and her white coat differentiating her from one of the nurses. The scrubs were wrinkled because interns and residents slept in them – allowing them both to get in bed and back out if called with a minimum of time expenditure. Many of the staff doctors referred to the clothing as 'pajamas' and expected the house staff to be better dressed; this was often the rule during the regular hours but not after 5:00 PM.

"Mr. Harding, I'm Doctor Pedersen."

"What's wrong?

"Oh, nothing's wrong. I just came by to check on your wife. And ask you some more questions."

"Why's that? Don't you know what happened to her?"

"I'm the doctor on call tonight. I've read her chart and I wanted to see how she was doing. That's all."

"Oh. OK." Benjie seemed pleased about this extra attention and he sat down and scooted his chair slightly away from the bedside as Sally moved over there.

Sally spent a minute or two holding Patricia's hand, feeling her pulse and opening each eyelid. She listened to her heart and the lungs in the front of the chest and then opened her mouth and placed a tongue blade on her tongue and tried to get a good look at her back teeth.

"What're you doing?" asked Benjie. "Nobody else ever looked at the back of her throat like that."

"Mr. Harding, does your wife take any medications?"

"What do you mean?"

"Prescription medicines."

"Like what?"

"Well, particularly we were wondering if she might be taking a diuretic."

"What's that?"

"Commonly known as a 'water pill'"

"I don't know anything about that."

"Would you know if she were taking something like that?

"Well, yeah, probably." He frowned and wondered whether his wife would have had a secret like that from him. "I mean, we have only the one bathroom."

Sally looked at Benjie with a questioning look in her eye; she wasn't sure about his meaning until Benjie clarified, "Like, we only have one medicine cabinet and I keep toothpaste in there."

"So, you would have seen any prescription medications?"

"Yeah. Like that."

"I see." Sally then changed her line of questioning to fill in some gaps in the medical history. "Are you aware of your wife having any other medical problems?"

"Like what? I mean, like I told the other doctors, she was fine and all."

"Did she seem concerned about her weight?"

"Not really. I mean she always ate real good – and scolded me about eating too much meat and fat." As he said this Benjie grabbed his mildly overweight belly fat with both hands and pinched a big roll to show Sally.

"Did she ever indicate that she thought she was fat?"

"What? No. I mean, look at her, she's not fat."

"Did she like to eat licorice?" Sally didn't feel comfortable about asking this question because she had not yet looked up the relation of licorice intake to potassium loss but she was by then fairly certain that Benjie wouldn't question her too deeply about it.

"Licorice? Ick, no, we both hate it."

"Are you aware of any times when she might have vomited after eating?" Sally intended this question to be along the same lines but Benjie clearly thought she was chasing another possibility.

"Yeah, of course."

"Of course?" Sally asked, wonderingly. Sometimes using different questions will get at a truth that is stubbornly resisted when responding to other questions. "Tell me about those times."

"Well it was only that once. We had some bad Chinese and we both puked most of the night." Benjie seemed proud to have remembered something that he could answer positively and help the doctors with his wife's care.

Sally tried not to be deflated. "Were there any other times?"

"Nope. We both have kinda like iron stomachs."

"How about diarrhea? Did Patricia ever have diarrhea or maybe frequent bowel movements?

"Well, I wasn't around her all day but there was nothing like that when we were at home."

Now Sally did feel disappointed. She had so hoped to get a scoop on why this apparently healthy young woman suddenly tried to fall off the edge of the earth. But she was just as puzzled now as everyone else. She paused and looked at the urine bag hanging on the lower rung of the side rail and took a sample tube from her pocket and knelt at the bag to obtain an aliquot for testing. As she did so, Benjie began peppering her with questions.

"What are you doing there? Do you think there's something wrong with her kidneys? Is she gonna be all right?"

"I'm just taking a sample of her urine to test for potassium."

"Why? Do you know something about her?

"Yes, we know that her body is low on potassium and we are not sure why. It could be that it's in her urine."

"Why didn't anybody tell me this?" Benjie looked alarmed and began pacing around the room. Once Again, Sally had the idea that she may have stumbled upon an important hint to Patricia's condition.

"Why is that important, Mr. Harding?" she asked capping the tube and rising from the bedside.

"What? Why is that important? Because it has something to do with her being out like this and nobody told me?" Benjie seemed amazed at the question.

"Does a low potassium level mean something to you, Mr. Harding?"

"No. I mean, not really. I don't even know what that is. But its like somebody shoulda told me what was wrong."

"I see."

"I mean, like if it was your wife, or . . . you know what I mean, you'd want to know what was wrong, wouldn't you?"

"Of course I would." Sally indicated that Benjie should sit back down and then she said, "Let me tell you what we do know."

She explained briefly that a low potassium level was one reason for the heart rhythm disturbance that was probably what had caused Patricia to have the abnormal heart rhythm and to pass out at work and it was only discovered after the emergency of her arrhythmia was stabilized and attention was directed to her comatose state. Even now the intravenous fluids were intended to replenish her levels but did not seem to be effective and other doctors consulting on her case suggested she might be losing it in her urine, hence the sample tube.

During that 7-minute explanation Benjie visibly calmed himself and was only bouncing his heels up and down a little when she finished. "Thanks, doc," he said, "I guess that helps."

"All right then. I'm going to take this down to the lab." Sally let herself out leaving Benjie staring at his wife motionless on the bed, just as he had been when she entered.

Sally went back to the Nurse's Station and retrieved Patricia's accession number. She grabbed a miscellaneous Test requisition slip and stamped it with Paticia's name. She took a sticker and stamped it, too and put it on the tube of urine and started for the elevator. One of the nurses passed her in the hall and asked who she was seeing on the Ward.

“Patricia Harding,” Sally said,

“I hope you didn’t stir up her husband,” the nurse responded and went on down the hallway.

Wondering what that was all about, Sally punched the button for the elevator. Downstairs at the In Door for the lab she wrapped the tube in the requisition, secured it with one of the rubber bands provided and laid in the In Box before heading back upstairs, already thinking of other patients’ needs and things she had to do before getting any sleep.

A few minutes later one of the new lab technicians passed by the In Box and noted the tube lying there. She picked up the tube and noted the label on the requisition for Miscellaneous Test. “We don’t do those on the weekend,” she thought to herself as she walked over to the area where the laboratory staff put tests drawn over the weekend that were to be run by the daytime technicians, who were better staffed and usually paid better, too. She put the tube in the box marked Week Day and returned to her station.

Chapter Six

Saturday, March 6

The longer Benjie sat and looked at Patricia lying in the bed and he played the recent conversation with Sally around in his head, the more jumbled it became. And the more confused and agitated he became. His thoughts began centering on why no one had told him about the potassium level. Not that it made any difference or meant anything to him. It's just that, it's his wife and they should have told him what they knew. I mean, he thought, I tried to call her parents to tell them she was in the hospital and what if they had asked me what was wrong and I didn't have anything to tell them except the doctors said she'd probably be all right in the morning? Of course, it doesn't really matter since they didn't answer the phone.

But she wasn't all right. And her stinking potassium is screwed up and I didn't know that – I don't even know what that is, anyway. I wonder what else they aren't telling me, he thought, getting more upset as he did. Now he was pacing the room again and grabbing his head and looking at the monitors. Every little wiggle in the lines on the monitor might mean something but – of course – no one tells me anything, he almost shouted out loud.

And, he noted to himself, that doctor just said something about 'one of the other doctors consulting on her case' or something like that. Who were these other doctors? Why were they, or she, 'consulting' on Patricia and he, Patricia's husband, not aware of that 'consultation'? Were they all hiding something?

No, he decided, that doctor had explained about the potassium. And that urine sample. But she had asked a lot of questions first. It was like they didn't know what was actually going on. Or maybe they did and they weren't ready to tell him about it. What could that be? It couldn't be anything good.

He thought, I bet the nurses know, too. They always sneak in on those quiet shoes and they look at me with those sad eyes. I've gotta find out what they know.

Benjie then made several trips to the nurses station to ask about minor little things and pushed the nurse call button an additional several times to ask them for interpretations of the various squiggles on the monitor or why the blood pressure readings changed.

By 9:00PM the nurses were fed up and confronted Benjie. Nothing was changing, he was clearly tired and needed his rest and they promised to call him as soon as she woke up. He was sent home and Patricia's room became still and quiet. Except for the beeping of the monitors and the intravenous pump. The room lights were lowered and the patient slept quietly and did not move except when the nurses came in to shift her around in the bed.

Chapter Seven

Sunday, March 7

Sally Pedersen grabbed a light breakfast consisting of a fruit Danish, a glass of orange juice and a traveling cup of coffee; she was up on the ward checking on her patient responsibilities by 0730. Once she finished those responsibilities she could go home. The STAT potassium level on Patricia was in the electronic system by 0815 – it was still low, but slightly higher at 3.4. Sally's interpretation was they were gaining on it and she made some calculations to increase the replacement rate slightly. She had already been in the room, noted the absence of Benjie, and had checked Patricia's condition. There had been no change. She was pleased to note that the nurses were attentive to turning the girl every so often to prevent bedsores. Sally was aware that acute care nurses often were not as attuned to this kind of prevention as those who worked in chronic care or spinal cord injury units.

As she was writing orders for increasing the potassium infusion rate, she thought, "there's something else I was going to do about this" but just then her beeper went off. She returned the call. It was another ward. The pneumonia patient was crashing; mucus plug they couldn't suction, he needed to go to the unit and get intubated. All hands on deck. Sally signed her orders and took off for the unit.

Over an hour later, with that patient stabilized and Sally's main thought was now she could go home. Her out-brief with the intern on call mentioned Patricia as a probably solved case – forgetting that she had not seen a report on the urine potassium level. And then she was gone.

Chapter Eight

Sunday, March 7

Benjie actually was at the hospital early on Sunday; he came by for a short look in on Patricia on his way to church. He and Patricia were in a group of Young Professionals at their church that usually got together every Sunday afternoon. Benjie realized he had not told any of these friends about Patricia's illness and made sure he checked on her before going off to meet with his friends at worship and Bible Study. He didn't arrive back at the hospital until shortly after noon on Sunday. He had been to worship and had solicited prayers for Patricia. Two other young couples from the church came with him and hung around in the room and the waiting room for several hours while Benjie paced around.

His friends did not leave until they had calmed him down and got him to stay and sit by Patricia's side again. Both couples left their names and telephone numbers with the nurses in case there was any need for them to come back.

After supper that evening, some of Patricia's coworkers at the law firm came by to see what they could do to help. They sat in the room with Patricia while Benjie walked between the hospital room and the waiting room several times and seemed unable to sit down. The whole group moved out to the waiting room after twenty minutes or so. They tried the vending machine and circled around Benjie in hopes of providing him some comfort. The discussion tried to take an upbeat tone but there was some heated discussion at one point. The nurses asked the group to keep their discussion quiet as becoming a hospital area. Shortly after that the coworkers left. And Benjie, newly agitated, began his pacing back and forth between the room and the nurses' station and the waiting area.

Benjie again began to wonder about a lot of things. He was disturbed by some of the comments from Patricia's coworkers; they really didn't know him, only hearing of and about him through comments Patricia had made at work. But they thought their comments would lift his spirits while they actually had the opposite effect. And, on top of that, there was the continuing question of why there was no news about what was happening in Patricia's condition and whatever therapy they were administering. Every time the nurses came in to check things or to turn Patricia he asked them "what's going on?" and "Why are you doing that?" as if he hadn't asked before or hadn't heard the answers they had given.

But when he started coming back out to the Nurses' Station and asking who the doctors were that were 'consulting' on his wife's case and what happened to the "Posium" levels in her urine that they knew another intervention was necessary.

This time they were able to get him to leave before 9:00 PM and the ward and Patricia's room settled down to routine, quiet care.

Chapter Nine

Monday, March 8

New City hospital was an amalgam – part reaching back to The War and part gleaming newness pushing patient care towers upward in the western sun. The original building, near the railroad, was red brick and narrow, only fifty feet wide. At five stories it was, in 1947, one of the tallest buildings in that part of the city. Located on a rail spur in the western part of town, it originally had been The Railway Hospital and it provided inpatient care for railroad workers and their families. When the new University Hospital was built in 1947, that 'modern' building – one of the earliest to have air conditioning – was originally conceived as the contemporary way to train medical students and residents. For a number of obvious reasons the University Hospital became an immediate attraction for patients. Even though the recognized 'cure rate' for most diseases was abysmally low, the national exuberance with the 'science' that ended the war began to be an attraction for patients. For some time, hospitals had been seen as the place to go to die – primarily if you had no other place. But after 1945 that attitude began slowly to change. First there was the 'marriage' between medical academia and the Veterans Administration that brought medical students and medical faculty into the nation's largest hospital system. Shortly, recognition of a shortage of hospital beds across the nation would lead to the construction of shiny new buildings with previously unattainable amenities. As a consequence, the Railway Hospital census began to steadily fall as its intended pool of patients increasingly chose to go elsewhere for their care and it looked for a time like the facility would have to close its doors.

The city decided to use available federal funds to upgrade the facility in the early 1950s with new construction and more inpatient care capability. But the new attached building was flat and dull in appearance and did not itself serve to attract either physicians or patients. Further, the potential for 'comparison' of their quality care with the University Hospital and the Veterans Administration hospital left Railway in a distant third place. Cash flow was a problem and the city held two referendums on sale of the property and closure of the facility in order to give more support to the University.

Then, in 1955, a local group, Regents Incorporated, offered to buy the facility from the city; the group successfully lobbied for continuation of the Certificate of Need, renovated some of the buildings and opened a nearby lot for parking and thus was born the "New City Hospital", as a for-profit venture. Not immediately attractive to locals, New City marketed its services and capital city location to the outlying areas where small hospitals were having financial difficulties. Within just a few years the foresight of the Regents Group was rewarded as their outreach began to show some success. Building on the steadily increasing load of patient referrals from surrounding counties the for-profit business began to operate in the black.

Real change began after passage of Medicare in 1965. With the tension about 'socialized medicine' in the physician referral base especially in the city limits, New City Hospital became one of the first hospitals nationally to develop a program for recruiting Medicare patients and ensuring the full collection of engendered fees. Three years later the system was financially strong and had developed a new reputation within the community as a progressive medical care institution. As the medical profession developed additional technical skill, techniques and technology, New City Hospital built a new medical tower and opened the city's first open heart surgery program. The University hospital also started a cardiac surgery program and the two programs functioned cooperatively and collaboratively for education and training issues. New City soon became a major teaching hospital for the University.

The 1970s and 80s saw further technological developments and New City seemed always on the cutting edge. A new neurosurgical program was opened, then a Neonatal Wing on the Research Tower. Further, New City kept adding staff physicians recruited from major medical schools and increasing their local reputation and expertise. When the Board funded construction of a new Façade and circular drive on Front Street a little more than five years ago they completed the amalgam stretching from the New Emergency Department sprouting from the Railway building across two city blocks and up into the flaring top of the Medical Tower. New City was visually arresting and visible from Interstate 75 by commuters going north and south.

Many of the leading specialty groups in the city had decided to add updated offices in the old Railway building, turning the old offices into swank outpatient care arenas with easy access into the adjoining new hospital building. Further, the State Forensic Laboratory opened a branch toxicology and microbiology center in the old laboratory space. New City was many things but especially it was New.

The rain has stopped. The front of the hospital is still wet and shining in the oblique morning light. The rising sun is shaded by the receding rain clouds but occasional flashes of brilliance break through and give parts of the building an iridescence that seems almost celestial – but then it fades and the sharp shining glass and the ancient brick facing reappear. The contrast between the old bricks of the early building and the steel and glass of the new addition is striking in the early light. By noon the contrast will be more noticeable and quite conspicuous. Car lights are now bouncing off the façade as workers pull into the parking lots for the 0700 shift. Available slots begin to slowly fill, the ocean of parked cars starting close to the building and walkways but ever pushing outward on the surface lots and upward in the parking deck. The cars stop and remain still and motionless for varying periods of time as their occupants finish a travel cup of coffee and gather their personal belongings rather as did soldiers of the past gather their weapons to take on the challenges of a new day. Once so heartened, these health care laborers slowly exit their vehicle and bundle their coats against the slight wind as they head for the doors leading to the challenges they have come prepared to fight.

As the workers enter the building the bricks and gleaming metal seems almost to wake with their presence. Lights go on and activity can be seen through the open doors. Another day of beating back death, misery and sickness has begun at New City.

Chapter Ten

Monday, March 8

Tom Bolling stood in his kitchen, leaning against the counter and eating a bowl of cereal. His wife, Sandra, came in behind him and opened the door to the refrigerator to get some fruit.

"Whatcha thinking, honey? You look like you're already at work."

"I'm thinking about the Urology thing."

"Again . . . or still?"

"Probably still. I've been thinking about this for the last couple of weeks. It might be a break through."

"Why's that? I thought you were just tired of Sam harping on it."

"Well, that, too. But there's a couple of things I haven't told you about it.

"Really? After all the conversations we've had on this topic in the past three months – I wouldn't think there is anything left unsaid, or even unsaid twice."

"Have I told you about the financials?"

"Which part?"

"I know I told you way back when this all started that I had checked their income – charges and collectibles and all – and noticed how low and flat they'd been."

"Yes. And Brad told you the numbers had been like that for years."

"Well, Mary gave me a new bunch of numbers for the last quarter Friday morning. They are much higher and steady."

"Because of what?

"I think I'm going to find all that out this week."

They were discussing a topic that had been 'cussed and discussed' for several months in their home. At issue was a concern by the hospital director, Sam Mastone, that the brother of the Chairman of the Board at New City was told a new patient appointment for himself in the Urology Clinic there would be 7 months in the future.

Sam had accosted Tom with the charge that "No one can get in the Urology Clinic" and demanded that he immediately "fix this problem – no matter what it takes!" Sam Mastone was known for his "fix it!" mentality and abrupt approach to every problem. As Director of New City he apparently felt that any and every problem, no matter how small, should be something of which he was aware and could command repair. Once, on monthly 'walk around' in the hospital, he had asked a junior nurse if everything on her ward was going well and she noted there was a leak in one of the hand washing sinks in the back hall. Sam stopped the rounds, called the chief engineer to the ward, pointed out the problem and waited while one of the plumbers came to fix the leak. Sam felt particularly good about doing this and talked about it for a week or more. Everyone else was puzzled why he would have paid such intense attention to so minor an issue.

Tom had talked with Brad Biggers, Chief of Urology, after checking the Urology financial statistics. Brad was aware that the Urology earnings were lower than most of the surgical specialty areas but he pointed out, that had been true for years and their income stream was pretty flat – nothing new to see here.

Nonetheless, Tom called a meeting with Brad and several others from Urology – including the Chief Resident, the Physician Assistant who worked in the clinic and a two Urology nurses, one from the clinic and one from the ward and both the ward clerk and the clinic clerk. He remembers well the negative body language at that meeting – legs crossed, arms folded, lack of eye contact and everyone repeatedly looking at their watch as if to say, "doesn't he know how busy we are?" They did talk, however, and after Tom asked each of them to describe the process by which a new patient got an appointment in the clinic, they individually described a different method and process from each other. There were headshakes and mumbled, "oh, no" from various members and at the end, they admitted they were surprised to hear of all the various ways that an individual patient could get an appointment into the Urology Clinic - it all depended on which staff member they contacted.. In fact, none of them were aware of all the different ways. They were aware, however, of what the Director had said about the clinic and were surprised and a little pleased to find out the Director was wrong with his conclusion that "no one can get in the Urology Clinic." When they first heard of the issue that brought their work to the attention of the Director, they all agreed there was a simple solution.

"Tell us the name of the Chairman's brother and we'll get him in the clinic tomorrow," someone said. It required some discussion for them to realize that didn't solve the problem of long appointment wait times for all other patients. As they slowly became aware that in contrast to what the Chairman's brother had encountered, their multiple mechanisms for appointments meant that actually "anyone could get in Urology" and that they had a real problem.

Their defense: "this is an academic program" carried a very real implication. Perhaps all of their patients were "teaching patients"? This was a favorite excuse for the Chief Resident; under questioning from Tom, however, even the Chief Resident agreed there were a lot of patients he saw that had no teaching function. They had agreed to collect some data on the next 100 consecutive patients in the clinic and to analyze that information for another meeting. But when they got back together about 10 days later they got defensive again. Their own data showed that about 88% of the patients they had seen that week had been referred for that visit from a previous Urology visit. That information clearly showed a "do loop" in the care of these patients. In addition, when they examined the recommendations made by clinicians at the end of the visit they were taken aback that more than 90% of those same patients had been given a return appointment to Urology. In fact, the most common disposition from the clinic was "RTC 3 mos" meaning Return to Clinic in three months. The data were found consistent on a second collection.

Further, the residents argued that most of the patients were not 'teaching patients' and they reappointed everyone because that's what was the routine thing to do and – most importantly – they personally would not be there in three months to see that patient again, it would be the responsibility of the next resident rotating through the New City Urology clinic.

At that point the entire clinic staff, physicians, nurses, technicians, assistants and clerks agreed to take ownership of the of the issue and make some decisions. They also agreed that the goals of their decision-making should be to develop a program for a set of steps for each entry point to the clinic, determine medical reasons for reappointment and circumstances that would allow them to discharge a patient from Urology back to their primary care giver. All that was more than four months ago.

"Apparently those changes that Brad and the residents made in their program were effective," Tom said. "I don't know if it was all of them or not and maybe I can get Brad to tell me about it this week."

"You need to get Brad to tell Sam about it," rejoined Sandra.

"I'm actually going to get the whole shooting match together and let them all tell him how they solved their problem."

"Watch it. You sound like you're trying to make a different point there, cowboy."

"What do you mean?"

"You know what I mean. Don't go in there with the idea that you're going to change Sam's mind about how to get things fixed."

"Oh, that never crossed my mind," Tom said grinning into his cereal. He was aware that Sandra had this uncanny ability to see right through his carefully laid plans. She had only 'allowed' him to surprise her on birthdays and anniversaries for the first dozen years of their marriage. Now they planned celebrations together . . . and things always seemed to go more smoothly. Surprising.

"On my way," Tom said grabbing his briefcase and jacket and heading for the door.

"Don't get in fights with the other children," she called to him as the door closed.

Chapter Eleven

Monday, March 8

Lila Ralston, RN, parked in her usual area of the parking lot and walked to the rear of the lot where it intersected with the rear of the 1950s building. She walked up the small staircase on to the loading dock and then through the large double doors into the rear hallway. In the darkened hallway from the loading dock past Central Supply and the Pharmacy storeroom, Lila stood out. She was not a large woman, 5'6" at best, but her coloring is distinctive. Her skin is almost alabaster, sprinkled with a decent amount of freckles and her blond hair appears almost white against her fair skin. Even at this hour of the day, her step has a spring to it and she walks with shoulders back and head held high.

Lila loved her job as a day nurse at New City. Divorced with a teenage son at home, she needs the income and the day shift allows her to be home when Jason gets home from school in the afternoons. Of course, leaving home by 0600 every day means leaving it up to Jason to get himself up, fed and off to school on time. It has been working so far but Lila still worries. It would be so easy for him to just lie back down after the alarm she set for him goes off. And easy to sleep right through the morning. Lila knows this because she has actually seen him do that on Saturdays and holidays so the concept is not foreign. She has considered calling him when she gets to work to ensure that he's up and fed and ready for school. But she knows that Jason would see her call and her questions as intrusive and would take them as evidence that she doesn't trust him. She has to trust him, she knows, and after all, this arrangement has been working for nearly an entire school year. But she still worries about him.

She worries about how to increase her income, too. She knows she's ready to advance in nursing, get a supervisor's job and take on more responsibility. Lila spoke with the Chief Nurse about it a few weeks ago; she was told she could start off on one of the smaller clinics if a position opens up – and if the committee selected her.

Lila knows a little about the committee activity and how they make their decisions: more on the basis of who you know than on what you know. Nursing politics is only barely subliminal. She has been thinking about how to make the 'right' impression on the supervisors who will make the decision about whether she should join their ranks. She knows the importance they put on education and advanced degrees in nursing but that's not something she wants to pursue as that would take money and time – she is more interested, and capable, of showing everyone that she is a very competent nurse and a good leader here in the 'real world'.

Lila's approach to most things, however, doesn't usually include worry. Her gait down the hall was springy and loose. She turned at the end of the hall down the walkway to the new building. She passed the service elevators where some of the food service people were bringing their carts back to the kitchen area. She didn't ride the service elevators; she walked on toward the Food Court where she knows some of her co-workers were eating.

As she passed the entrance to the Food Court she once again thought about the signage in New City that refers to the floor she is on as Ground Floor in the Railway Building but that same elevation is termed the First Floor in the New Building. That jargon was part of a hangover from an earlier century in the Railway Building, she remembers she was told in her orientation. Apparently when the building was first erected the designers were overly influenced by the English tradition of naming the bottom floor of a building "ground", as in contiguous with the outside grounds. American tradition has always been to call that floor "First Floor". As New City grew and new buildings were erected someone decided on the compromise that the new structures would start on a First Floor and the old Railway building would remain starting on Ground – even though the two buildings connected and the floors were on the same level. Just confusing, she thought as she turns down the new hallway toward the staff elevators in the rear of the main lobby. Two other nurses rode up with her to the third floor; they turned toward Ward 3B while she turned toward 3C.

Lila ducked into the nurses' lounge and opened her locker to put up her purse and jacket and greeted the other nurses. She was welcomed, as always when she opens the locker door, with a eight by ten glossy snapshot of Jason showing his impish grin. And, as always, the image gave her a boost of morale and energy to start her day with a purpose.

"Hello, girls. Everybody ready for a new week?"

"So, Ms. Congeniality is back." This with tongue stuck out and a funny face.

Lila smiled at this and rejoined, "Good to see you, too, Bobbie."

Someone asked, "Anything BIG happen on the ward over the weekend?"

"We'll find out at report."

"Anything BIG happen in your life this weekend?" Lila asked of the group in general. There were some assorted snorts and shakes of the head but at least one nurse smiled at her and nodded.

And they moved off to sit around the small table where the charge nurse was flipping through her Cardex. A couple of the nurses moved to the small table nearby where an old percolator sat with its bottom light on indicating contents. Each one grabbed a Styrofoam cup and one poured three-quarters cup of black liquid in the cups held by the other. Both reached for the sweeteners at the same time, fumbled a bit, then one took a yellow packet and the other grabbed a pink one. After dosing their drinks they joined the others at the large table.

The charge nurse begins the routine; every patient on the ward is mentioned starting geographically from the end of the ward closest to the elevators. The Night nurse responsible gives the update including whether there are any new conditions or orders to be carried out and the Day nurse assigned to that patient makes a few notes for her own later reference. Then it is on to the next patient and so on through all twenty-eight of them. Lila notes there are two empty beds and knows that means the ward is likely to get some new admissions. Each new admission is more work for the nurses, just as a discharge is. The admission work is critical for the nurses to get to know their patient. Lila knows her job is much easier if she can just provide the care needed for people she already is familiar with. That reminded her of a saying from one of her colleagues years ago: "I love this job. And it would be even better if I didn't have to deal with all these sick people!"

Twenty minutes later the nurses left the Nursing Conference area and headed for various duties – some stopped at the chart rack, one went to the Medication Cart to check on something and Lila walked down the hall toward Patricia's room. She stopped at the room next to Patricia's and slipped in the door, calling the patient's name. About five minutes later she reappeared stripping off some purple gloves to throw them into the trashcan at the doorway.

Lila opened the door into the dark room where Patricia was lying. She entered and purposefully did not turn on the light. After putting on some gloves from the box near the door, she called out to the patient.

"Ms. Harding?," she calls softly from the door. There is no answer.

"Ms. Harding?" a little louder, but still without response. Lila stepped to the bedside still without turning on the room light and quickly checked the machines and the patient's vitals. Patricia was lying on her left side breathing quietly with her eyes closed. Lila examined the bag hanging from the iv pole and used her flashlight to read the attached label, assured herself that the bag was due to run out at 0900. Silently she stood at the bedside and watched the drip rate in the bubble trap and compared that to the amount of fluid left in the bag. As an experienced nurse Lila knew the drip rate that was set on the pump and she was confident that the bag wouldn't empty all its contents before she was due to hang the next one at 0900. She turned off her flashlight, patted the patient gently on her shoulder and started for the door. A quick glance at her watch told her it was 0742. Now satisfied things were stable for the patient and the infusion is set properly, she stripped off her gloves and left the room. She would be back in plenty of time to change the intravenous bag and start the infusion from the bag hanging on the pole. But she had some other patients to care for first.

Chapter Twelve

Monday, March 8

Tom Bolling was part of the work force coming to the hospital. As always, he drove his four-year-old Ford F-150, enjoying both the elevated height it gives him over the rest of the traffic and the quiet and peaceful interior. Tom didn't play the radio except when driving a long distance and then only to listen to books-on-tape. He preferred the quiet. Partly he enjoyed the quiet time because he likes to think about things that are going to happen that day and begin to move the chess pieces in his head to get things done in the right order and in the right way. Tom is a very educated man – he thinks in complete sentences, sometimes rephrasing them in his head, complete with punctuation.

Right then he was remembering that the Director of the hospital, Sam Mastone, asked him some time ago to look into whether or not to start a new program: a Beating Heart Cardiac Surgery Program. As the Chief of Staff at New City, Tom Bolling, USAF Brig Gen (ret.) knew the key parts of this decision were going to come down to how he presented the facts to Sam – and to the Board. The whole thing only came up because of Sam's brother-in-law; he was operated on in Cleveland and heard all about the 'new advantages' of avoiding the use of the heart-lung bypass machine. Tom was savvy enough in the history of medicine to know that the original coronary artery surgeries were always performed on 'beating hearts.' The reason for such approaches was really quite simple: there were no such things as heart-lung machines back then that would allow the patient's heart to be stilled for the surgery and still provide oxygenated blood to the body.

That came much later – and was seen at the time as the 'new wave' of cardiac surgery. Now, Tom thought, "I'm being pushed back to the past like it's all new and shiny." Things like this often came down to the way they were presented. An enthusiastic presentation might pull in some less-informed individuals but usually just made the others look more warily at the prospect.

As a major teaching hospital of the South West Ohio Medical School, New City had a very good cardiac program for the major invasive treatments like CABG (coronary artery bypass graft), stents and PTCA (percutaneous transluminal coronary angioplasty); but now one of the other medical schools in the state had started a Beating Heart Bypass program and they were getting a lot of coverage and apparently a lot of money from the state. New City Hospital was one of the oldest cardiac programs in Cincinnati and had largely overcome its previous reputation when it was the Railway Hospital. In fact, Tom had the data to show that New City was now the equal of the other hospitals in the metropolitan area in terms of quality and outcomes, but that damn JCAHO recommendation still stuck with him.

Tom often would drive through various neighborhoods on his way to the hospital, taking in sights of new growth and flowers in the spring, fall colors in autumn and always on the lookout for attractive porches. He had always had an interest in porches, especially ones that that ran the length of the front of the house and were wide enough to gather on and stay out of the rain. His grandfather's house had a porch like that with wide steps leading down to a broad sidewalk. Tom had spent many days there in summers and the porch was the centerpiece of his world when visiting.

When he was a kid, Tom used to hide underneath the porch and build small tunnels and indentations in the dirt, imagining battles of tiny armies. Later, after a long game of baseball, the shady front steps were a place to get rejuvenation with Grandma's lemonade while recounting events of the day with friends. His teen years involved cutting the lawn and then getting sweet tea from Grandma while sitting on the wicker furniture and remembering Grandpa with her. Porches were now a major architectural aspect of home life to Tom and his morning commute was a way to see as many as possible.

But this time he stayed on major roads and saw only other cars and drivers. Nonetheless, he occasionally saw the flash of color off to the side of the road; early spring daffodils and crocus and even the faint blush of the redbuds starting to bloom. This was a part of the drive that Tom enjoyed, seeing the evidence of life and nature springing back after winter. He liked having that encouragement from God's world as he prepared himself for being immersed in pain, suffering and unhappiness in his work world. That discouragement with the 'down side' of medicine had something, perhaps more than he wanted to admit, to do with his choosing orthopedics for a career. Throughout his third year in medical school he had felt himself surrounded by the 'down side'; he had trouble sleeping when he rotated through Pediatrics because he was upset about seeing sick children every day. He had rationally excluded oncology from possible careers – who could live a contented life if every day was spent battling some dread disease like cancer? Similarly, medical subspecialties all seemed focused on near catastrophic illnesses and cures: dialysis, transplantation, implantable defibrillators, respirators, and such. He had considered obstetrics for a short while but, after looking around the specialty, discovered that it was becoming a woman's profession – at both ends. Tom had always been relatively good with his hands, and since he had a disciplined and three-dimensionally capable imagination he found himself drawn to orthopedics. Of course, there were always going to be those unusual kids with bone tumors but most of his work had turned out to be just what he expected and wanted – repair of damage and return to function both of limb and patient. And he had been daily strengthened by that feeling that his work was both honest and helpful. Even in the midst of the trauma in Balad when he was often called to amputate a limb damaged beyond repair he had known that return of function was an increasing possibility for most of the young men he worked on. Progress in prosthetics was impressive even if it did seem to gather its momentum from war.

He started north from his home and swung on to the I-75 after just a few blocks. Then it was in and out of traffic and dodging those who were late and hurrying to some office space downtown. Twice already he had been caught in a "K-wave" of slowed or stopped traffic when the road ahead was clear but the compiled effect of several dozen drivers touching their brakes because someone ahead of them had done so had slowly and inexorably brought a whole lane of interstate traffic to a halt – often for no obvious reason at all. Sitting high on the road in his truck, Tom could see the effect and the lack of cause and often would get annoyed about the vagaries of interstate driving. A small sports car suddenly cut in front of him and accelerated to keep from being hit. Tom almost absent-mindedly tapped his brake to allow the driver to escape. He thought to himself, "That's one of the perks of driving a big truck. If we were to collide, he'd be rolling over for a week." That was one of the disadvantages of taking the major roads to drive to work in the mornings – other drivers. However, Tom's mind was only partially on the road and partially on the fact of the JCAHO's RFI, or requirement for improvement, which could create a significant amount of trouble for New City. Resident training accreditation was dependent upon JCAHO approval of a hospital and this RFI could put all the training programs at New City in jeopardy. But that wasn't the only thing on his mind. He was also sitting on several months of work with the quality improvement team in the Urology Clinic and his own personal imprimatur with the hospital Director was clearly on the line in this instance.

The Director, Sam Mastone, was laser focused on the profitability of the hospital's various programs; he was also not a committed fan of the academic affiliation and was aware that the affiliated training program in Urology was routinely failing to make financial goals. His initial decision was to cut out the training program but he was aware that a very similar program at other hospitals was clearly a financial boon – the 'Men's Gynecology Clinic" he called it. Tom was highly committed to maintaining the affiliations across the board and had virtually promised Sam that he would see to the turn-around in Urology. That was almost six months ago and Sam had been uncharacteristically quiet about any trends in the data and Tom's time was about up. This week he knew the Urology clinic team was scheduled to make a report to him and Sam and he was only partly aware of the results; that worried him and kept creeping into his mind.

But the biggest worry Tom had was the push from Sam for the major change in the cardiac surgery program. It started with Sam's brother-in-law having surgery in Cleveland but now that Sam was aware that the Boston hospitals were developing "beating heart" surgical programs he wanted one, too. Further, Sam wanted to have the first such program in the Greater Mid-West here in Cincinnati at New City. And Tom didn't think the concept had much merit but had agreed to get some data and lead a discussion. Now, a month later, he knew that Sam was going to be asking him about this discussion and presentation every time they came together – and that was way too often for Tom's comfort. He had to get a handle on this or he would never get time to work on other things.

Chapter Thirteen

Monday, March 8

Tom edged into the exit lane and left the I-75 at Exit 2B and swung slowly down in traffic to merge into the east bound lane on Western Hills. The traffic was always lighter here at this time of day and he was able to slide over to the left turn lane in just a few car lengths. At Spring Grove he turned north toward the hospital joining a short line of others arriving for work.

He pulled into the parking deck behind another truck and stuck his access card up to the proximity reader at the gate. He then drove to the end of the drive and turned back toward the front of the hospital and found his marked parking space on the first deck. After he had parked, Tom walked to the hospital entrance in the garage, entering about 0730 still thinking about the recent JCAHO inspection. He made rather desultory greetings to some nurses leaving the building and a couple of other employees entering at the same time. He was distracted and starting to get a little bit grumpy about the whole JCAHO affair. Inspectors at the recent review of their programs had become unhappy with the hospital's review of codes and arrests. Tom had learned that the leader of the team had lost his father to an inpatient heart attack sometime in the previous year and now was determined to push for programs that could make possible improvements in outcome from inpatient cardiac arrest. In an attempt to pacify the inspectors, Tom had created a new program: every code or arrest during regular hours would be attended by a senior staff member who would, mostly, observe and intervene only in unusual circumstances. The Staff member would also run a detailed 'after-action' review or AAR, of the code with all participants, make the appropriate teaching points and write a short but detailed review for the record. That's the way he did in the Air Force – even though the U. S. Army piloted the concept of an After Action Review initially. Tom's military background was simply going to come to fore – he did have 22 years service and he was never going to be other than a military physician, and a General Officer as well. He was also aware that his plan was not well received by many of the senior faculty staff; they felt they already had enough to do and this was just another piece of 'busy work'. Tom had tried reasoning with them and using the teaching aspect for leverage but they were resistant – they ultimately became involved and they were organized into getting the task done – but very few of them were happy about it. Nonetheless, they had been at it now for more than two months and he was already seeing some added value in comments from the residents and students. All that remained was for Tom to write the results of the program in language that would convince the Joint Commission not to censure New City. But first he had to wait for the program to have a six month experience to report. That would not be easy but Tom was confident they had the data to make a persuasive case.

As he entered the main lobby he could see that the Green Bean coffee kiosk was already crowded with faculty and students. As he approached, however, the barista looked up and caught his eye, "The usual, Big Doc?"

He nodded and Nick, the barista, turned to the machines. Tom took up position at the far end where finished drinks were placed. He nodded to the faculty clustered around and one asked, "What's the 'usual'?"

"Americano. With two shots."

"Like a 'Red eye'."

"Sorta. It's actually more like a Black Eye. Just the way I like it."

"Nice to have your own special barista, eh?"

"Nick? He was Air Force. We have a bond."

"I get it. Did you guys serve together?"

"No. He spent his time at Sig and fell in love with Italian cooking and coffee."

"What's Sig?"

"Sigonella. Naval Air Station in Sicily. There's an Air Force detachment there. Then he went to Aviano and finished his tour."

"Italy, too?"

"Right. And now he's a most accomplished barista. Thanks Nick!" Tom said, reaching across the bar for his coffee.

"You got it", said Nick accompanying the cup with a quasi-salute of two fingers touching his right eyebrow.

Tom took the cup and turned toward his office and was immediately stopped by the Director.

Sam Mastone looked like he belonged in Sicily. He was not a tall man and was somewhat bulky with dark, slicked down hair and a complexion of pale olive color. As usual he was wearing a dark, pinstriped suit and patent leather shoes. And, also as usual, he was not smiling; his lips were pulled together like his teeth ached. His voice did nothing to dispel that impression. And, also as usual, he began the conversation without pleasantries, "When are we going to talk about Richard's idea?"

Tom understood the question as coming from Sam's brother-in-law in Cleveland. He needed to get some answers together for Sam – and maybe for the Board. "I'm still looking into it."

"How much longer?"

"I don't know – a couple of weeks maybe."

"Tom, we need to move on this."

"No, we don't" Tom thought to himself but instead he said, "Look, we have very good results with what we're doing and moving in that direction could cost us a hell of a lot of money – and we would likely do less well for a while."

"But, this is what the science is moving to, right?" Sam posited this with a pair of firm head nods as if to get Tom to agree with him before going on.

"Really not sure of that, Sam." Tom was wise to this maneuver of Mastone's, a trick to get the other person in the discussion to first agree with Sam's position and then try to defend their own. He slowly shook his head to indicate the failure of the ploy and said, "I told you I'd get us an answer. Just give me the time to get it right."

"Speaking of getting it right, are those Urology guys doing any better?" The abrupt change of topic was also typical Mastone. Whenever he deemed himself in a more defensive position, he often changed the subject – sometimes in mid-sentence. Again Tom was not surprised or taken aback by the change in topic but he was surprised by the admission that Sam didn't know what was going on in the Urology Clinic yet.

"Let's talk about that at the morning meeting," Tom said pulling himself up and squaring his shoulders in an attempt to signal that this conversation should be over, inappropriate as it was to be held in the lobby.

"OK," Sam walked off to get in the line for coffee and Tom turned the corner toward his office. It was 0742.

Chapter Fourteen

Monday, March 8

Mary Brighthouse prided herself in always being in the Chief of Staff's office when he came in each morning. They had been together since he arrived, four years ago and they were a good team. He once said to her that there were only two times when he absolutely needed to have her in the office – when he was there and when he was not. He trusted her judgment about people and her ability to both prioritize her work and to get it done without calling a lot of attention to herself.

As Tom stepped into the office, Mary looked up smiling and said, "Good morning, doctor. Have a nice weekend?"

"Pretty much, at least until I got my coffee."

"Nick not there today?"

"No. It's not Nick. It's Sam. He grabbed me before I could get the first sip to talk about that beating heart idea of his brother-in-law's"

"What are you going to tell him?"

"I'd like to tell him to stick to the accounting and personnel issues and let me take care of the medical decision."

"But you won't." Mary was a good sounding board for Tom. She was about his age, with a little gray showing in her dark black hair. "Every one of these gray hairs is an obstacle overcome in my life," she was prone to say. "Why would I ever want to hide them? They are the sign that I'm a winner." Tom admired her and desired her sage advice; she had risen through the secretarial ranks at New City over the past 18 years and was wise to the politics and personalities of the place. She had liked Tom from the start, her husband had been a Marine sergeant and she understood the military mentality. Her advice had helped Tom get over more than a few small crises in the first year, ending with him being considered by the faculty and staff as a very good leader for them.

"No, I won't. Probably. Well, not today." Bolling looked at the small pager sitting in a charge at the end of Mary's desk. "Who's got the duty today?"

"I'm not sure. I can look it up," she turned toward her computer to pull up the call schedule.

"No. Don't worry about it. It's still early. But let me know if that's not picked up by the end of the morning meeting."

"Will do," she said, smiling at him as he went toward his office. She liked the way he kept everything and everyone busy around him. She had worked for the previous Chief of Staff who was much more laid back and who tended to act as if there were no emergencies that couldn't be waited out. He was a surgeon, too, but one who motto seemed to be, "All bleeding stops – eventually."

Tom stopped in the doorway to his office and turned back to her, "Have we heard anything from those guys I asked to do the business case analysis?"

"Not for awhile. I'll check with them today."

"See if they're in now. I need to tell Sam something this morning at the meeting."

Mary turned to her phone, cradling it to her ear as she typed in a name to the computer. When the number appeared, she dialed it as

Tom walked on into his office to hang up his coat. He sat down at his computer, logged on and was starting through his email when there was a knock on his door.

"Hmmm?"

" Doctor Bolling?'

"Yes. Come in, Andy." He said, looking up and recognizing the caller.

"Mary said you'd like a quick update on the BCA."

"I would, can you do that before my morning meeting?"

"Sure. It's simple enough."

"Alright, Go"

"Well, we don't have an answer but we do have all the data."

"That's a little too simple. More." He gestured with his hand like telling a car to pull on through the intersection.

"We have now compiled a five-year database of all our cardiac procedures and outcomes and we have gotten the latest census data for all the major referring counties."

"Which allows you to . . ."

"Determine the probable rate of incidence of cardiac disease in our catchment area for which we could do either a CABG or stenting procedure over the next five years. Plus, we have captured all the cost data on each of those procedures so we can quickly come up with an average to use for cost calculations."

"And the answer is?"

"Not yet calculated. Getting the data has been a major issue. But we're ready to crunch now." Andy McCall was a slim man of about 30 who was starting to see thinning of his brownish hair. His long face and rounded glasses began a picture of a man more accustomed to computer screens than interactions with people. And the picture was completed with his untucked shirt of some 1950's pseudo-plaid print and the pocket protector filled with pencils of varying length.

"All right. Good. How do we stand on the start-up costs for a beating heart program?" Tom was aware this was going to be the big stumbling block but he would need the possible case volume to work out the return on investment and the time to profitability.

"We have two scenarios: Buy a surgeon and team from the Northeast or send one of our guys for training. And either way we have to buy some specialized equipment and do a little construction. It's the usual dilemma of Buy or Make." Seeing Tom's hand making the traffic signal again, Andy jumped to the bottom line. "Either way we're looking at a minimum of $2 million before the first case."

"When can you give me the BCA?"

"Actually, maybe even later this week."

"Really? That would do just fine. What does it look like to you now?"

"We can't tell yet. But we can soon."

"Get back to it, Andy. And thanks."

Now, Bolling thought, there is something I can tell Sam that'll get him off my back for a while. He smiled and sipped at his coffee. Then, rising and grabbing his white coat and the cup of coffee, he left the office and walked across the hall to the Director's Conference Room for the morning meeting.

It was 0755.

Chapter Fifteen

Monday, March 8

Whitney Albright, Junior Admitting Resident, had been sitting in the ECG Reading room since 0745 Monday morning. In front of her were several pages of ECGs run by various personnel during the night. Some were from the ED, others from the wards and even several from the CCU. Part of Whitney's training program involves reading every one of these ECGs, making comparison with the unofficial computer interpretation and annotating any necessary changes in the patient's records.

Whitney was a stocky brunette wearing her white coat over a brown skirt and red blouse. She was wearing sensible and comfortable black ABEO Rocs. She learned to wear comfortable shoes while in medical school in Minnesota; the fate of every medical student involved running up and down stairs in the multi-story hospital to deliver samples or requests for tests, even messages between residents. And, of course, to respond to every code in the building no matter how far away. Those stairs helped her learn the lesson regarding comfortable footwear very quickly. She had gone to Minneapolis after graduating from the University of Colorado from a small town in Eastern Wyoming and was comfortable with her cowboy boots until she hit the wards as a third-year student.

She was sitting comfortably at her desk with a fresh cup of coffee from the lobby barista, Rocs up on the adjoining desk. Before taking up the first of the ECGs she reflected a little on her medical journey so far. She was definitely moving east – and moving up in both culture and society. She was now a second year resident, two months into her Cardiology rotation, and very adept at reading ECGs. The skill of interpreting the jiggling lines on the red paper was becoming as comfortable to her as tracking deer on the family farm back in Wyoming. She had hunted with her father and brothers in every deer season after she turned 13 – rifle, muzzle loader, bow and arrow, it made no difference – she knew each weapon well but more importantly, she understood the deer and how to track them and find them.

Of course, no one in Cincinnati knew any of that information about her – she was "from" Minneapolis as far as they know. And she was still content to let that piece of her background be an 'unknown unknown' to the rest of her fellow residents. She preferred being thought of as a 'city girl' to the public; even on her infrequent dates she was not one to reminisce about the 'good ol' days' back on the farm; she talked of the food and night life in Minneapolis like it was home.

And now she was slowly becoming more of citizen of Cincinnati, urbane, a fan of the Bearcats, the Reds and Mad Tree beer – but thinking about a Nephrology Fellowship in Boston in a couple of years. That's really getting east!

Suddenly her pager alarmed with a Code Page. She swung her feet down, gulped a big swallow of her coffee and headed for the stairs. In the stairwell she bolted down the two flights from the Heart Station and burst through the door onto Ward 3C. As she approached the nurses' station, two nurses there pointed her in the direction of Patricia's room.

Chapter Sixteen

Monday, March 8

Like many hospital directors, Sam Mastone held a morning meeting to be aware of significant happenings in the past 24 hours. And, like in most hospitals, there were few matters of sufficient significance to spend much time discussing. As a consequence of feeling the need for a meeting and having little of timeliness to discuss, Sam tried to push the conversation to addressing his list of important items. Unfortunately, most of the time he did not have the necessary players in the room to make that discussion pertinent and so most of the time these conversations were groundhog day occurrences – same points made, similar decisions determined to be correct and virtually no plan made to turn those decisions into action.

This Monday was not different. All the players arrived just before 0800. Roslyn Burke, the Chief Nurse, arrived with her cup emblazoned with the slogan 'World's Best Nurse' and sat across from Tom at the head of the table. Tom, and others, who had had occasion to disagree with Roslyn harbored a secret belief that she had bought the cup for herself. She was accompanied by her executive officer, Alena Preston, RN, Ph.D. Where Roslyn was white and well-filled out, Alena was black and very thin. But both wore nurses white with Nursing association pins on their collars like soldiers campaign ribbons. Both of the women felt there still was a contest between the medical and nursing profession – not a war over how best to deliver high quality care but a contest to see who was going to be 'in charge'.

The response of nursing service to any physician order they did not approve was to claim that physicians were trying to make nurses their 'handmaidens'. Tom had spent much of his first two years battling these issues, winning most but losing some. The seating arrangement for the morning meeting with Tom and his executive officer on one side and the nursing members on the opposite created a sense of conflict from the beginning, something Tom did not care for but that he was sure was a goal of the nursing executives.

Sam Mastone entered directly from his office, also carrying his coffee cup from the lobby kiosk. He had shed his suit coat for the more relaxed look of office work but the tightly tied and noosed tie against the bright white of his shirt said anything but 'informal'. As he always did, he entered carrying the printout results of the hospital activities for the past twenty-four hours: bed occupancy rates on various services, admissions and discharges, number of visits to the Emergency Department and volume of clinic visits in all the specialties. Tom got the same printouts at 0745 each morning and asked that his executive officer, Beverly Hancock review them and warn him if he were going to get static from any side in the morning meeting. This morning she had indicated there were no problems.

Sam tossed his pile of reports on the table in front of his seat at the head of the long conference table and said, "At least things were quiet all weekend," as he sat down.

Others all nodded agreement. Tom had a reticence to bring up any topics at this meeting because of the nature of the discussion and the lack of planned follow-through. He tried to make his contributions of two types: answering previously asked questions and taking ample notes about any questions so they could be answered in one meeting at some later time.

"Roslyn, you have any issues?" asked Sam.

"I'm hearing from the ward nurses that the Code Review is taking a lot of their time away from patient care," she said, tipping her head and glancing sideways at Tom.

He responded, "not too much, I'd say. Most of the reviews are finished in a half hour and most of them have had important teaching points."

"Perhaps that's all true for the doctors," said Roslyn, "but the nurses spend much more time getting ready for the review and cleaning up afterward and they haven't given me any information about 'important teaching points' for nurses."

"Perhaps that's true, too," Tom said smiling at her. "Maybe you could assign one of your 'clipboard' nurses to attend and help us develop more nursing directed teaching." He was referring to the several nurses who roamed the hospital daily carrying clipboards and doing various kinds of assessments. Whenever Roslyn raised the issue of needing more nurses for patient care, Tom's first suggestion was to move the 'clipboard' nurses back to the wards.

"That might be a good idea," said Sam before Roslyn could respond. "In fact, that might make the response to the JCAHO even stronger, right Tom?"

Tom looked directly at the director and said, "We would like to have that kind of senior nursing input into out review process." And there was silence on the nursing side. Tom and Beverly noted that Alena was not making any notes regarding this suggestion, however.

After a little more discussion about the JCAHO and when the hospital would make its follow-up report, Sam shifted the conversation to the Urology issue.

"Do you have any results from that 'intervention' of yours, Tom?"

"Actually, yes. And I'd like to note that the nurses in the urology clinic and on the ward were very helpful in identifying processes that needed improvement. Dr. Biggers was very strong in his praise for them." Tom hoped what he was saying would put a little oil on the water from his previous comments.

Roslyn smiled and Tom felt he might have averted a clash, until she said, "they tell me that the residents are the ones causing all the problem."

"I think everyone had a little part in creating the problem," Tom said, turning back to the director. "I'll try to put something together this week about where we are, OK?"

Mastone nodded and moved on to another topic. Without much to say on these topics, both sides of the table were nodding and making a few notes for collecting information about an issue for future discussion.

When Sam ran out of coffee, he threw his cup in the corner trashcan, stood up and said, "Thanks everyone. That's all," and exited back into his office closing the door firmly behind him.. The other players nodded to each other, gathered up papers and notes and left through separate doors heading for their own offices. It was 0835.

Chapter Seventeen

Monday, March 8

Wilford Adamson, MD, Chief of Cardiology at New City and Associate Professor of Medicine at the Medical School arrived at the parking deck at almost the same time every morning. He had a route from his home in Northside, straight down to I-75 to the off ramp near New City. He drove this route everyday, left home at the same time and fought the same traffic every morning in order to arrive at almost exactly the same minute every morning. Order was a way of life for Wilford. Things out of order – or out of the ordinary – were best avoided in his opinion.

Wilford was almost 6 feet tall and broad of shoulder. His grayish hair was thinning ever so slightly on top but the effect of his broad face, shaggy brows and wire-rimmed half-glass spectacles presented exactly the mental Rembrandt one would expect if asked to imagine a Professor of Medicine. Except that he wasn't wearing a tweed jacket with elbow patches nor did he drive a Volkswagen Squareback. He was dressed, as most every day, in a dark suit, white button-down oxford shirt with solid color tie and black wing-tip shoes and a lightweight overcoat. And, also as usual, on his head was his favorite houndstooth fedora. Also predictably he was driving his pride and joy – a three year old Porsche 911 Carrera 4S, gray with black racing stripes.

At 54, he was one of the six cardiologists at New City and was the first of them recruited eleven years ago to keep step with the University program that had just performed its first heart transplant. He was brought in as a new Chief and given the direction to recruit some of the brightest and best for the New City program. Now, eleven years later, Wilford Adamson was chairing a section that had a national reputation. His own research involved the arcane work of recording His Bundle electrophysiology from the surface electrocardiogram instead of requiring right heart catheterization.

His research funding was secure, he had found a niche where his technique was not previously known to be helpful – patients with advanced pulmonary disease – and was collecting recordings and analyzing them for ways to show relevance of his technique. This involved amplifying the signal from the His bundle over three dimensions so as to create a hologram of the signal as opposed to the two-dimensional one conventionally studied. Adamson's conviction was that a three dimensional model would uncover broad new applications for surface recordings.

He entered the hospital lobby at 0735, nodded to the guard on duty and approached the coffee kiosk. He saw the Chief of Staff, Tom Bolling, on the other side of the kiosk, chatting with one of the hematologists. After a moment waiting in line, the barista noted him and signaled asking whether Wilford wanted his 'usual'. Wilford nodded and started around the crowd to the cashier. As he did so he noticed the Chief of Staff and the Director having an intense conversation. He wondered if that had anything to do with the question the Director had asked him about the Beating Heart surgery program. Such a program wouldn't have a direct impact on him or his cardiology staff but he might be able to get attached enough to the project so as to find a little funding, too. One of the Internal Medicine residents was coming away from the stand as he noted his uncapped drink being placed on the counter. The Baristas always put names on the cups and Wil was known to not care for the type of cup lid they used as he often burned his lip with the first sips. The resident greeted him and asked a question about one of the ward patients being followed by Cardiology. Wilford was peripherally aware of the case, one involving a young woman with an atrial myxoma so he paused for a minute of two and chatted with the resident.

While chatting with the resident, he made a mental note to talk with Tom Bolling about the Beating Heart program someday soon. Wil broke away from the resident and pushed up to the pick-up area and noted there were now two other drinks on the bar and individuals pushing to pick them up. There was no confusion, however, over which one was his; the missing top clearly identified Wilford Adamson's morning coffee. He picked it up, paid the cashier and got his Reward Card punched. As he looked up he realized that Tom had headed for his office and he followed him down the hall since he had business there, too. He entered just as Tom, in his office, was stepping over to his desk.

"Good morning, Mary."

"Good morning to you, Dr. Adamson. Can I help you?"

"Oh no." Wilford said as he set his briefcase on the floor and put his coffee cup on the low counter in front of Mary's desk. "I'm just coming by to pick up the Old Ball and Chain."

He reached over and plucked the pager out of the charger in front of her and wiggled it as he spoke making a little toothy grin. She knew that many of the senior cardiologists did not care for the way the Chief of Staff had created another responsibility for them to attend and observe any in-house codes during regular working hours. Mary smiled at him without speaking.

He clipped the pager on his belt and picked up the briefcase and coffee cup. " I would like to talk with Tom about the Beating Heart program sometime."

"He's working on a business case analysis."

"Are we going ahead, then?"

"I really don't think there's been any decision until he finishes the analysis."

"Well, I'd like a minute to chat with him about it."

"I'll tell him of your interest."

"OK. Thanks" he said as he turned and left, heading down the hall back toward the lobby and then down the hall to his office in the Cardiology Suite.

Chapter Eighteen

Monday, March 8

Don Horvath had just gotten his coffee at the kiosk and was walking toward the elevators when Wilford Adamson walked in front of him.

"Dr. Adamson, can I have a minute?" he asked.

Adamson looked up, already a little annoyed by his having the Code pager and was not pleased to see Don. He had been expecting Don to press for this conversation for more than a month but he was not looking forward to it.

Don Horvath was a pleasant enough looking young man, brushed back hair, earnest face devoid of hair, eyes that were always ready to smile. He was middle height, maybe five foot seven or eight and average in build, but his halting mannerisms belied the basic look of comfort that Don might have had in his body. He was constantly moving one of his extremities and he rarely was able to hold a look, his eyes wandering away before jerking back to look at the other person in his conversation. It was more than annoying; his inability to be still and answer questions had given the faculty reason to be unenthusiastic about his request for extension in the cardiac fellowship program.

Don had not matched in the Fellowship Program the previous year but had applied for the New City-South West Ohio program secondarily. He had finished a Straight Medicine Internship in Tennessee and had been left out of the Fellowship match. Given his record and medical school grades, the fact that he did not match was a little surprising but not completely unusual; several good candidates went unmatched in various disciplines each year. New City had benefitted from this kind of happening a couple of times in their early years of developing a training program. Wilford and the Fellowship Committee considered his application without a personal interview and thought he was a possible good fit in the First Year Fellowship. But that fit was only because one of the other Fellows in that year, Bennie Goings, had been recently diagnosed with lymphoma and was certain to miss much of his first year and possibly all of the Fellowship. The committee reasoned, Horvath could fill in the clinical work that Bennie won't be able to do and if Bennie wasn't available for a second year the program won't have a gap in positions. The plan always was, however, that the second year slot belonged to Bennie if he recovered. The Committee was taking a bit of the NFL playbook to heart: 'you don't lose your position because of injury'.

So, Don Horvath made a trip to New City and went through the recruitment process. Most everyone was under-whelmed. If he had been considered for one of the regular positions, no one on the faculty would have supported him for the position. But, with the future uncertain about one of their actual stars, Bennie, they convinced themselves that they would be better off with Don Horvath than without him. They could not have been more wrong.

Now more than eight months into his planned and promised one-year Fellowship Don Horvath could not be considered a success by any standard. Other Fellows found him distant and patients he interviewed often asked if he was a real doctor. Don tried to look professional by not taking notes during interviews with patients but then found he could not recall specifics of their history later. He generally kept to himself, reading cardiology texts and looking eager – if unable – to please. On several occasions he volunteered to take care of a particular procedure or task only to explain he had no idea how to perform it. Faculty had developed a coping mechanism of allotting another Fellow to follow up on all assignments given to Don in order to assure completion. When

Bennie was recently declared free of disease at the end of his therapy and showed himself ready to return to full duty, the Committee agreed that Don Horvath needed to be let go at the end of the academic year.

They wrote him a letter reminding him that his contract with New City was for only one year and that the contract would not be renewed. They thanked him for his work and service, wished him good luck with his future and signed off.

Don was devastated. Somehow he had convinced himself that he was doing very well in the Fellowship and would be staying on for the final years. He had been taught that hard work equaled success; his Little League team had floundered but he was awarded a Participation Trophy anyway. Other similar experiences throughout his college and medical school career enforced the idea that if one worked hard success was guaranteed. And he had worked hard during this past nine months; he was always in the hospital both early and late and in the library whenever there was a break from his assigned duties. Tom thought this dismissal must be a mistake. He showed the letter to other Fellows and asked their opinion about its interpretation; he asked secretaries in the Cardiology Division their opinion about how he should go about 'getting this fixed' and he called some of the Committee members at home at night to lobby them for his extension. So far, the wall had held.

Adamson looked up at Don, noticed the immediate break in eye contact, and said, "Don, I'm really scheduled pretty tight today. And I certainly think the issue has been settled." He turned and walked down the hall to his office in the vain hope that such a clear signal to disengage would be rightly interpreted by Horvath. That was truly a vain hope.

Horvath tagged along behind. "I just want to know whether it was something I did or something I didn't do. And how I can fix it. I mean, why?"

At the door to the office Wilford paused and said, "Look, Don, you knew from the outset that this was most likely a one year position. And that's the way it turned out." He then entered the office area, nodded to his secretary, Sheila, who always seemed to be at her desk when he came in the mornings. The pair crossed in front of her desk on the way to Wilford's office. Sheila smiled at him and started to get up to block Don from following Wilford into his office but Wilford signaled her to leave the issue alone.

Don actually followed him all the way into the office and right up to the desk where Wilford turned around to face him. He set his coffee cup on the corner of his desk and put his briefcase in the chair in front of his desk blocking any attempt by Horvath to sit there. Then he turned and faced the Fellow directly. "It's a done deal, Don." Wilford stepped back toward the office door and with his back to Horvath slowly took off his coat, hung it on the coat hanger and then placed the hanger on the hook on the back of the door, removed his hat and placed it on the same hook, taking his time. Again he had vainly hoped that Don would just leave. Wilford sighed to himself and turned back to Horvath at the same time indicating with his right arm that the door was open.

Even Don Horvath understood that gesture and moved toward the door saying, "I just want to know what I did . . ."

"You signed a one-year contract, Don. That's what you did. And the year is coming to an end. Get over it. Start looking for some place that has a vacancy. And leave all of us alone while you do it." Wilford delivered that last sentence forcefully as he stood in his open doorway and in full view of Sheila. His intent was clear; Don Horvath could not look to anyone in the Department of Cardiology to help him locate a position nor to write him a letter of recommendation. With these words Wilford took Horvath by the arm and firmly moved him out of the office. He then stood and watched him leave the secretarial area. Wilford remained there until the door had closed behind Horvath before moving. He turned, looked at Sheila and rolled his eyes and then returned to his office.

Wilford crossed to his desk, picked up his coffee cup from the desk, and left his briefcase on the chair and went to his own chair behind the desk. The briefcase contained several folders, some on his current research projects, and two about interesting cases he and the residents had come across in the last month when he was attending. One or the other of those might make a decent case study for a publication, he thought. He had reviewed the available medical data and was going to get the responsible residents to start the literature review and write the cases for his review.

He sat at his desk, sipped at his coffee and signed on to the computer so he could check his email when he saw movement at the door. Wilford looked up and smiled as Angela Pirini walked in, moved the briefcase from the chair and sat in front of his desk like she belonged there. She actually did belong there – Angela was Wilford's Assistant Chief of Cardiology and many days started off just this way: her coming in without knocking or being asked, sitting in the chair in front of him and controlling the conversation for 15-20 minutes. He had recruited Angela from the finishing cardiology fellows the year after he came to New City and they had been close ever since. Wilford thought she was not only a fine physician but also a very good administrator; she ran the CCU efficiently and without causing waves among either nursing or administrative personnel; she had built an impressive teaching program in the Unit. He had actually recommended that the folks at Tulane talk to her when they were searching for a new CCU Director. He would rather she not leave but thought it right and proper that he endorse her capabilities – and he was surprised that she did not take the offer. That was last year and they had never really talked about it since her return. Initially, Wilford thought she was possibly considering the idea, but as time went by and he heard back from his friend at Tulane that she had declined their offer, he decided he would give her time and space to come discuss the issue with him. That time had not yet come even thought the two of them talked daily, including almost every morning just like this when she would drop in before the day got started.

Angela was not tall and her thin physique and pageboy haircut of her light brown hair projected an appearance that others initially took of her being younger than she was. She was wearing her usual pair of dark slacks with plain skimmers and a colorful blouse with a large bow in front. In spite of her young looks, she had an air of complete confidence. She was also carrying a latte from the kiosk. "Good morning," she said as she sat and took a big swallow of coffee.

"And to you." Wilford responded, leaving the computer and turning to her.

"So, my question is should I put money on the Over or the Under if the number is 115." Angela asked this with her eyebrows arched.

"Are you talking about the Match?"

"Of course. How does the chairman of the Intern Search Committee see the results coming down? Over or Under 115?"

She was talking about the results of the National Internship & Resident Matching Program, the results of which were announced nationwide on March 15th. Academic programs advertised their available positions each Fall, winnowed through hundreds of written applications, invited as many as a hundred individuals to visit their program for interviews and then ranked all these candidates in a single list. Candidates did the same, ranking their choices from first to last and both parties then sent their confidential lists to the NIRMP. Candidates and programs alike signed declarations that they would not seek agreements outside the program and that they would abide by the match. The Program then did the digital 'magic' of matching each candidate with the highest rated program of their choice that had also chosen that candidate on their list. Results came out all at one time on March 15th – Match Day. Next week.

The programs rated themselves internally by two measures after Match Day: the medical school GPA of their matched interns was a key bragging point, but so was how far down their list of names the process went before their slots were all filled. Although each department had responsibility for their individual programs, the medical school and New City had appointed an overarching Intern Oversight Committee for coordination of visits, assisting with some of the paperwork and confirming that departmental slots were completely funded. Wilford had served as chair of the search committee this past year. Now he said, "I have no new information since we talked about this at the Christmas Party."

"I know, but now it's time to place the bets," she responded.

Just then, Sheila Hester, Wilford's secretary stuck her head through the doorway, "I'm here," she said smiling at them both. "Need anything?"

They both said they did not and she went to back her desk and returned to setting up for the day.

Back in Wilford's office Angela persisted, "See, I always do better on the March Madness Pool if I at least came in on the right side of the Match Pool. What's the likelihood of Under 115?"

Wilford took another swallow of coffee and said, "Medicine and Surgery are both going to come in in the 30s, so really the question comes down to what happens in Peds."

"They haven't done that well in years."

"Right. But they weren't pushing a program with a chair who is the outgoing President of the American Academy."

"Oh come on! Graduating medical students aren't interested in that kind of stuff." Angela poo-pooed that concept, sat back in mock disdain and took a big draught on her coffee.

"The ones that came through this year seemed pretty knowledgeable and impressed about it." Wilford wasn't arguing with her; he was simply giving her his interpretation of facts he had observed in his committee role.

"That wasn't me. I don't think I even knew about national organizations when I went for interviews."

"Or me. But we need to realize, it's a very different game now than when you and I went through the match. These guys were already talking about opportunities for Fellowships."

"So, will they do well enough to bring in the 'Under' vote?"

"I'm really not sure – obviously this is the first year we are advertising a Past President of the Academy. It's a hard call."

"I'm gonna top up my cup," Angela said, rising and starting toward the door. "Want me to hit you again?"

Wilford looked at his half-empty cup and said, "Sure" as he handed it to her.

Angela stepped out into the secretarial area and went to the Keurig coffee machine in the corner. She quickly chose a pod, put it in the machine and filled the room with the sound and smell of fresh brewed coffee. She repeated the maneuver on the second cup she had and reached for the small container of packets to get some sweetener.

"Sounds like a toss-up," she said to Wilford through the open office doorway. " Probably why the pool organizers chose 115 for the break point." Her attention on the cups finished, she walked back in Wilford's office and retook her seat.

"What do you win in this pool anyway?" Wilford asked. He was not a person to get deeply involved in faculty and staff activities. Somewhat aloof in his dealings even with those in the Cardiology Division, to whom he referred as 'those who work for me', he was not really any closer with other Division Chiefs and did not know any of the secretarial staff in the hospital except for Sheila who always relayed his messages to other divisions. His big involvement in staff affairs outside of work was to attend the Chief of Staff's annual Christmas Party.

"Everybody puts in $5 to bet either Over or Under or to pick a particular number," Angela answered. "All the money on a specific number goes to anyone hitting the exact number. If there's no 'exact hit', all the money is evenly divided between those who guessed the right side of the break."

"Is the Chair of the Interview Committee allowed to bet?" he asked sipping at his coffee, but not really interested. He was not a gambling man.

"Oh, sure," she said "we'd be happy to take your money. But you're not allowed to win."

"What did we get this weekend?" he inquired losing interest in the discussion of the Match and the betting game afoot. Almost every morning he had this conversation with Angela about new cardiology cases admitted the preceding day. He wanted to be abreast of things but not really involved.

"A couple of MIs – both stable and settling in to the CCU. And a young girl with unexplained V Tach and torsade in the ED." Angela was the on call physician for the CCU over the past weekend and usually discussed all admissions with the house staff.

"She make it?"

"Yeah. She's up on the ward now, sleeping it off as I understand." She quickly told him particulars about Patricia's case including the response to magnesium.

"I heard that Bolling is about to finish his evaluation of the Beating Heart project," he offered wondering if her opinion about the project mirrored his in any way.

"I don't see that for us right now. You've seen the presentations at the meetings – nobody has any data that it's any better." She shook her head at him while speaking to indicate her own lack of interest.

"Well, I haven't seen all the data and somebody is keeping the issue alive and I bet . . ."

Just then the pager on Wilford's belt went off. It wasn't loud, just totally unexpected and he jumped and twisted to see the message. "Damn! Here we go. An arrest and I just got here." He grabbed his coffee and drained it and headed for the door, grabbing his white coat and stethoscope as he left. It was 0824.

Chapter Nineteen

Monday, March 8

Angela remained sitting in the chair in front of Wilford's desk after he left. She sipped her coffee a couple of times and replayed the conversation in her head.

Pirini, 38 years old, unmarried and without a steady interest in anyone to pair with is an important part of New City. She grew up in a small town in Northwest Ohio of quite modest means; her father ran the local garage and her mother was the town librarian. She spent much of her free time in the library, did her studies conscientiously and scored high on her SATs and later on her MCAT. She was clearly bright and hard-working and well thought of by her coworkers.

And she was ambitious about climbing the academic ladder. In her early years she pursued two or three different paths in research, successfully getting one of the efforts funded with a start-up grant but the work in the laboratory was less clear than expected and turned out to be explicable by one of the process steps she had employed to purify the component she was testing. When the results didn't pan out, her grant was not renewed.

On the other hand, Angela was quick to recognize things that were out of the ordinary in the clinical arena and, after not succeeding in the research laboratory, she turned her attention to teaching and clinical care. Her recognition of unusual presentations of common conditions or uncommon conditions led to her working with students and residents to develop individual case reports publishable in reputable journals. Students and house staff alike came to her with questions about ECG interpretations.

After more than 10 years in the field, she was now the Associate Director of Cardiology at a mid-level medical school, an Associate Professor of Medicine, member of the American College of Cardiology and a regular presenter at various scientific sessions in her field. But she was not particularly happy. Nothing to do with her social life, the unhappiness was generated by a feeling inside that she lacked fulfillment. She had taken the New City CCU under her wing and developed systematic protocols for admission, transfer, discharge, etc. She had taken responsibility for approving the credentials of other specialty technicians such as respiratory therapists to work in the CCU causing some arguments and discord with certain physicians. Nonetheless, her 'credentialing' process did not involve professional capability but success in interpersonal relations: other disciplines ultimately followed her lead. In a clinical arena often beset with tribal and internecine conflict that occasionally hindered prompt and high quality patient care, she had asserted a fact-based leadership that allowed all practitioners in the area to work smoothly in every patient's best interest.

Angela believed in process improvement and preached it from the bedside in the CCU. Every event or untoward occurrence was carefully studied by all disciplines with Angela leading a search for ways to improve the way the process was done 'next time.' She began to publish medical articles on improved CCU processes and some of the residents wanted her to work with them on one or more case studies for publication. Within just a few years she had not only an enviable curriculum vitae for academic advancement but also a growing national reputation in critical care quality improvement.

After all that, she was invited to Tulane last year to interview for a position there only to find out that all they had wanted was for her to do what she was already doing: run the CCU, build a program like the one at New City and be second in command in the cardiology division. She had been embarrassed when this came clear during her interview. Later as she thought on it she had become angry and disappointed. She knew that Wilford was puzzled about why she did not take the position and she knew that someday she would have to have 'the talk' with him about it.

But for now she would keep the conversation on lighter topics and the usual 'what went on last night?' Over the ensuing months since she returned and got past the first conversation without explaining her action, it became easier to dodge with each passing day. Their subsequent interactions had comfortably left that topic alone. She had time, she knew, before it would come up again.

She finished her coffee, grabbed Wilford's cup and left the office, throwing both cups in the trash next to the Keurig machine. Sheila was not at her desk, probably off running some errands or paperwork to other offices. Angela went into her office, closed her door, turned on her computer and began checking her email.

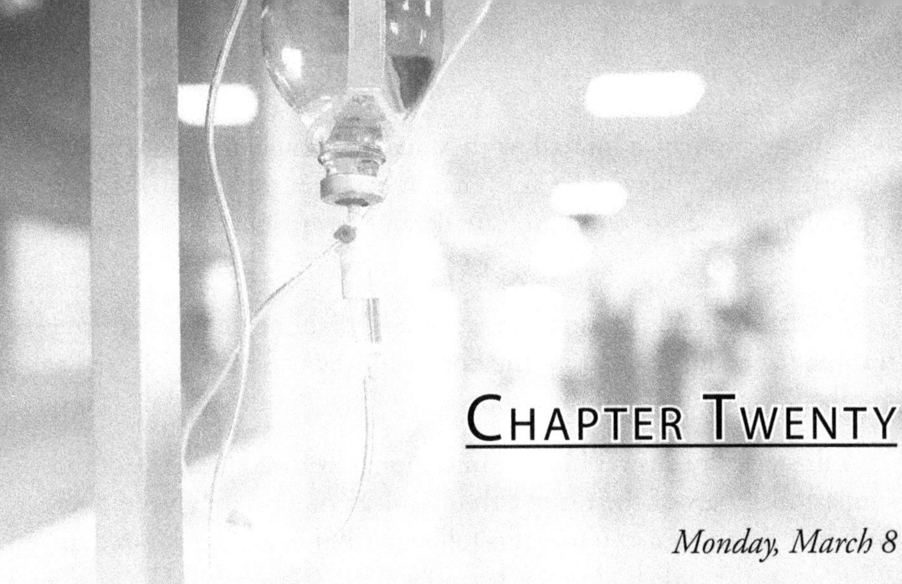

Chapter Twenty

Monday, March 8

At 0822 the cardiac monitor in the paralegal's room started alarming and its shrill beeping and wailing sound was heard all over Ward 3-C. Everyone stopped whatever he or she was doing at the sound and each made quick mental assessment of the source then started running toward it. Lila put down her tray of medications at the nurses' station and made directly for Patricia's room. When she entered she noted that Patricia is lying quietly on her back and Lila felt what was almost a wave of relief as she thought, "a lead fell off". Then Lila turned and glanced at the monitor and could immediately see the saw tooth pattern of ventricular tachycardia – a runaway ventricle thrashing the heart to run 180 beats a minute, so fast that the heart could not fill with blood between beats. Even as others were coming in the room, Lila hit the intercom and the ward clerk answered promptly. Lila said, "call the code team" and hung up. She spun around and with gestures and muted orders to the other nurses started preparing the patient and the area for resuscitation – lowering the head of the bed and moving the intravenous pole out of the way. Within 30 seconds the Code cart was in the room, and the area around the bed cleared just as members of the Code Team started entering the room.

Whitney was the first physician in the room and immediately began to take charge. "What have got here?" she asked pushing up the sleeves on her white jacket as she stared at the monitor.

"Young woman admitted with v. tach through the Emergency Department on Friday," Lila answered in the calm monotone medical professionals use to communicate key information as quickly as possible.

"What's gone on during the weekend?" Whitney queried before turning to the nurse entering the door with the crash cart. "I need a number 7 trach tube and the 'scope."

Lila started to answer but was interrupted by the appearance of the surgical members of the team. The Resident came through the door with two interns and two students following and immediately sized up Whitney as the code leader. "What do you need?" he asked her.

"Get me a cutdown," she responded hardly looking up from her attempt to insert the tracheostomy tube.

"Do you want a subclavian?" one of the interns asked.

"Not until I get this tube in place!"

"Right," he said and stepped back while the other intern started a cutdown on the left ankle.

Whitney felt the tube slide into place and hooked the Ambu bag up and gave a couple of tiny puffs listening to the anterior chest. "In place. I'm bagging."

Lila noted, "Pulse Ox is coming up."

Whitney again stared at the monitor. That wasn't run-of-the-mill V. tach. she thought. What the . . . wait, that's torsade, she thought.

At about the same moment, she and the surgical resident asked, "What's her treatment?"

Now Lila got her chance. "We've been pumping her full of potassium but her levels have stayed low all weekend."

"What's her K now?" asked Whitney.

A medical resident who had joined the effort had been looking at her chart now spoke up. "Last measured was 3.4 yesterday. One was drawn this morning. Looks like she converted with Mag sulfate in the ED."

"OK, then. Let's get some mag sulfate running," said the surgical resident.

The crash cart nurse looked at Whitney who nodded and said, "two amps in 250 of saline. And somebody call the lab about her latest potassium."

"How's that cutdown?" asked the surgical resident. The intern performing the insertion didn't raise his head but said, "having trouble threading."

The surgical resident looked at the bag hanging from the intravenous stand and asked, "What's this?"

"Saline, thiamine and potassium," said Lila.

"Pull that out of the pump and hang the mag sulfate and open it up."

Lila was already on the task and when the magnesium sulfate bag was ready she had the connection ready for it and started it running through the intravenous line as quickly as it would go – but that wasn't very fast.

Whitney decided something has to be done about the rhythm and it couldn't wait for the intravenous medications – especially when the line was running so slowly. Loudly enough to be heard over the several different conversations in the room she said, "Get me the defibrillator."

"Start at 100," she directs.

Lila pulled Patricia's top up so the paddles could be placed; the bared breast gained no attention from the team members; each is glued to their single responsibility. They were recalling coursework and trying to be helpful while not getting in each other's way. Every so often someone squeezing the Ambu bag says, "I need a break," and another team member stepped to the head of the bed and assumed the responsibility for breathing for the young woman. Nurses were preparing medications and physicians and students were attentive to intravenous lines for medication administration. Whitney had the paddles in her hands and had greased them. Now, as she rubbed them together to spread the gel, she glanced at the settings then turned to the bed with the paddles held up so everyone could see.

"Clear!" said Whitney; everyone backed up and raised their hands in the air, including the intern working on the cutdown and the one pressing the Ambu bag. Whitney placed the paddles on the bared chest, wiggled them slightly to get a seal with the gel and pushed the button.

The shock caused Patricia to arch her back but not viciously. As her body settled back on to the bed, almost everyone turned their total attention to the monitor showing the electrical heartbeat. The intern working the Ambu bag stepped back to the head of the bed, grabbed the bag and began the regular inflation of Patricia's lungs as the surgical intern immediately bowed his head over the cutdown site in Patricia's left ankle. Their work had not changed no matter what happened on the monitor – and the monitor showed no change; Patricia remained in V. tach. with a barely palpable pulse; she could not long last in this condition.

"BP down to 90 systolic," called one of the nurses.

"Bump it up to 200," Whitney said, picking up the defibrillator paddles again and moving to the bedside.

This time the shock had desired results. Patricia had a pulse and a normal sinus rhythm on the monitor and everyone started to relax and even an occasional smile was seen. The regaining of the normal pulse is the usual prelude to the blood pressure stabilizing at a normal level and spontaneous respirations starting up again. It is the first step on a very long staircase in a successful resuscitation. There was a reason to be happy with the result but no reason to let down one's guard or to think the battle was won.

"BP down to 70 systolic," calls out one of the nurses.

"Give me a cc of 1:1000 epinephrine," cries Whitney. The crash cart nurse was already preparing for that request but while they waited everyone in the room watched the blood pressure slowly fall toward zero. Then Whitney had the drug and syringe; she pushed the pajama top up and quickly identified specific anatomic marks on Patricia's breastbone and ribs. Then, choosing her spot, Whitney pushed the long needle between the ribs and the medication was injected. "Now, pump her," she called out, with more than a little tremulousness in her voice.

Chapter Twenty-One

Monday, March 8

Meanwhile, Wilford left his office and turned down the hall toward the elevator bank. As he strode purposefully into the area, fully intending to catch one of the cars going up, he looked up at the indicators over the doors and noted that all cars were above the lobby area and rising. No telling when they would be back down to take him to the code. He thought to himself, "Good thing I'm not the first responder, I guess. Ward 3C is only three flights up and down that hall. I can make better time on the stairs."

He turned to the far side of the elevator bank and pulled open the doorway to staircase and started up. These stairs were not part of the area commonly used by patients and family members. The stairs were concrete and the handrails were metal pipes. Because patients or family members did not use these passages between floors, Wilford knew there would not be much traffic to get in his way. He wasn't exactly hurrying but he decided to take the steps two-at-a-time. The staircase was in part of the newest construction of the hospital and the first two floors were interspersed with interstitial space for engineering to access pipes and conduits in the space between one ceiling and the floor above. As a result of this construction the usual staircase between ground and the first floor and between first and second floors were divided into two partial flights that added several additional steps and two landings. Each staircase came to a landing halfway between floors where the direction of the stairs made a 180-degree turn around the landing. Entrances into the staircase were located at each floor; there were access ports on the intermediate landings.

Wilford began to note some shortness of breath and a little light-headedness as he turned on the first landing and he slowed his pace to one step at a time. He reassured himself, "I don't need to be there at the kickoff, anyway." However, even with the slowed pace he realized he was feeling a little light-headed after he passed the door to the Second Floor. As he continued up the stairs he noted that his visual field was darkening. At first he thought the lights were just dimmer in the rarely used staircase but within a few seconds he knew that was not the explanation. His vision was blackening out and the tunnel through which he could see was narrowing with each step. He thought, "what the hell? I'm not in this bad a shape. But I gotta sit down." He felt weak and stumbled on the stair as he reached the interstitial landing between second and third floors.

And he paused a second on the landing he thought, "I've got to get out of these stairs." But he couldn't decide whether to keep trying to go up or to turn around and descend. Then he thought again, "I need to sit down and let this pass." But as he turned to try to sit down, his feet slipped and he fell against the outer wall of the staircase with his head on the landing and his body on the top steps leading up to the landing.

Wilford thought, "Gotta get head down." But he couldn't get his feet to move and his head slumped. "Got to move," he thought again but didn't, because he did not have the strength to move. He felt his heart beating in his chest very fast and the darkness continued to close in on the central point of his vision. He was lying with his face to the wall on the top step and his entire visual field was the concrete joint where the landing met the top step. Then that blacked out, too. And Wilford no longer felt his heart beating fast. Or beating at all.

It was 0828.

Chapter Twenty-Two

Monday, March 8

The third year medical student reading the medical record and watching his first real code spoke out loud, "Wow! Her potassium was 2.7 when she came to the Emergency Room." With all the hubbub in the room her statement almost went unnoticed. The surgical resident said, "Wait a minute! What?" and looked at the student.

Semi-transfixed for a second, the student looked up at the momentary quiet and found everyone looking directly at him. "Her potassium was 2.7 when she got here," she said, a little uncertain.

One of the medical residents grabbed the chart from the student and shortly announced, "That's right and they gave her replacement that night!" At these words, everyone started moving more quickly, some doing what they had been doing and others taking up new tasks.

"She needs more potassium," called out the surgical resident.

Whitney was already calculating in her head. "Put 40 of K in a liter of saline and hang it," she commanded to the crash cart nurse who jumped to comply.

"Why isn't there a central line?" asked the surgical resident. "Somebody find out what today's potassium was!"

In the middle of the tumult another nurse's voice cut through, "BP down to 60!" And the resuscitation efforts began anew to address the rhythm, the possible electrolyte imbalance and the falling blood pressure simultaneously.

One of the students was now handling the Ambu bag hooked to the endotracheal tube while another was straddling Patricia on the bed to apply chest compressions. The intravenous fluids were wide open but running very slowly. Then, in the middle of the activity there came a familiar and dreaded sound - a steady beeping from the monitor. Everyone stopped their activity, even the Ambu bagger and the chest compressor. They stopped and turned first toward the monitor that was showing a flatline for a heartbeat. Then everyone looked at someone else for a clue as to what would happen next. And the monitor beep continued.

Except for the chest compressions and the Ambu bagging, everything came still. "How long has it been?" asked the surgical resident.

The crash cart nurse checked her watch and said, "Thirty-seven minutes."

"Your call, Whitney," said the surgical resident looking at her standing at the head of the bed.

Whitney stared at the monitor for a couple of seconds and then, began to strip off her gloves and said, "I'm calling it at 8:59. Thanks everyone."

One of the nurses switched off the sound coming from the monitor and almost before the sound had faded, people were leaving the room, not wanting to be so closely associated with a failure to save a life. Within ninety seconds, everyone had left except for Lila, Whitney, and the crash cart nurse.

Whitney picked up the medical record and took out her pen, preparing to make the final entry but she stood for a moment deciding whether to go sit at the Nurses' Station. Lila automatically started to clean up some of the debris on the floor and was reminded by the crash cart nurse that all the materials need to be left in place – tubes in the body and all that – for the pathologist and for the AAR.

"You remember, the General wants to have everything left like it was to see if there's something out of place," she said.

"I know," said Lila, thinking to herself, "*I've actually helped with several of these reviews and I know what I'm doing.*"

At that moment Jimmie Harper walked into the room and stopped in his tracks, he stared at the mess and the other people he did not expect to find there. "What's going on?" he asked, truly surprised about all the mess and its implied activity in a room he thought would be still and quiet.

"She coded, Jimmie and we couldn't get her back," said Whitney. "She's yours, isn't she?"

"Yeah," he said with a sinking feeling. What could have happened? He began to run things through his mind about how Patricia was when he left on Saturday morning. Had he checked everything? What was the potassium then? Had he not ordered enough replacement? These thought were clashing in his mind as Whitney was trying to tell him what had happened.

"She went back into V. Tach and we just couldn't get her into normal sinus."

"What about her potassium?"

"Oh. I don't know. We didn't have today's yet. We gave her magnesium and shocked her twice. She just wasn't coming back. I'll write the note."

Jimmie just stood there, staring at the bed and his now very dead patient.

"Who's going to call the family?" asked Lila.

"That would be you, Jimmie," said Whitney as she left for the nurse's station.

Chapter Twenty-Three

Monday, March 8

Wilford was lying still and quiet on the staircase landing between the second and third floors. Twice someone bolted out of the door on the third floor and headed up the stairs, away from where he was laying but Wilford was not aware.

Only when three residents were leaving the third floor and heading down did anyone notice him. As they turned the corner, talking about baseball spring training one of them saw the figure lying still and quiet on the landing, "Hey, who's that?"

And then there was the flurry of activity that always accompanies someone lying on the floor in a hospital; the attempt to wake them up, the checking for vital signs and, usually, the initiation of cardiopulmonary resuscitation. And for these three, there was also the recognition that this was one of them: the white coat and the stethoscope were first clues but the real awareness came when one of them paid attention to the face of the fallen man.

"Geez! It's Dr. Adamson," he said, actually taking his hands off the dead man's chest as if he were violating some tradition.

"We need to call a code!" said another reaching for his cell phone.

But it was obvious that Wilford Adamson would not be responding to any resuscitation. He was cold, pulseless and had the glassy discoloration of his eyes that were the hallmark of death.

The code team was not called; there was nothing for them to do. After standing around on the staircase for a few minutes one of the residents had the idea to move the body; he re-entered the ward and a gurney was brought to the stairwell. The three of them lifted the body and carried Adamson up the half-flight and placed him onto the gurney. One of the other residents found a sheet to cover the body.

The conversation then turned to where to move Dr. Adamson. The senior resident noted that they had to get him out of the main hallway and suggested the morgue. They all agreed and one of the younger residents was sent to summon the freight elevator. The senior resident assigned the task of escorting the body to the morgue to the other resident and then personally took off to notify the Chief of Staff.

Tom Bolling was in his office when the resident came in. Looking through the open door the resident could see that the Chief of Staff was alone at his desk.

“Sir?” he said in a rather small voice for him. He actually started speaking to the Chief of Staff while walking past the front of Mary’s desk.

As Mary stood to try to intervene, the resident walked directly into Tom’s office and said, “ Dr. Adamson, sir. He’s dead. On the stairs.”

Tom bolted from behind his desk and grabbed the resident by the arm. The resident was pale and looked like he was going to fall and Tom steadied him and steered him to a chair. “What did you say?” he asked.

“Dr. Adamson. We just found him lying in one of the staircases. He must have had a heart attack! I mean we tried. But he was already dead. You gotta believe me.”

“Who was there?” Tom immediately sized up this development as a multilevel crisis. It was obvious to him that he needed to keep some kind of lid on this news. He couldn’t have everyone running around with all the rumors that would get started. At the same time in his imagination he began to think through how he was going to have to tell Elizabeth Adamson about what had happened. He needed more information and he needed it kept somewhat quiet for now. And, on a haunting and unsettling different level, he began to think about how he was going to deal with the loss of a Division Chief and all the trouble associated with going through the recruiting process. He was ashamed of that last thought and pushed it to the back of his mind. To handle the immediate issue he needed more information, quickly. He turned back to the resident and asked, "Who, exactly, knows about this?"

"There was just the three of us. I mean we didn't call the code team or anything. There wasn't anything to do. Honest. I mean he was dead."

"I believe you. Where is he now and where are the other guys? And was there anyone else?"

The resident named his companions and Tom looked to the doorway where Mary stood with pen and pad. As she wrote down the names, Tom issued orders to page those individuals directly and have them come to his office. Then, hearing that the Chief of Cardiology was now in the New City morgue, he grabbed his own white coat and headed out the door. "When you get those guys here, keep 'em here," he said to Mary as he left. "And don't let them talk to anyone till I get back."

Chapter Twenty-Four

Monday, March 8

Jimmie Harper was surprised to see that Patricia's husband was not in the room or even in the hospital when he set out to find him for notification of her death. After checking all over the Ward and asking several nurses, he learned that Benjie had not yet been seen that day. But he had left his cell phone number and Jimmie was able to get him on the phone quickly. Jimmie told Benjiethat there had been a 'change' in Patricia's condition and that he needed to come to the hospital right away. Following a common policy, Jimmie did not tell Benjie that Patricia had died – that was information that needed to be handled personally. They arranged to meet in her room.

It took Benjie about fifteen minutes to arrive, still a little disheveled, anxious and flustered. Jimmie met him at the door to Patricia's room and steered him quickly into a small consultation room.

"What's happened?" Benjie wanted to know.

"Mr. Harding, your wife had another attack of that abnormal rhythm."

"But you fixed it, dintja?"

'Mr. Harding, this was a very serious kind of rhythm disturbance, and . .

"What happened to my wife?" Benjie demanded.

"Sir, if you would just sit down here . . ."

"I don't want to sit down! I want to know what's going on!" Benjie was starting to shout again and Jimmie closed the door to the room and indicated that they should both sit down.

"Mr. Harding," he began.

"Benjie, dammit! Call me Benjie"

"All right, Benjie. Your wife had a very serious rhythm disturbance and we could not pull her out of it."

"What does that mean?"

"She died while we were trying to get her back into a normal heart rhythm. She was just too sick for us to make any difference."

"Died? Patricia's dead?"

"Yes sir. I'm very sorry for your loss."

"How did this happen? You had all those monitors and things on her?"

"It was very fast. And the monitors picked it up and we were right on top of it but it was too severe for us to get her back. I'm really sorry."

"If I'd been here this wouldn't have happened, you know. The nurses kicked me out and if I was here I could have done something. I know it." Benjie seemed to have lost all the air in his body as he slumped further in the chair.

"Don't blame yourself, Mr. Hard . . . Benjie. We were right there and spent over a half an hour working to bring her back. I'm sorry we couldn't do better."

"Do you know what went wrong?" Benjie was almost pleading now.

"Not completely, no. We are aware that her potassium was very low but we aren't sure why," Jimmie explained.

"What's that got to do with it?" asked Benjie.

"The heart rhythm goes haywire when the potassium level is too low," Jimmie said, preparing to give a short explanation of the electrical system of the heart.

"But why was the level so low? And how come we didn't know about it before?" Benjie asked, jumping right to what he considered the heart of the matter.

"That's part of what we don't know . . . Benjie. And that's why I want to ask for your permission to do an autopsy on Patricia," Jimmie laid his hand on Benjie's arm as he said this and tried to make eye contact.

Benjie began shaking his head and wouldn't look directly at Jimmie. "I don't think so. She's been through enough," he said in a monotone.

"We can do the autopsy very quickly, Benjie. You do want to know what really happened, don't you?" This was followed by silence from Benjie so Jimmie again laid his hand on Benjie's arm and spoke quietly and earnestly to him. "Look, someday in the future you are going to want to know more than what we can tell you today. With the autopsy we are much more likely to get to the bottom of things."

"She's been through enough," Benjie persisted but without a lot of conviction.

"No one is going to hurt her, Benjie. We will take good care of her. I promise."

"How can you say that when you let her die?" Benjie was almost in tears.

"Because we want to know whether we could have done something else. We are here to learn about this, too, Benjie," Jimmie said.

"Really?

"Really. And the autopsy is how we do that. Will that be all right with you?"

Benjie sat there for a minute apparently thinking and finally slowly he nodded. Jimmie patted him on the back and said, " I have some papers for you to sign and we'll take care of everything."

Minutes later Jimmie left the consultation room with permission slips all signed, leaving Benjie and one of the nurses in the room. Other nurses had called Benjie's friends from the church and they arrived shortly and were shown into the room with Benjie. The nurses left them there comforting him and went about the business of moving Patricia's body down to the morgue.

Chapter Twenty-Five

Monday, March

Lila was standing in the hospital room where Patricia had been. She looked around at the post-code mess: wrappers, tubing, needle guards, even discarded syringes. There was the usual other material out and around the crash cart and scattered over the floor of the room – even under the bed. Her job now was the usual of getting the crash cart re-stocked and ready for the next code but also, under the new guidelines from the General, arranging for the AAR.

Lila thought the AAR was a good innovation. She particularly liked the closure of putting the events in order and understanding what had worked and what may not have. Of course, the initial organization of the materials was not the most enjoyable part of the drill. And that's what she was looking at right now. She needed to follow the course of the events and lay out the involved and utilized materials on the bed in the order of their use.

To an inexperienced nurse, this might be a near-herculean task, but for Lila, who had now done this arrangement more than a dozen times, and who had been present during the attempted resuscitation, there was an invisible order – a pattern that had emerged from familiarity.

As she gathered the various bags and instruments she performed some of the functions that she knew would be part of the AAR: she checked that the laryngoscope light came on when the blade was clicked into place, she turned all the bags so their labels could be read and she grouped the various 'sharps' together.

The purpose of the AAR was, essentially, to replay the events in the code. Beginning with the alarm, and whatever it was that caused the alarm the team would walk themselves through the steps taken by the code team. The new cardiac monitors had a recording function that looped the findings from all the various leads to a 'last hour' recording. The review team would be able to trace the event that led to the code and match the tracings with the record of medication administration kept by the crash cart nurse for everything that happened in the last hour of Patricia's life.

For obvious reasons, the team needed to replay their efforts soon after the event in order to recall the major events and to get those events in the right chronology. Lila's job was to preserve all the materials in a usable and interpretable state so the team did not waste time arguing over recall of minor – or even major – events. Her technique, now evolving out of the habits she developed with previous reviews, was to line up the bags and instruments by the timing of their usage across the patient bed; she noted that her attention to these details had helped more than one of the residents to better recall events from a chaotic code in the past.

And she paused and looked at one bag particularly. It was nearly empty but as it lay against the white sheet of the bed, Lila thought the color didn't look quite right. As she was about to read the label, another nurse came in the door and asked, "Do you need any help? I'm free for the next few minutes and I know how long this stuff takes sometimes."

Lila spun around and smiled. She didn't count on getting this kind of help and this offer would help her focus more on what happened rather than getting ready for the next one.

"Hey, thanks, Rebecca. Yeah. Would you take that sheet from the crash cart and get Pharmacy to start collecting the replacements?" This, of course, was a key requirement after a code. The cart and its medications and instruments might be needed somewhere else in the hospital at a moment's notice. One couldn't leave the cart depleted or standing idle in an AAR when it was needed for life-saving interventions elsewhere. Immediately after a code was finished, Pharmacy service personnel took the sheet of medication administration and began replacing the used items in the cart with new bottles; instruments like the laryngoscope were also replaced and the used one left for the review.

Lila remembered one review where some key items – sharps – had been deposited after use in the container on the top of the cart during a code. And that cart had left the room and created some question about the order of medications and even whether one particular medication had been given. She reached up and grabbed the sharps disposal box from the top of the cart and said to the other nurse, "You can leave the cart here for now but I've got all I need and they can have it when they're ready to restock."

"Sure." And she was off with the list in hand, leaving Lila momentarily wondering what she had been doing before the interruption.

Chapter Twenty-Six

The morgue at New City was a study in contrasts. Every morning the angled sunlight gleamed coming through the high windows at the rear of the main room. Highly polished floors reflected the light onto the surfaces of the stainless steel tables and countertops. The stark white of the cabinet fronts added to the lightening effect. At some time each morning, the sunlight streaming into the room would catch the reflection from the table top and illumed the glass doorway so that anyone entering at that moment seems otherworldly, a person suffused in light that makes them appear, if only for that instant, radiant. But the bright and shiny cleanness of every surface – even here in the newest hospital in the city – was not 'clean' from a medical perspective. Every day these surfaces were coated with various body fluids, some infected and some not, a few necrotic and foul smelling. But at the end of the day came the ritual washing of the surfaces and all surfaces wiped dry. Clean, yes; sterile, most certainly not.

Monique Song, 42, is the Chief Laboratory Service at New City and the head of Anatomic Pathology. She was five foot four inches and round of face reflecting her Philipino heritage. Her black hair was swept back into a tight bun at the back of her head. She was wearing surgical scrubs but no booties. Her feet were enclosed in a pair of dark blue gel-fit Asics and her trademark bright orange knee-high socks. Hanging around her neck was her identification badge.

Monique originally trained in Cleveland and served as the medical examiner for Cuyahoga County for four years after finishing her training. During those years she became known, and respected, as very organized and thorough. She was seen by the District Attorney as a reliable witness and was frequently called to testify; she came to dislike the practice and when her research interest began to center on cytocellular damage from chemotherapy agents, she realized she needed a different work environment and decided to move.

When she entered a room, there was little doubt in anyone's mind that she thought she knew as much – if not more – about anything or anyone else in the room. Monique was not afflicted with any deficit of confidence, yet she was not an abrasive personality. It was as if she understood the old adage about pathologists, 'knowing the final answer but too late to do anything about it.' Her time in the Medical Examiner's Office was spent in an unofficial attempt to reverse that concept and to provide a 'final answer' to families and the police so that something – 'justice' if needed – would be done about the death. She was largely able to do this, making few enemies but gaining even more non-supporters along the way. And feeling ground down by the whole experience, she began thinking about a different path after only a little more than three years in the Office.

Monique came to New City more than eight years ago, drawn by the academic setting and the opportunity to continue her research. From the very beginning, however, she organized the morgue and the technicians there as if she were setting up another medical examiner's office. There were protocols for everything and samples were taken from everywhere. Monique's theory was, "if I don't need it I can always throw it away. But if I need it and didn't get it, we're out of luck." Because of her interest in cytotoxicity, it was almost universal that a sample tube of blood and other fluids available for testing accompanied every autopsy. Two of her autopsy technicians had come with her from Cleveland and they knew her habits and protocols by memory – with them it became a semi-religious set of steps.

There were many adjectives the medical staff used to describe Monique's running of the laboratory. "Efficient" was the most common – and the most kind. That efficiency butted heads often, however, with the medical staff desire to invade her area to gaze through her microscopes and watch her slice up organs at autopsies. Early on she had to retract policies that prohibited non-technical personnel from entering the various division areas. Her reasoning was based in her former life and belief in the sanctity of a 'chain of evidence'. Previous Chiefs of Staff and Chiefs of Medicine were unable to unravel this belief of hers to any significant degree but she and Tom Bolling had come to an understanding very early in his term as Chief of Staff.

Tom was able to understand her background and the resulting underlying concept of the 'chain of evidence' and led her to an understanding that such methods might actually slow or impede pre-mortem diagnosis. He also managed to get her to make thorough explanations of pathophysiologic mechanisms to the staff and students who came to the lab. His point were that these were the people who were looking for answers and she had many of those answers and could become the one who unlocked much of the mystery of medicine for these students and residents. Monique was ultimately persuaded and, after a period when her discussions became a little too long and the word in the hospital was, "Don't go to the lab for information unless you have an extra hour to spend," she learned to pare her discussions to the needs and time constraints of the questioners. Rather quickly she became one of the more renowned teachers at New City.

Monique knew what Tom had done in making her change her thoughts about multiple people wandering in and out to watch her perform an autopsy. But she maintained her demeanor of command of the scene and of the facts whenever these interlopers showed up. Students and residents were no longer reticent to travel to the laboratory to get vital information, but no one went there for a casual chat.

Chapter Twenty-Seven

Monday, March 8

When Monique started her first autopsy of the day, she approached the body of the man who died in the Intensive Care Unit over the weekend, aware that blood and urine samples had already been taken, labeled and set to the side for her to determine which tests will be run. Monique's first steps in performing an autopsy were similar to those of many pathologists: she started from the 'big picture' and moved carefully through to the microscopic. For this case she started with a thorough examination of the body, including turning it over to examine the back - a feat that required the diminutive Dr. Song to enlist the aid and assistance of one of her technicians. Then she activated the floor switch on the recording and gave her name, the date and the autopsy number as posted on the whiteboard to her right.

"This is a large, well nourished white male who appears the stated age. In place are two intravenous lines, one in the right forearm and one in the left subclavian. The endotracheal tube is also in place as is a urinary catheter." She raised her eyebrows at one of the technicians who, understanding this as a question about whether a urine sample had been taken, nodded affirmatively and Monique continued, "Urine and blood samples have been obtained without difficulty." Monique would leave the catheter and various tubes in place until she came to that part of the dissection. She routinely examined the placement of such tubes and lines and provided feedback to house officers about any misplacement particularly if the adverse placement had anything to do with the death or the lack of success of any resuscitation. Although such instances were rare, Monique did not waver in her instructions that all tubes in place at death were to be left there when the body was transferred to her for autopsy.

She proceeded with her description of the external aspects of the body describing body hair, tattoos, bruises or other skin abnormalities. Monique's team would complete the autopsy in slightly more than an hour, never moving with haste or seeming to be in hurry. The body was opened with the usual "Y" incision and the various organs were removed singly and, after close gross examination by Monique, were handed to a technician who weighed them and called out the weight for posting on the whiteboard. Then she sliced the organs searching for internal abnormalities. Finally a small fragment was detached and placed in formalin for later microscopic examination and analysis.

Monique had taken a brief opportunity to look at the patient's medical record before beginning the autopsy and knew this was related clinically to a massive heart attack. Paying close attention to the heart, she was able to see the intensive build-up of plaque in all major arteries and the definitive findings of softened and pale muscle tissue plus the presence of tough scarred areas on both sides of the heart. The scarred areas indicated previous injury from loss of blood and cell death – 'infarction' to the doctors, 'heart attack' to patients. The area of softened and pale tissue corresponded to the findings on the electrocardiogram of a new, fresh infarct. The area was large and encompassed a major amount of heart tissue on the left side. Clearly this was the cause of death. She sighed and passed the heart to the technician.

Just then the doors swung open and two young residents noisily entered pushing a gurney holding a body covered with a plain sheet.

"Hold on. What's this?" Monique frowned at the intruders. She insisted on correct process regarding dead bodies brought to the morgue. There was paperwork and proper notification. Something was amiss here; she had not been notified of the arrival of another body. This intrusion was completely out of order. She turned her back to the autopsied body and crossed her arms across her chest, the bloodied gloves evident as she faced the intruders. Her very attitude stopped the residents in their tracks.

"Sorry, Dr. Song," said one of them. "It's Dr. Adamson."

"What about Dr. Adamson?" she inquired. "No one sends a body down here without notifying me! And that includes Dr. Adamson." She took in a deep breath and stood as tall as her five-foot frame would allow.

"I mean, this is Dr. Adamson," one of the residents said pulling back the sheet to expose Wilford's face.

"Oh, my God! What happened? When did it happen?" Monique dropped her arms and stepped closer to the gurney, aware that she was not able to touch anything while still gloved. She again crossed her hands on her chest and gazed at Wilford's face and then indicated that the sheet be replaced. Monique looked up at the resident and said, "What happened?"

"We just found him. On the elevator stairs. Probably had a heart attack," the resident said but his voice began to trail off at the end. He certainly knew better than to tell the pathologist about a cause of death.

Monique frowned and said, "We'll see about that, won't we?" feigning abruptness at the presumption of the resident as she turned back to the first body. "Well, put him over there," she said indicating the rear of the room.

She was more than a little shaken by the sudden appearance of Wilford in her autopsy room; they were not close friends but together they had developed a unique method of opening a heart at autopsy following the blood flow. This had allowed them to inject the major arteries with contrast and take a flat X-ray of the organ to show all the anatomy of the vessels. It was a wonderful teaching tool and their colleagues had given them many pats on the back for developing the technique. But that was a few years ago and Monique recently had only seen Wilford on odd occasions and never for a protracted talk.

And now he was dead – no longer available for a new research idea. Not even available to chat in the cafeteria at lunch. Unexpected, as death almost always is, and far too early, as most people believe. And she, one of many left behind, would be the one deciding what the cause of that death was. Not a task she wanted as a friend and colleague but something that, unfortunately, was part of her job.

Pushing these thoughts away so she could finish the job in front of her, Monique actually turned her back to technicians who were moving the gurney carrying Wilford's body into the autopsy room, placing it almost gently against the rear wall as if not to disturb its resting occupant. She let them do their job without her gaze. The residents then stood around for a minute or two and, realizing they were not needed, quietly left the room.

After they were gone Monique stopped what she was doing for a moment, took a deep breath, closed her eyes and bent her head in a silent prayer for her former co-worker and for his wife. Then she released that breath, took another deeply into her chest and determinedly returned to her work.

Only a few minutes later and the doors opened again. Tom Bolling stepped into the room and made gentle eye contact with Monique who turned to see who had entered, and nodded quietly before stepping over to the table where Wilford lay. He looked down on the covered body of his friend as the technicians considerately took a step back from their work of preparation. Tom gently removed the sheet from Wilford's face, confirming it really was him underneath. For perhaps the first time Tom noted the gray hair at the temples of his friend and colleague and that the eyebrows were predominantly gray. "How did I never notice that?" he wondered to himself.

"Is he here for a post?" asked Monique not really looking up from her work.

"Don't know. I haven't talked to Elizabeth yet."

"There's no rush, you know."

"I'm going to go see her in just a few minutes."

"No. I mean there's no rush on the post – I can do that tomorrow or later." Monique looked up at Tom. "What do you think happened?"

"I have no clue," Tom said, as he shook his head slowly. "He seemed healthy and happy and then he died running up the stairs. I just don't know. Maybe could happen to any of us."

"Could. And does," Monique said. "I see it all the time. And it never gets easier – and not when it's a friend."

Tom turned away toward the table where she was working and asked, "Do you know about the young woman who died this morning in a code?"

"No."

"I've got to go to the Code Review before I go see Liz. Is there anything you can tell me that I can tell her?" Tom indicated Wilford's form as he spoke.

"I really don't know any more than you. He was just wheeled in here about ten minutes ago. You said he collapsed running the stairs. Sounds cardiac but don't quote me on that."

"That's what I was thinking but . . .'

"That's why we do the post." Monique was becoming more involved in her work and needed to use the recorder. She didn't want to talk about her friend in the abstract anymore. She looked at Tom, tight-lipped, and stepped on the switch. "Lungs and trachea are normal without obvious disease." Tom recognized he was being dismissed and stepped back to the door. As he left he noted that the technicians had resumed their work assisting Monique.

Procedure rules.

Chapter Twenty-Eight

Monday, March 8

Nelson Humphries was all business. He was the senior cardiology fellow in the New City training program and already had an offer to join one of the prestigious practices locally when he finishes in just a few months. He was recognized throughout the hospital as bright, savvy and politically smart. At six foot two inches with a full head of dark brown hair and light brown eyes, he is also not bad to look at – as many of the nurses and female doctors have noted over the years.

In the past few months, ever since the offer from the local cardiology group, Nelson has changed his daily work clothes. Where he formerly wore chinos and running shoes with a golf shirt, he now arrives wearing pressed dress slacks, a long-sleeved white shirt and colorful tie with shiny, black, Italian slip-ons under his long white coat.

Tom had asked Nelson to fill in on the AAR by taking the role that should have been occupied by Wilford Adamson, checking all the steps in the process of the code and confirming that all was done properly. The task was somewhat more difficult for Nelson because he had not witnessed the code and the resuscitation; that was the role of the faculty monitor. Nelson was proud to be asked and was ready to assume this responsibility, although he was saddened by the death of his teacher and mentor, Wilford. Nelson had decided on a career in cardiology primarily because of the role played in his education by Wilford. As the attending when Nelson was an intern, Wilford's clinical skills had impressed him, from bedside diagnostics to incisive readings of complex electrocardiograms.

Now, as he tried to perform the review duties of his former mentor, Nelson was the complete professional. He noted and mentally catalogued the various bags and equipment arrayed on the patient bed and quickly checked these against the list of those used in the resuscitation efforts.

Tom Bolling stood off to the side in the room, watching the process he had initiated, troubled about the absence of Wilford but determined to add the meaning of his office to the proceedings. Tom knew he was going to have to go see Elizabeth Adamson soon and he was not looking forward to that at all. While he watched the AAR his mind was more on the conversation he was dreading with Elizabeth. He had met very briefly with the residents who had found Wilford in his office on the way to the AAR. His admonition to them was clear: No talking about the event to anyone for the next couple of hours. Tom tried to impress on them the importance of not letting the news about Adamson's death leak to his wife before he, the Chief of Staff, got to the house to talk to his wife. They had agreed but he was uneasy about leaving the task undone for very long. He had called Sandra to have her go with him. She was out but would be at the house for pickup within the hour. Tom mentally came back to the review as he watched Nelson sort through the materials and check list with ease.

"And these are still in order?" Nelson asked the nurses.

"Exactly," replied Lila.

"Which ones were up when the code started?" he inquired, checking her answer against the medical record.

"Right here," she said indicating the yellow tinged bag at the far end.

"And that was taken down to run in the extra potassium?"

"That's right. When the morning lab came back, Dr. Hollings ordered us to add more potassium and use that access."

"OK." Nelson laid the medical record down and started checking the labels on the next few bags in the sequence. "Was that before or after the mag sulfate?"

"After," said Whitney, who until this moment had been quiet. She was remembering the sequence vividly and thought her dallying about the potassium might have made a difference in the outcome.

"Tell me about that," Nelson said without looking at Whitney.

"We didn't know about the hypokalemia until Lila mentioned it. But it had been almost normal and we thought she needed the magnesium."

"Probably right," nodded Nelson. "Depends on why she was hypo to start with and what the level was then. What was her K?"

He was answered by a short silence as those in attendance remembered the sequence.

"I don't think we ever got today's number," said Whitney. "We just knew she was very hypo and started pushing the K sometime after she got the mag."

"So, this is the bag with the magnesium? He asked holding up a small plastic bag.

"That's right. We started that right after we got here." Whitney then relayed the information about the initial discovery of the hypokalemia and the reversal of her tachycardia in the Emergency Department with magnesium sulfate.

"And what's this? " asked Nelson pointing at the first bag in the sequence.

Lila responded, "That's a banana bag she had hanging when this all started. That came down when we started the magnesium." Nelson nodded at this and moved down the line looking at subsequent bags. Lila, on the other hand, stood there looking at the banana bag and trying to remember something that had run through her head before. For a second she thought she had it but then the 'memory' – or thought of a memory – was gone and she tried to get back into the conversation of the review.

Twenty minutes later they were through. The review concluded that the code personnel had acted appropriately in the face of serious rhythm disturbance and that the probable electrolyte depletion had limited the responsiveness of the heart. Tragic, but understandable. Consideration was given to the lack of a central line when the patient came from the Emergency Department. There was a question left unanswered about why Patricia was admitted to the ward and not to the CCU. Nelson agreed to review these with the Director of the Emergency Department. Notebooks were closed and everyone started for the door. Tom, stood quietly by the door, nodding to individuals but really not paying attention as the review team filed past him on their way out of the room. He was in no hurry to get to his next task of notifying Elizabeth about Wilford's death.

He looked up intending to smile his thanks at Lila and caught her holding the first bag in the sequence and staring at it. He stood quietly and watched for a few seconds but she did not look up.

"Lila, everything all right?"

A pause. "Ah, no sir. I don't think so."

"What's up?"

"This bag isn't right."

"What about it?"

"Does that look like a banana bag to you?"

"Pretty much, they're all yellow like that, aren't they?"

"Yes. And, no. I mean they're yellow all right but really much darker than this," she held the bag up toward the light.

Tom was not convinced. "Look, it's yellow like it's supposed to be. Right? And that bag wasn't part of the resuscitation. It was hanging when this began, right?"

With a discouraged sigh Lila admitted, "Yes."

"Well, then. Are we done?" Tom wasn't really pushing but his attempt at closure for the conversation might have worked on another nurse.

"I think something's been added," Lila said, her mouth and lips firming up into a solid line. And she met the eyes of the Chief of Staff and nodded her head. "I'm sure of it."

"Nobody brought that up during the review," Tom said but his voice was no longer trying to shut down the conversation. He knew from long experience that when one of the nurses told him something with this degree of certainty, it was in everyone's best interest to listen, and to listen carefully.

"I know that." Lila nodded looking back at the bag. "But it could have been added before. And I didn't see it when I came in to check on things at the start of shift."

"Do you think it was added later?" Tom asked.

"I don't know. I didn't see anyone in here until the code. And I don't recall anyone adding anything to that bag during the resuscitation." And she went on, emboldened by Tom's manner of questioning. She told him of her visit to the bedside about an hour before the code. She mentioned checking the bag with the flashlight and opined that was why she didn't notice the off color. She also mentioned that she had calculated the infusion rate from the drop rate and realized there was plenty of fluid in the bag – later realizing there was too much fluid in the bag for it to end at 0900.

"What is really wrong with the bag?" Tom inquired.

"The color. It's way too light. Banana bags are a deeper yellow. I've mixed and hung hundreds of them and this one is the wrong color." Lila was now emboldened to her belief and Tom could see that in her eyes.

"Tell you what. Let's send it down to the lab and ask them what all is in it. That way we can know for sure." Tom was still not convinced but he was more than willing to support Lila in her conviction. How many times had nurses told him about something he had missed and saved him in his career? Specific instances from Emergency Rooms, Operating Rooms, Post-operative Care Units and even bedsides came immediately to mind. How many were there? Enough to make this extra test more than worthwhile.

In any event, Tom knew he had a more important task waiting for him.

Chapter Twenty-nine

Monday, March 8

Tom called Sandra and alerted her, then left the hospital and drove to their home to pick her up. They sat in the car in front of their house for a minute and Sandra asked, "Any idea what happened?"

"Probably a heart attack. He was going up the stairs and probably thought he could run through it – or something like that. I don't know."

The drive over to the Adamson's was quiet. Tom had made trips like this before. As a commanding officer, duty called him to be the official that visited the home to notify the family of the death overseas of one of his officers who was deployed. In the military family, that kind of visit from the commanding officer to your doorstep requires no lengthy explanation – but there was no telling how Liz was going to understand this visit. And there was no way Tom could soften the blow.

Once arrived, the Bollings again sat in the car for a minute, quietly composing themselves. As they walked to the door Tom had a closer look at the signs of spring: daffodils were in high profusion in the beds beside the door. Somehow their presence gave an otherworldly feeling to their visit. Together they stood for a brief spell before ringing the bell. Liz answered the door with a smile and a pleasant greeting, "Tom. Sandra. What in the world are you doing here at this time of day?" Then she saw Tom's face and immediately understood that there was some tragedy. "What's wrong?" she asked opening the door and gesturing them in. She was dressed in a simple skirt and blouse and had a short-arm splint on her left arm and a wrist splint on her right.

"Something's happened to Wilford," Tom said. Sandra took Liz by the arm and helped steer her to a chair. After she was down, Sandra slipped into the kitchen and got a glass of water and brought it back. Meanwhile, Liz asked, "What happened? Is he all right?"

"No, Liz, he's not all right. He died. We think he had a heart attack." Tom's words were gentle but the effect was as if he had shouted at her. Her head snapped back and she started to cry, "Oh no. No. NO."

Sandra was comforting her with pats and hugs but Liz pushed through to ask, "What happened? How could this have happened in the hospital? He was in the hospital wasn't he? Where is he now?"

"Yes," said Tom. "He was going up the stairs by himself and apparently passed out and before he was found . . . well, it was too late."

"Oh my God. All alone." She slumped in the chair and put her face in her hands.

Sandra went through the drill of finding out about family member's contact information and making arrangements for getting in touch with them. Liz's sister and her husband also lived in Cincinnati and Liz called them to come over right away.

Tom had taken the time to find out about the New City insurance policy and had written information to leave with Liz. He knew that was not important to her right now, but she and the family would have to start doing some kind of planning for burial and the hospital had a policy to help with those expenses.

Sitting on the couch a little later, sipping on a whiskey, Liz said to Tom, "I really don't understand it. A heart attack. You know we went on that hiking trip just a few months ago up at Leadville and he didn't have any trouble at all."

"I really didn't know where you had gone on that trip. I do remember your homecoming, though."

Liz ruefully raised her bandaged right arm. "Yeah. Go on the Big Trip and come home to smash up your car. And now this. Tom, What am I gonna do?"

"Your kids are both out West, aren't they?" Tom asked.

"Yes, Ken is in Colorado Springs; that's why we were out there hiking. To see him and the grandkids.'

"And Katie?"

"She's still in Portland, working on that degree."

"You haven't contacted them yet?"

"No. I'm waiting until Virginia gets here. I don't think I can do it alone, Tom."

"I understand. It'll be better if you have Virginia here for support."

"I don't. Understand, I mean. How could he have a heart attack on the stairs if he's able to do our yard work, play racquetball, and walk the trails at the top of Colorado without trouble? How could that happen, Tom?"

"I don't know all there is to know about that, Liz. But things like that do happen, we know that."

"Can you find out if it really was a heart attack? I mean aren't there tests and things like that?"

"Sure. We will get the autopsy if that's what you want and that should answer that question."

"I want that. I definitely want that. Willie was so .. . vigorous, you know. I just don't believe he had a heart attack."

"I'll see to it, Liz. And I'll let you know whatever we find, I promise. I'm so sorry."

"What's going to happen at the hospital?" Liz asked, suddenly.

"What do you mean?" Tom asked, puzzled by this line of questioning.

"Who's going to take his place? He really focused a lot of time and energy on that program, you know." Liz started to tear up again at the thought that Wilford's life work was now hanging empty.

Tom spoke quickly saying, "I'm going to ask Angela Pirini to take over right now. At least until things settle down. She knows what Wil was doing and she's the senior one in the Division."

"Oh, that's good," said Liz, taking a deep breath and willing the tears away. "Wil always thought so highly of her. He thought she had the potential to run a department someday. Remember, he recommended her for that Tulane job, and he was thinking that maybe she'd like to look at what the Cleveland Clinic is doing in terms of CCU care and like that. Things will be fine if she agrees."

Liz's sister-in-law, Virginia, arrived after a cross-town trip. The two women hugged and cried and sat on the couch together. Virginia had called her husband Charles and told him she was moving in with Liz for a few days so she had brought a suitcase. Sandra helped her get it into the back bedroom but she declined any help on unpacking. "Liz and I can do that later. It'll give her something to do with her hands and we can talk things over while we do it."

"That's smart," said Sandra as they returned to the front room. Tom had given Liz the paperwork from the New City personnel office and explained briefly the help they were prepared to provide. As Virginia and Sandra returned, Tom said to Virginia, "This is some information the two of you might want to go over. Insurance, burial cost defrayment, things like that."

Virginia nodded, "We'll have time for that later, but thanks."

Tom and Sandra collected their things, exchanged brief hugs and said short goodbyes after making sure that their phone numbers were well distributed.

Tom drove Sandra back home and the car was once again mostly quiet. As they neared the house, Sandra noted, "He's about the same age as you, Tom."

"I know. I've been aware of that the whole time. But I'm fine, I promise you."

"Sounds like exactly what Wil was telling Liz."

"I'm fine. I promised you years ago that I would not hide my medical conditions from you and I won't. As you well know, I had a complete physical just a few months ago and nothing new was found – and the mild hypertension is well controlled. I am fine and I have no angina or ulcers or anything else – right now. Except a really bad headache." This last was said with a bit of irony and Sandra recognized the drift.

"You mean that's a 'Sam effect' don't you? Is he getting to you?"

"That's right, and he won't."

"I remember you saying once that you were convinced that he had flying monkeys and wouldn't hesitate to use them."

"Yeah, well, I've got guns and ammo and I know how to use them."

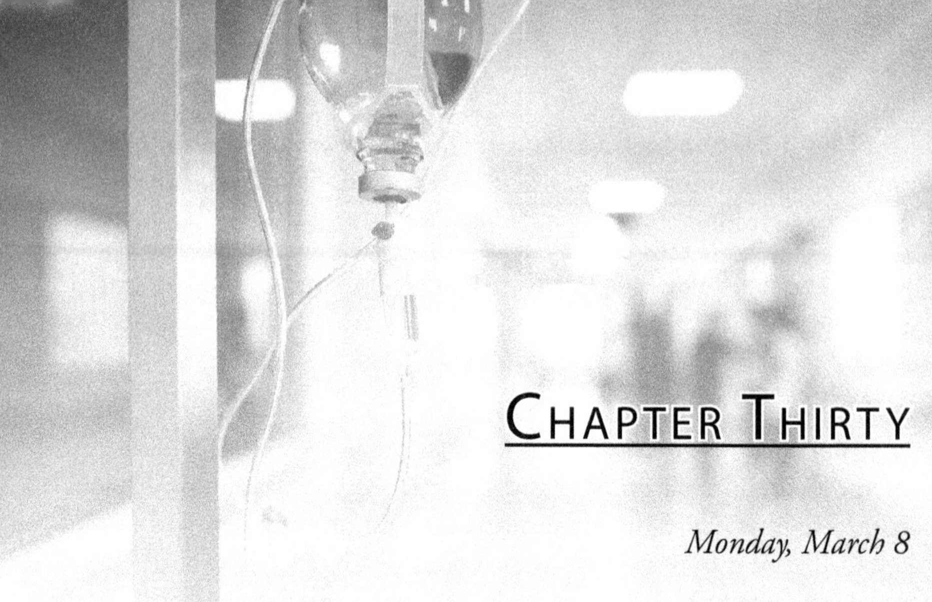

Chapter Thirty

Monday, March 8

Tom was back at his desk, sifting through some of the usual detritus that collects on the desk of an administrative physician. None of the various items were declaring itself important enough to pull his mind completely away from the conversation he had recently had with Elizabeth Adamson. Nonetheless, having done most of the required actions many times in the past, he was automatically reviewing paperwork, signing some, forwarding others and trashing a few.

After leaving the Adamson home and taking Sandra back to their home, Tom had faced the dismal task of telling the medical staff about Wilford's death. He had called an immediate 'all hands' meeting on his return to the hospital and met with everyone in the large auditorium where special events were held. He made his announcement simple and direct and told the crowd that he had already spoken with Elizabeth and that his office would keep everyone posted about funeral arrangements.

Just before the announcement he was able to corner Angela Pirini and asked her to assume the leadership of the Cardiology Division. She seemed particularly distressed and distracted about Wilford's death but was able to nod her assent to Tom's request. That forestalled the major question he had been asked after the announcement. The faculty and staff seemed calmer after hearing of Angela's appointment.

He had called Monique on his way back to the hospital to tell her that Liz wanted an autopsy on Wilford so when someone knocked on his door interrupting his administrivia detail, he was not surprised to see her standing in the doorway with a handful of papers. They nodded to each other and he indicated the chair in front of his desk and she sat down but clearly did not relax.

"What's up? Did you find something about why Wil died?" Tom asked putting down his papers.

"No. That's not why I'm here. I'll do his post in the morning. I wanted to talk with you about that girl, Patricia Harding," she said, checking the paperwork to get the name right. "You asked me about her earlier, right?"

"OK. Why?"

"I found out some stuff after we completed her post and I wanted to compare that with your Code Review findings."

"Well, we didn't have anything big from the Review. What did you want to talk about?"

"I guess you knew that she was very hypokalemic when she arrived, right?

"Yes, we knew that. And she had been given replacement over the weekend," Tom said, remembering that the Review had noted that the morning lab value for Patricia's potassium was apparently not known during the code.

"Well, her potassium this morning, drawn about an hour before the code was 2.3," Monique said with a little cocking of her head to the left and raising her eyebrows.

"What? No wonder they were unable to convert her. How in the hell did that happen? She was getting replacement . . . at least I saw orders for replacement."

"Oh, I think she got replacement – it just wasn't enough," Monique said this with a wry smile and went on, "I also found a urine specimen sent down on Saturday for a potassium level. It was 227. 227! And the chloride was high, over 200 and the magnesium was 56. All while she was profoundly hypokalemic."

"So everything poured in just went right back out? What causes that?"

Remembering she was talking to an orthopedic surgeon, Monique said, "It's a rare condition involving renal tubular reabsorption capacity."

"Oh, no," said Tom. "Not one of those fleas' disease!" Of course, he didn't actually mean a disease carried and transmitted by fleas. He was referring to the Internal Medicine physicians' nickname among other specialties. The old adages were: a surgeon won't care what you have, but will cut it out anyway; an internist will figure out what you have but it will take a thousand tests; psychiatrists can't figure out your problem in their lifetime and the pathologist knows the truth – but far too late. Internists were reputed to only figure out what was wrong with a dead dog after all the fleas had left – and now they were generally called "fleas". Tom's comment was in response to Monique's words "rare" and "tubular reabsorption". This would be a disease or condition only a 'flea' would love.

"Exactly," said Monique. "And I already talked with Jim Donaldson. He actually came down to the lab today to ask about the urine potassium. Seems he talked to one of the house staff about it over the weekend and didn't get any feedback." Jim was the Chief of Nephrology; this confirmed Tom's fears about this being a 'flea disease'.

"What's Jim say about it?"

"It's a variant of Bartter's syndrome – called Gitelman's syndrome. It's less rare than Bartter's. It looks for all the world like someone taking too much diuretics."

"And how did we miss this?"

"Well, that's what I came to talk about. To see if there was any comment at the Review."

"Not really. I was there and heard about the hypokalemia and everybody knew she was on replacement. Nobody said anything about that urine potassium."

"That's because the value wasn't known until after her death. The request was set aside as 'Special' and only done during regular hours." Monique knew this could be a problem for her and the laboratory. She had developed the process of certain tests only being done in the regular hours when she had a full complement of people to spend the time on an unusual test. This test, however, was not one of those tests; it was just 'unusual' to the technician who moved it into the Week Day box for measurement.

"And there's treatment for this Gitleman thing?" Tom asked, almost afraid to hear the answer.

"Yes. And it's pretty simple, really. Potassium sparing diuretics and maybe an ACE inhibitor. She still would have needed replacement potassium and magnesium but she probably would have walked out of here."

"What's the key to diagnosis?"

"According to Donaldson it's what we had in our hands – high urine potassium in the face of low serum levels."

"Damn it!" said Tom. "Then we probably could've saved her."

Monique had to slowly nod and look down.

"Was there anything else about her post?" he asked, wanting to talk about something else while he digested what to do about the missed laboratory finding.

"She had an IUD."

"What's odd about that?"

"Well, her husband was telling everybody that they were trying to have a baby."

"Again. The husband doesn't know what's really going on. And, let me ask my question another way. What's odd about that?"

"Maybe not anything. I just thought I'd mention it." Monique stood and handed Tom a batch of papers with notes on the autopsy and the permission slip for Liz to sign about Wilford's autopsy and walked to the door. "Maybe she should have been in the CCU, Tom. Just maybe."

"Okay. Thanks. I'll look into it. Actually, I'll ask Donaldson to look into it. Thanks for the 'heads up' ". Tom waved to her as she left and realized his headache had just gotten much worse.

Chapter Thirty-One

Tuesday, March 9

Tom recognized the need for some positive actions in the hospital after the disastrous events of Monday, so he had scheduled the Urology group to present their findings, actions and results to Sam Mastone on Tuesday morning. They all trouped dutifully into the Director's Conference Room at 0900 and sat around the table; each had their own coffee cup and a pad of paper with some notes.

Sam entered promptly at 0900. Jacketless, wearing a white shirt and muted purple tie he sat at the head of the table and looked around at the assembled group, he smiled and realized that he did not know the names of most of the people there. So, he turned to Tom and said, "Your meeting," before leaning back to listen.

Tom began the report by summarizing the issue as it had been presented to him and concluded with the statement he had originally heard from the Director: "No one can get in to the Urology Clinic". He then fleshed out that statement with some of his own research into the financials of the Urology clinic. He was aware that during this phase of the presentation many of the urology team members were smiling and even winking at each other. After all, Tom wasn't making a case for scolding them. They knew the answer. Fortunately, Sam was mostly paying attention to Tom's presentation or looking at Brad Biggers for reaction to Tom's statements. Those reactions were mostly muted nods of agreement.

The presentation by the Chief of Staff did not take long and then Tom turned to Brad and said, "And Dr. Biggers will provide the direction for the remainder of the presentation. Brad."

Brad Biggers was a 55-year-old academic urologist. A man of average height and weight, he had a striking head of lush, white hair topping a head of square jawed honesty. His dark eyes were framed by an ever-present pair of half-glasses so that when he looked at anyone over them there was an immediate feeling in the one so viewed that they had been caught in arrears. Biggers was an accomplished public speaker that had made numerous presentations at the national level and he was not the least intimidated by the setting of the Director's Conference Room. Tom knew that Biggers' presentation would be thorough, accurate and pointed. But that's not what Tom wanted at this time and place.

Tom had talked at length about the concept of the presentation with Brad over the weeks leading up to this moment. Tom wanted the Director to see the work done by the nurses and clerks and residents – in their own words – rather than a polished academic presentation. He had encouraged Brad to get each person on the team involved in the presentation; Brad had told Tom just that morning that he had pushed the concept with the team and they had actually rehearsed their parts.

So Tom sat back in his chair, already knowing the facts, and watched the dynamics of the team presentation and the look on Sam Mastone's face during the various speakers' expositions. And he thought back to the first meeting he held with this group and their highly negative body language and contrasted that with today's relaxed and even convivial approach to the story of their process improvement.

Each of the team members had a part, some more than one, and under Brad's guidance they related their journey of discovery about their own day-to-day activity and their home clinic. They recounted the early resistance to Tom's suggestion that their work could be improved, smiling and even laughing quietly at themselves as the facts were recounted.

They particularly enjoyed telling about their astonishment after collecting the first round of data to discover that they – personally – were responsible for most of the overload in the clinic by reappointing so many patients to return back in a few months. They even offered some of their well worn, but now discounted, theories about why they believed they were doing the right thing. To his credit, Sam sat mostly quietly, sipping on his coffee and nodding or smiling at the various presenters. His usual pattern of interrupting someone to get to the bottom line more quickly was not in evidence.

The team really had some fun presenting the director with the information they had learned about all the different and variant ways that a referral patient could get an appointment in the clinic – and they recounted to him the amazing fact that none of them, including the Chief of Urology, knew every one the different ways. That allowed them to sum up their initial findings by explaining, "So, it wasn't that no one could get in to the urology clinic – it was that everyone could get in!" That statement seemed to back Sam up for a second or two, but then he caught the message, smiled and nodded and indicated the presentation to continue.

The presentation became more serious at that point as each of the disciplines pointed out how they could improve their own triage and communication with others and how they ultimately agreed on a simple set of rules regarding how a patient could get an appointment and which patients should have return appointments. Tom thought this part of the presentation far understated the distance everyone was apart from each other at the beginning and the wrangling that had occurred before they had come to consensus. But he did not interrupt.

After what might be considered a slow windup, the end came more like a fastball on the outside corner. The team noted minor difficulties in implementing their plan and how almost immediately they had noted more clinic openings, more time available to spend with individual patients and less stress over what they had previously seen as inappropriate referrals. Then Brad ended with updating Tom's financial history noting how the clinic was now actually seeing fewer patients in a session but earning more money by seeing more new patients and more complicated cases. Plus there were far less no-shows making the clinic more cost-effective.

Sam, naturally, had a few questions at the end of the presentation. Tom and Brad tried as much as feasible to get the team members to provide the answers. This initially was a little uncomfortable for Sam but he seemed to quickly grow into it. Tom was beginning to feel good about the day when, toward the end of the hour, the door into the hallway cracked open about a foot and Monique Song peeked through and indicated she wanted to speak to Tom. The formal presentation was completed and the team was involved with the Director in conversation that was congenial back-and-forth so he excused himself, knowing she would not have interrupted a meeting in the Director's Conference Room without good reason.

"What's up, Monique?' he said as he stepped into the hallway.

"I've got some new information. Let's go in your office."

She clutched a folder tightly as they walked down the hall to the office of the Chief of Staff. She didn't loosen her grip on the folder or say anything until they were in Tom's office with the door closed.

"You remember that intravenous bag you sent down for analysis?" she asked.

Tom nodded.

"Well, it had insulin in it."

"Come again?"

"Regular insulin. I can't tell right now how much since I'll have to back calculate the concentration but . . ."

"What the hell is insulin doing in that bag?" he said coming to his feet.

"I don't know. That's why I thought you should know. That didn't come up at the Review?"

"Of course not! There's no reason she should have insulin in her i.v. Are you sure about this?"

"Yes, Tom. Don't start that with me. I checked the results twice before coming up."

"Did you go through the chart, too?"

"Yes. And 'No' there's no order for insulin anywhere in the record."

Tom slumped into his chair. "You know what this means?"

"Either some giant mistake occurred . . . or this was deliberate."

"That's exactly what I'm thinking. How else could that have happened? We've got digital coding on all medications and double-checking by nurses against the armband. Oh, man! Do we have a problem."

"Well, nobody knows about this except you, me and the tech who ran the sample – and he doesn't know where it came from."

"Let's keep it that way for now. I've got to think this through – all the implications. Like the Joint Commission. Right after they already dinged us once. We really, really, really, don't need this."

"Well, neither did she – Patricia Harding, I mean."

"No, of course not. Did anything else turn up on her post?"

"No. Speaking as a former M.E. I'd have to say that even though we have the electrocardiographic evidence of a fatal arrhythmia, her cause of death is suspicious and I now believe it was due to a deliberate dosing of unnecessary insulin."

"You mean murder."

"I mean murder."

"Have you told anyone else about this?"

"No, I came straight up here to see you. I was about to start the post on Wilford when the technician told me the results of his analysis. I decided you should know that right away."

"So, this technician knows?"

"Well, he knows what was in the sample I gave him to run. He doesn't know where that came from or that the results indicate anything sinister – if that's what you're looking for."

"I just want to be sure we have a lid on this until we figure out what the next step is."

"No one else in the lab will be part of this, just me."

"Good. Let's try to keep things looking normal, OK? You go on with the usual day's work and I'll think about what to do next and who we can involve without this blowing up in our faces." Tom flopped back down in his chair as if his legs were unable to hold him upright.

"I'm heading down to do the post on Wilford, then. You going to come by?" Monique said as she started for the door.

"Yeah, sure. In a little. This is a bit much, you know?"

"Yes, I do. You know this used to be my daily life. Except no one was surprised when I said 'murder', because that's why I had the body to start with."

Tom sat up straighter and looked her in the eye. "I'm going to need that expertise to help us get through this."

"I know," she said, nodding to him and then slipping through the door. He leaned back in his chair and stared at the ceiling.

Chapter Thirty-Two

Tuesday, March 9

Monique and one of her technicians were nearly an hour into the autopsy before Tom arrived. He didn't look any more certain of 'next steps' and was understandably tight-lipped about observing the autopsy on a close friend. "How's it going?" he asked after a moment.

"Well, there are a few things to concern me," said Monique, looking up and brushing a lock of hair out of her face with her forearm.

"Was it a heart attack?" he asked

"Tom, you know better than that. This is not a television program where people make cellular or dynamic diagnoses from the X-rays and call electrocardiographic changes from looking at the heart."

"Are you giving me a hard time?" he asked, with a wry grin.

"A little. I have opened the heart and he had almost no coronary atherosclerosis. There was a single lesion in the distal right coronary – maybe 40% at most and no acute changes around it. Hard to settle on a diagnosis of an acute MI with those wide open vessels."

"Really? So, what did kill him then?"

"Not so sure about anything right now but there are these things that concern me," she said and turned from her work on the body to the tray holding the various organs. "He had some marked lividity in his feet and his abdomen was congested. Like he was in shock. I've seen those changes with big burns and one case following a lighting strike. All the blood just pools in the lower parts."

"Is that what happened here?" Tom asked, puzzled since he knew that Wilford had been apparently quite healthy just moments before collapsing on the stairs.

"I can't be sure until I do some histology work," Monique said holding up the liver. "But just look at this. Congested and 150% of normal weight. And the bowel was also congested. But the lungs and heart held very little blood."

"Neurogenic?"

"Probably. Brain is usually preserved, you know. We haven't gotten to that yet. If it was neurogenic we may never know from what. I really need to look at some microscopic samples before I can say, but from the history it looks like he was running the stairs and went into shock."

"What would do that other than an MI?" Tom queried.

"Electric shock will do it. Maybe some drugs. Anaphylaxis. I don't know for sure but I'll find out." Monique said this with an intense nod in Tom's direction.

"But no heart attack?"

"Don't go running off and telling anyone that just yet. I need to have a look at the tissue samples. I suppose it is still possible he had an acute infarct resulting in cardiac standstill. That would explain some of the findings."

"You know this is a guy that recently went hiking at altitude."

"It has to start sometime." Monique was acting her wise woman role.

"Helluva time for it to happen now."

"I doubt that Wilford chose this time in order to inconvenience you, Tom."

"Yeah. I know. By the way, I'm going to visit a friend about that other matter we were discussing," Tom said trying to be nonchalant in the presence of the pathology assistant. "He may want to talk with you about specifics."

Monique didn't raise her head from her work. "Fine. I'll finish up here and we can talk about that later. Just please don't tell Liz anything definite until I have a chance to do a little homework, OK?"

Tom nodded as he turned and walked out the door.

Sensing his chance to ask a question, the pathology tech interjected, "Want a full tox screen on this case?"

"Just like every case, Jeremy; just like every case," Monique said without raising her head and not really paying that much attention because she had just realized something unusual about the liver.

Chapter Thirty-Three

Tuesday, March 9

Tom drove slowly out to Ron Looney's house. He wanted some time to think – partly about what he had just come to realize, that someone had actually tried to kill a patient in the hospital. But he also needed to think about how he was going to raise this subject with Ron. That might be a little tricky since Ron was an active homicide detective in the Criminal Investigation Section of the Cincinnati Police Department. Tom had called Ron from the office and reached him at police headquarters. He had explained, in very general terms, that he wanted to have a serious talk with Ron and that he didn't want to do it at the police station. Ron quickly agreed and they set a time for Tom to come by the Looney's home after work that afternoon.

Although it was spring, the trees were not budding enough to produce shade and the afternoon sun cast vacillating streams of alternating light and shadow on the windshield as he drove. The flickering sunlight and the quiet interior of the truck might have created an atmosphere conducive to letting one's mind wander – or even to allow the knitting up of raveled sleeves. But Tom was not sleepy and certainly not letting his mind drift very far from the purpose and intent of his drive. In fact, all he thought about was what – and how – he was going to talk with an old friend about a murder that apparently had occurred right under his nose within the hospital.

Tom and Ron had been friends since the Air Force. They met at Sheppard AFB. Tom was a relatively new military physician, a Major in rank but still unfamiliar with much of the military life. He had some experience during two weeks in the summers with his reserve unit wearing a uniform and learning which shoulder insignia to salute. His unit was mostly medical officers and some enlisted techs. Most of the time he wore BDUs and boots and spent time on the firing range where the battle dress uniform was standard. The men in the unit were not gung-ho military but they all tried to abide by the rules during the weekend drills. The officers in the unit were regulars and yet still had a somewhat relaxed way of dealing with their charges that were not 'real' airmen – yet.

As a consequence, when Tom learned that his initial two weeks on active duty would be spent in Air Force Orientation course, he wondered exactly what he would be learning. But, after his two week 'orientation' to the active duty Air Force and still pretty new to the culture, he knew the history of the Air Force, his chain of command, how to dress and act like an officer and – very important – how to shine his shoes.

Then the wisdom of the Air Force sent him Balad and then to Germany where he worked as staff orthopedist at the hospital unit in Landstuhl for three years. During that time he became mostly familiar with the ins and outs of military life and somewhat enjoyed the freedom of not having to decide what to wear every morning when he got dressed. Sandra said he looked very professional in uniform.

When he returned from Germany, very glad to have had an 'accompanied' tour, he was posted to the Hospital at Keesler AFB to be the Director of Orthopedic services. He was an 'Officer in Charge' primarily by the date of his agreement with the Air Force; since he signed on for financial support during his residency his 'date of service' was earlier than the other orthopedists on staff at Keesler. Turned out, the OIC stuff didn't get any additional pay and meant more paperwork.

One day, early in his short tenure at Sheppard, he was sent from the hospital to the stockade to check on a prisoner who had a cast on his leg and was complaining of pain inside the cast. He remembered talking with the Air Police MSgt on arrival at the stockade and hearing the familiar twang of an Arkansas' accent. Tom remembered he was also impressed with the way the MSgt had arranged everything for his visit and made it go smoothly. Later, he had joined a basketball game at the gym with the MSgt and some other noncoms and didn't embarrass himself.

Over the next few months he got to know the MSgt – Ron Looney – and they even visited in each other's homes. Tom finished his stint with the Medical Service School and within a month was spending 20 hours a day as the Chief of Orthopedic Surgery in Trauma Bay II, Balad AFB, Iraq. But the families had kept up and exchanged Christmas cards regularly. Then Looney retired and moved back to his wife's hometown of Cincinnati and they both thought that was that. Even as Looney's military career was ending, Tom's was already on an ascendant course. Over the next several years he was rated exceptional in all evaluations and was promoted 'below the zone' three times – making Brigadier rank in Feb 2009. He served in various capacities as Director of Orthopedics, Chief of Surgery, Executive Officer and finally as Hospital Commander at Wilford Hall, Lackland AFB in San Antonio, Texas. Even though he was not given a second star at the first opportunity, his chances for that promotion were still good when he decided to retire and seek a civilian position.

Tom had actually forgotten that Ron and Meg Looney lived in Cincinnati when he visited New City, but Sandra, who always checked the return mailing addresses on the Christmas cards, was very aware. She made the contact and arranged for the families to meet again on the Bolling's second recruiting trip. They had dinner together in a mid-priced downtown steak house and talked over dinner and drinks and dessert and coffee until wee hours of the morning. Ron's presence in Cincinnati was a positive factor in Tom ultimately deciding to take the Chief of Staff job at New City Hospital.

And they picked right up with their friendship when Tom and Sandra moved to Cincinnati. But it was almost always a friendship outside their respective professions. Tom didn't probe for inside details on active murder investigations and Ron didn't ask medical questions except for names of respected physicians for referral. But of course, they did exchange some stories about their work place issues and even discussed the eccentricities of a few of the individuals they had to deal with in the work place that were not as clear thinking as the pair of them. They had shared a few stories of things that went wrong but mostly talked about how their respective systems worked to do the right thing – no matter how they were portrayed in the media whenever something did go wrong.

Tom remembered a time when he was overseeing a multiple injury automobile accident in the Emergency Room – three cars involved and four patients brought to New City. The emergency room was well staffed but two of the injured had broken legs and the doctors wanted some orthopedic guidance to stabilizing them for further studies. Tom and one of the Senior Orthopedic residents went to the treatment area to help out. When he looked up from his task, Tom saw Ron Looney staring at him through the glass door. He excused himself and went out to see Ron. Turned out that someone thought the accident was deliberate – murder, or at least attempted murder, hence Ron's involvement. They talked about the possibility that Tom might have heard any comments from the individuals injured in the accident. There had been no great revelation from any of the injured and Tom and Ron settled down an hour later in Tom's office with a cup of coffee. As he remembered the event, Tom was cheered by the memory of how their interaction in an event that overlapped their two spheres had been comfortable and certainly not strained.

However, laying out a probable murder in front of the expert – and admitting it happened while he was in charge – did not make Tom feel comfortable this time, even dealing with this old friend. As he neared Ron's house Tom thought, "I really should have asked Sandra how to handle this."

Chapter Thirty-Four

Tuesday, March 9

Tom pulled his truck up in Looney's driveway. The house was a modest rambler with an attached two-car garage all faced in red brick. The wide window expanses had always seemed inviting but now Tom was feeling conspicuous as he looked at them. The drive went straight to the garage and he sat in the truck for a few moments before getting out and walking up the bricked walk to the red painted front door. Before he could knock, the door opened and Meg, Ron's wife, greeted him.

"Hello, Tom."

"Hey, Meg."

"Come in. He's up changing clothes. He told me you were coming."

"Yeah, I called to make sure he'd be home."

"Didn't want to talk at the station?"

"Well . . . no."

"You aren't trying to get him involved in another of those all night poker games are you?"

"What? No. It's just . . . a little problem I want to consult with him about."

Just then Looney came down the stairs in jeans and a loud short-sleeved shirt and wearing sandals with dark blue socks. "Boy, you got here quick."

"Really? I thought I was driving slowly."

"Want a beer?"

"Sure."

Looney went to the refrigerator, pulled two longnecks from the bottom shelf and indicated the back door. "Patio, OK?

"Sure, thanks," Tom said, thankful to not have to be rude and ask Meg to let him talk with Ron alone.

The patio was not yet ready for summer. The wire chairs were still covered with a canvas cover and the little table between the chairs was littered with empty pots and planters that held some drooped and dried plants that had weathered the winter outdoors and looked ready for the compost heap.

Looney cleaned off some pots and jerked the covers off the chairs. Both men brushed at the seats before they sat down.

"So?" said Looney, eyebrows raised. "What's the reason you want to talk?"

"Well, I kinda need a consult?"

"Whoa." Looney gestured with both hands outstretched, palms up toward Tom.

"No, I'm serious"

"You do know that when a homicide detective gets asks for a 'consult' there's usually somebody dead. Or about to be."

"What?"

"Are you looking for a way to get away with it?"

"Get away with what?"

"Killing someone – like that jerk director of yours."

"No. It's . . ." Tom stared off into the darkness gathering in the distant bushes.

"Come on, Tom. I'm kidding. Talk. Nobody here but us chickens."

"I think there's been a murder at the hospital."

"You think?" Looney sat up at this disclosure.

"Well, it's a little uncertain what actually happened."

"You pulling my leg?"

"It happened a couple of days ago, and . . ."

"What? And just now I'm hearing about this?"

"Well, we didn't know."

"Why not?"

"It happened during a code and we didn't think it was anything but an unfortunate death until we did a review."

"One of your AARs?"

"Yeah. And we might have missed it otherwise."

"Tell me about it."

Just then Meg stepped out the door with a small tray that she brought over to the table and set down. It was loaded with chips and salsa. "I thought your consult might go better with chips and Ro-Tel," she said, smiling at Tom.

"Damn straight," said Looney, getting up and heading for the back door. "You need another beer?"

"Sure."

When he came back, Meg went back in the house and they touched bottles and Tom started the story:

"It's a young girl, late twenties, paralegal. She collapsed at work – no, we don't know why that happened – and was brought to the ED. She was very depleted of potassium and had a cardiac arrhythmia but we shocked her out of that and seemed to have that under control but she didn't really wake up."

"Hit her head at work?"

"We didn't think so. Apparently she went down in her carpeted cubicle but we didn't really have any first hand witness."

"So, what do you think happened?"

"We got a CAT scan of her head and that was clear and she looked stable otherwise. We put her up on the ward for monitoring."

"What does that mean, monitoring?"

"She was hooked up to a cardiac monitor that would alarm if she developed anything irregular. And we had her blood oxygen level monitored and her blood pressure every 15 minutes or so. Plus, the nurses went in the room every 15 minutes or so, as well."

"But she was otherwise left alone."

"Yes. But that happens all the time. We had no reason to 'put her on a watch'."

"Who all was there?"

"Her husband, of course."

"Tell me about him."

"Squirrelly dude. Unemployed computer geek. Wanted to know everything that was going on and clearly couldn't keep it together."

"What do you mean?"

"He was asking the same questions over and over like he didn't hear the answers – or didn't believe them."

"What kinds of questions did he ask?"

"Is she gonna make it? That was his big question, right from the start."

"And she didn't, did she?" said Looney, sipping his beer.

"Yeah, actually she did, for a couple of days. She never really woke up and the house staff were pouring potassium into her and she was still low on every measure."

"What caused that?"

"We don't know yet."

" Seems like a lot of stuff you don't know. Why do you think someone murdered her?"

"Monday morning she had another arrest – she actually came in on Friday night. She was all alone in her room and the monitor went off and the nurse ran in and called a code right way. The Code Team got there promptly and did all the right things but she went back into a terminal arrhythmia and died."

"No one else around?"

"No. The husband had been such a nuisance to the nurses that they convinced him to spend the night at home. He had been there all night Friday and most of Saturday."

"So, it's a really sick, 'depleted' young woman – maybe like one of those anorexia girls – and she circles the drain for a few days and dies. What makes you think murder?"

"It's what I found in the AAR, Ron. There was a bag of i.v. fluid hanging up and attached to her pump that had insulin in the bag."

"And I'm guessing that shouldn't have been there?"

"Absolutely not. Insulin would lower her potassium and it was already scary low."

"So, who put insulin in her i.v.?"

"We don't know and there is no order for it. And it never should have been there."

"Don't the nurses know anything about it?"

"It was one of them that actually caught it. She wasn't the one that hung the bag but in the AAR she noticed it was the wrong color."

"Wrong color?"

"Yeah, they were giving her potassium with some magnesium and vitamins – the vitamins color the bag contents yellow. We call it a 'banana bag'. She noted that the color was too light and that's why I had the lab run some chemistries on the contents."

"Why didn't anybody notice that earlier?"

"Probably because the lights were off during the night."

"And your lab found the insulin."

"Right. And that looks like murder to me."

"I agree it's damn suspicious. When did you get this information about the insulin?"

"About two hours ago."

"Who else knows?"

"Only me and the pathologist, right now."

"And now me," said Looney with a sly grin as he finished his beer.

Chapter Thirty-Five

Ron Looney was not a complicated man. Probably because he was not a complicated child. One of four Looney children on the small farm outside Squashton, Arkansas, he had regular daily chores. Even after he started school he knew there were things to be done at home when the school day was over. He walked the three miles home from school every day and completed all the chores before suppertime. The chores were not backbreaking: feeding the hogs and the chickens and occasionally mucking out the barn and, in the fall, chopping some firewood every day. But they were routine and regular.

What the routine produced in Ron was a set of characteristics that he exhibited as a man: reliability, dedication and capability. Ron Looney's word was considered like a fungible commodity and no one doubted his ability or his work ethic. He did not participate in school sports because of the chores but he was active in hunting and fishing with his father and brothers. Before he graduated he had likely walked every road and streamside in the county.

But, familiar as he was with the county and the homestead, when he graduated he got a ride to Pine Bluff and enlisted in the Air Force. The draft had put out its last call two years before but he still had to register with the Selective Service System right after his eighteenth birthday. That experience got him to thinking about military service and traveling and having experiences he had little knowledge of except through his reading. When he completed his schooling he decided the time was right for the next phase of his life and he chose the Air Force because, "I'm likely to get sea-sick if I went in the Navy." Apparently joining the Army was never a strong consideration, either, but that topic didn't get much attention in his explanations.

After Basic Training, Looney became a member of the Security Police, Law Enforcement Branch where he demonstrated skill, clear thinking and perseverance and rose fairly quickly through the ranks. After a posting to Osan, Korea that only lasted a little more than a year, he applied for and was granted ta position in the Air Police at Maxwell AFB where he got special training in investigations. The only marks in his record that were less than 'fully satisfactory' occurred when command tried to put him on desk duty with supervisory responsibility. Ron Looney was not a man to sit when others were working and he truly did not want to have oversight and supervisory responsibilities. To him, if a man had a job and that came with responsibilities, then he was supposed to do the job, and it shouldn't take someone else hanging over his shoulder to get him to do it. Fortunately, that experiment didn't last long; his supervisors recognized his discomfort and he continued his meritorious service working in the field.

Very early on he decided he wanted more than just to rise in the Air Force ranks and began to take some distance learning courses in Criminal Justice from Arizona State University. Years later when he finally earned a degree, the Air Force tried to make him an officer but he demurred citing his uneasiness with having to tell others how and when to do their job.

At one point, stationed at Wright-Patterson AFB in Dayton he had met the cute and very charming Margaret Andicott. She lived in Cincinnati and was visiting a friend in Dayton. She stayed long enough for the relationship to get serious and soon they married. She had been with him at every posting after that and when asked, 'How long have you been married?' his usual response was "As long as I can remember." At the time of his discharge from active duty Looney and Meg moved to her home town – Cincinnati – and he joined the police force. His GI Bill allowed him to take refresher courses in Criminal Justice while working and that quickly led to his assignment to Homicide.

Looney had his own memory of the first meeting with then-Major Bolling at the stockade on Sheppard. The Major had looked a little uncertain about parts of the protocol when he got out of the car at the stockade. Looney had put the stockade personnel on notice and had arranged for the prisoner to be examined moved up front to a holding area. He expected the whole thing to be a smooth visit. But, when he opened the door to the anteroom and someone shouted, "Officer on ward!" and everyone –guards and prisoners alike – snapped to attention, the Major froze. Looney, standing beside Bolling, whispered to him, 'as you were' and, after a momentary pause, Major Bolling repeated that out loud and everyone relaxed. The NCOIC later introduced himself to Bolling and showed him where the prisoner was located and everyone took care of their business. In later years, Tom would tell that story on himself and explain his indecision as an example of not being accustomed to folks standing up when he entered a room. Looney thought, "I bet he got used to that pretty quick when he put on that star!"

Looney also remembered asking the young Major to join a pickup basketball game at the gym and being a little surprised how aggressively Bolling played, as well as having a killer jump shot from 18 feet. Of course their camaraderie on the court led to them sharing a beer or two and becoming friends – as much because they shared their Arkansas background as anything else originally. Even though they only had a few months together at Sheppard before Bolling was promoted to Lt. Colonel and shipped off to Balad, the friendship between the two men had grown solid and their wives were more than acquaintances, too.

The Cincinnati connection worked out well, too. Meg's brother, Paul, was on the Cincinnati Police force and helped Looney to get the right interviews and certainly helped hustle the paperwork so that he was employed within a few weeks of his retirement from active duty. Paul was in Robbery, a unit just down the hall on the fourth floor from Homicide and when Looney had worked his way up there, they often met for lunch. He definitely 'settled in' to the civilian life and had largely put his memories of airlifts in the Balkans and uniformed service on a back shelf in his memory vault.

So, Looney was surprised when Tom called and told him that he was considering the position at New City and might move to Cincinnati, too. Their dinner had brought back several warm memories for both men and Looney even arranged a "Welcome" party for Tom and Sandra at his home with a couple of folks Tom told him to invite from the hospital when the deal was finally set.

The two former colleagues continued to see each other occasionally, almost always at a Christmas Party at the Bolling's with all the high rollers from New City and later at the Fourth of July barbeque in Looney's backyard attended by several of his friends from the CPD. But they also met now and then at a sports bar to share a beer and burger and watch the Razorbacks. Just a comfortable friendship, telling stories about growing up in different parts of Arkansas and laughing at their own individual cluelessness back then.

Looney was aware that the former Major, young and not attuned to the military, had matured into a very capable senior officer. But he was also aware that Bolling had a reputation of 'not suffering fools gladly' and he wondered how long his friend was going to be able to deal effectively with the hospital director who was always meddling in things on the clinical side. His concerns in this regard were lessening with the passage of time as he sporadically had occasion to visit the ED with injured individuals and saw the respect the staff had for his old friend; clearly he wasn't creating any waves – yet.

And then, out of nowhere, Tom Bolling, retired U.S. Air Force Brigadier General came and sat on his patio and told him that a murder had been carried out at New City Hospital apparently during the usual activities of the day. To complicate the matters further, the murder was now days old and the scene had been thoroughly cleaned. "It will be almost like a cold case," Looney thought to himself, "and I'm gonna have to tell the Captain sooner or later."

It didn't take long for him to choose 'later' and then Looney turned to Tom and said, "I'll probably need to talk to some of the folks involved. Can you get me a list of anyone you know had access to that room? And can you tell me a little more about the layout and how this could have happened?"

Tom was certainly pleased that Ron had agreed to help. "Get me some paper and I'll make a list," he said.

Chapter Thirty-Six

Tuesday, March 9

Working on another beer, Looney was making some brief notes in a small flip top pad. Actually his memory was pretty good but he used the notes as a way of lowering tension in many cases – and he always liked going back later to see if the key issues or points had made it into his pad. When he found that a key piece of information had not been recorded he had the makings of a dense review of the case, at least in his own mind. Plus, he rather liked the image of the pain-staking detective with a stubby pencil working his way meticulously through the details of a case. Except that he used a special ballpoint pen that had been a present from his children years ago. Apparently they were not as taken with the image of the hard-working detective working with a stubby pencil. So they had given him a sterling silver Parker T-ball jotter and three refills. Since then the stubby pencil was a thing of the past and he cherished his new image.

Clicking the pen, Looney said to Tom, "OK. Let me see if I have all this right. The girl's room is on a dead end hallway and it's close to the Nurses' Station where there are usually some nurses working."

"Well, the number of people at the station varies with the shift. Daytime there's almost always someone there, a clerk or one of the nurses."

"And at night?"

"Fewer nurses, no clerk. And the same number of patients."

"But less going on?"

"Usually. Certainly less scheduled things. But people get sick."

"I understand that. So, its possible that someone could get to the room and not be seen from the nurses' station.

"Yes. That's what I'm saying."

"And that would be most likely during the night shift."

"Yes. Any other time during the day or evening, there's just too much activity to believe someone could waltz past the nursing station without being seen – or challenged."

"What if that someone looked like they belonged there?"

"You mean like if that was one of the nurses?"

"Or anyone else. Say a janitor or somebody bringing a food tray or someone dressed like a doctor. Would that attract attention?"

"Ron, we are a relatively closed system. We don't have strange doctors or even unknown janitors showing up and walking around the wards. Especially not at night. I don't think that's realistic."

"You do know about the 'Purloined Letter', don't you?"

"Sure. And I know the concept of not seeing something, even something very obvious, if you are watching for something else. But there wasn't anything else going on that night."

"And how do you know that?" Looney asked with a sly little grin, leaning back in his chair and raising his eyebrows at his friend. "Seriously, you weren't there. You don't know what happened that night. Somebody could've created a small disturbance away from the girl's room and slipped in when everybody's attention was elsewhere."

Tom sat back and thought for a moment. Certainly the morning meeting was supposed to keep the senior executives aware of major mishaps occurring during the night, but no one would think twice about reporting something like a dropped dinner tray. Maybe Ron was right.

"I guess it could happen," Tom grudgingly noted. "I'll check with some of the nurses from that night shift and see if there was anything that could have distracted them."

"OK. Good. But be subtle. I don't want to get everyone thinking we're looking for someone stalking the halls at night. By the way, are you absolutely certain this wasn't just an accident that that medicine got in that bag?"

"There was absolutely no reason for that patient to be getting any insulin at all," Tom said firmly. "Insulin would lower her potassium level and cause exactly what happened, a fatal arrhythmia." He shook his head and continued, "There was no order for any insulin for her and her medications are checked by bar code against her wrist band."

"So, it absolutely had to be added on purpose?" queried Looney.

"Yes, of course. But right now we don't really know that the insulin was added during the night," Tom said just to make the point. "Remember, that bag had been hanging for several hours."

"Was it hanging before the husband left the night before?"

"I'm not sure. Again, I can ask the nurses about when he left and let you know."

"Good enough – for now," Looney said making another notation in his little notebook. "I'd still like to talk about the nurses, though."

"You mean like as suspects?"

"Of course I mean as suspects. Don't you guys have some doctors and nurses that go around killing folks in the hospital like some kind of 'angel'?"

"You guys? You act like that's some kind of secret society we have in the medical profession!" Tom guessed that Looney was just pulling his leg with the suggestion that such activity in the medical profession was either sanctioned or widespread.

"Well, how does this one not fit?" Looney asked.

"From what we know of those 'angels of mercy' they are usually serial killers and this is the only case we know of."

"So far. I mean, could it be the first of a series," Looney suggested.

"Maybe, but let's come back to that later – if there are any more deaths like this. The usual 'type' for angels of mercy is someone who thinks they are making things better for the person they kill – usually because they are stopping their 'suffering'. That happens mostly, I think, in patients with long-standing disease or debilitation. And that's not what I see here."

"I thought there was another type of 'angel' I remember you telling me about one a long time ago. Some guy in the operating room."

"Oh yeah. There is a type of person who creates a 'hero' situation for himself so he can get credit and recognition for saving the day."

"And you don't think this is one of those kinds of situations?" asked Looney.

"Well, there certainly wasn't anyone who stood out as a 'hero' on this one. She sure wasn't saved."

"Still, that might have not been the intent." Looney was really pushing an envelope here. Tom began thinking that if one of the medical staff wanted to appear heroic by pulling someone back from the brink of death, they might have actually gotten to the room, added the insulin to the iv bag and been waiting for the code. He would have to recheck the whereabouts of the code team – including all those medical students.

Suddenly, Tom was hit by another idea; he was going to have to tell the Joint Commission about the murder. If ever there were a Sentinel Event, this would be it. Damn.

Seeing his friend's face, Looney knew something bad was rumbling around in his mind. "Of course," he ventured, "we have really only talked about one aspect of the case, so far."

"What do you mean?" said Tom snapping himself back to the present.

"Well, we've spent all our time talking about the access to that room – that's what we call 'opportunity' in the so-called murder triad."

"And what are the other topics we haven't gotten to yet?" asked Tom.

"Motive and Means."

Chapter Thirty-Seven

Tuesday, March 9

Tom and Ron Looney were sitting at the dining room table at Looney's. It was after supper and the dishes had been cleared and Meg was reading in the living room while the two men drank coffee and talked. Looney had explained that he was prepared to do a little 'off-book' interviewing of the people who might be involved in Patricia's death but that he couldn't do that for very long and it would have to start now. He couldn't keep this kind of information from his Captain for long; his intent was to be 'exploratory'. He said he would later explain to the Captain that he had a tip that something might be amiss in the death of a young girl at New City and he was just examining the facts to determine whether the police should be involved. However, he told Tom, he couldn't drag out that review of the facts. He needed to get moving the next morning with his review.

Tom was persuaded to stay and continue the discussion and give Looney all the facts, as he knew them. He called Sandra to tell her that he was having dinner with Ron and Meg and would explain the reason when he got home.

"Why do you think someone would want to kill this young girl," Tom asked. "I mean, in general, why do people do that?"

"Well, motive is a big part of solving the puzzle in a murder case." Looney sipped his coffee and followed on with, "But mostly it comes down to love, money, revenge or power. Let's start with what you know about this girl. Who is she, who were her friends and family? What is she involved in, like at work or in the community? Stuff like that."

"I really don't know much of that. All I have is her medical history. She was married, no kids. Apparently worked as a clerk or something like that at a local law firm. That's it."

"I've got a buddy on the force that says 'its always the husband'. What do you know about him?"

"Probably even less. Seems he was around on the ward a lot after she was admitted but had to be called in from home when she died."

"Isn't that a little odd?" asked Looney. "I mean, if he's so interested to be there a lot why isn't he there at the end?"

"Well, people do have to go home occasionally, you know. Change clothes, bathe."

"Still. That's enough reason for me to want to talk to him first."

"OK. How do you want to do that?"

"I'd like to do it down at the station. That gets everyone's attention right quick. But if I do, it will have to be an official investigation."

"Meaning?"

"Meaning that I will have to tell the Captain what's going on and 'Murder at New City' will be the next morning headline."

"Can we avoid that? At least until we know a little more?"

"Then I'll have to interview him somewhere else – like maybe at the hospital." Looney squinted a little at this idea, thinking through how he would explain why a homicide detective was questioning someone at the hospital. But, he figured, maybe he wouldn't have to explain that at all if he never told the husband who he was. "Maybe I can make that work. What do we know about the wife?"

"Local girl as far as I know. Working at local law firm, like I said."

"Oh, another kind of case I really enjoy. Lawyers from the get-go!" said Looney with a wry grin.

"Why do you want to know about her?"

"She's the one that's dead. We usually start by looking at the victim, Tom. That's sort of 'Homicide 101'."

"Of course . . . sure. I don't know much else. But I'll get our Admin people on it in the morning to get you everything we know – address, religion, date of birth, etc. Will that be enough?"

"I don't know till I see it. Let me know when you've got something. In the meantime, who else should I talk to?"

"I can arrange for you to talk with the nurses on the night shift but that should also be done at the hospital, shouldn't it?"

"Yep. And probably during their regular shift."

"I'll talk with the Nursing Service and get their names." Tom wasn't looking forward to having to explain this to Roslyn or Alena without rousing reservations. He imagined that they would immediately think he was trying to cast suspicion for any wrongdoing on the nursing staff. It would certainly be easier if he could just say "Official Investigation. Nothing I can do about it." But, of course, that's exactly what he had to avoid. He frowned at these thoughts and rubbed his face.

"What's the trouble with that?" asked Looney.

"Only that they will cause me more trouble than you can imagine unless I tell them the truth and then the cat's out of the bag."

"You at war with these people, Tom?"

"Not openly. Just some sniping back and forth. Tribe versus tribe. A little one-upmanship at times."

"How about if I talk to them?

"How is that going to help?"

"Well, first off, I don't tell them that I know you at all. Second, I could tell them that we have an 'unofficial' reason to be concerned about some patient injury during the night shift – and I can't be more specific at this time. I can even make it sound like the nurses are the only ones I would trust. You know, get them in on helping me find potential bad guys, who just happen to not be nurses."

"That might work. But don't lie to them."

"I'm actually pretty good at getting people to believe what they want to believe about me and my doings," Looney said with a smile.

They talked on for a while but Tom had nothing more to offer in the way of names for Looney to interview. Looney made notes in his little notebook and finally said, "OK. That's enough to start with. Husband and the nurses and you're going to get me the name of that law firm she worked for."

"Right. First thing in the morning."

"So, next thing I want to know is who can get hold of insulin?"

"Well, that's not really going to help us."

"Why not? That's the 'Means' in this case, right?"

"Yes. But the access to that 'Means" is not very limited. For years anyone could walk up to a pharmacy and ask for some over-the-counter insulin and get it."

"Really? I didn't know that."

"Diabetics need insulin to live and making it difficult to get is not always in patients' best interest. It is possible to get insulin now without a prescription. Anyone can do it. Of course, the new generation of insulins that you hear about on television aren't included in this blanket approval – you still need a prescription for them"

"You mean anybody can get insulin? Wouldn't they have to show a diagnosis card or something?"

"No. They just ask the pharmacist for over-the-counter insulin and pay the price. It's much cheaper, by the way. Largely because it's the generic form of regular insulin, not the newer forms. But that's what someone would need to tide them over a few days to get to their regular physician."

"But isn't that dangerous?"

"Not as much as keeping a diabetic from getting insulin at all."

"Records of those sales?"

"Maybe, if someone used a credit card. Not likely if they paid cash."

"Crap. There goes our best chance to narrow the field."

"Sorry," Tom said, not really feeling sorry now that Ron had said 'our best chance' indicating that he was now invested and going to help.

Looney leaned back in his chair and summarized, "So, I'm unofficially looking into a death that *might* be a murder but we don't have any idea of a motive, everybody on earth has the means and we can't talk to the people who could help figure out who might have had the opportunity. What did I miss, old buddy?"

"You didn't mention that the best homicide detective in the city is working the case?" said Tom.

Chapter Thirty-Eight

Wednesday, March 10

"Benjamin. I'm Ron Looney." Looney's entrance into the interview room was slow and deliberate. He quietly pulled up a chair and sat across the table from Benjie and looked at him expectantly.

"Benjie. Everybody calls me Benjie." Head down, voice low and despondent, Benjie made no effort to make eye contact or to shake Looney's offered hand.

"OK Benjie. I just want to talk with you and ask a few questions."

"What's this all about? I mean, why did I have to come back here to the hospital?"

"I want to talk with you about Patricia. And find out some things"

"What about her? She's dead." Suddenly, Benjie's head came up and he stared at Looney with eyes reddened from crying.

"Was that something you wanted, Benjie?"

"What?" Now the eyes flashed at Looney as Benjie almost spit out his words. "Hell, no. I loved her and we were gonna have kids and all. And now she's dead an' nobody can tell me what happened. It's like it's a secret or somethin'." And then his head went back down and he became silent.

Looney waited for several seconds then, realizing that Benjie was not going to continue, he asked, "What can you tell me about her?"

"She was just great, ya know? Funny and smart and like that." Benjie actually started to smile as he remembered Patricia's fun-loving attitude toward life. He was still smiling when Looney asked, "Was everything all right with her?"

"Whadda you mean, 'right with her'?"

"I mean did she get along with everyone?"

"Oh yeah, everybody loved Patty." Vigorous nodding accompanied this statement.

"Any quarrels with neighbors or friends?"

"No, man, we had no troubles. Until now, of course. What's gonna happen next?"

Ignoring this question, Looney pursued his own line by asking, "Was she happy at work? Have friends there?"

"I think so. She talked about it a lot."

"Were you aware what she was working on?"

"Not really. She would tell me about how some things worked in the law but she never got specific about what she did all day." That memory seemed to trigger another wave of dismay in Benjie – his head went down and he pounded the table with his hand. "An' now I'm never gonna understand what she was doing!"

"Did she talk about people at work?" Looney wanted to know.

"Yeah, there was Elaine and some guy – Duane. They worked together a lot. And had lunch together, too. So,yeah. And she told me all about them." This last was said halfway defiantly, as if Benjie thought that Looney was implying Patricia kept secrets from him.

"Do you know what they did? I mean what kind of paralegal work they were doing?"

"No. Like I said, she didn't tell me much about that. What's this all about? Why do you care what her work was about?"

Again ignoring the direct question, Looney pressed a different line. "Did you know she was sick?"

"No. She never said anything."

"Did she act healthy and seem active all the time?" asked Looney, probing for any break in the picture of health and happiness.

"Pretty much. We were trying to have kids, you know, so she was eating and exercising to keep fit."

This declaration caught Looney a little by surprise. He sat back and looked closely at Benjie who met his eyes, at first, and then let his gaze wander to the right and then downward. Looney wondered just how much Patricia had actually shared with her husband and whether Benjie had lately discovered something was amiss in their marriage.

"Benjie, how did you and Patricia meet?"

"At a party on campus."

"Campus?"

"Yeah. Here at Cincinnati State."

"When was that?" Looney asked.

"Maybe six years ago."

"Tell me about that and what happened after you met."

"We dated a year or so and decided to get married."

"She was a student at State, too?"

"Yeah, she was taking some paralegal courses. I thought that was really cool."

"And when did you get married?"

"Four years ago. Right here in Cincinnati. At the same church we go to now."

"Did you meet her family then? At the wedding I mean."

"No. She said they couldn't come."

"Do you remember why not?"

"Not really. I wasn't paying a lot of attention right then. I was trying to finish up my Associates Degree."

"I see. Have you met her family since?"

"No. They have some kind of work thing that keeps them out of the country a lot. She said they would come visit soon. But they never did."

"Benjie, do you know where they live?"

"Somewhere in Minnesota, I think. I don't really know. Patty used to address all the Christmas cards and maybe she's got an address book or something."

"Do you know any of her friends from when she was at State?"

"Not really. There were some girls in her classes but they all left town."

Looney recognized that this line of questioning was going nowhere and paused for a moment to think and remembered what Tom had said about the change in Benjie's attendance at the bedside in the last day of Patricia's life and decided to pursue that.

"Benjie, you spent a lot of time at the hospital, didn't you?"

"Yeah, I guess. I didn't know what else to do."

"You stayed there overnight the first night didn't you?"

"Yeah. Slept in that recliner chair. It's not very comfortable."

"But then you didn't stay the night anymore, right?

Reluctantly, Benjie nodded, "No, I got sent home."

"Tell me about that, Benjie," Looney said in a voice he thought was calm and inviting. He was surprised by the harsh reaction from Benjie.

"The damn nurses were conspiring against me and wouldn't tell me what was going on and they said I had to go home and let them do their job!" he shouted, clearly very angry about the memory. "Do their job, my ass! If they'd done their job she wouldn't be dead, I bet. And if they'd let me stay, I probably coulda told them something was wrong – but, NO, they didn't want me around and they sent me home!"

"Did they tell you to stay away?"

"No. They just said 'go home and get some rest!'"

"Then you could have come back early the next morning?" Still Looney was soft, spoken and gentle in his inquiry. Benjie was calming down from his outburst but was still obviously tense.

"Yeah, I guess so. And I did on Sunday." He said proudly remembering.

"But you didn't come back early on Monday, did you?" Looney asked, still in the quiet calming voice. Benjie's head did a double-dip, first up at make eye contact and then down again and he became quiet. Looney decided to wait for Benjie to ask the next question, which came about twenty seconds later. "Yeah, so what?"

"Well," Looney said, sitting up straighter and leaning forward slightly while raising his voice just a little, "I wonder why the difference? You want to be there all the time at first – even spending the night in an uncomfortable chair. Then you come back early on Sunday morning but not on Monday morning. Why was that, Benjie? What was different on Monday morning?"

"I don't know." Face down, voice a little muffled.

"I'm sure you do have an idea, Benjie. Tell me about it."

After another pause Benjie spoke in a more quiet tone. "It was those guys from her work. They said she was trying to do something." Looney remembered that Sunday afternoon Benjie had been visited by some of his friends from church and some of Patricia's coworkers. The nurses had told him they sat in the waiting room and talked for a long time and that Benjie had been agitated after they left.

"What did they say about her?" Looney probed.

"They said she was talking about going to law school."

"Had the two of you ever talked about that?" Looney inquired.

"Well, yeah, like a dream or something – I mean, she couldn't do that and us have kids, right?" He looked at Looney for confirmation of this.

"Well, I don't know. Maybe there was a way she could see . . ." Looney said, trying to elicit further insight from Benjie.

"That's what they said. She was looking to get a scholarship or something from her law company."

"I see. Well, that might have allowed things to happen."

"No. You don't see!" Benjie was back to his loud voice again. He hit the table sharply with his hand and said, "We hadn't talked about this at all. This wasn't our plan. We were gonna have the kids first and then she could go to law school. And I woulda been able to support her then. No 'scholarship' or other funny business."

"What do you do, Benjie?" Looney realized he had no information about employment for Benjie and he wondered how he was planning to pay for professional school without his wife's income.

"I, ah, am . . . looking right now."

"Looking for what?"

"A computer programmer job." Head up, spoken proudly.

"Is that what you used to do?"

"Well, sorta. Yeah. I learned the tricks working in the stock room at Wal-Mart. I taught myself how to do some programming and they promoted me into a job doing just that."

"And then what happened?"

"Well, a couple a three years ago we got a new manager and he wanted someone with a degree and I got laid off. Now I can't find anyone that will hire me for programming work without a degree."

"Did you and Patricia have any life insurance?"

"Nah. We thought that could wait till we had the kids."

"Was there any insurance for her at her job?"

"Only medical, I think. I don't know. She kept up with all that."

"What is your training and education, Benjie?"

"I got an Associate's degree from Tech."

"But not in programming, huh?"

"NO. And that's what I really wanna do."

"What are you going to do now?"

"I don't know. Patty kinda helped me make those decisions. Say, listen. Can you tell me something?"

"What do you want to know Benjie?"

"What's going on here? I mean, why all these questions about her work and all?

"Well, you know she got sick at work?"

"Right."

"And you said she was not sick before that?"

"Ahuh."

"So, when she died we got to thinking maybe something happened at work, you know?"

"I see. . . Wait, do you think somebody did something to her at work?" This was clearly a new thought to Benjie.

"Do you think that could have happened?" Looney pushed.

"I don't know. They all seemed to like her."

"Do you think they could have hurt her, Benjie?"

'"I said I don't know." I don't really know them very much."

"Would you have ever hurt her, Benjie?"

"What? Hell no. She was everything to me. Why do you ask that?" Benjie was starting to get angry again and Looney quickly turned the conversation. "You were going to have kids, right?

"Sure, soon's I get a programming job we were gonna get started. Or maybe before."

"What do you mean, 'maybe before'?"

"Well, if she got pregnant and had to quit that job we'd be on the way."

Looney was only slightly taken aback that Benjie apparently didn't see any difficulty with the family breadwinner having to quit her job. By this time he had figured out that Patricia was the brains of the family and Benjie didn't really have clue about how things really worked. Of course, that might actually put him higher on the list of possible suspects since he might not be deterred by obvious consequences. Looney switched lanes again, "But you did know she was talking about going to law school?"

"Sorta. I mean, maybe. That wasn't nothing for sure. We were waiting."

"Waiting to see if she got pregnant?"

"Yeah." Benjie was nodding in agreement to this and Looney wondered again about the level of communication in the marriage.

"Benjie, did you know Patricia had an IUD?"

"What's that?"

"An intrauterine device. It prevents pregnancy."

"NO. That's not right. We were gonna have some kids!" Hands slamming on the table again, eyes flashing as if Looney was telling lies about Patricia.

"Benjie, she was wearing an IUD to keep from getting pregnant. Did you know that?" Now Looney was leaning over the table, his eyes flashing back at Benjie. And Benjie immediately retreated and slumped in his chair.

"No. How could I know? She didn't tell me that. Why would she do that?"

"That's something we are trying to find out," Looney said as he realized that Benjie likely really did not know about the IUD.

"Why would she do that? We wanted kids," Benjie was muttering almost to himself.

"Listen, Benjie, you sit here for a minute. I need to talk to some other people." Looney waited a second or two for some recognition from Benjie. When he got no sign he opened the door and went out.

Chapter Thirty-Nine

Wednesday, March 10

Looney met Tom just outside the door. He shook his head gently and said, with a wry smile, "I don't see this guy killing her – or anybody. Unless it was in a car wreck. He is totally clueless about her and the ways of the world."

Tom responded, "Would have been nice, though, to wrap it up that easily."

"Oh, sure. But it never is that easy. Maybe once in a while somebody says, 'I did it and I'm glad and I'd do it all over again!' but that's actually pretty rare. My experience is they keep denying everything all the way to prison. And even if they do admit it, they have umpteen reasons why it was someone else's fault."

"I guess that would be like a patient coming in the Emergency Department with their diagnosis tattooed on their forehead."

"Just about."

They were silent for a moment and then Tom started back toward his office. Looney put a hand on his arm to stop him and said, "Why don't you show me her room?"

"Her room? Oh, you mean where she was . . . Well, certainly. I should have thought of that. It's up on the Ward 3C."

As they came off the elevator on the third floor, Looney again put his hand on Tom's arm and said, "Let's just walk slowly around the whole ward like you are giving me a tour or something. Don't show any particular attention to the room – or to me. I'm going to act pretty uninformed."

They strolled down the hall from the elevators to the Nurses Station as Looney had his little notebook out and made a few notes. Tom introduced him as an 'old friend' to the two nurses in the station and then pointed out to Looney the computer terminals on the desktop behind the counter and motioned to the area in the rear of the station where the medication cart was kept. As they stood there talking other nurses came by and spoke to Tom briefly. One the male aides grinned at Tom and asked if they had come up to help him take a man down to Radiology. Tom laughed and said his Union card wasn't up to date and he'd have to take a pass. This got a laugh and then any tension about having the Chief of Staff walking around on the ward seemed to dissipate.

Tom led Looney around the nurses Station and down a hall to the right. "Is this her room?" Looney asked at the end of the hall.

"No," said Tom, "I wanted to show you the whole layout. Come in here." He led the way into a small area at the corner of the ward. It was a waiting area with a few padded chairs and a good view up the river. No one was in the room and the two men sat down.

Tom said, "There's another hall that runs off at right angles to this one; there's another little room like this at that end and another right angle hall back to the one where we came from the elevator. It's actually a big square with five or six rooms on each arm of the square on both sides of the hall."

"And Patricia's room was back here?"

"No. This hall where we came from the Nursing Station runs back away from the Station in the opposite direction to a dead end. It's actually part of the old hospital complex and is joined at a big seam just on the other side of the station."

"Which side of that hall was Patricia's room", asked Looney making a quick diagram of the ward layout.

"That ward on the old hospital side has rooms only on one side, the right as we walk down there. The hallway is wider and has windows opposite the rooms. It's usually a little more quiet down there." Said Tom.

"So, Patricia's room is down a hall with fewer patients?" asked Looney making a change to his drawing.

"Yes. And it's also more quiet because that's a dead end hallway."

"Really? You mean there's no way in or out?"

"No, I don't mean that, exactly. I meant there's no connection to any other hallway. There's a staircase down there but it just goes to other wards. If you are in that hall and need to leave, you have to go by the Nurses Station to get to the elevators or the central stairs."

"How far down this hall is her room?" asked Looney. Tom said it was a little over halfway to the end and Looney made a note on his drawing. "Can I see it now?"

"Sure," Tom said getting up and leading the way back to the Nursing Station where Looney stopped to tie his shoe. As they went down the hall Tom kept pointing at things out the windows on the outside of the hallway. Looney gave little notice, however, to things outside the area where a murder had probably occurred. When they arrived at the room where Patricia had been hospitalized and where she died, Tom stopped but Looney again urged him to walk all the way to the end of the hall.

When they got there, Looney looked up the hallway before trying the door to the stairs. It opened without a sound but was very heavy. He looked into the staircase but saw only concrete steps about six feet wide running up two and down three flights. The stairs did not look like they had been cleaned in some time and there was dust on the handrails.

"This was a fire exit in the old building," Tom said. "When the new building was erected they just built right around it."

"Where does this staircase go?" asked Looney.

"Well, it doesn't go outside anymore. They closed off that exit with part of the expanded laboratory facility on the first floor. So, this staircase only connects the five floors here to each other. No roof access and no exit at the bottom."

"Huh," said Looney letting the door close behind them with a heavy sound and an obvious click.

Then they walked back to Patricia's room and Looney stood in the doorway to the room looking down the hall to the Nurses Station where he could see the counter portion that ran along the hallway they were in. He looked up at the ceiling and asked, "These lights on all night?"

"No," Tom said and went on to explain, "Sleep is very important for hospitalized patients and we turn the hall lights out at 10 PM to facilitate sleeping. And yes, I am quite aware of all the jokes about patients being awakened by nurses trying to give them their sleeping pill. That's why I know this wing is so quiet."

"How?"

"I've been up here visiting patients at one time or another, sometimes at night and I can tell you this area is like a graveyard."

"Wrong simile there, pal," said Looney. "But I catch your meaning." They both laughed lightly and Looney stepped over to the outside windows in the hallway. He looked back at the nurses' station and noted that he could not see the outside of the counter. He called this to Tom's attention by saying, "If someone was in this hallway and kept up against the windows he wouldn't be visible from the nurses' station until he crossed the hall and entered the room."

Tom looked at Looney and walked himself through the same paces that Looney gone through, checking visibility from the nurses' station down the hallway on both sides. “I see what you mean, Ron, but you're wrong. They can't see anyone in this hall until that person gets right up at the seam.”

“I can see that counter very clearly from about halfway down here.”

“So what?”

“Well, anyone standing at the counter could look down the hall and see anyone there, couldn't they?”

“Oh,” said Tom, “Now I see what you're saying. But it is still wrong, Ron. Nurses hardly ever stand on the outside of that counter. Their work area is all on the inside of the counter. From that position they couldn't see the door to Patricia's room.”

“And I thought I had a major insight.”

“Just one of those little things you have to work here to know.”

“Well, unless someone came from another floor down those back stairs, the only way to get into this hallway is by the nurses' station, right?”

“That's correct. And, if they came by elevator, like we did, their arrival would be ‘announced’ by the elevator bell. Making it even more likely the nurses would have looked up and seen the person.”

“Unless they were invisible.”

“Of course, I had completely forgotten about that possibility. It's a good thing we have cops on the force who are cognizant of the supernatural and acquainted with the possibility of teleporting and invisibility. Whoever it was probably had a Cloak of Invisibility, right?”

Looney smiled tolerantly at Tom. “Not what I'm suggesting, but if you know where I could get one, that'd be great for tracking criminals without being seen.”

“Then what are you talking about?”

"How many people have we passed in the hall on this ward since we got here?"

"What's this, a test?"

"Yes. How many? And who were they?"

"I'm not completely sure. There were the two nurses I introduced you to. Then three others and the two aides. And I remember a man coming to visit his wife and the girl delivering the meal trays. That's nine, I guess."

Looney smiled and said, "That's really pretty good. But it's a couple of people short. Did you see the janitor cleaning the room at the end of the hall where we sat and talked? Or the pharmacy tech who dropped off a package at the desk?"

"I do remember the tech and I forgot that one."

"And the janitor?"

"I guess I remember him, but I really didn't notice."

"Right. You didn't notice him because you expect him to be there, like the tech. And if I waited until tomorrow to ask you who we had seen on the ward, you likely would not have remembered either of those."

"So you're saying the nurses could be correct that they didn't see anyone but really they're just forgetting to report on someone they expect to be there."

"That's what I call being 'invisible'. People look right past them. Like panhandlers on the street."

"Why did you notice them, then?"

"Because that's my job. And sometimes it takes somebody who doesn't work here to notice that."

Chapter Forty

Wednesday, March 10

Most of the large law firms in Cincinnati are located in a several block square in the Central Business District within easy walking distance from the Great American Ball Park. Patricia's firm was no different. Looney took the little jog on East 5th Street past Fountain Square and began looking for a parking space. Most of the buildings had large glass doors with large, expansive lobbies presenting visible shiny granite and marble flooring and elevator casings. Elegant and upscale; open and inviting even while being a little imposing. Many also had guards in the lobby, uniformed and posted at a desk or podium – not to prevent visitors from entering but to keep vagrants and the homeless from taking up residence in the comfort of the lobby corners. They also provided minimal assistance in locating certain tenants.

Looney eased his seven year-old Nissan Sentra into the parking deck next to the law offices. Circling up to the fifth floor he noted the high number of import cars – BMW, Mercedes and Lexus – in the deck. Not for the first time it occurred to him that maybe he was in the wrong line of work, at least on this side of the law. Even putting his military retirement income together with his current salary he knew he wouldn't be able to afford one of those cars. One of his buddies at the station knew the man who was the premier salesman for 'pre-owned' Mercedes in Cincinnati and had made the referral a year or so ago. Looney talked it through with the guy - Lamont something or other – and even drove a 350E around the neighborhood. Really slick, comfortable and out rigged with seat warmers and Sirius radio. But even with a five-year payment plan he knew that he and Meg would be cutting corners for the entire time. Not the car for him.

But he also knew he wasn't cut out for one of these office positions, pushing paper and writing opinions. He preferred the getting out and moving around and sitting with people and talking to them and watching how they reacted. Looney was convinced that stories about detectives who stayed in the office or their home and still figured out the mystery and directed the catching of the killer from afar were all figments of the crime fiction genre. He was more a believer in the "shoe leather" school of detecting. No, he wouldn't have been happy with a desk job. And he had been certain of that since the Air Force tried to put him into one and that didn't turn out well for anyone.

When he made Tech Sargent, the Air Force decided he should become a supervisor and sit in the main office and make assignments for the other SPs out on various duties. That lasted less than two months as he was not very subtle about assignments and repeatedly sent the guys he thought were slackers off to 'rat patrol' while giving the better assignments to men he was convinced would do a better job. Sure enough, there were complaints and his explanation didn't help the Captain see things his way. So he was 'busted' back to patrol and found that he wasn't the least bit resentful.

When he joined the Cincinnati PD and took right to the patrol aspects of the job he made a little name for himself – 'Walker' – and was well known in his assigned neighborhood for being so visible. Even when he moved up to car patrol he often got out and walked around the area just to be more familiar with the territory and the people. And, now, after making detective, 'Walker' Looney was the partner everyone wanted to have with them out in the field. His sense of what was important and how the geography played into whatever case they were working became a piece of the legend.

But, whatever the reason, Looney would not want to change jobs with these office bound guys. Not even for one of the BMWs . . . although that black one over there is really pretty . . .

He parked next to a new Cadillac Escalade and spent a minute staring through the tinted windows at the leather appointments and the 16-speaker Bose sound system. Sure, that would be fun to drive. And think of all the people you could get in there. "Well, that's a bit of a downer; why would I want more people in my car?" he thought. He walked to the staircase and entered the building.

The offices of Tillson and Martin were just down the hall on the fifth floor. The doors were double and made of polished oak and carried the names of the partners in gold lettering on the right-hand door. It opened almost silently into a medium sized room carpeted in beige with pale blue walls covered with modern art paintings . There was very little furniture in the room, two short couches – Meg would call them 'loveseats' – that were centered and facing each other across a small glass-topped table that held a couple of art catalogs.

A pretty blonde woman of about 35 sat at a Queen Anne writing desk in the rear of the room wearing a headset. The desktop was essentially empty except for an intercom set, a ledger and a small writing tablet. She looked up at Looney and said, "Good afternoon. May I help you?"

"Hello, I'd like to see Mr. Hall." Looney consulted his notebook. "C. Wayne Hall."

"Do you have an appointment?" This was asked with the obvious recognition that she knew all Mr. Hall's appointments and she was certainly aware that Looney was not one of them.

"No. Is that a problem?"

"Well, he's quite busy today. Perhaps I can set something up for you later." She turned from Looney and began ruffling through the pages of the ledger.

"No. I'd really like to see him now," Looney said firmly as he flashed his badge. "I don't intend to take up much of his time."

"Oh." The secretary sat up straighter in her chair and dropped the fake smile. "Let me see where he is right now."

She clicked on the intercom and spoke quietly into the headset. Then she rose and indicated for Looney to follow her. She opened a door at the rear of the room and escorted him down a hallway richly carpeted in a deep burgundy color. He could not hear their footsteps as they moved down the hallway. Looney thought, "If they ever shoot someone in here, we'd never notice the blood." The blonde paused in front of a solid oak door at one corner of the building. C. Wayne Hall's name was painted on the door. Just next to the room was a large area cordoned off into small cubicles from which came a steady low noise of subdued talk and fluttering of paper.

She knocked gently on the door and heard "Come" from inside. She opened the door and indicated that Looney should enter past her. As he did, the man behind the desk stood and advanced toward him.

"Officer."

"Detective." Looney handed him his card.

"Of course. How can I help you? Is this about Patricia?" C. Wayne Hall was nearly six feet tall and shaped almost exactly like a pear. He was bald and wearing wire framed glasses and had a narrow graying moustache. His thick neck disappeared into a bright white shirt behind a muted rep tie of black and gold. He wore a gray suit of barely visible pinstripe and black Allen Edmonds wingtips. His lips were pursed as if he were about to ask a very important question. He looked every bit the lawyer.

"Yes. Just a few questions if you don't mind." Looney wasn't inclined to put people he was questioning about a death into a comfortable setting at first. He preferred that they be uncomfortable and wondering just what he knew about them. He signaled to C. Wayne that he should return to his seat behind the desk.

"No. Not at all." Hall said, as he sat on the front of his seat and placed his elbows on the desk and his hands together in front of him. "What's this about?"

"You know she died." Looney wasn't exactly accusing him of anything but his tone and raised eyebrow seemed to suggest that C. Wayne just might be trying to put something over on him.

"Yes, of course. We were all devastated. So young and all. There at her desk one minute and the next . . ."

"So you thought there was something wrong?" Looney used the same tone but added a lifted eyebrow.

"What? No, I mean its just wrong for someone that young to die, that's all." Now he did begin to look a little flustered.

"You weren't thinking maybe something else had happened?"

"No, of course not. I mean . . . Why? Did it?"

"Do you know what happened?" Looney was moving closer to the desk with each question.

"Not really. I mean I was here but I didn't see anything."

"Why not?"

"Well, I was here . . . you know, in the office and she was out there." He indicated the open space outside his office.

"Was anyone else with her?"

"Yes, I believe some of her co-workers were there."

"Can you give me those names?" Looney asked.

C. Wayne seemed only too happy to give names of others who might deflect this attention from him. "Oh, yes. Certainly. I know who they are."

"What did you hear about what happened?"

"As I understand it, she just fell out."

"Fell out?" Looney seemed incredulous at this description, as if no one had ever done that before. Eyebrow up again.

"Yes, someone heard her hit the floor and they found her like that."

"Had anything like that ever happened before?"

"Not that I'm aware of."

"Would you be aware of it if it happened?"

"Oh, I'm sure I would. Why? What do the doctors think happened."

"They don't think she should have died."

"Oh, that's really tragic."

"That's why I'm asking about what happened."

And, finally, slowly dawning on C. Wayne was a realization that this detective was asking questions that were far from routine. "Wait. You think something happened to her here at the firm that caused her death?" C. Wayne was now openly perspiring on his bald head. He pulled his handkerchief and wiped his head.

"What do you think?" Looney asked, somewhat conspiratorially, leaning forward and lowering his voice.

"No., that's just not possible." C. Wayne Hall shook his head vigorously. The thought of that was almost too much for him.

"What was she working on?"

"Ah, some mergers we are involved in – nothing unusual," he said and then his mouth twitched and he made furtive glances both to the right and the left.

Looney saw the furtive glances and probed, "Really? Nothing unusual about them . . . at all?"

"Well, they are somewhat touchy."

"Touchy?" asked Looney, leaning forward again to encourage more detail.

"Yes. I mean, it would be injurious if any of the information got out."

"Why?"

"Nothing illegal, you know. These mergers are routine business. Just something that will change the liquidity of a couple of big local firms and their stocks will go up sharply when the deal is finished."

"Is that some kind of information that someone would want to get at?"

"Of course, if anyone knew what was about to happen they could make some astute purchases on the stock market and make a lot of money. That's why it's touchy. Sensitive. But we keep the lid on those things very tightly here."

"Could Patricia have let something slip?

"I suppose but that's not terribly likely."

"Why not?"

"Patricia was one of our most trust-worthy paralegals. Completely tight-lipped. Even in the office. Everyone respected that." C. Wayne was on more solid ground here. He leaned back and put his fingertips together as he pronounced his faith in Patricia.

"So, if she didn't talk about it, could someone else have looked at her work and figured it out?"

"Maybe, I really don't know. Everyone keeps their records in their own ways and I don't know if someone else could have figured out her system."

"What exactly do you know of her background, Mr. Hall?"

"Actually, as I thought about it after she got sick, and it's not very much. She came to us as a student at Cincinnati State. Very bright. Talented. We promoted her shortly after she came."

"Where was she from?"

"I don't know. I always thought she was from around here."

Looney looked steadily at C. Wayne for a moment and then went on, "For the record, are you aware of any office tensions with her?"

"With Patricia? No. Everybody liked her."

"How do you know that?" Looney probed. He liked to follow up on such generalizations as if there was a hidden meaning. Sometimes there actually was.

C. Wayne looked a little flustered at the question but responded frankly, "The staff here are usually quite close because of the nature of their work and need for cooperation. Any significant tensions would have had an effect on the work and I certainly haven't seen that!"

"Of course. How about romance in the office?"

"She was married."

"Let me ask that another way. How about romance in the office?'

"No. There was never any hint of anything like that." He sounded very sure of himself here.

"Jealousy?"

"Of what?"

"Her position. Her trust. Her work."

"I don't think so. The paralegals all seem to be a close group and not prone to in-fighting or back stabbing."

"How closely did you work with Patricia?"

"Off and on, fairly closely. I am in charge of the kind of mergers she was working on and we consulted several times a day."

"Ever work with her after hours?"

"What? Well, there were some long days . . ."

"Alone?"

"No. There were always three or four of us. What are you implying?"

"Nothing. Just trying to understand the way she worked."

"She was a very valued employee. All of us in the firm thought highly of her and of her work."

"And you don't have any idea why someone might want to kill her?" Looney said this quickly while staring directly at him.

"What? Kill her? I thought you said she died from whatever it was that made her fall out?"

"Actually, I didn't say anything like that. The doctors don't rightly know what that was just yet."

"But, she was in the hospital and we understood she was getting better."

"That was never really true. And then someone gave her an overdose and killed her."

"Oh my God! Do you think someone here . . .?"

"I'm just starting out, Mr. Hall. Just getting started on finding out about this young lady you think so highly of. I'd like our forensic accountants to take a look at her work." Both eyebrows now were up, daring him to deny that possibility.

"Well, I can understand that but – My God, man! You really think someone here may have murdered her?"

"Like I said, I don't know and I'm just getting started. For all I know she was into something pretty deep and it ended up getting her killed."

"Well, I really can't let you take her records out of the office."

"I can subpoena them. And then it will be public that we are thinking something is going on here in the firm."

"I'm sure you can do that, Detective. And, I'm not really trying to be difficult. But her work is so, you know, sensitive." C. Wayne's own eyebrows went up as he said this, an unspoken request for Looney to back down from the threat of subpoena. After a few seconds with neither of the men saying anything, C. Wayne said, "Wait, can you send your folks over here to look at them?"

"Possibly. Why?"

"Like I said, there's a lot of potential insider trading in this deal and I'd rather if we could keep the cap on it here." It did appear that C. Wayne Hall was making a real effort to be helpful while protecting his firm and its work product as best he could.

Looney relaxed a little and said, "Yeah, I think we can do that. As long as you're open with us."

"Of course," C. Wayne said, almost sighing with relief.

Looney stood up and said, "You have my card. If you think of anything . . ."

"Right. Sure."

They shook hands and Looney left, back down the rich carpet, into the pale waiting area and out into the hallway. He waited until he had left the office area before taking out his handkerchief and wiping his hand; as calm as C. Wayne appeared to be at the end of their conversation, his hand was clammy and sweaty on the handshake.

Back in his car, the reliable 2007 Sentra, Looney settled down and looked at his notes. Probably nothing there, he thought. Nonetheless, he would come back and talk with the co-workers. But he would let them stew a little on the news about a murder in their midst first and see if that helped turn any stones over.

Later, when he told Tom about the interview with C. Wayne Hall, Tom asked if Looney was convinced that there was little to pursue at the law firm.

"Yeah, I didn't get the feeling that the guy was holding out on me or anything like that. But there still could be something he doesn't know about. You know, like the officers never knew what the non-coms were thinking, right?"

"I know that was the theory – on the non-com side, anyway," Tom replied, not feeling like rising to the obvious bait his friend was putting out. "So did this information really change anything for you?"

"Well, for one thing I'm no longer comfortable skating around without talking to my Captain. I'm going to have to tell him soon – probably today."

"Is that going to bring the press into the act?" asked Tom.

"Maybe it doesn't have to. Believe me, I do understand that you would rather this be cleared up before it hits the newspaper. But it is going to be in print at some time and we have a better chance of getting to the bottom of things if we have the resources to follow leads quickly. That's what I think I need from the Captain."

"Why did you say, 'maybe the press doesn't have to be involved'?" asked Tom, looking for any sign of positivity in the proceedings.

"Because I think I may be able to get the Captain to understand a need for less publicity."

"How?" asked Tom.

Grinning for the first time since he entered the room, Looney said, "I have some ways."

Chapter Forty-One

Wednesday, March 10

Tom was sitting in traffic on Martin Luther King. It was Wednesday afternoon and he was on his way to the VA Orthopedic Teaching Clinic. When he was discussing the Chief of Staff job at New City he had made it clear that he wanted to have some regular clinical contact and input into the teaching program at the University. The for-profit Board at New City was initially uncomfortable about his request, thinking that such involvement might either pull him away from the job at New City or give rise to a conflict of interest at one or another programmatic level. There were several discussions about how to arrange some protected teaching time for him that wouldn't compromise his functions at New City and the final decision was to make his teaching time a set piece of the week when his presence away from New City could be expected. That left only a decision about where he would best play a role in the surgical residency program. The Chief of Orthopedics at the University had been deeply involved in the discussions and wanted Tom to have the opportunity to teach in the program. He was aware of the unique experience Tom had had serving in a war zone – multiple injuries requiring immediate triage, horrific tissue damage with potentially devastating long-term consequences if not handled properly plus the necessity for calm team leadership to see that everything ran smoothly for the patients. He wanted his residents to come out of the program capable of handling those kinds of situations and he personally did not have the experience to give them. So he was all in favor of Tom's desire to be involved in the teaching program.

It was the Chief of Orthopedics, Harry Bolten, who had come up with the idea of Tom being a major player in the Wednesday afternoon clinic at the VA. There Tom would have a natural "in" with the veteran patients and the usual bevy of patients seen in the clinic provided a wide array of problems, some of which were service-connected injuries. Although the mix of patients was mostly older and from conflicts that occurred before most of the students had been born, there were almost too many teaching moments there for even the former general officer to handle. And Tom thought the idea to be exactly in tune with his desire for involvement – and the federal nature of the VA would keep any likelihood of a monetary conflict of interest with New City out of the question.

Tom had been going to this clinic every Wednesday afternoon since the first month of his arrival in Cincinnati five years before. He looked forward to his time with the residents and had developed a few short teaching 'lectures' that he could deliver at the whiteboard in the clinic conference room at the end of the day. In the past residents and students had always been able to slip away from clinic after they finished with their last patient of the day but under Tom's tutelage, everyone had to stay until all patients were seen and discharged. And then they sat in the conference room and reviewed some of the common issues they had seen that day; short presentations of patient complaints and examination findings followed by Tom showing how the different presenting pictures were similar in causation. After a few months of grumbling about losing their "easy out" clinic, almost everyone realized how they were getting a powerful educational experience and quit grumbling. And the senior residents started a tradition of providing food for the end-of-clinic-conference; one of them made a run to a local coffee house for a box of prepared coffee and the other brought cookies. By the end of the first year, the Wednesday afternoon conference was attracting even some of the orthopedic staff. Academic discussion tended to start fairly high and rose over time.

Tom had even convinced one of the medical librarians to come to the conference each week. Audrey Hausland was herself interested in medical education and she and the senior residents had developed a mechanism to make the conference a key educational activity. Tom and the staff physicians served as mentors in the discussions to push the students and residents to ask "the right questions" about diagnostic tests, treatments and long-term outcomes. Then Audrey took those questions to the library and searched out answers. She made paper copies of the publications she could find that addressed the questions raised and also put electronic copies on the department's website so everyone could get the answers promptly. The residents had been so intrigued by this innovative process that they gave Audrey and Tom a joint teaching award the next year.

Tom loved his time in this clinic and always looked forward to it. But now, as he idled at a stoplight, his mind was not on what he was going to do in the clinic that day, he was thinking about Patricia. Although he didn't have extensive information about her or her legal work, it did not seem evident that she was killed because of some nefarious activity she had gotten herself involved in. Couldn't rule the husband out entirely but that also seemed a bit thin. Which left, what? A random act? Who would do that? And for what reason? Or, worse still, could this be the beginning of a string of seemingly senseless deaths in the hospital?

How long could he and Looney keep the implications of Patricia's death from others? Like the press? Tom knew he couldn't let that happen before he told Mastone and the Board, but he wasn't ready to tell anybody anything just yet. Nothing was clear; no reason for the killing, no obvious suspect, not even a clear method to start trying to prevent another similar attack. Telling anybody right now would be catastrophic – and once that cat was out of the bag, there would be no putting it back in. But already too many people were aware of the oddities in Patricia's death and just a little leak about that and the dam would break. He wondered how long they might have until . . .

The horn behind him was anything but pleasant. Tom looked up and realized that the light had changed and he was blocking traffic. He jerked forward and waved to the driver of the car behind him. He proceeded on to the VA grounds without getting distracted again. He used his key card to enter the physician parking lot and purposefully chose a space far away from the clinic entrance. This was how he got his steps in every day, after all. He always parked far away from his destination and by his estimate added a good 1000-1500 steps a day to his walking regimen.

Later, after all the patients had been seen and the residents were off in their conference room writing notes and preparing for the conference, Tom was sitting with the last patient he had seen. Joe Gibson was a 59 year old Army veteran, one of the first to enlist in the all-volunteer Army in 1974. His reason for visiting the clinic is his non-service connected amputation of his left leg below the knee for diabetic vascular disease. Joe had been a large man and was well-fed during his time in service. He actually left active duty partly because he could no longer make the weight restriction and his weight pushed even higher after his discharge. He developed insulin dependent diabetes but was not compliant with diet and medications and now has both some visual loss and serious vascular disease in his feet. He had the amputation because of infection and gangrene in the left foot nearly three years ago but has had problems with his prosthesis since then.

"You ever seen anything like this before, doc?" he asked Tom after the resident had left. "You sounded like you had some experience with this."

"What is 'this', Mr. Gibson?"

"This trouble with the leg and it not fitting right. You know." Gibson was obvious about wanting to talk about his issue with the prosthesis. Tom knew from his history that Gibson had blamed the physical therapists and prothestists for a poorly fit artificial leg and was not going to get into an argument about that with him.

"There are many reasons why prostheses don't fit perfectly forever. But, yes, I have seen that problem quite often."

"I guess you've done this procedure a lotta times, huh?"

"Yes. Many times." Tom probably didn't realize how his voice sounded when he made this confession. But Gibson looked up and saw the look on Tom's face. He said, "they weren't all fat diabetics, were they?"

"Oh no, they certainly weren't."

"It wasn't Nam was it, doc?"

"No. I was in Iraq. Balad."

"Lot of action?"

"A lot in the operating room. Not so much in the area. We were a forward operating base and took some attacks but our patients were mostly brought in from around the country for immediate surgery before shipping them to Germany."

"That must of have been tough," Gibson said.

"It was." Tom said and then hesitated. Why did he want to tell this man about his time in Balad? The guy wasn't a war injured vet. But he had a story that was all too familiar to Tom. "Yes. It was tough. Mostly because we never got to see what happened later. They came in our O.R. and we went to work and they went out, woke up and shipped out to Germany without us having any chance to find out if we had done good or bad."

"Any of them have something like what I got?"

"I'm not certain what you mean by that exactly."

"Well, it's kinda complicated. And it's probably more my fault than anyone else's." This was said with a soft voice and a shamed look on his face. Tom immediately wondered whether the information about Gibson's complaints in the chart were accurately reflective of his thoughts. "What makes you think that?" he asked, sitting back down beside the examining table where Gibson was sitting.

"Well, when they fitted me up the first time, it felt pretty good and all that. I had just had my foot lopped off because I wasn't doing right on eating and my insulin and all that and I was feeling kinda down." Tom was quite familiar with those feelings having 'lopped off' a number of feet and legs from poorly controlled diabetics; he nodded and encouraged Gibson to go on with his story.

"Well, see they also got me with this psychologist who helped me see that I needed to be more involved in my care."

"That sounds very positive," said Tom, nodding at the insight.

"Well, sir, I got involved and was pretty good after that on my diet and taking my medicines and doing my exercises." As he said this, Gibson sniffed and looked down at his feet. The story seemed to stop there until Tom said, "And then what happened?"

"I lost weight. Got down to about 265 over the first year after the amputation."

"Again, not unexpected – and very positive," Tom said. Now he was sure he knew where this was going.

"Well, sir, with all that weight loss, my leg got smaller and the leg they give didn't fit me anymore. It rubbed around and gave me some sores and then it hurt to wear the leg. I went back to see the guys in the clinic and the lab and they tried to pad the thing and I just got worse sores."

"And then . . ." Tom was almost able to finish the sentence for Gibson, but he wanted him to say it himself.

"And, then I quit doing the exercising and got a little down on myself and like that." He seemed only slightly defensive about this revelation and then went on, "They had tried everything to make the leg fit and it didn't work, so they re-fitted me and ordered another one."

"And how long did it take before that one was available?"

" A few weeks. But the thing was, I was just lying around and eating and I gained a lot of weight and that second leg didn't fit when I got it either."

Tom nodded. This was a familiar problem especially for obese patients. "I know what you're talking about. This happens a lot and it is not all your fault. It would have been better if your weight weren't so dependent on exercise. But the science of prostheses has been improving because of these kinds of problems. And there may be some help for you in the near future."

"Whadda you mean?" Gibson was interested but not highly encouraged. He imagined some kind of devilish exercise machine he would have to endure while not having the prosthesis.

Tom said, "There are two breakthroughs happening right now. One is using 3-D printers to help create a better and more form-fitting pad on the prosthesis. But the second development is the use of materials that are able to allow for weight gain and loss – to a degree – and not let the prosthesis rub and cause injury."

Now Gibson was sitting upright and looking much more interested. "Can I get one of those?" he asked.

"Don't know," Tom answered truthfully. "I don't know what the VA policy is on that process," he said. "But I will find out and get an answer to you." He stood up and wished Gibson well, shook his hand and headed for the conference area.

Tom got a cup of coffee and sat on the side of the conference room thinking to himself. And, as occurred several times since Balad, his mind wandered to the question of PTSD. He remembered having this conversation with Susan before – why didn't he have any of the PTSD he has seen in so many vets? He had been right there in the busiest operating theatre man has ever seen, day after day, long shifts running together while a seemingly endless stream of wounded pushed through the doors and needed immediate attention. He certainly saw the trauma. Sometimes he could call up a memory of some of those events, perhaps brought back by the smell of the bone saw in the O.R. But he slept well – even while he was in "the Sandbox" he had been able to sleep when he got the chance. And there were no nightmares. He had no easy explanation. Was he somehow inured to pain and misery? He didn't want to think of himself as an unfeeling bastard.

His own theory was since he was 'relatively' safe most of the time (a few incomings to the contrary) he was able to 'just do the job'. His life was not immediately and repeatedly threatened like those of the men with full-blown PTSD. Further, his medical and surgical training had provided him with an experience where he had seen the devastating effects of high velocity injury prior to being put in the war zone. The blood and gore and limb salvage was not a shock to him like it surely was to the uninitiated. But he has always felt a little guilty that he didn't come home with the PTSD like so many of those who went through Balad.

"At least," he thought to himself as the residents began to gather their paperwork for the conference, "at that time I didn't have to wonder who was causing all the death and destruction. Today has been a nice respite from the events at New City. But pretty soon I'm going to have to get back to figuring out who killed Patricia."

Chapter Forty-Two

Wednesday, March 10

Looney's office was on the fourth floor of the Cincinnati Police Department Building. The Detective Bureau operated out of the southwest corner of the building using their slightly less than a quarter of the floor to house a large open space with desks pushed face-to-face for partners, one corner dedicated to printers and copiers with a large table for spreading out work and another accommodating an enclosed locked room containing active and inactive files. The doorway entering the "Dick Pen" as it was known was near the center of the floor; on either side was a short wall with coat hooks where personnel left their heavy coats during the winter. Otherwise, coats and sweaters and caps took up residence on desks and backs of chairs when the wearers were 'at work'.

The corner outside office was the Captain's; it was enclosed with walls that were thin plaster up to waist height then frosted glass up to the ceiling. The door also had frosted glass on which was lettered "Arne Thorason, Captain, Chief of Detectives" in bold Copperplate font. The door to the Captain's office was almost always open. When it was closed someone was getting explicit information about how his or her recent work was falling short of the standard expected by the Captain. Fortunately, this did not happen often as the homicide detectives, individually and as a group, were solid achievers.

The Captain, Arne Thorason, or 'Thor' as he was known behind his back was a 23 year veteran of the Cincinnati police department and, perhaps more important, a former college linebacker. Still built like he could plug holes in a defensive line, he was just short of six feet tall and was a solid 235 pounds with only a slight waistline bulge. He liked wearing three-piece suits but always left the coat in his office while in the building. His bulky appearance, squarish head and bushy eyebrows, clad in vest and shirt with loosened collar was the least reminder of his former occupation. The eyes were the most important. When Thor squared up his body, tucked his head ever so slightly and fixed you with his solemn, wide-eyed stare you felt like a freshman running back about to hit the turf on your back. 'The Look' was known throughout the department and probably accounted for a major part of the work ethic in the detective bureau – no one wanted to explain why they had fallen behind the standard to Thor and become the recipient of 'The Look' not to mention not to be a recipient of 'The Talk' behind a closed door in Thor's office.

Looney had a good relationship with Thorason primarily because he understood that the Captain was willing to allow his detectives some latitude in working their cases but the lane was narrow and rather well defined. Stay in the lane between 'whatever it takes' and 'don't embarrass the department' and you were unlikely to face 'The Look'. Looney felt he could safely tell Thor about his delinquency in bringing a probable murder to the attention of the department because of the unique circumstances of the hospital death: late discovery, cold scene thoroughly cleaned, etc. Nonetheless, he was a little uncomfortable and hesitant to bring the subject up with the Captain because he still wanted a broad lane in which to work – and that lane might need to be broader than Thor would allow. He knew the Captain had gained the confidence of the department because of the division's high closure rate; plus everyone knew his reputation of covering for his detectives. What was known only to those who worked directly for him was that he had a sincere willingness to listen to their 'hunches' and 'gut feelings' about cases. But he wasn't a softie; conversations with him were usually short as he didn't want to spend time circling a subject – his tendency was to treat it like an opposing running back. Thor's conversational style was to use short, direct sentences, often jumping over the next two normally expected sentences to get to the point. He also interjected the word "Huh" into conversations often usually without inflection so one would have to pay very close attention to understand when "Huh" was a question, a comment of mild surprise or simply the Captain's way of indicating that he was still listening.

Looney knocked on the Captain's open door and was waved in.

"Captain, I may have just picked up an interesting case."

"Huh."

"You remember my friend for the Air Force that's now Chief of Staff over at New City, right? Well he has discovered that one of the deaths there recently looks pretty suspicious."

"Meaning?"

And the whole story came out with Looney bringing the Captain up to speed on the details and timeline of Patricia Harding's death and the reason the medical examiner was suspicious about the cause of death. He mentioned that he had known of the event and the possibility of murder for two days but had taken it upon himself to question Patricia's manager at the law firm before bringing it to the attention of the department. That revelation brought a brief confluence of Thor's eyebrows and a hint of 'The Look' but Looney just shifted his gaze to the top of Thor's head and pressed on with the story. At the end he gave his best guess that the events seemed more like an insider than family or friends but he wasn't sure and had no real leads at that point. And he asked the Captain for some help and leeway in progression.

"Why do you want the forensic team?"

"It's still possible that our perp is one of the coworkers and the reason has something to do with her job. I do think that's a bit of a stretch but her boss really broke out in a sweat when I mentioned going over her books. It just didn't feel like I was getting the whole story there."

"Alright. One day."

"That should be enough. Thanks."

"You told Gene?" This was a reasonable question. Gene Novalchek was Looney's partner. Regulations were that murder cases were to be worked in pairs for many reasons, safety among the highest on the list.

"Not yet. I'm really just on the way in. He and I can talk right away."

"Huh."

"I've got some additional interviews lined up and I'll keep you posted."

"Yeah. OK." Thor broke eye contact and turned back to whatever he was working on at the desk. Looney took that as dismissal and turned and left.

Out in the Dick Pen, Looney found Novalchek at his desk, facing Looney's desk. In that setting it usually took only a short conversation for them to apprise each other of what was going on and what was needed. Gene Novalchek did not resemble the conventional mental picture that most people would get when they heard the name. He was not overly tall, about six feet, nor was he bulky, weighing in just under 190 pounds. His face was narrow with a high hairline and eyebrows that nearly touched. His nose was shorter than expected but gave adequate room to a broad mouth that was often smiling and revealing a set of teeth that often appeared too large for the mouth. Gene was, in general, more of an optimist in the Homicide group than many of his compatriots. He was also the best-dressed man in the room, showing up in a new suit every few weeks and always wearing a tie no one could remember seeing before.

"S'up partner?" Novalchek asked, "Showing up in time to go home?"

Looney grinned at him. He was aware that he would have been called if anything came up that required his presence.

"Gotta sign in so I can get paid," he said.

"That's not what the look on your face says," Gene said, leaning back in his chair expectantly.

"Well, actually, I did run across a little funny thing we should look into," Looney said sitting at his desk and pulling the chair close while leaning forward.

Gene took the hint and also leaned forward, pushed a couple of items on his desk out of the way and, leaning forward, made serious eye contact with his partner. "Go ahead," he said quietly, "I got your message that you were out 'looking into something' and I was hoping it was about getting a new car."

"There's nothing wrong with my car and you know it. You're just so sensitive that you feel every bump in the road."

"Prince and the pea, that's me."

"You know that story is about a Princ*ess*, you dope. Want me to get you a tiara?"

"I'd rather you just got some padding in your passenger seats or maybe fixed your suspension."

Looney shook his head over the never-ending critique of his seven-year old Sentra. "Listen up," he said, shifting the topic, "I've been asked to look into something funny at New City."

Over the next fifteen minutes Looney sketched out the events involving Patricia Harding and why his old friend, the Chief of Staff, had called him for 'consultation'. For personal reasons, Looney went a little light on the medical terminology and reasoning but convinced Gene there was something amiss in this girl's death. He also told of his drop-in visit to Tillson and Martin and the feeling there might be something being covered up there. He outlined his plan and Gene agreed to oversee the forensic review at the law firm while Looney carried out additional interviews of Patricia's coworkers.

With that settled, Gene asked, "You gonna get in the Bracket Pool? I'm sure you can do better than last year?" He was referring to Looney's next-to-last finish in the point totals from the NCAA basketball tournament pool in the office the previous year.

"Sure. We all know that wasn't representative of my expertise and knowledge of the college basketball scene. The 5-12 upsets were what got me."

"Expertise, eh? Where do you think the Bearcats will go, then?" referring to the local University of Cincinnati team.

"Ranked in the middle like they are, they sure won't be playing here in the Mid-west bracket. I'd guess they'll end up in the West."

"That wouldn't be all bad. We can probably catch most of their games, then." Gene paused and went on, "You remember my friend Lucas from down the block?"

"Yeah?"

"He's got tickets for First Round action."

"Really? Where?"

"Dayton. He'd like me to go with."

"Gene, we got a case, here."

"Maybe it'll be done by then."

"When are these tickets?

"Friday and Sunday. Might get to see the Bearcats!"

"Nope, they're going out West. You'll see."

"Anyway, I'd really like to go."

"You planning on driving?"

"Yeah, it's only 70 miles and these are night games. But we'll stay the night and come back Monday."

"I don't know, Gene. This is a puzzler at New City. I don't think you should plan on it."

"Yeah, well, let's just wait and see."

Chapter Forty-Three

Thursday, March 11

The Director's conference room was almost half full on Thursday afternoon. Tom had assembled the analysis team that worked on the beating heart program and also asked all of the cardiac surgery and medical cardiology groups to attend. Trying to fit such a meeting into known schedules and the unknowns of daily operations in a hospital had been surprisingly less stressful than anticipated – or perhaps because Mary Brighthouse knew how to get the principals to attend. But, of course, it took second place to scheduled operations and clinics and medical school lectures. Whether the individuals were just interested in the topic or interested in the inside scuttlebutt about the death of the chief of Cardiology didn't seem to matter. Schedules were juggled where necessary and arrangements made and almost all of the primary participants that had been invited found the time on their calendar to be present even if it was at the end of an otherwise busy day.

Surgeons arrayed themselves on one side of the long table wearing scrub suits under their white coats. Many of them also wore either a scrub cap or left a surgical mask dangling from their neck. These were not individuals who would pass up a chance to remind everyone in the room of their importance and the high-stakes activities in which they trod every day.

Cardiologists, on the other hand, were snappily dressed in suits and ties, with an occasional vest, often with collars buttoned down. And they sat mostly across from the cardiac surgeons as if they were joining an arbitration council.

Once Sam joined the table, Tom set the stage for the presentation and introduced the members of the analysis team. He had decided to push for the presentation on the basis of information provided by Andy and the analysis team. They said they had the models populated and had run several scenarios though the computer modeling system. And, the analysts said, the models were very consistent on key points – so consistent that they felt strongly about their recommendation.

Tom had spoken with most of the cardiac surgeons about the proposal of the Director and knew that they were less than enthused about the concept. Their position essentially was, 'Look we are doing quite well, we are a leader in the city and the state in our outcomes, so why make a change?' Underneath this valid argument, Tom knew, was the very real possibility that any such new program might cause financial disruption in their practices and ultimately could lead to lower incomes if they were not part of the new surgical program. He understood their reticence and even agreed with it to some degree.

But Tom Bolling was a physician with a background in quality improvement; a man who did not believe in "if it ain't broke, don't mess with it!" He had long before adopted a personal policy of "everything can be done better" and was prepared to push that concept – but only if the financial analysis showed some actual reason to think harder about the proposed program.

When he had been on active duty, Tom Bolling had been thought of as a 'change agent'. He had effectively created an environment at different bases where the average worker and their superiors all up the line seemed to agree that 'everything could be improved.' Tom knew from his reading in history that an 'agent of change' would find resistance. He was particularly aware of the writing of Nicolo Machiavelli about change and often had paraphrased the 16th century political theorist saying, "the agent of change has no friends." But that thought only helped him to recognize opposition early and to take a variety of steps to contravene that resistance. Over time he became effective in pulling even dedicated resisters over to his side. Of course, some of those opposed to him thought his success had been related to the hierarchy in the military since many flag officers liked Tom and his programs. And, having his own star became the 'answer' to his success in the eyes of some. He was ready to see if those naysayers were correct when he left the service and entered the world of private medicine. So far he was ahead in the change game, but aware that Sam Mastone wanted him to make even agreed upon changes much more quickly than he did.

Tom knew that Mastone would have made a terrible officer in the military because he had no sense of the need for followers to be informed and in agreement with goals and tactics. He had learned over the years the need to talk things through with those who opposed his efforts, find a common ground and enlarge it and rarely use rank to close out discussion. He looked around the room now and briefly thought of the many conversations he had held with the surgeons and the cardiologists about this topic. He was about to see whether his preparatory work was going to be effective in creating a unified decision.

There had been many conversations between Tom and the cardiology staff members in the past few months. At least as much as the surgeons, they were aware of the growing number of beating heart surgical programs in the country and of the heated discussions between the two camps. To many of them it appeared more as the tempest in a teapot – not so much difference in the outcomes but very deep feelings regarding the craft on the part of the participants. Tom was hoping to get everyone on the same page with a financial business case analysis. If the literature and the science were not able to show a decided advantage in terms of throughput or outcomes, the hinge for the decision was going to turn out to be how much it would cost.

Andy began his part of the presentation by going back over some of the points made by Tom in his introduction. Andy did this in order to answer the first question of importance in the development of the business case analysis: why are we considering doing this? Of course, his 'explanation' of how the question arose was not so simple as to say 'the Director made us do it' but he did not pad the presentation with any implications of non-worth. He laid out the question as it appeared to many hospitals in the nation at this time: 'Is there a valid reason for us to abandon our current processes for open heart surgery to embrace the new trend?'

Andy and Tom had discussed the way Tom wanted the analysis to proceed and Andy stuck with that playbook: emphasis was placed over and again against the notion that there were different outcomes. Andy's presentation of three large studies underscored the lack of any such difference when all was said and done. This presentation plan kept the focus on the costs of the program and the ultimate question of whether the hospital – and the practices – would benefit financially from change.

Tom knew the particulars and was very familiar with how Andy would make the case; he sat back and allowed his mind to wander a little from the conversation. He watched the faces of those in attendance, trying to read their reaction to various points. Mostly, however, he thought that Wilford was missing from the table. He wondered what Wilford's face would have revealed; after all Wilford had told Mary that he wanted to talk with Tom about the program just shortly before his death. They had spoken twice before and Tom recalled that the first discussion was relatively short and to the point. At that time, at least, Wilford was unable to see any impact on the Cardiology division by opening the new program – and, therefore, he was not interested in spending time on a discussion of something that was of no impact, or interest, to him.

The cardiologist had instigated the second encounter with Tom. He had pulled Tom into the office one afternoon and asked several questions about the proposed program. Tom remembered being more than a little surprised by the show of interest from Wilford but he was, at the time, distracted by other issues and in a bit of a hurry. His answers to Wilford were short and he did not take the time to determine why there appeared to have been a change in interest in the program by the chief of Cardiology. Now, he thought, I'll never know what Wil was thinking about. He also remembered now, for the first time, that Wilford had asked whether Jennings Crawford had talked with Tom about the program. Tom had said 'no' and closed the conversation.

Now he began to wonder why Jennings' name had come up. Jennings Crawford was a very interesting man. A graduate of the University he had been in general practice in a small town north of

Cincinnati for 4-5 years and then came back to the University for a Cardiology Fellowship. Then he joined the staff of the VA for 4 years before moving to New City at the behest of Wilford. Jennings was an invasive cardiologist and widely regarded as one of the best in the Midwest. He believed – and his results backed him up – that he could put a stent into any artery of the heart. Tom wondered if Jennings was concerned about a new open-heart program taking away cases from him?

Surprisingly, Andy was able to keep the attention of the physicians through his explanation of the market assessment. Although such dull information is at the heart of business case analysis, he had anticipated that the attention of the physicians would wander. They were, on the other hand, actually very interested. Andy's presentation looked at the demographics of the catchment area for New City and, using well-documented incidence rates for coronary heart disease, projected the probable number of heart attacks, patients needing stents or bypass and coronary deaths for each year in the next decade. This was the work product for these physicians and the numbers caught them.

But it was Andy's presentation of the financial cost for start up that really got everyone's attention. He presented the two most common scenarios used by other hospitals to develop a new beating heart program: buy or make. The 'buy' option would involve recruiting a talented surgeon to come to the area and develop the program: recruit and train operative assistants and oversee the purchase of equipment. The 'make' scenario required one of the current surgical staff to leave the area and go to an ongoing program to learn the particulars of both the surgery and the program support before returning to the area to set up the program. According to Andy's analysis, start up costs of slightly more than $2,000,000.00 would be necessary regardless of the 'make' or 'buy' scenario chosen. That got everyone's attention. But the 'make/buy' scenarios were the tipping point for the surgeons. They did not want a new surgical member coming into the area and none of them wanted to go away for additional training in order to build the program locally. The financial costs were a good focal point but their interests were predominantly personal.

Tom noted that a couple of the cardiologists seemed to perk up their interest when Andy mentioned that there might be some research program capabilities with the new program but their interest was desultory and almost fleeting. Tom noted that Jennings Crawford seemed no more interested than anyone else and thought he could not discern any particular interest in the program from anyone sitting at the table – and he was fairly certain that Sam Mastone was just as aware of that lack of interest.

Andy's presentation wound down with a brief recap of the start up costs, the operating costs and a possible 'break-even' point in the future. That point, more than three years away, was highly dependent upon the volume of cases selected for the beating heart program and was thought by many to be far overestimated. By that time Andy's recommendation against the initiation of such a program at New City was expected and accepted. Even Sam Mastone seemed to understand the uphill battle he would have to engage in to get started on such a program and he was now willing to step down his push to get underway. He could explain to the brother-in-law about the fiscal aspects.

The meeting was about to break up when Monique Song slipped in the back door and quietly moved over to sit next to Tom. He raised his eyebrows but she just shook her head a little and pretended to be fascinated by the end of Andy's presentation.

Shortly, as everyone was moving toward the doorways, Monique said, "We need to talk," and headed off toward Tom's office.

Once there she closed the door and said, "I calculated the amount of insulin in that bag." She leaned back against the door and seemed to get a little smaller when she said this.

"In Patricia Harding's case," said Tom.

"Yes." Monique looked directly at Tom and said, "Tom, there wasn't enough insulin in that bag to kill her."

"What do you mean? I thought you said that insulin would lower her potassium and cause those arrhythmias. Now you're not sure?" Tom had been about to sit at his desk but now walked toward her in puzzlement.

"That's not what I said. But you're right about the potassium. The bag had only 10 units of insulin in it but it also had a lot of glucose. Someone probably put insulin in D-50-W and injected that into the bag."

"So what? Is that really different from injecting 20 or 30 units of insulin?" This was starting to be a bigger puzzle than he had thought.

"Yes, I suspect it is. Especially with the added glucose. That way she wouldn't develop the usual cause of death from insulin overdose – hypoglycemia. What would happen is she would lower her potassium and have more arrhythmias. And she had a history of recovering from the arrhythmias."

"What are you suggesting here, Monique? Was someone trying to kill her or not?"

"I don't know for sure but I think we have to consider that the low dose of insulin was just intended to cause her to arrest – not to kill her."

"Jesus. This makes the whole shebang into a rat's nest. We better get Ron over here to discuss this. It was bad enough when we were dealing with a murder, what changes when it becomes attempted murder?"

Monique smiled wryly and said, "Don't fret. It's still murder. Patricia Harding is very definitely dead."

Chapter Forty-Four

Thursday, March 11

The four of them sat in Tom's office. Tom was behind the desk, slumped in the chair with his head resting on the back. Looney sat in an upholstered chair in the corner that Tom usually kept for dignitaries. Monique sat in a straight chair at the side of Tom's desk, back straight, hands folded in her lap; Gene leaned against a lateral filing cabinet. Looney had introduced his partner and recapped what he had told him about the case.

Monique brought the detectives up to speed on the chemical nature of Patricia's condition and the attempts by house staff to make corrections. Tom laid out the results of the AAR confirming what Monique had said had transpired. And he added the key catch that Lila had made as everyone else walked out the door. Monique reviewed the chemistry findings of insulin and high glucose levels in the banana bag and they all agreed that their initial thought of murder was justified.

Then Monique explained her calculations concerning the contents of the banana bag; back calculating from the volume and the glucose concentration she was able to determine that about fifty milliliters of D50W containing only 10 units of insulin had been added to the bag. She ended by noting that the rate of infusion of that banana bag would have added only about one unit of insulin per hour to Patricia – not enough to cause significant hypoglycemia, especially not with the added glucose in the D50W. Her conclusion brought on the silence: Someone had added insulin to the banana bag but likely not with intent to kill.

After this revelation and the issues the new information raised, the four of them talked for nearly twenty minutes but had reached no conclusion. After several minutes of silence, Gene spoke. "Help me understand why you don't think this is attempted murder. She could have died from the rhythm thing couldn't she?"

"In fact she did die from her rhythm," said Tom as Monique nodded in agreement. "The thing that is puzzling to me is that the insulin was given with extra glucose."

"Why is that puzzling, again?" asked Gene.

Monique leaned forward and answered, "If someone wanted to kill her with insulin, the way to do it is without any extra glucose."

"Because . . ." Looney asked.

"Because the way the insulin works is to move blood glucose into the cells of her body and . . ."

"Yeah, I got that.

"When we treat a diabetic with high blood glucose levels with insulin the immediate effect is to start a movement of that high amount into the cells of the muscles and throughout her body. If you give insulin to someone with a normal level of glucose, it could easily cause the level of blood sugar to drop to dangerous levels."

"OK. I'll buy that." Looney said. "But two questions. One, what's that going to cause? And Two, is that likely to happen with this small dose of insulin?"

""That's part of what's troubling us both, Ron," Tom interjected. "If the intent was to kill Patricia, the glucose goes against that. And, yes, even this small a dose could cause that because it was in an intravenous bag and being slowly and continuously delivered."

"So, you think this was not an attempt to kill Patricia?"

"It's somewhat confusing, I'd say," Tom put in, holding up his hand to stall a comment from Monique. "The addition of the glucose seems incontrovertible evidence that the insulin was not intended to lower the glucose level to dangerous levels."

Monique added, "Plus, the action of insulin to move glucose inside the various cells of the body is accompanied by movement – in the same direction – of potassium and phosphorus. We know she was getting this extra insulin and at the same time she was getting extra potassium in her fluids, her blood potassium level fell from admission to Monday morning."

Looney nodded and said, "So, if the intent of giving the extra insulin with glucose was to lower the potassium level, it certainly worked."

"Right," said Tom. "And we think that's what triggered her rhythm disturbance again and that's what killed her. So, the question for me is 'was the intent of the added insulin to kill her?' "

"Well, it certainly does seem more complicated than necessary for a straight-forward murder. But, as you say, if the girl's death was not the object, what else could be the reason?" asked Gene. "And how does that change our inquiry into who was responsible?"

His question to the room was met with another prolonged silence as each of the three leaned back in their respective chairs and broke eye contact. Finally Tom spoke, a little slowly as if he were thinking his way through the sentence. "Maybe the intent wasn't for her to die but just to be really sick and have a prolonged hospital stay. Although I can't imagine what the reason for that would be."

Looney shook his head and said, "It could still be the husband. He was really unaware that she had an IUD but if he was just thinking about getting her to stay home and have babies, this might have been a way to do that. Did you find out anything more about her from your Admin guys?"

Tom shook his head and answered, "No. They told me this morning they have no other information than what her husband gave when she was admitted. He apparently doesn't know where her parents are."

"Yeah. That's what he told me, too. Maybe he's covering something up. Right now I don't think he had anything to do with this. Especially since he was so keen on them having kids and all. Unless he really was just trying to get her sick and fired so they could get started on that family"

"I don't think that makes any sense. They would have no income if she left her job, right?" asked Tom.

"Well, right. It doesn't make sense to you or me. But maybe this guy was thinking if she got pregnant then she would quit her job and they would be 'on track'. I don't think his elevator goes to the top floor." For a moment there was quiet head nodding. Then Monique said, "But from what you said about his lack of insight, you really can't remove him from the suspect list, can you?"

Sighing, Looney agreed, "I guess not. But if he has that little insight I just don't see him having the ability to plan this out."

"I think I agree," said Tom. "Besides, I think we're maybe missing something else about the 'means' of this plan."

"What's that?" asked Monique.

"Well, we know anybody could walk into any drug store and get the insulin that was used, right?" Heads nod. "But where did that guy get the D-50-W?"

"Oh," said Monique, "I see what you mean. That looks like a medical person – someone from the hospital?"

Gene put up his hands and asked, "What are you guys talking about?"

"It's really simple," said Tom. "We've been focused on the insulin but the real clue may be the D-50-W – the sugar water that the insulin was mixed in. You can't just waltz in to a drugstore and get a bottle of that."

"All right!" said Looney. "Now we're talking. This cuts out everyone except the medical personnel. Can we be sure there have been no other cases like this in the hospital?"

"You mean 'do we have a serial killer on staff?' " asked Tom, while Monique sat back in her chair and opened her laptop. "No, I can't categorically state that there have been no other cases in the hospital similar to this until we have looked at damn near every death we've had in the past year or so."

"But if you had any hints at all it would really help narrow down the field of suspects I have to take to the Captain," Looney sounded almost like he was begging.

"Time out!" said Monique, looking up from her laptop. "Turns out the second item listed on Amazon under '50% Dextrose' is a 500 milliliter bottle for veterinary use."

"What?" both detectives said almost simultaneously.

"Let me see that," commanded Tom. She swung the laptop over to him and he quickly looked at the page and then grimaced at Looney. "She's right. Anybody could get this and it's injectable"

"So the idea limiting us to the hospital personnel is bogus, huh?" Looney was really deflated by this turn of events. "That's a real kick in the shins."

"And we are back where we started," added Monique. "Unless you think there's something going on with her work at that law firm."

Looney was quiet for a moment re-thinking his interview with C. Wayne Hall. He had come away thinking there was not likely anything going on between him and Patricia but there was obviously something about his visit there that had made the man sweat. "Actually, I haven't pursued that as far as I should have," he admitted. "There needs to be another visit. The Captain said I could get an accounting look at her records. Plus we will sweat her co-workers some to see if there's anything there."

"You know," Tom said as Looney finished and started to stand, "This all started at the job site. Maybe we shouldn't be overlooking that piece of information."

"Or from somewhere else in her background," commented Looney. "I didn't get much on that from her husband. Do you know where she's from?"

Tom thought a second and responded, "No. I guess not. We needed next-of-kin permission for the autopsy but we got that from the husband. I don't know if the family was ever notified."

"Can you find that out for me?" Looney asked. "This could be someone from the past harboring a grudge or something."

Monique spoke up, "It's possible that someone at work was jealous of this girl – Patricia – jobwise, I mean, you know wanting her position and responsibility. Maybe all they wanted was for her to be unable to work so they could get ahead."

Tom added, "And if that's true it wasn't really attempted murder – more like 'attempted sickness'."

"Even if that were true," said Looney, "that might only change the charge from first degree to second degree murder. I still have a murder charge to pursue. The girl is dead – and because of the actions of whoever put that insulin in her i.v."

They sat there for another 20 minutes or so, each with their own thoughts about what had happened, why it may have happened and who would have had reason to cause such medical turmoil. But it was clear that no real answers were popping into anyone's mind.

Later, as they walked to their car, Gene said to Looney, "You were right, this is a can of worms. First, we aren't sure it wasn't an accident. Now we aren't sure if it's first degree or second degree and that makes a difference about who might be involved."

Looney nodded and followed up with, "But one thing's sure: the docs are pushing for this to have roots in the law firm where Patricia worked. They are really trying hard not to see a connection to anyone in the hospital."

"Well, right now I kinda think they're right."

"Good thing that we're set up to spend the day at the lawyer's office, then. We've got every incentive to find the thread that helps us track down the killer."

"Plus, I want this thing over and done with by next week – 'cause I got a basketball tournament to get to."

"And then, there's that," said Looney getting in the car.

Chapter Forty Five

Friday, March 12

Beverly Hancock was sitting in her office next to Tom Bolling's. They had a short meeting with the Director that morning and she was able to get her coffee freshened and get started on her day. She was working on credentialing and privileging packages for two new ophthalmology consultants, putting the paperwork into the style and packaging that Tom had instituted when he arrived when she was interrupted by a faint knock on her door.

Rather pleased to have a reason to step away from the boring work she was doing, she called out, "Come in."

The door opened to reveal the Public Affairs Officer, Johnny Taliaferro. "May I come in?"

"Certainly, Johnny. Have a seat."

Johnny Taliaferro, 31, resembled his Italian forebears in many respects. He was five foot ten, with an erect posture. His skin tone was short of swarthy but slightly richer than a common suntan. His black hair was swept straight back from his forehead and his open face and dark eyes gave an immediate impression of openness and honesty. Perhaps that's why Sam Mastone had chosen him for the Public Affairs Office. Mastone obviously had an Italian heritage and Johnny looked really good in his Italian suits – good enough for several of the female staff to comment that he looked like he belonged in one of the men's fashion magazines. Certainly, since his appointment there three years ago, Johnny had represented New City very well and had a personal reputation with local newspapers and news outlets as both friendly and honest. That reputation served the hospital well in the last year when a citywide outbreak of MRSA occurred and Johnny was talking to the press every day about the cases, thankfully few, at New City and what the staff was doing to limit the in-house spread.

Johnny came in and closed the door behind him. Bev thought that a little strange and sat up straight, paying close attention to the body language Johnny was exhibiting. He was hesitant, almost apprehensive and tentative as he sat in the chair in front of her desk. These were not the usual characteristics of Johnny's behavior and Bev unconsciously frowned at him as she asked, "What's wrong, Johnny?"

Bev herself was not an imposing figure. Short at five foot two, prematurely gray and quite pale in complexion, she almost looked ill. She had a congenital hip dysplasia that made her walk with a sideways cant and she almost always carried a batch of folders in front of her held by both arms as this made her gait look less awkward. Now she was frowning and leaning forward looking intently at the Public Affairs Officer.

"Bev, is there something going on I should know about?" he asked

"Exactly what do you mean, Johnny?"

"I mean is there something going on that I should know about in the office?"

"What are you talking about?"

"I don't know. I just got a call and I wonder if there's something I should be aware of and help to handle."

"What was this call?" Bev knew that Johnny had a very good network of informants throughout the hospital and often knew of things that had occurred on the wards or the clinics before even she and Tom were aware. So it wasn't unusual for him to have information very early in many events but he rarely came to her or the Chief of

Staff to bring the matter up; he was much more likely to wait for them to approach him. Now she wondered what kind of a call would make him break his habits.

"Daniel Edderman"

"Really," Bev said, wondering aloud what the local news reporter would be up to by calling Johnny. Daniel Edderman wrote a week day column for the *Beat,* usually with comic relief but he had already won one local award for his pursuit of a story about the death of a local youth basketball player from drugs that led to a successful police sting operation in the neighborhood and the conviction of 12 members of the drug ring. He was a bit of a local celebrity and his column, *Daniel's Den,* was a first-read for many in the city. Even though he was not a classic investigative journalist, Edderman had the history of latching on a story and never letting go, often using his biting humor to call attention to slow or inadequate response to issues by authorities.

"What did he say?" Bev went on.

"He asked me if there had been a murder involving staff at New City. What the hell is that about, Bev?"

Bev was aware of the death of Wilford Adamson but not aware of anything suggesting murder. She knew that Tom was particularly stricken by the death but he had certainly not shared anything with her about foul play. She had no idea what Daniel could be referring to.

"Why would he ask that?" she queried Johnny.

"He said he was sitting in the lobby waiting for a friend who was visiting her father who had just had heart surgery and he saw two homicide detectives go into the Head Shed." He was referring to the Director's Office suite where Sam, Tom, Bev, the Assistant Director and the Chief Nurse and her Executive Assistant had their individual offices.

"They could have been here to see anybody"

"I know that, Bev. I want to know if there's something I should know about and be ready to answer questions about."

"Johnny, I don't know of any reason why homicide detectives would be visiting one of our executives. If I did, I'd tell you. I'm simply not aware of anything. And I'm certainly not keeping you out of the loop."

Johnny looked calmer even if a little skeptical. "Well, if Edderman is on to something, you know he's not gonna let go."

"If he calls you again, tell him we don't know of any reason for their visit and if he wants to talk to me, I'll tell him the same story. Because it's true."

Johnny knew that Bev was a person whom he considered honest. Unlike some of the executive assistants he had known, Bev always seemed interested in helping her boss get things done and not in helping him cover something up. But, if this really was murder . . . well, he had no experience in something that big and didn't think Bev did either. But her calm demeanor and firm resolve that she was unaware of any such doings, lead him to believe her and then to believe there really was nothing there.

"OK, Bev. Thanks. I just hope he doesn't call again."

"Well, so do I. But if he does, he'd better have a better reason than a single drop-in."

Johnny nodded and left. Bev thought about the visit for a moment or two and considered going in Tom's office to talk to him but remembered it was Friday and he was walking around the hospital wards as he often did at the end of the week. Instead she turned back to her work and within the hour the incident was all but forgotten.

Chapter Forty-Six

Friday, March 12

This time as he parked in the law office parking deck, Looney didn't pay much attention to the cars around him. He had a list of names from C. Wayne Hall of the people who had been supervisors or part of Patricia's work; the list included those in her immediate work circle and he needed to get some leads from someone. Things were not progressing in his investigation so far and he was slightly worried about that. By this time in almost every investigation he was beginning to get a feel for the way interviews would go and where he was likely to hit the right set of questions and answers. This time, however, he just couldn't quite put a finger on what was going on in the case.

Patricia appeared to be well liked; her husband was probably clueless about her plans for the future – and her lack of interest in getting pregnant on which he seemed to be so adamant. The interview with her boss was plain vanilla; no rise at all about the possibility of office romance. Maybe the guy was just out of the loop – the old guys frequently are. Or, maybe there really wasn't anything going on in the office. Still, Looney had that feeling that something wasn't completely above board at the firm. He had this feeling at times in the past and most of the time – or at least most of the time he remembered having the feeling – it turned out that something really was up. Today's session with the coworkers would have to give Looney some indication of a track to follow or he and Gene would be standing there scratching their heads.

He parked on the same level as before and walked to the fifth floor entrance and down the hall to the firm but paused in front of the double oaken doors. How common, he wondered, was it for law firms to have the ostentatious entry way and exterior waiting area but keep the individual offices rather bare and Spartan? He had come to expect rather bare office space from the prosecutors – not the District Attorney, of course, but the run of the mill prosecutors. But he had always had a picture in his imagination of very plush and swank private lawyers' offices but Tillson and Martin didn't completely match that picture in his head.

He opened the door and once again walked silently on the carpet to the receptionist desk. Same woman looked up at him and smiled. Clearly, she had been alerted of his coming and was prepared to be the most gracious person he would meet that day.

"Good afternoon, Detective."

"M'am."

"Mr. Hall has arranged a room for you just back here," she said, and rose from the desk and walked to the rear door and opened it for him. She escorted him down a short hall at right angles to the one he had taken earlier to get to Mr. Hall's office and showed him into a small conference room. The room was comfortable, a client conference room, no doubt. Centered in the room was a small round table with four chairs. On the back wall was a credenza with water carafe and glasses and the tabletop held a box of tissues, a couple of legal pads and several ballpoint pens. The pens carried the logo of the law firm and were held in a large pewter mug in the center of the table. The cup was emblazoned with a large Red O and the insignia of Ohio State. Pictures of woodland ducks rising from a marshy lake hung on both sidewalls. Comfortable.

"Mr. Hall said you and he had arranged an interview schedule?"

"Yes. I have my copy right here."

"Would you like a moment or are you ready to start seeing folks now?" she asked.

“Could I get a cup of coffee?” Looney asked, interested as much in how much she was going to act like things were completely normal as in actually having something to drink.

“Of course,” she said with a smile that looked for all the world like it was real and unfaked. “Cream? Sugar?”

“No. Just black, thanks.” He nodded and she left leaving the door open. Looney took off his jacket and hung it on the back of a chair and then sat in it. He pulled one of the legal pads to him and thought, ‘If I took notes on something that big I’d need one of those boxes with wheels to haul everything around in.’ He pushed the legal pad away and took out his small pocket notebook and pen and entered the date and the setting.

The receptionist reappeared with an actual cup of coffee – a china cup sitting in a matching saucer – which she placed in front of him and then looked up expectantly. “Are you ready for me to call someone?”

“Yes, please. I think Elaine Johnson is scheduled first.”

“Yes, sir. I’ll get her.”

Elaine turned out to be Patricia’s age, slightly shorter and a bit more plump than Patricia. But Looney could see right from the beginning that she was quite hurt by Patricia’s death. She sat in the chair across the table from him very straight and not quite able to hold his gaze; not guilty but certainly very uncomfortable.

‘Ms Johnson?”

“Yes.”

“Can I presume you know why I’m here?”

“You think somebody tried to kill Patricia, right?”

“Can you think of anybody who would want to hurt her at all?” Looney started off the interview in his soft, interested voice. Over the years he had found that getting the confidence of people allowed them to tell him things they would not have considered under different circumstances. He had actually thought of this after watching a short skit on television one night where Art Linkletter was shown interviewing children and his first question always was, "What did your mother tell you not to tell me?"

Elaine shook her head and looked down at the table, "No. I mean not really. Everybody liked Patricia. Well, almost everybody. But there wasn't any reason to try to kill her."

"Of course not. Who had trouble with her?"

"Really no one. Well, maybe Deidre. But not really. I mean they weren't friends or anything but it wasn't like that."

"You and Patricia were friends, weren't you?"

"Oh yes," Elaine said, much more comfortable with this line of questioning. She made eye contact, nodded and went on, "We often had lunch together."

"And shared feelings and secrets, right?" Looney said smiling at her.

"Well, sometimes."

"Did she ever tell you that she thought someone was trying to hurt her?"

"Oh no. Nothing ever like that. Mostly we talked about the work and what we were going to do on the weekend."

"I see." Looney paused and seriously wrote something in his notebook taking a few minutes to let the previous conversation percolate.

"Ms Johnson, did the two of you ever talk about growing up, family and friend stories and like that?"

"Well sometimes we would talk about the 'old days', you know, but not very much. She was focused on the future and didn't want to spend a lot of time looking back."

"Did she mention where she was from?"

"Some small town in Minnesota, I think."

"Do you remember the name?"

"No, I'm sorry. Why is that important?

"We would just like to know more about her background."

"Do you think this could have been someone she knew before she came to Cincinnati?"

"We never know until we look into those things."

"Well, I don't know but I'm sure Mr. Hall could tell you."

"Why would he know?"

"Well, maybe not him exactly. But he can get the personnel records where she put all that down when she was hired."

"That's a good idea, Ms Johnson. Thank you for that." Looney leaned back and smiled at Elaine. He didn't mention that the same thought had occurred to him earlier about checking the personnel records. He made a note in his little book.

"Then what about this Deidre, Ms Johnson? What was between her and Patricia?"

"Well, it was just assignments, you know. Deidre thought Patricia was getting better ones than she did."

"What about that? Was it true?"

"I don't know. Maybe. Patricia was very smart and she wanted to go to law school and all."

"What did Deidre say about that?"

"Only that she thought Patricia was getting special treatment."

"What are these 'better assignments'? Do they involve less work?

"Oh no. Patricia often got the longer and more involved assignments. Ones that even the partners were interested in."

"And other assignments?"

"Well, most of us work on cases that are being handled by the associates. Working on a partner's case is a big deal?"

"Why? Does it earn more money?"

"Oh no. We all work on salary. I mean, there's bonuses at the end of the year and maybe some get bigger ones because of the work they do. But mostly it's just because everybody knows if the partners are giving you their cases they think you're pretty good."

"What has Deidre said about this?"

"Look, I don't feel comfortable talking about this. She never said anything bad. She just said little catty things like referring to Patricia as 'the office favorite' and like that."

"I see. And, as her friend, did you ever defend her?"

"Not really. I mean, the comment was so off-hand, you know. Not like it was anything to start a fight over."

Switching to another topic, Looney asked, "How often did you and Patricia eat together?"

"Two, three times a week. Sometimes one of us would have too much to do and the other would grab a sandwich or a salad and bring it back for the other."

"And the two of you ate lunch together the day she got sick, didn't you?"

"Yes."

"What did she have to eat?"

"A pasta salad. She always ate pretty light for lunch. Sometimes soup but most often just a salad. She gave me her pickle," suddenly Elaine's eyes filled with tears and her shoulders slumped. Looney sat quietly and gently pushed a box of tissues across the table to Elaine. She took one and wiped her eyes and blew her nose then turned to him and said, 'I'm sorry."

Looney smiled at her, gave a brief nod and said, "Nothing to apologize for. Did she eat with others in the office?"

"We usually go at different times to keep up the coverage if somebody needs something right away . . . but a couple of times Duane wanted to eat with us but it was uncomfortable."

"That would be Duane Solomon?" Looney said, checking his list of names.

"Yes." Now she was looking uncomfortable again.

"What was that all about?" Looney asked conspiratorially.

"Well, you know, I mean . . . I think he was kinda interested in her."

"Was he aware she was married?"

"I'm pretty sure he knew. But I don't think he was trying anything. I mean, he was just wanting to be around her."

"Interested?"

"Well, yeah. Interested. But Duane is not going to do anything. And she let him know we were having 'girl talk' so he sat somewhere else."

"And did that upset him?"

"I don't think so. I mean, he was disappointed but he wasn't mad or anything."

"Did Patricia have any other close friends here at the office?"

"No. She was pretty much a 'do the job and go home' kind of girl."

"Was that different from the other girls in the office? And boys?

"Not really. I mean, we don't have after work parties or anything like that."

"And does that include you and Patricia?"

"Yeah, I guess. Once we went to movie but really that's all."

"Did you visit Patricia in the hospital?"

"Sure. A couple of us went up on Sunday night. We saw her on that machine and we sat and talked to her husband some. He got pretty upset about not knowing what was going on. We didn't stay very long."

Looney went on to find out who exactly had made the trip to the hospital, what they had talked with Benjie about, and what time they left.

"And where did you go after that?' he asked.

"I went home." She replied.

"Anyone there who can confirm that?"

"Well, sure. There's my mother and my cousin and her husband. Mum and I live here but Ceci is from Idaho. Her husband – that's Jack – is looking at going to graduate school here. We all sat around and talked until bedtime."

It turned out that Elaine slept in her upstairs bedroom and Ceci and Jack had slept on the sofa bed in the living room – right in front of the door. It was highly unlikely that Elaine could have slipped out, or back in, with them unawares.

After another cup of coffee and making sure his notes included all the relevant facts, Looney called for the next employee.

Duane Solomon was a tall drink of water, probably at least three inches over six foot, and still skinny like an adolescent. His shock of unruly hair tumbled into his face over a pair of wire-rimmed glasses sitting on a quite prominent nose. Overall the impression was 'gawky" and Looney thought, 'Now I know what that word means'. He started his interview similar to the way he began with Elaine.

"Mr. Solomon, do you know why I'm here?"

"Sure." Solomon spoke a little nasally accompanying his response with a slow deliberate nod. It appeared to Looney that Duane was not about to give anything away – and certainly was not about to be chatty.

Still using the soft, inquiring and friendly voice Looney then asked, "Do you know of anyone who would want to hurt Patricia Harding?"

Again, Duane slowly nodded and took a breath.

"No," he said continuing to nod.

Puzzled momentarily by the mixed signals, Looney asked "Anyone at all. Here at work or anyone else."

Again, this question got a slow nod and the short response, "No."

Looney paused and thought. After a moment, he tried another tack. He had each interviewee's personnel record and so he shifted his line of questioning to areas where he already knew the answer.

"Have you lived in Cincinnati all your life?"

Nod. "No."

"Really? Where were you born?" Looney asked with apparent sincere interest.

Nod. "Hillsboro." Looney already knew this fact but had learned something about Duane Solomon in those answers. Every question would be acknowledged by a nod, almost as if he were saying, 'Yes, I heard your question.' The subsequent oral answer was unrelated to the body language.

"How long have you worked here at Tillson and Martin?"

"Two years." The nod was slightly more vigorous.

"And were you a friend of Patricia Harding?"

"Sorta. We talked sometimes." Finally, an answer with detail, however small.

"Do you know who her friends were? In the office, I mean."

"There was Elaine. You know that already. I think that's about it."

"How well did you know Patricia? Did you ever go to lunch together or get together after work?"

Slow nodding. "No. She and Elaine ate together but they didn't want others with them."

"I see. Was there anyone that didn't like that arrangement? Other than you?" Looney was still using the quiet voice of sharing a confidence between friends.

A slow nod. "There's Deidre, I guess."

"What about Deidre?"

"I kinda think she thought Pat was stuck-up and like that."

"Why do you think that?

"She said so." The nodding was of shorter stroke and increased timing with this statement.

"What did she say?"

"She said she was sure Pat thought she was better than everyone else because she was married and 'cause she got all the good cases."

"Do you think that was true?"

Thoughtful nodding. "Not at all. Pat was kind, but shy. She didn't get involved in the office stuff and she went right home after work. She didn't do any bragging."

Looney went on to find that as Elaine had said, Solomon did not go to the hospital on Sunday night. He never did visit the hospital and on the weekend in question he had gone home to Hillsboro where he had stayed through Sunday night, leaving early on Monday to get to work.

After he dismissed Duane, Looney reviewed his notes and made a couple of calculations. Then, rubbing his face he left the room in search of a toilet and another cup of coffee. He ran into Gene coming out of the toilet and they quickly compared notes. Gene was finding nothing in the firm's records or accounting to suggest anything out of the ordinary. The lack of any leads was already depressing him and the morning wasn't over yet. He complained that something had to break or he might miss that basketball game.

Chapter Forty-Seven

Friday, March 12

Before Looney had a chance to finish that next cup of coffee, Gene joined him in the conference room for a formal debriefing. He had nothing to add to what he had said in the hallway.

"This girl was completely organized," he said. "Every thing we looked at was wide-open, clean and as transparent as anything I've ever seen. She really was good."

"So there's nothing to suspect her work was behind the killing?"

"Not unless Oscar Madison works here," he said dropping into one of the chairs.

"What the hell does that mean?" asked Looney.

Just then the secretary opened the door and asked if the detectives wanted more coffee. Both indicated yes and she disappeared. Looney quickly flipped through his notes and looked at the employee list.

When the secretary re-entered she brought Gene a new cup and left a small pot of freshly brewed coffee on the table. As the door closed behind her, Looney looked up and asked, "Who is Oscar Madison?"

Gene looked back with widened eyes in mock surprise, "What are you, a Luddite? Really? Oscar Madison from the play 'Odd Couple'."

"Oh, yeah," said Looney really only vaguely familiar with the reference.

"Oscar was the slob and he had this roommate who was a neat freak that drove him crazy."

"I get it. Patricia was a neat freak."

"Almost obsessive. Contents of every drawer were arranged just so. Nothing like your top drawer with all those cough drops and pencils rattling around."

"OK. I get it. Stay out of my desk drawers. And this Madison guy isn't on the employee list so what does all that mean?"

"It means the forensic guys are done and there's absolutely nothing about anything she touched that's looks even a degree out of kilter." Gene accompanied this announcement with a motion of brushing his hands to indicate the absence of findings.

"Yeah," said Looney, "I didn't do so much better." He explained the conversations with Elaine and Duane then said, "They've both got good alibis."

"Well, what about this Deidre person?" Gene inquired. "Seems like she may have a little grudge thing going."

"I asked to get her in here and I'm going to talk to her right after lunch."

"Lunch? And I thought you'd never ask," said Gene standing and moving toward the door.

"Yeah, I've heard of nice little place nearby. I'll get a table and you can pay."

About 1:30 Looney was back in the conference room with a new cup of coffee that he brought with him from Starbucks and the secretary introduced Deidre Kirkland.

She was about five foot eight or nine and wearing heels. She was also wearing a tight form-fitting skirt and a white shirt that was at least one size too small. Her face was pleasant with almost delicate features but her hair was styled in what Looney knew from his youth was called simply, 'big hair'. It was shoulder length and seemed to radiate out from the sides of her head at least three inches. And on top of her head, the forelock was turned up and back in a pronounced wave. Although everything about her was good to look at, the first thing you saw was the hair.

"Have a seat, Ms Kirkland." Looney said without rising from his seat. "Do you know why I am here today?"

Settling into her seat with a slight wriggle, Deidre batted her eyes at Looney and said, "I'm sure you're going to tell me."

"Are you aware that Patricia Harding died in the hospital?"

"Yes, so tragic. At her age and all." This was said without any conviction, almost taunting Looney to challenge her.

"Were you two friends?"

"Not at all."

"There seems to have been some friction between you two, right?" Even though Looney was still using the quiet voice he was adding a little tone of imperiousness to get her attention.

"What makes you say that?" Deidre opened her eyes wide in contrived surprise.

"Gossip in the office. From several sources. Is it true?" slightly harder but still sounding just interested.

"Not really. She was getting more of the cases I wanted, that's all."

"And why did you want those cases?"

"Look, in this business you get ahead more on who you know and she was getting cases from the partners and I was seeing only ones from the associates."

"So what?"

“So, if anybody’s going to get a raise or a supervisor job, it will be decided by the partners.”

“And you wanted more exposure at that level?”

“Is that a crime?”

“No. But eliminating your competition just might be.” Now the hardness was very evident in Looney’s voice. It would have been clear to even a casual observer that he was not being affected by the flirtatiousness of Ms Kirkland.

“What are you implying?” She dropped the vamp and became the shocked schoolgirl.

“Did you kill Patricia Harding?”

“I did not!”

“OK, then let’s just get a couple of things straight. Where were you when she was killed?”

“How would I know? I don’t know when she was killed.”

Sliding past the failure of that little trick, Looney asked, “Did you visit the hospital to see Patricia?”

“No.” He knew she hadn’t gone with the others from the office. If she really hadn’t gone at all perhaps she would not have known about the access up the back stairs.

“Can you account for your presence from late Sunday night until Monday morning?” He was forced to use such a broad time frame because Monique could not tell exactly when the medication had been added to the iv in Patricia’s room.

“Well, I wasn’t at the hospital.”

“Where were you?”

“Someplace else. Personal.”

“Were you alone?”

"That's also personal."

"You know, Ms Kirkland, in my business there's nothing more personal than murder. If you can't account for your whereabouts that weekend, I'm going to have to take you down to the station for more serious questioning." At this, Looney noticed that she sat up just a little straighter and her pupils dilated slightly. So he added, "And we will have to jail you for a couple of days while we get your story straight."

Deidre clearly believed him because she seemed deflated when she finally spoke, "It can't get around. Nobody can know."

"It certainly doesn't have to get around. But I do have to have the facts before I can rule you out as a suspect."

"You can't tell anyone about this."

"Ms Kirkland, I'm conducting a murder investigation. I don't make deals with witnesses about their whereabouts or what I can or cannot discuss. Where were you?"

"I was with someone."

"I gathered that. Were you together all weekend?"

"Yes. We even came to work together on Monday."

"So, it's someone in the firm?"

"Yes. But you can't let anybody know."

"Like I said before, no deals. Was it a guy?"

"What? Yes. Of course."

"Who?"

In a very small voice with her head bowed she said, "Tommie Everest."

"And who is he?" Looney made a note in his notepad.

"One of the associates."

"I see. I will have to ask him if he can verify your story."

"But no one else has to know about it, right?

"Where were you two Sunday night and Monday morning?"

"At a motel on the other side of the river."

"Anyone see you there?"

"Tommie registered. I didn't get out of the car."

"OK. I'll get his side of this story. Until then, don't go leaving town."

Deidre stood, shook her shoulders – and her hair – and walked out the door with the same carriage and bearing she had coming in. No one watching would suspect she had not won the confrontation.

Gene joined Looney in the conference room a half hour later. Looney had finished his notes on the interviews and was reviewing them for inconsistencies when Gene came in.

"Hey," Gene said. "Anything?"

"Not really. Got one more thing to do before we leave. You and the audit guys turn up anything?"

"Nope. I know you had a feeling but it is not panning out using these tools. What's your additional thing?"

"Probably just a little thing but we can't nail down her folks and where she came from. My buddy C. Wayne may be able to clear some of this up with her personnel file."

The two of them navigated the hallways back to C. Wayne Hall's office and knocked. They heard "Come," and entered to find the man seated behind his desk. He looked up expectantly and asked, "Find everything all right, gentlemen?"

To keep all his avenues open, Looney said, "The auditors are finished looking at the records. Their report will be available in a couple of days. Actually I'm here to find out more about Patricia."

"What's that?" Asked Hall.

"I want her personnel records. Information on her background and stuff."

"We have all that in our personnel files. I can get you a copy."

"How about the original, Mr. Hall? You know she's not going to be making adjustments to it."

'Well, certainly. I guess." C. Wayne looked at the card Looney had given him previously and said, "I can have it sent over right away."

"You do that, Mr. Hall. Just as soon as I leave."

The two detectives stepped out of the office and closed the door.

Gene looked at Looney and asked, "Beer?"

"Does the Pope go in the woods?" was the answer.

Chapter Forty-Eight

Friday, March 12

A little before one o'clock on that Friday, Tom approached the busy Green Bean coffee kiosk in the lobby. He was not wearing his white coat but had on a gabardine overcoat over his suit. He was on his way downtown where he was scheduled to give a deposition in a National Labor Relations Board hearing concerning the case of an individual he had fired a few months ago for unprofessional conduct. Tom was being charged with racial discrimination and was not looking forward to the experience of testifying even though the allegation was completely false. He wanted to grab a quick cup of coffee to take with him to the hearing and he noted the crowd of people around the kiosk. Students, residents, staff all trying to get the necessary sustenance before going into the auditorium for the one o'clock lecture series on clinicopathological correlations. Since all cases in the series were based on recent patients seen at New City everyone had an interest. But that put several people ahead of him in line. Tom was about to turn for the lobby door when two things happened to stall him.

First, Nick caught his eye and winked at him pointing at a cup. Tom nodded and Nick went to work. Just then, Tom felt a tap on his shoulder. He turned and saw Monique at his side.

"What's up?" he asked.

"I just got the Tox Report on Wil's blood."

"Is it bad?"

"Just puzzling."

"Why?"

"He had nitrates in his system."

"Huh, that is odd. Didn't you say he had no coronary disease?"

"Yes, but."

"But what?"

"Well he did have that 40% lesion in the distal RCA. Maybe he had a little angina of effort."

"Maybe. But Liz didn't seem to know about it."

"I just thought it a little odd. That's all. Wanted you to know."

"OK, thanks," Tom said as Nick caught his eye and handed him his cup over outstretched hands of several others. "Let's go over things again Monday morning. I've got to run."

"Sure thing," Monique said to his back.

The crowd around the kiosk filled in the space Tom had left and the serious business of mid-day coffee resumed.

The NLRB litigation seemed rather like a kangaroo court to Tom at first. Although it was being held in the Potter Stewart Courthouse, the actual room for the hearing looked more like a classroom, partially filled with folding chairs. The judge was balancing two open notebooks in his lap and the two lawyers and the witness sat in folding chairs arranged in a rough semi-circle around the judge's chair.

There were several witnesses called by the employee and Tom's turn to testify was delayed for almost two hours. By the time he was called and entered the room the air was stuffy and stale and no one looked happy. He was sworn in and pledged to tell the truth and nothing else.

The judge, looking a little harried, spoke first and recited the charge against Tom and New City for racial discrimination in the firing of this employee and asked Tom if that was correct. Tom answered 'no' and the fired employee began to talk loudly at him demanding that he tell the truth.

After the judge called the employee down and warned her and her lawyer about similar outbursts, he allowed Tom's lawyer to walk him through the circumstances of the firing. As Tom was explaining that the employee was in a probationary period and had thrown her pager at her supervisor for an alleged scheduling disagreement, the employee again began to rave about the racism exhibited by her supervisor. Following another intervention by the judge, Tom finished his story and the employee's lawyer began to ask him questions. When Tom's lawyer objected to some of the questions, the employee, who was black, again spoke up, this time addressing Tom's lawyer saying she didn't know what happened, she wasn't there and it was clear to her that the lawyer was also racist.

It so happened that Tom's lawyer was a prominent black woman in the legal profession in Cincinnati asked "What? Are you calling me a racist?"

And the employee responded, "Yes. Yes, I am. It's clear to me that y'all are every one racist, including you!" This last sentence was aimed at the judge who closed both books and said, "everybody out. Right now. You attorneys, stay."

Tom sat in the waiting area for another 45 minutes before his lawyer joined him and said, "It's over. Dismissed. Judge had the evidence that you were in the right and wanted to see if you sounded like a racist. When you didn't and she blurted out all those ridiculous charges the judge saw there was no case. We've been in there with the judge scolding her and her lawyer about these kinds of frivolous charges.

"All over?" Tom asked.

"Yes. Go home. The day is shot anyway."

So Tom was in his truck heading home when Looney called. He left the Courthouse and cut up to Sixth and then headed west to join the 75 going north. When the phone buzzed, he hit the 'answer' button on the steering wheel and his cell phone picked up the call and transferred it through the radio.

"Hello."

"Tom, it's Looney. Can you talk?"

"Sure. I'm driving home but it's all hands free."

"All right. Just listen. I can repeat it later if you need to hear it again."

"And what are we talking about?"

"Patricia Mulligan Harding."

"OK. Shoot."

"First, let me set the story. You know that your Admin people didn't have any information about this girl and her husband was no help."

"Right."

"I said, just listen. Keep your eyes on the road."

"Yes, sir" Tom said in his most sarcastic voice. Generals don't like being told what to do even if it's in their best interest.

Looney started again. "So, the law firm sent me Patricia's personnel file. Says she was born in Minneapolis, Hennepin County Medical Center, lived with her parents in Elko, Minnesota and went to high school in Lakeville. Maiden name was Mulligan."

"That's good information . . ."

"And my folks have now confirmed that there was no Patricia Mulligan born in Hennepin County on the day she listed as her birthday."

"Did you . . ."

"Dammit, Tom, I'm telling this story. Yes, we checked a week on either side and the two years before and after. No such birth."

Tom was silent. Where was this going?

"She said she lived in Elko and actually gave the law firm an address. Fake. One of my guys called the PD up there and found out the address never had been residential. Right now there's a strip mall at that address but back 15 or so years ago that was a Dairy Queen and a parking lot. Like I said, fake."

Tom said quietly, "So . . .?"

"And that's not all. There never has been a Patricia Mulligan having a driver's license in Minnesota. The very first public record of this girl is in 2009 when she applied for both an Ohio driver's license and a Social Security card."

Tom remained quiet and Looney went on, "She's a ghost, Tom. She appeared out of nowhere in 2009 as a waitress downtown. She was registered at Cincy State and we know she was hired as a temp at Tillson & Martin in 2010. But before that, nada. Ghost."

"What do we do with that information?"

"Yes, you may talk now. I don't know what to do with it and I sure don't know what it means. Except that we don't know where she's from or anything about her that might help us with this case."

After a short pause he went on, "I've got a buddy in the Marshall Service. If she's in the WitSec program maybe I can get him to let me in. That might explain the 'ghost' and it might point us at a reason someone might be after her."

Tom spoke as he turned off the Interstate nearing his home, "I need to think about this. And there's something that Monique has turned up that we'd like to talk to you about. Can you come back to the hospital on Monday?"

"Is it about this girl?"

"I don't think so. It's just odd, that's all."

"OK. I'll see what I can find on Mystery Patricia by then."

"Thanks for calling. Now I need a drink."

"Wait till you stop driving."

"You sound like my mother."

"She was right."

Chapter Forty-Nine

Saturday, March 13

That Saturday morning was cool and sunny. The brightness of the sunlight reflected off the front of the church and gave an odd sort of uplift to the funeral. There was a sense of purpose and spirit in the gathering; men dressed in dark suits with subdued ties still walked with heads up, shoulders back and shook hands with each other vigorously. The women were similarly dressed in dark colors and hats; they hugged each other and all moved to the steps leading up to the front doors of the church building. There was little talking but the mood was not somber or downcast. Tom and Sandra had attended many funeral services over the years and they noted a subtle but real difference in the attendees from their previous experiences even before the service began.

Wilford Adamson, MD was a life-long Lutheran, like his forebears before him. If he had had the opportunity to make a choice he would have preferred to be buried in Pioneer Memorial, the historic - and oldest – cemetery in Hamilton County. His forebears back six generations were buried in Hamilton County, many of them in Pioneer Memorial. At one time, Wilford had become interested in the genealogy of the Adamsons in Ohio and had traced the family back to its arrival in "the Northwest" as it was then known in the 1820s when still primarily pioneer country. The patriarch of the Ohio Adamsons was Louis Adamson, farmer, carpenter, and small businessman. In the early days of the community, he had been well respected in the growing town of Columbia and best known for helping many of his neighbors erect their own homes and barns and stores. Louis was buried in Pioneer Memorial, as were his sons and grandchildren.

Pioneer was now a Historical Park and archeological site, burial grounds for many of the pioneers to the area and a presumed former site of a Native North American pre-Columbian village. The archeological finding of the pre-historic use of the land initially caused a great stir. After some time of careful limited excavation, however, major findings were scarce and interest in further study of the site began to fade; the excavation team decided to leave the site untouched and the city responded by deciding to halt any further intrusion by burials. Since the cessation of excavations and burials at Pioneer Memorial, Adamsons had been buried at the Vine Street Hill Cemetery. And that was where Wilford would go on his last trip through the city. But first there was a typical Lutheran service downtown.

Many of the mourners were from New City; Wilford had few outside interests over the years but several civic leaders knew him and many of them also were in attendance. Tom, still a military man in his own mind, looked around the crowd gathering at the church to see if there were any uniforms present. He knew Wilford had not served in the military and so he was not surprised to note the absence of Navy blue and Army green uniforms. But there were uniforms present; one was dark blue of the Cincinnati Police Department in the form of the Assistant Chief for Operations. Wilford had taken care of the Chief during a heart attack a few years before. The second uniform was khaki shirt and olive dress pants with an olive drab neckerchief. The shirt was decorated with shoulder patches and left shoulder loops of blaze red. The neckerchief was secured at the neck with a slide. As different as the color scheme was from all the surrounding dark suits, the feature that most caught Tom's eye was the man's headgear – he was wearing a campaign hat of the type favored by Park Rangers and Smokey the Bear.

Tom indicated the man in the hat to Sandra and began a slow move sideways through the crowd entering the church on an intercept course with the campaign hat. As he neared the man he became aware that it was an unfamiliar person but the uniform was certainly something he had seen before. It was a Class A Boy Scout Leader's Uniform. As he neared the man, Tom made eye contact with him and held it as they approached each other. The man stuck out his hand and said, "Howard Jefferies."

"Tom Bolling. I'm the Chief of Staff at New City."

"I'm an old friend of Wil's. He was a big help in getting our troop organized 12-15 years ago. I thought his effort should be noted."

"I'm sure that Liz will appreciate that, Howard."

"Maybe not." This was accompanied by a droll smile. "Wil spent so much time with the boys she got a little annoyed. We had some talks about it. I know she was happier with him when he finally cut the cord with us. We had a big dinner for him and she was beaming. I haven't really seen her since then."

"When was that?" Tom asked.

"Oh, eight or nine years ago, I think. We still have his picture on the wall in the meetinghouse. Only a few of us left who remember him from the time he spent but everyone knows him by the picture. 'Knotty Wil' we called him."

"What? What's that mean, 'Naughty Wil'?"

"Oh, sorry. That's K. N. knotty Wil. He was a master at knot tying and loved to show the boys the use of every knot in their book. He had a length of rope he carried around the building with him all the time."

"I didn't know that about him. I got here four years ago from the Air Force and he never mentioned his time in the Scouts to me. And neither did Liz."

"As I said, she probably would rather just forget that time," said Howard.

"We better get inside," Tom said, taking his arm and starting for the door.

"Right. At least I wore the long pants so as not to embarrass anybody."

They found seats but not together; Sandra had saved a space for Tom and Howard moved closer to the front on the other side. Tom explained the uniform and Howard's presence to Sandra and then turned to estimate the turnout. Sprays of flowers nearly overwhelmed the front of the church. The colors were vibrant and bright and seemed perhaps even more so than in life due to the morning sun coming from the eastern windows through stained glass and hitting the flowers with brightness one could almost feel. The effect was heartening and inspiring, not the feeling that Tom usually associated with funerals.

The church was nearly full; Tom estimated close to two hundred people in the sanctuary. As he was completing this survey, the rear doors opened and in paraded the procession; a young man carrying a large silver and enameled cross followed by another young man with a large candle. Immediately next in the procession was a man robed in a long white garment who had over his shoulders a white stole with Greek characters imprinted in gold on it. Six men carrying the casket of Wilford Adamson followed him and behind the casket were Elizabeth with her sister Virginia and Liz's children, Ken and Kaitlyn and Ken's wife and their two young boys. The pallbearers were men from Wilford's Sunday School Class; they carried the casket to the dais at the front and set it down on the stand set up for it there.

Tom noticed that, oddly different from other funerals, the casket here was situated in the center aisle with the foot toward the front of the church. And it was completely covered by a white cloth. The candle from the procession was placed, still burning, on a small table at the head of the casket.

Tom, both with and without Sandra, had been to many funerals in the military. But those had been more Congregational in nature with a definite blend of military on top. His overall impression of Wilford's service was a little put off by the pageantry and heavy organ music. His upbringing had been Evangelical, although after he left home for college, the first time he was back in a church building was when he married Sandra. He mused about the components of the Lutheran service, recognizing one of the Scriptural readings and the recitation of the Lord's Prayer but little else. He was also struck by the minister's words not mentioning much at all about Wilford's life.

When the service was over and attendees were waiting their turns in their cars to follow the hearse out to the cemetery, Tom asked Sandra her opinion of the service.

"I thought we'd hear more about Wil. But I noticed that Liz wasn't crying; she watched the minister like what he was saying was just right and what she had expected," she responded thoughtfully.

"Well, it wasn't what I expected. At all. I know that doesn't make it wrong or anything like that. Of course, I knew he hadn't served so I really didn't expect the usual military honors."

They were more than twenty cars back of the hearse as the vehicle procession pulled away from the church parking lot. Cincinnati police on motorcycles manned intersections so the flow of regular traffic came to a halt to allow the procession through. They went west on Sixth Street to the I-75 H ramp and then headed north. As they settled in to the 35 mile an hour pace in the middle lane heading north with their headlights and flashers on, and the motorcycle police positioned themselves in front and the rear. As they got north of the city proper and curved east on I-75, the lead motorcycle pulled in to the left hand lane and began to slow down, preventing other vehicles from passing on that side. The hearse slowly tracked over in to the left lane and took Exit 6 then turned right onto Mitchell Avenue and then right onto Vine Street. Even though there was an entrance to the cemetery near the off ramp, the hearse headed southerly on Vine to Ehrman before turning right into the cemetery grounds and proceeding around some curves. The procession passed the mausoleum on the right and shortly the hearse came to a straight stretch of road where it pulled off the right shoulder. All the cars in the motorcade kept their relative positions and also pulled off on the shoulder.

Pallbearers emerged from the first few cars and carried the uncovered casket the short distance to the prepared grave. Within a few minutes all the cars had emptied and the occupants gathered around the casket perched on a stand above the grave and surrounded by artificial grass. The minister appeared, without robe, wearing a dark suit with the stole over his shoulders. His graveside comments were short and reminded everyone that from dust they came and to dust they would all return. His benedictory prayer offered some solace for the family and then repeated the Beatitudes. And everyone filed past the seated Liz and her family to offer condolence. Tom and Sandra were toward the rear of this line and when they left the graveside, the bulk of other cars had already departed. Nonetheless, Tom sat in the car without moving for a moment. Sandra looked at him, waiting for an explanation.

"I missed seeing the flag," he said.

"I know. And you missed being involved."

"Yes, I did. I guess that's selfish but it's something I could do that honored the life and something that said, 'Thanks' as well as 'I'm sorry and will be there to help you' to the family. Just being one of whole herd of people leaves me feeling like . . . I don't know, maybe unimportant."

"You know this was about Wil and not about you."

"Of course I do. And I'm also feeling ashamed about how I feel. A little ashamed anyway."

"They warned you at TAP that there would be days when you would wish you were a General again," Sandra said, reminding him to the lessons the military Transition Assistance Program had presented to both of them.

"Yeah, yeah, yeah. I know. Let's go home and put our efforts into finding out why he died and who was involved."

Chapter Fifty

Monday, March 15

Monique met Tom in his office right after the morning meeting; she brought the folder with the autopsy results on Wil. They began their discussion by discussing the Tox screen findings and confirming that the nitrate really was in Wil's bloodstream when he died.

Tom said, "I've thought about this the whole weekend and the only way it makes any sense is if he was having some angina – probably started when he was in Colorado."

Monique said, "I agree that makes sense. Of course, there's no way I can tell how long he's been taking nitrates but I am sure that he didn't have serious coronary disease. But I do know why he died."

She opened up her folder and began a thorough presentation of her key findings. First, even on external examination she had noted that he was extremely pale over the face and upper extremities but had venous distention and mottling of the legs. She noted how the lungs were relatively light but the bowel and liver and kidneys were all heavier than usual. She recounted the dissection of the heart and the finding of only a single coronary lesion and that was in the distal RCA.

Then she turned to the microscopic findings. The scant amount of blood in the lungs and the cerebral slices and the congestion she found in the liver, gut and kidneys were conclusive for her. "He died in shock."

"He was perfectly fine earlier that day – just an hour before. What could do this?"

"Well, I thought about that, too," Monique said. "So I went looking for some cause. Like I reminded you, this isn't like television where the medical examiner can make a mechanism diagnosis of ventricular arrhythmia from looking at the heart. We both know that takes an electrocardiogram and a live patient. But I can often find some microscopic changes around an infarct even very early."

"Did you?"

"No. I checked specifically around the RCA lesion but even if it was there, that is not likely to cause a rhythm disturbance. So I also checked around the AV node and the bundles. Nothing there."

"Meaning?" Tom was gesturing with his hands again, telling her to get to the point.

"This wasn't likely a rhythm death. He went into shock for non-cardiac reasons."

"Such as?"

"Well, not to be too obvious about it – nitrate and exercise – he was running up the stairs, right?"

"But he would have known not to do that." Tom was puzzled about this new finding and uncertain how to make it fit with the circumstances. "You have any other ideas?"

"Not right now."

After a bit of silence, Tom said, "I don't know why I'm thinking this but I want to talk with Ron about this. I already asked him to come by today. Are you free enough for me to get him over here now?"

Monique quickly ran her schedule in her head, indicated she was available and Tom picked up the phone.

Chapter Fifty-One

Monday, March 15

Looney drove and Gene talked. They were on their way to New City to meet with Tom at his request. Tom had called and reminded Looney that he had asked him to come by New City. He was non-committal about whether his new information would shed light on Patricia's case but both detectives would be glad if it did because they were at a near standstill. Interviews at Tillson and Martin uncovered a few possible leads but alibis had checked out and no motive was found in Patricia's paperwork. The cold case was just getting colder by the minute.

Gene was trying several different approaches, trying to think like the killer. "Let's say I don't have anything against her, Patricia I mean. So, I'm trying to get back at somebody else by killing her."

"OK," said Looney. "Who would that be?"

"Maybe her husband?"

"Have you talked to him?"

"No, why?"

"Well, I just think it's unlikely that a killer as sophisticated as this one seems to be would take these risks to get back at Benjie. He's likely to be much easier to get revenge on than concocting this elaborate a scheme."

"You mean because he's unemployed and mostly just sitting at home?"

"No. I don't think he runs in the same circle."

"Still. I'm keeping him on the list. What about Patricia's family?"

"She's a ghost, Gene. We don't know anything about her or her family."

"On the list then."

"Is this a list of the Most Unlikely?"

"Cut it out. I'm serious here."

"If you want to be serious, think about what might be in her missing background. I mean why not a jealous former husband or an abusive father or uncle who wants to be sure she keeps quiet about things back in Minnesota. Since we found out that she has run away from somewhere and changed her identity, I'm thinking we have a whole world of options and possibilities that we have not yet considered."

"So, Detective SmartAss, how are we going to filter our way through this mess when we have nothing – zero – to go on regarding her background before she showed up in Cincinnati. Are you planning on interviewing everyone in Minnesota? And how do we even know she came from Minnesota?"

"All right, calm down. I admit we don't have a place to even start right this minute. But it sure does look like she was running from something and that whatever that was it just might have caught up with her." Looney wasn't going to be dissuaded from staying on point. "We should do some more interviews with people she knew at Cincy State and at that place where she was a waitress. Perhaps she told someone something that will help us get into her background."

"Or not. And we could waste a lot of time. I believe we should stick to the people she was around recently. We can surely push the law clerks a little harder – and her husband, too."

"Anyone else for your list?" asked Looney, grinning. "How about their landlord?" he shot at Gene.

"Why? What do you know about him?"

"Absolutely nothing. That seems to be a key component for getting on your list."

"All right. I'm quitting the list business. Your turn. You think it's somebody starting a serial at the hospital?"

"That's actually a real possibility. Tom and I talked about that. He doesn't want to think about it but it's too early to rule that out. See, I think if it is someone in the hospital they didn't expect that it would be caught as a murder so soon. That nurse upended their time line." Looney had not given up on this theory just because his friend Tom was not in favor of the concept. Looney could understand why Tom wouldn't want to think about having a serial killer on his staff but Looney didn't have the luxury of wiping possibilities off the board because they made him uncomfortable.

"How would we prove that?" asked Gene.

"It'd be hard without another case. I hope that's not what Tom is calling us about!"

After parking in the Visitors Lot, they entered the lobby and noted the cluster of people around the Green Bean. They had intended to stop for a cup but the line was sufficient to make them go straight to Tom's office.

"Everyone here drinks a lot of coffee, don't they?" said Gene as they surveyed the line.

"Not sure if its everyone but the ones that do are very serious about it," said Looney. "There's usually a line when I get here."

"You'd think we were in Seattle, huh?" said Gene. "Oh, and by the way, speaking of Seattle where the West Regional Final will be played, have you finished your bracket yet?"

"No, dammit, I haven't. And I probably won't as long as this case keeps dragging on. Unlike all you yo-yos in the office, I have a murder case on my hands right now."

"Geez, will you calm down? Anyway, you've got till Wednesday to get it done. Dickey said his son showed him how to set up a bracket on the internet that keeps a running score of all the players."

"Have you told your neighbor you can't go with him to Dayton?

"Not yet. C'mon, man. We still might get something on this case. Maybe that's what your buddy has called us for." Thus brightened, if only in his own mind, Gene stepped out briskly in the general direction of Tom's office.

Mary Brighthouse met them at the door and led them to Tom's office. She asked if the wanted some coffee and both laughed and said, "not right now."

Tom greeted them and Looney and Gene nodded greetings to Monique and everyone found a seat. Tom was behind his desk, Monique in the overstuffed wing chair near the window and the detectives in the two chairs in front of the desk. As they faced each other, Tom asked Monique to explain the reason for the call. As she started through Wil's autopsy findings, Gene leaned forward and asked, "Has this got something to do with Patricia?"

After a brief pause, Tom spoke up. "Maybe," he said. "Or at least we are thinking so. I told Ron I didn't think so last week when we talked but the more Monique and I have batted this around the more I think there's got to be something tying them together. I presume you both have a good grasp of the particulars in Patricia's case?"

Gene replied, "We are aware of the circumstances and all that and you thinking she was murdered because of medicine in one of the i.v. bags. But I haven't heard anything about this guy, Wil."

"Neither have I," said Looney. "This is new. And you think it's related?" he asked Tom and included Monique with a glance and raised eyebrows.

"We think so," Monique nodded. "But let me give you the facts we have before we try to connect the dots."

Both detectives nodded and sat back in their chairs.

Monique realized that her audience did not have medical terminology sophistication and so she slowly went through the facts of the autopsy trying to use everyday words and to give an explanation where it was needed. She painted the picture of a robust man in his early fifties who suddenly collapsed on a staircase and exhibited findings of being in shock. She then carefully excluded the obvious first concern of a heart attack and paused.

Both men realized she was not finished and sat quietly waiting for the other shoe to drop. When Monique turned to the results of the toxicology screen and mentioned the finding of nitrates in Wil's blood, they both developed questioning looks on their face and she hurried to explain.

"It looks like he may have had too much nitro. It would drop his blood pressure and especially if he was exercising – like running up the stairs."

"Enough to kill him?" asked Looney

"Probably not with a usual dose. That's why I said maybe he had too much. But yes, enough to make his blood pressure fall and when he stumbled on the stairs and landed with his head elevated everything just pooled in his feet and legs."

"Wow." Said Gene. "I always thought that nitroglycerin was good medicine for people with heart trouble."

"It usually is," said Tom. "But in the right dose. And the other important point here is he didn't have heart disease. That's what she was telling you about his coronary vessels."

"So, why would he be taking nitrates if he didn't have the heart trouble," asked Gene.

"That's the puzzle," Tom noted. "And the reason we asked you here today."

Looney spoke up then, "Are you thinking this was given to him by someone else, like Patricia got that 'extra' medicine?"

"Well, it's a theory," said Tom as Monique added, "And that might all fit in with a theory about this being part of a serial set of murders."

"Ain't you the tough one?" Gene said. Tom remembered that Looney's partner did not know all the players like he did and explained to Gene that Monique had considerable experience with murder in her role as the medical examiner prior to coming to New City. "It's that experience and practice that probably accounts for us being aware of these deaths at all."

Gene looked at Monique with new perspective and gave her a slight nod of approval before he asked, "But don't these hospital serial killers usually act like angels of mercy?"

"Yes," she said, "And your meaning is what?"

"Well, unless the good doctor was a patient here, that doesn't seem to fit with the usual mercy killings I've heard of."

"You're right about that, detective," Tom said while Monique nodded. "But if this is another case of unexpected medication side effects the similarities are too much to ignore."

"Do you know if he was taking nitroglycerin on his own?" This question from Looney seemed out of place at first but then everyone realized that the concept of Wil being 'dosed' would be harder to prove than Patricia.

"No, I don't," said Tom "But there was no obvious medical call for it."

"But you don't know," said Looney.

Slowly both doctors nodded in agreement.

"Well, I guess the first thing we have to do is figure that out. Where's his office?" Looney asked, rising from his chair and edging toward the door.

"What?" said Tom. "Oh, I see. It's just down the hall. I'll show you." He led the way out of his office and down the hall with Looney close behind and Gene and Monique keeping up.

Chapter Fifty-Two

Monday, March 15

A half hour later they were back in Tom's office, sitting exactly where they had been before. Now they had a new concern: the small bottle of nitroglycerin pills they had found in the top drawer of Wil's desk.

When they arrived at the Cardiology Office suite, Sheila Hester was sitting at her desk beside the closed door to Wilford Adamson's office. The door was not locked and not sealed – not a surprise to any of them since this had not previously been considered a crime scene. They told Sheila they wanted a quick look around and went in.

Tom and Monique stood close to the door and watched as the detectives began a quick search of the room. They donned their latex gloves and with surprising ease and quickness began looking for the evidence. Gene stood in front of the desk and began examining all the desktop items, especially those that could contain a small vial. Looney sat in Wil's chair and one by one examined the contents of the desk's drawers. He looked first in the column of drawers on the right finding only papers in the top two and a shoeshine kit in the bottom one.

The top middle drawer of the desk was cluttered with pens and pencils, paper clips and a small stapler plus an array of business cards from various pharmaceutical detailers. At the front of the drawer was an organizer tray of short and long compartments. One of these compartments contained a mass of rubber bands and a small, dark brown glass vial. It was unlabeled but when Looney lifted it up and showed it to Tom and Monique they both said, "Nitro." And the search stopped.

As the four left the suite, Looney asked Sheila, "Anybody go in that office in the last couple of days?"

She replied, "I did once to get a copy of a manuscript he was proofing for one of the residents. It needs to get back to the publisher."

"Where was it?"

"Right on the top of his desk. I think he was working on that last," she looked like she might again start to tear up and Looney moved on quickly. "Anyone else?"

"Not while I've been here," she said straightening her shoulders and looking more like a guardian. "But, of course, I'm not here all the time."

"Right," said Looney smiling at her to put her at ease. "Thank you."

Now they were sitting there in Tom's office looking at the little vial and pondering how that finding fit in with the various theories they had been discussing.

"C'mon, Tom," Looney said. "You're the guy's boss."

"That's not the same as being his doctor."

"You really didn't know he was taking?"

"Of course not. His medical condition is his own. And he was a cardiologist. He would know better than most how to take this medicine."

"Right," Gene threw in. "Docs are always so much smarter than the rest of us."

"All right. I was wrong about this," said Tom. Monique nodded her assent to this admission and then added, "We were thinking we were looking at another, ah 'dosing' and thought it was significant."

"You two thought this was related to the girl's death?" asked Gene.

"Well, not really, Monique said. "We were just struck by the coincidence. But now it looks like it's just a case of wrong medicine at the wrong time. I'm sorry we got you guys here under a false flag."

Looney turned to Tom and said, "So, now you're thinking the good doctor was taking these nitros for cause? And that he took too much or what?"

Tom was slow to respond initially. "I think its clear he was taking the drug. I don't really know why. He did have some minimal coronary artery disease. Maybe he did have some angina symptoms and this was his way of handling it."

"And what happened?"

"Well, I'd guess he knew he was going to run the stairs and took it prophylactically. But maybe he was little dehydrated or something and it dropped his pressure too fast for him to react. That's my guess, anyway."

"OK, then. Anything else turning up on the girl's death?"

"Nothing else medical. You get anything from the interviews?"

"Nope. Nothing in her records and the co-workers stories all match. But like I told you Friday, her probable status as a runaway, changing her identity and all that raises a whole specter of possibilities we haven't thought of yet."

"Like what?" asked Monique. "You mean like someone from her background showing up and sneaking into the hospital to kill her?"

"Well," said Looney, "let's remember this whole ballgame started at her place of work. Maybe only because it didn't work there, someone had to follow through at the hospital."

"If that's true then the incident with Wil . . .Dr. Adamson would not be related at all."

"Possibly. Or the killer might have found out that Dr. Adamson would show up at her Code thing and likely be able to save her. So the hit on him was simply to preserve the likelihood that Patricia would die in the Code thingee."

"Oh," said Tom, "That really gives me a headache. How would someone from outside even know that?"

"Well, I don't rightly know," said Looney. Gene picked up on the thought and offered, "Maybe the girl saw someone from her background on the street or in a restaurant and that person happens to now be working here at the hospital. So when they made the attempt at the law firm and she gets shuffled off to New City, the killer would know how to get around and also might know the role that Adamson would have in her recovery."

"Look guys, you're not helping my headache." Tom shook his head and looked down at his feet. "I'm going to have to tell the Director and the Board and the Joint Commission something very soon."

Looney stood up and said, "Give me a couple more days before you jump off a cliff, OK? My partner here is betting we can crack this case soon. He's so sure that he's betting his tickets to the NCAA Regionals on it." Then he and Gene said their goodbyes and left and walked back out through the lobby.

Looney took a quick turn across the lobby and re-entered the Cardiology office. Sheila was still sitting at her desk and looked up at him with a little alarm in her eye. "Yes, Detective?"

"I wonder if you could tell us little about that Monday morning when Dr. Adamson died," he asked.

"I guess. What do you want to know?"

"Usual Monday? Anything different? Did he seem upset? You know, like that."

"Well," she said, straightening her back a little and raising her chin, "I was in the office when he arrived. And that Horvath fellow came with him."

"Who is that?" asked Looney, pulling out his notebook.

"One of our trainees. He's being let go and he's very upset about it."

"I see. Any chance we could talk to him?"

"I think so. He seems to always be around."

"How long was he here?"

"Not very long. Dr. A let him in the office but after he took off his coat and hat he walked him right back out. Told him he was done and to get over it. And to leave everybody alone. That's what he said."

"Can you give me his full name and where to find him?" asked Looney. Sheila indicated she could and began writing down the pertinent information. Looney took the note and tucked it into the front of his small notebook.

"Then what happened?" Looney asked.

"Well, I had some schedules to deliver so I left the office, too. I was only gone about 5 minutes."

"And when you got back was Dr. Adamson still here?"

"Yes, he and Angela were talking."

"Angela? That's the Assistant Chief, right?" Looney opened his notebook back up and started making a short note.

"Yes. They frequently start off the day in there for 15-20 minutes."

"Every day?"

"Mostly. And I'd say always on Mondays or after a long weekend."

"Why's that?"

"She is the Assistant Chief and she hears what went on in the hospital during the weekend so she would come in and tell him about it. I think it was more a personal connection; he never seemed to do anything about whatever she told him. It was more like they wanted to talk to each other."

"Were they talking when you first saw them?"

"Oh yes. I put my head in the door to tell them I was back."

"And then what happened?"

"When he got the page he ran out and that was the last we saw of him." Again the tears began to form. Looney quickly moved to give her something else to focus on.

"Did anyone else come in while they were in there?"

"No. Of course she came out and fixed their coffee."

"Tell me about that," Looney asked nonchalantly.

"They always get a big cup at the stand in the lobby. I can't remember the fancy name for it – it's the middle-sized cup. And they sit in there and drink some it and one of them comes out and puts another shot of espresso in each cup from our machine over there." She indicated the small little area just outside Wilford's door where an espresso machine sat on top of an old bedside table. Also on the top were a large pitcher of water, a can of powdered creamer and some packets of sweeteners.

Sheila went on, "Angela came out and fixed each of them another shot of espresso. She was standing right there and smiled at me. They were still talking through the door about something on the resident match. She stirred their cups and went back in and a little bit later he got that page."

"Did he say anything to you as he left?"

"No. He was looking at the pager to see where the Code was."

"And Angela?"

"She came out after him and said, "Better him than me." and went in her office right there," she indicated the door to the left of her desk.

"I know we asked you this before, but who does have access to these offices?"

"The doors are wide open all day. I lock them when I leave and unlock them when I arrive in the mornings. Housekeeping has keys and so do all the cardiologists."

"All right. Thanks so much." Just then Looney's cell phone buzzed and he pulled it from his pocket and answered. "Looney," he said and then listened for a few seconds, nodding. "Fine. Good. Just set it on my desk, please . . . Thanks." He looked up at Sheila and nodded to her

"I hope that helps," she responded and turned back to her work.

"Is Angela in right now?" Looney asked indicating her closed door.

"I think so," Sheila said picking up her phone and hitting a button. "Dr. Pirini? There are some detectives here about Dr. Adamson's death. They'd like to talk to you." After a pause she looked up and nodded at Looney and indicated the door, "She said, 'of course'."

Before they could get to the door, it opened and Angela Pirini stood there beckoning them to come in. Even though she was only five feet, four inches tall and slight of build, both detectives could feel a presence of command as she waved them in, closed the door and indicated that they could sit in the chairs in front of her large desk.

"Detectives? And you're here about Wil's death? We all thought it was an accident," she said looking back forth between them.

Gene spoke first. "Well, that may still turn out to be the obvious answer but there were some things about it that seemed a little odd."

"Really?" she said. "I hadn't heard that. What was odd about it?"

Looney scooted forward in his chair and asked, "Is it true that you were the last one to see him?"

"Well, I don't know who might have been on the staircase but, yes, I was in his office talking with him when he got the page."

"What were you talking about?"

"Just medical stuff. I told him about the weekend admissions and asked him about the Match?"

"Match? What's the Match?" Looney asked remembering that Sheila had mentioned this topic of discussion as well.

"The Resident and Intern Matching Program. It happens every March 15th. That's when the residents find out where they will be doing their training and training programs like us find out who we will have."

"Only once a year? Then it must be a big deal, huh?'

"Well, medical schools only graduate a class once a year. And, yeah, it's a big deal for them and for us."

"Was there some problem with the Match this year?" asked Gene.

"Oh no," Angela replied. "It hasn't even happened yet. I was trying to get an inside read on how well we were going to do."

"Why?"

"Look, Wil – Dr. Adamson – was the chair of the Resident Admissions Committee; the chairman of each department gives him an idea of how well they think they will do in the match. And we have a pool among the faculty every year trying to guess whether we will go over or under."

"I don't understand, what do you mean 'over or under'? asked Looney now truly puzzled.

"It's really not that difficult to understand," Angela said, "but it is very difficult to predict. See every program – I mean like Medicine, Surgery, Pediatrics – has a set number of slots we can afford to support for residents. And everybody interviews many more than that number of potential residents. Plus, the average graduating medical student will interview at five different programs across the country."

"That sounds like a scramble for jobs," said Gene.

"And it really was until the RIMP was developed many years ago. Now each student makes a list of the training programs they would like to match with and ranks those programs from first to last. And the hospitals do the same with the names of the students they would like to have in their programs. And everybody sends their list to the RIMP in February. A computer matches the lists and gives both students and programs the best possible match. And that's what gets announced on March 15th."

"So what's that got to do with 'over and under'?" Gene pressed.

"Say a program puts down fifty names of students, ranked from top to bottom, for their six or eight positions and the lowest ranked of their positions that was filled was by someone they placed at number forty-two, then they had to "go down to forty-two" to get their eight. That's not considered a good indication of the strength of their program."

"And you have a pool on whether they match at a specific number?"

"Yes. Sorta. We have training programs here for Internal Medicine, Surgery, OB-Gyn and Pediatrics. We have 29 first year positions and the combined lists have gone down to 122 or more each of the last three years. This year the Chief Residents who organize the pool have set the number at 115. That seems low but this year Pediatrics is a real wild card. There's a new Chair with a National presence and no one really knows . . ."

Before she could go on, Looney interjected, "How did you actually do?"

"We won't know until right after noon. The NRIMP tries to get in touch with any unmatched students before releasing the results of the match."

"Was Dr. Adamson interested in all this?" asked Looney.

"Actually, no, he wasn't."

"What else did you two talk about?"

"The usual. I gave him the rundown on the weekend admissions and then he got that page."

"And then what happened?"

"He got up and left."

'Did he do anything first?"

"Oh, well, yes. He opened his desk drawer and got his stethoscope then went to the door and got his white coat off the back of the door and went out."

"Sheila said you got both of you some coffee."

"Yeah, I did. I often get an extra shot in the first cup. He did, too. Some patient a few years back heard about how much Wil liked his coffee and got us that espresso machine. That was before the Green Bean opened in the lobby."

"Did Dr. Adamson seem his usual self that morning?"

"I'd say yes. He wasn't interested in helping me pick Over or Under but he wanted to know about the patients who'd been admitted."

"Was he alert or did he seemed tired?"

"Pretty much normal, I think. I haven't really thought about it so I guess he didn't seem off to me."

Standing up and moving toward the door, Looney said, "Well, thank you for your time." He held the door for Gene and then almost as an after-thought turned back and said, "One last thing. You said to Sheila after Dr. Adamson left, 'Better him than me.' What was that about?"

For a second Angela looked puzzled, then said, "Oh, nobody likes the Code Observation and AAR activity. We think it's mostly a waste of time and we do it just to keep the Joint Commission happy. I was glad it wasn't my turn to waste a half-day, that's all."

"Alright then, thanks again for your time," Looney smiled and left closing the door behind him.

Gene waited until they were back seated in the car before asking, "What's up partner? You got some idea you didn't want to tell the docs about?"

As he answered, Looney pulled out of his pocket the small plastic envelope containing the small amber bottle they had discovered in Wil's desk drawer, "Didn't you think the big doc science guys were pretty quick to accept they were wrong when we found this?"

"Whadda you mean quick?"

"Well, first how do they know what's in this bottle? I know it looks like a nitro bottle but that doesn't prove what's in it. Could be aspirin. And they weren't thinking about testing the contents, they just gave up on their theory of suspicious behavior. And all it took was seeing a small brown bottle."

"OK. I'll agree with that. But they wanted to be wrong – about there being suspicious behavior, I mean. You could see that when we walked in."

'Yes. That's true. But there's more. The fact that the bottle was in his desk was accepted as evidence he was taking the contents. And I don't get there as fast as they did."

"That's why you got the bottle?"

"Right, and very soon Forensics will tell us whose fingerprints are on the outside and what's actually on the inside."

Chapter Fifty-Three

Monday, March 15

Tom came back from a late luncheon meeting with the Cardiology Division. They wanted to talk with him about plans to fill the vacancy in their ranks left by Wilford's death. They had met in the small doctor's dining area in the cafeteria from 1230 until almost 2 o'clock discussing the issues. Angela helped arrange the meeting but left it to Tom to lead and run the discussion. The cardiology faculty were mostly concerned about workload and not about leadership. It took them some 45 minutes, along with eating, to get that point out in the open. Tom had come to the meeting expecting to hear their concerns about replacing their Chief of Cardiology and had prepared some thoughts for their consideration. He intended to get their opinions about whether they thought recruiting for a new head of the division should focus on finding and attracting a proved leader, an excellent teacher or a renowned researcher. He was prepared to take any one of those directions in his attempts to find a replacement; he thought he could rely on Angela's leadership and mostly wanted to hear confirmation of that from the group and their desire on future direction.

What with eating and interruptions, however, it took some time before Tom realized that the faculty concern was predominantly with the impact the loss of a consulting cardiologist did to their composite income – and, of course, to their individual salaries secondarily. They gave Angela a pass on the promotion; she was known as a good worker and did her share in production in the income stream. It was clear no one thought that adding the administrative duties to her would lessen her earnings for the group. However, that still left them 'a man down' as one of them put it. There was then some considerable discussion and difference of opinion about the specific skill set needed by Wilford's replacement. Some wanted non-invasive clinical acumen; others thought the workload suggested a need for another invasive cardiologist. No one seemed to be pushing any particular interest for a replacement to have research interests.

Tom finally summed up the meeting by recognizing their having pared down their collective understanding of their need to a clinician who might have research interests. And he recognized their split decision about the sub-interest in cardiology that they would agree would be best for the group. He then charged the group, under Angela's leadership, to continue this discussion among themselves and get an answer to him in about a week. He thought that timeline was adequate since the hole in their income-making capability provided ample incentive.

He circled past the coffee kiosk in the lobby for another 'black eye' and returned to his office. He had barely had time to assess the paperwork needs on his desk before Bev walked in and sat down in front of his desk.

"Boss, we may have some trouble," she said, looking frankly at him.

Tom put down the papers he was holding and put his hands in his lap as an indication that he was listening and that she had his undivided attention. "What's up?" he asked.

"Last week Johnny Taliaferro got a call from Daniel Edderman asking about why two homicide detectives were visiting someone in the Director's Office last week," she said in a flat tone. She stopped and looked at Tom inquiringly.

Tom, on the other hand, felt like someone had placed a cold hand around his heart. Never having been one that could hide his emotions, he was sure that he had visibly blanched. That was confirmed when Bev said, "Hmmm. I see you know something about that," in the same flat tone.

Tom asked, "What does he know?"

"Well," Bev answered resuming her usual tone of voice, "all he knew last Friday was that two homicide detectives had walked through the lobby Thursday afternoon and came in here. He was sitting in the lobby waiting for someone to finish their visit and saw them himself. He called Johnny the next morning to ask about it and Johnny came and asked me."

"What did Johnny tell him?" Tom asked anxiously.

"He told him that he knew nothing about the visit or anything related to it. Which was true. Then Johnny came to see me because of the risk of something blowing up that he wouldn't be able to get in front of."

"And you told him . . .?"

"I told him that I didn't know anything either and blew the whole thing off."

"Then why are you in here now?" Tom asked starting to feel like the issue might be contained.

"Because Daniel called back just a little while ago. He called Johnny first, but I told him to tell Daniel that nothing was going on and if he didn't believe that he could ask me." She paused just long enough to recognize that Tom was blanching again. She went on, "So Johnny transferred the call in to my office. I had just walked in from lunch and found myself talking to a nosy reporter about something that sounds like homicide."

"What did you say?" Tom's question almost stuck in his throat.

"First, he told me what he had seen last Thursday." Pause. "Then he said he didn't believe Johnny so he started camping out in the lobby this morning and guess what he saw?"

Tom knew what Daniel Edderman had seen but he said nothing and gestured for Bev to continue with her story.

"He said he saw the same two guys come in about mid-morning and go in the Director's office. And about 20-30 minutes later they come out and cross the lobby to the hall across from here with you and some oriental looking woman. And the four of you stayed over there for maybe twenty minutes then went back in the Director's Suite."

Tom knew all of that and wondered how he was going to explain the big picture to Bev when she went on, "And then the two detectives came out alone and went back down that hall and stayed almost thirty minutes. When they came out they weren't speaking, just had stern faces as they left the hospital and went toward the parking lot. What's going on, Tom? He's describing these two guys going in to the Cardiology Division. Is this about Dr. Adamson?"

Tom nodded slowly and said, "Let me start at the beginning. I've been keeping quiet about this until I thought we knew what happened but it's just getting muddier every day." Starting with the puzzling circumstances of Wilford's death on the stairs and Monique finding nitroglycerin in her toxicology screen and him visiting an old friend who happened to be a homicide detective. When he explained that the four of them had visited Wilford's office they found the nitroglycerin bottle in his desk, Bev showed her surprise and shock with a sharp intake of breath and asked, "Tom, do you think he was taking nitro and overdosed?"

"I don't know, Bev. Sure looks like it with some in his desk and all that. But Monique did not find any reason for him to have angina. It's all just a big puzzle right now."

"Why didn't you tell me?"

"Until right now you had no reason to be involved. I thought I could take care of this alone. Now, I guess, it's pretty clear that I can't."

"Well, what are we going to tell Edderman?"

"Nothing for right now. Remember I still haven't told Sam about any of this. Plus we really should notify the Joint Commission before anything hits the newspaper."

"Edderman is waiting for my call back."

"Another good reason why you shouldn't be involved."

"Like you knew that was going to happen."

"Come on, Bev, I wasn't making a big effort to keep you in the dark. I just didn't want to talk about it any more than necessary. Plus, I didn't think you had any special answers."

"But I can't protect you if I don't know things."

"Your job isn't to protect me, it's too help me get things done."

"Like figuring out what's going on?"

"Well, yes, maybe."

"So, what do you want me to tell Edderman?"

"I'd prefer that you continue to tell him that you are unaware of these visits by detectives or what they were doing here or who they were with. Tell him if he thinks I was involved, he should call me."

"What are you going to tell him?"

"For a while I will be unavailable for him to ask me anything."

"That won't work very long."

"Maybe long enough for me to get some help from Ron. Either he will solve this damn thing or give me advice about how to handle the press."

"And Sam and the Joint Commission?"

"Give Ron a couple more days. That's what he asked for."

Chapter Fifty Four

Monday, March 15

Approaching four o'clock that afternoon Tom got a call from Looney.

"Tom, I've got some news for you."

"Good. As I told you I'm really feeling close to the edge of a cliff here."

"Not sure my news is going to make that feeling go away."

"What have you got?"

Looney took his time walking his friend through the forensics data he had gotten back on the little brown vial. "First off, the contents are definitely nitroglycerin. There were twelve tablets in the bottle, each of them containing a little more than a half a milligram of drug. They look 'fresh', in that the pills were not chipped and there wasn't a lot of dust in the bottom of the bottle."

"That's really not news," Tom said wondering where his old buddy was taking him with this line of discussion.

"Maybe not but now we're sure that it was nitroglycerin. And the bigger news is what we found on the outside of the bottle."

"And that was . . .?"

"Nothing. Nada. Zip. No fingerprints. All wiped clean."

"Wait . . . you think that bottle was planted, don't you?" Tom said with visions of new nightmare stories racing through his mind. "Damn! If we'd gone to his office right away we would've known that."

"Everything clearer in hind-sight, buddy. But we may have missed our best chance at catching the bugger."

"Triple damn!" Tom muttered putting his head in his hands.

"You ever do much hunting back in Arkansas?" Looney's question took Tom by surprise and there was a brief pause before he answered, "A few times. Just birds. Why?"

"Well, us old country boys who do some regular hunting understand there's three ways to catch your prey: if you're after something like a deer, you might catch 'em by tracking or sitting in a tree waiting for them to wander by and if you're after something more wily you might want to go for trapping them. I suspect someone did dose your friend and thought it would go undetected. When word got out about the nitro in his system, this guy put a bottle of it in his desk – and we missed a good opportunity to trap the perpetrator in the act."

"What can we do now?" asked Tom, even more discouraged after hearing how he had let a chance of catching a murderer slip away. "Are you thinking this is connected to Patricia's case?"

"I'm not sure yet. But, if you think about it she was telling us all along that she was faking something?"

"What do you mean?"

"Her name. Or, properly speaking, the name she came up with to come to Cincinnati."

"Patricia?"

"No. Mulligan. She virtually announced that she was putting on a second name and going to try making things work a second time."

"You really think so?"

"Yep. But I also think that Gene's right. I don't have the smallest starting place to begin to running down leads in her background. So I need to start somewhere closer."

"Such as?" asked Tom, fearful that Ron was about to ask for permission to start interviewing staff at New City.

"I said there are three ways to catch your prey. You likely used it when you were out bird hunting. We flush the bugger out. So, I'll make the assumption that the two 'dosings' are, in fact, related. And to do that I need to get more information about this doctor. Would you see if his wife would meet with me and Gene?"

Chapter Fifty-Five

Tuesday, March 16

Looney and Gene met at the station and drove out to the Adamson's home together. They had agreed with Tom's request to not ask Elizabeth about whether Wil had any enemies because he didn't want her thinking someone had killed him. They reluctantly agreed to this limitation on their usual approach and on the way to the house they discussed how they would approach the interview with this restriction.

Liz's sister greeted them at the front door.

"Hello," she said, opening the door and waving them in. "I'm Virginia Harper, Liz's sister."

Liz was sitting quietly in an armchair in the living room and she looked up and smiled at them as they entered. "Detectives, how nice of you to try to help Tom figure out what happened to Wil. Would you like some coffee?"

Both men agreed and Virginia stepped into the kitchen as they took seats across from Liz.

"Mrs. Adamson, we are very sorry for your loss," said Looney. "And we don't want to intrude."

"I know and I appreciate that but Tom said maybe this would help him to figure out what happened to Wil," Liz said.

"We thank you for being willing to talk to us about Wil," Gene said, taking out his own small notebook and opening it up.

"If it will help," she said, looking at the notebook. "Tom said he thought maybe your approach would help explain what happened to Wil."

This came as a complete surprise to both men; they thought, what could Tom have suggested to her as the reason he was asking for her to sit down with detectives from the Homicide Division? For a moment or two the two men sat quietly and Looney raised his eyebrows to encourage her to be more explicit. Liz went on to explain that Tom said he had spent some time in the Air Force with the military police when there were some odd cases and the medical history didn't seem to explain things. He had told her that he had noticed a couple of times how the military police questions about previous actions and activities had actually helped explain circumstances. And, Tom had explained, the key questions were things that the medical personnel would not have asked.

"Did he tell you why he was asking us in particular to come talk to you?" Looney asked.

"Oh yes. He said you were one of the military police that had helped him in the past. That you two went a long way back."

Just as Looney and Gene were taking a deep breath, Virginia re-entered the room carrying a tray of coffee and cups. She sat this down on the coffee table in front of Liz who then asked Virginia to be hostess and pour each person a cup. This struck Looney as a little odd until he noticed that both of Liz Adamson's hands were heavily wrapped around the base of each thumb. When they arrived at the house, Liz had been sitting with her hands held together and they were partially covered by long sleeves on her sweater. Thinking back, Looney remembered that Virginia had opened the door and Liz had not offered to shake hands with them; He was a little put out with himself for not noticing those things. Virginia sat and started pouring, beginning with Looney. As Virginia poured, Liz indicated the sugar and creamer were filled appropriately and available. And she added, "I hope neither of you would prefer artificial sweetener. Wil didn't even want them in the house."

"Why was that?" asked Gene, conversationally.

"He said the rush to artificial sweeteners in the American diet is why we have the epidemic of diabetes. So he pushed us all to quit using it."

"I haven't heard of that theory," said Looney taking his coffee black. "Is that something new?"

"Oh no," said Virginia. "Wil's had been on that hobby horse for years."

"Was he particular about other things in his diet?" asked Looney. "I understand he was a hiker."

The following twenty minutes were taken up with stories from the sisters about Wil's adherence to an active life style. He ate natural grains, avoided eating preserved foods (other than frozen), chose only antibiotic-free meats and never ate refined sugar. Except that the mention of refined sugar made both sisters laugh.

"What's that about?" asked Looney grinning at them.

"Well, before he found out how bad the refined sugars were, Wil had a love affair with Dunkin Donuts."

"Really?" smiled Gene, who was actually a bit enamored with Dunkin –both for their donuts and their coffee.

"Oh yes. When we were in medical school, our Saturday norming breakfast was half dozen donuts – he ate four and I ate two. With fresh coffee. In bed."

"Delivery?"

"Oh, no. He got up and went down the street to the store and brought them home for me."

"And then he gave them up?" asked Gene, who was suddenly thinking how good one of those donuts sounded right about then.

"Completely. Cold turkey. Just one day up and said 'No more donuts for me.' And that was it. Except for Christmas morning," Liz said smiling in memory. "He would get up before me, go out and find a store and bring home half dozen donuts. And we would eat them in bed." Her smile turned wistful and then bordered on tearful and Looney interjected, "And he had remained active?"

Liz sniffed back her tears and said, "Oh yes. I guess that Tom told you we visited our grandchildren out in Colorado Springs over the holidays?" Both men nodded. "We actually went out hiking while we were there. One of the lower trails, of course, but he wasn't showing any sign of heart trouble or angina."

She again seemed to pull away from the conversation a little and said, "He was a vigorous man. Very vigorous." And she brought her eyes back to Looney and said, "That's why him collapsing is so mysterious. I just don't understand it."

Gene stood up somewhat abruptly and asked, "M'am, May I use your bathroom?"

"Certainly, Detective. It's just down the hall there." Virginia stood as if to show him the way but Looney engaged her in pouring him another cup and Gene left the room. He walked down the hall to where he was out of sight of the living area, opened and closed the door to the half bath in the hall and then slipped off his loafers and quietly went down the hall into the master bedroom.

He identified the side of the bed that would have been Wil's and quickly looked in the drawers of the side table. Nothing unusual, some eye drops and cough drops. Next he moved into the bathroom. Probably 30 years old, one washbasin, single medicine cabinet with mirrored front. He carefully pulled the mirrored door open to prevent any squeaking and stood quietly perusing the contents. Then he took out his phone, opened the camera and flashed a picture of the cabinet contents.

Then it was back down the hall to the half bath and quietly entering. Then he flushed the toilet, slipped on his shoes, turned on the water and washed his hands. After drying, he opened the door and went back to the living room.

Chapter Fifty-Six

Tuesday, March 16

Back in the living room, as Gene entered, Looney was leaning back and saying, "That's an amazing story. On so many levels."

"What did I miss?" asked Gene as he again took his seat.

"Liz was just telling me about the neighborhood here," Looney said. "Apparently they have the best neighbors ever."

"Impressive," Gene commented as he sat down and picked up his cup.

"The middle school kids get out at first snow and clear all the sidewalks and driveways of the 'older' people."

"That's amazing. What's their incentive."

"It appears that their fathers are out there with them."

"Now that's the kind of neighborhood where I want to retire!"

"But," Virginia said, "maybe they won't be so eager now that there's a wolf in the area."

"What do you mean?' asked Looney.

"Oh, when they cleaned the snow while we were gone to Colorado, one of the fathers noticed a disturbance in the snow next to the driveway and thought it might be where a wolf might have snuggled down."

"Why did he think of a wolf?" asked Gene.

"In the Fall last year a couple of the puppies from a litter down the street just went missing and one of the neighbors thought she might have seen a wolf in her backyard. All rumors, of course. No real proof."

"Anyone seen any tracks?" asked Looney

"Apparently not. They had already cleared off all the snow from the driveway and sidewalks when they found the nesting place. But one of the fathers called animal control and learned that there have been several sightings up here over the past two years."

"Still, kids shoveling my walks, wow," said Gene.

After a few more minutes of discussion of Wilford's energy and activity level recently and a frank denial of any episode of chest pain or interrupted activity, the detectives thought they were about to overstay their welcome.

"Thank you for seeing us," Looney said, shaking both Liz's and Virginia's hand as they edged to the door. They waited until they were at the car before speaking. Looney said, "Just a minute. Let me see where that wolf was bedded down." He went back to the driveway and examined it from the street end. A single car affair at the right end of the house it ended at a painted overhead door with clear windows at the top. Wilford's Porsche was parked in driveway, up close to the overhead door and right at the corner of the garage. Any animal lying there would have a survey shot of the neighborhood and be able to slink off behind the garage if approached, probably without being seen.

"Huh." He said and returned to his care.

"Well, whadda you think?" asked Gene.

"Pretty much just like she said."

"Wait till you see what I found, then," Gene said taking out his phone. "And I just might be a lot closer to going to those basketball games than you ever believed!"

Chapter Fifty-Seven

Tuesday, March 16

Noontime that day found Looney and Gene again parking at New City and winding their way through the lobby to Tom's office. Once again they noted the number of people around the coffee kiosk stand and Gene commented, "These guys probably drink as much coffee as we do."

"And we don't have a barista or an espresso machine. I bet their intake would be lot less if they had to drink the stuff we do."

"Or they would go somewhere down the street – you know, like we do."

This line of conversation even continued when they waited outside Tom's office for Monique to show up. "Did you notice that there's a special coffee maker in the Director's Suite?" asked Gene pointing over Looney's shoulder. "They can't even be bothered to walk to the lobby for a specialty drink. Jeez!"

"Tom said most of the division offices have a pot of their own. The Dialysis Unit reportedly has the best coffee in the building outside of the lobby.

"Why's that? I mean what are they putting in it?"

"Something like the Cinnamon Toast taste drink at Starbucks, according to Tom. One of the docs sprang for the machine and the rest of the staff buys the flavoring."

"Where is this Dialysis Unit?" asked Gene rising from his chair.

" Sit down. We don't have time," said Looney just as Tom opened his door and signaled them in.

Soon everyone was sitting in the same chair they had occupied earlier followed brief handshakes. Monique had come up the back stairs from the basement and had entered the back hall. She and Tom were interested in what the detectives had found in their visit to Dr. Adamson's house.

First, Looney wanted to know about the accident that Liz Adamson had suffered. Tom explained, " She's got a typical Bennett's fracture involving both thumbs."

"I'm so glad you cleared that up," Looney said, sarcastically. "What the devil is that?"

"Sorry, doctor talk. She broke both thumbs in an auto accident a couple of months ago."

"And how did that happen?"

"I'm not really clear on all the details. Apparently she and Wil had just returned from Colorado and she jumped in his car to run to the store for some eggs and bacon or something for breakfast the next day and ran off the road. Probably a slick spot. And she rammed into a stone abutment on a bridge near their house. Going pretty slow, I guess. And, she broke both thumbs. It happens a lot in head-on collisions."

"Really? Why's that?"

"The driver has hands on the wheel and grips it tightly just before the impact. Even though the airbag will keep their head from hitting the steering wheel or the dashboard, the steering wheel is pushed straight back and just smashes into the joint at the base of the thumb, right here," Tom said indicating the area on his own hand.

"Why was she driving his car?"

"I didn't get that straight but something about he was unpacking the other car or something like that."

"Did she say that she skidded on ice or what?"

"All I remember was her saying she couldn't keep the car from going off the road. But she wasn't going very fast. Unfamiliar car and all that, I guess. The damage to the car was pretty minimal and Wil actually got it fixed and running. Liz's thumbs are a different story.

"In what way?"

"Well, I was able to fix her subluxation . . . I mean I got the thumbs back in place fairly easily and put her in a cast. We did an MRI to confirm there was no significant ligament damage. I've changed her cast a couple of times and now she's just in a cock-up splint and starting to go to physical therapy. But she's still got a way to go to get back to her usual strength and mobility."

"Was there an investigation of the accident?" asked Gene, puzzled why Looney seemed so interested in the medical details.

"Not really, I guess. I believe the insurance adjuster looked at the car and I think he went to the scene. The insurance paid for her medical care and the car repair so I guess they didn't suspect drinking and driving."

"OK. Thanks for the explanation. Next time I'm in a head-on, I'll pull my hands off the wheel," said Looney

"Good luck with that," said Tom. "Is that what you wanted to talk to us about? I thought you had something of interest for Monique, too?"

"Actually, we do," said Gene pulling his phone out his pocket. "Look what I found in the good doctor's medicine cabinet." He showed them the photograph he had taken.

"Is that . . .?" from Tom and "Oh my . . ." from Monique as they realized what the orange and red packet was that sat at one end of the lower shelf.

"That's Cialis!" said Tom, his voice indicating both surprise and sudden insight. "Was he taking this?"

"We didn't press Mrs. Adamson about it. She did say several times that her husband was both 'feeling frisky' and that he was 'very vigorous' since they had gone on their trip to Colorado. I think those are some code words for his frequent and capable interest in sex. But I didn't press her on that in front of her sister. I suppose she might not have known," Loony explained.

"But it was right there in the shared medicine cabinet," Gene said. "Do we really think she didn't know?"

"Well, that's at least consistent with his activity level," said Tom rubbing his face at this new revelation.

"But wait a minute," interjected Monique. "This doesn't jibe with a theory that he might have had a little angina and taken some nitro. Wil was a smart cardiologist; he knew better than to take nitro at all when he was taking Cialis." She turned to look to Tom for support for this idea and saw him seriously nodding his head.

"That's right," he said with firm emphasis. "And that means we were right about him being 'dosed' with that nitro, weren't we, Ron?" This was delivered with some emphasis directly at Looney who smiled back and nodded. Looney thought Tom was now conveniently forgetting how strongly he didn't want to consider foul play coming from inside his hospital just a couple of days ago.

"Yep. That's certainly the way we look at it. But there are still some unanswered questions about all this."

"For sure," said Monique. "Like who did this and why?"

"Yes," answered Looney as Gene nodded, "but there's a couple of things a little more basic we need to find out first."

"What's that?" asked Tom.

"Well, first question might be 'did the perpetrator here know that the good doctor was taking Cialis?'

"Why is that important?" asked Monique slumping back in her chair.

"It goes to motive and intent," explained Looney. "Let's say the perp wanted to kill your friend. Since the Cialis is an every day dose, the poisoning could happen at anytime, right?

"Right," came from both Tom and Monique.

"So, if the perp knows about the Cialis it raises the question 'why at this time? I mean, think about it, why in the world would someone try to kill somebody with a medical cause in the middle of an active teaching hospital? Really, there's medical personnel around every corner and a high likelihood that the event wouldn't kill him, right?"

"I suppose . . ." offered Tom and Monique slowly nodded her assent to this concept.

"That makes me wonder if the perp knew about the Cialis."

There was a long pause in the conversation. Tom was trying to put things together and the finding of Cialis at Wil's plus what had to be planted nitro sounded like intent to kill. And Looney's point about the foreknowledge of Cialis treatment raised additional concerns. Tom had actually begun to think perhaps the person dosing Wil was someone on the faculty or staff, someone close enough to him to have insider knowledge of the Cialis. But that meant that murder and the death of Wilford Adamson was the goal of the affair – and he was having trouble thinking like that about his own staff.

"But of course," Looney spoke into the growing silence, "if the perp did not know about the Cialis there are some other rather probable conclusions. First, if the perp was ignorant of the Cialis, then the 'dosing' was probably considered more likely to cause a recoverable episode, right? I mean, you wouldn't normally think someone would die from a little nitroglycerin would you? If they were otherwise healthy and all that? And that might mean that murder was not the point here. The fact of the death makes it a question of first degree or second degree and it's still murder but the intent has to be considered."

Again there was a prolonged silence as the detectives watched the two doctors try to assimilate all the repercussions.

Then Gene spoke up. "And, of course, if this wasn't attempted murder, the question returns to 'why now?" Is there a reason for the 'dosing' to take place in the morning of a regular workday in a hospital? That seems to us most likely to point to an incident that was not intended to kill – one that was intended to be responded to the way hospitals do every day. And to end up with a recovery."

"And there's always that last little question," stuck in Looney. "Is there any connection between this 'dosing' and the other one that same day in the hospital?"

All four sat quietly pondering this question and looking at each other with some wonder and concern about implications and, of course, next steps. Then Looney took a deep breath and said, "All right. I'll go first. We have to build on two different "truths" about the fact that the Doc was taking the Cialis. Let's say whoever knew about the Cialis did the dosing and we have questions about why now and maybe even how? But I'm gonna add one other question in front of those. Who would have known? About the Cialis, I mean. For sure the Doc knew but I'm ruling out suicide here. Probably the wife knew; she sure hinted around at a noticeable difference in his "vigor" recently - which both Gene and I took as polite conversational reference to his bedroom activity. Is there someone else he would have discussed this with?

Tom looked at Looney and slowly shook his head. "It surely wasn't me, but we weren't really all that close. Not close enough for 'bedroom talk' anyway. I don't know if there's anyone else – except maybe whoever wrote him a prescription . . ."

"This wasn't a prescription," said Gene. "This is the stuff you can get without a prescription.'

"OTC," said Monique.

"Huh?"

"Over the counter. It means you don't need a doctor's prescription, same as aspirin."

"Yeah, like that. So he coulda bought this on his own."

"So, that leaves us with only the wife knowing about it, and that's just a probable," said Looney. "Anybody got any idea why she would want to kill the Doc?"

Tom and Monique shook their heads.

"Well, we may have to go looking for some motive, then," opined Gene.

"Wait a minute," said Tom, just as Monique was raising her hand and also about to speak, "You are now acting like Wil's death had nothing to do with the girl's death."

"Well," said Looney, "If we don't have a connection maybe they are not connected. We now know that she wasn't who she said she was. There could be almost anything in her background that would bring someone to kill her if she was recognized. Could be revenge, could be getting even with someone in her family – her real family, I mean – or something else. Without knowing more about her and where she came from we really can't rule out her past as the main feature in why she got killed."

Monique spoke up, "But wouldn't that make the two deaths on the same day just an hour apart some kind of coincidence? That's a little hard for me to believe. Things I saw in the M.E,'s office that looked like they weren't related at all often turned out to be first degree relatives."

Looney nodded and added, "I agree with you. When other people say 'coincidence' I start looking for the connection. That's my job. But we have to agree that these two deaths may not be connected other than in time and space. At least, I've got to consider that until I get a better reason to put them together."

Monique took a deep breath and said, "The Taoist Liezi explained the way we see things is because of the way we look at them. He said something like, 'When two events occur together we say cause and effect if we think one caused the other. But if we think they are unrelated we call it a coincidence – and if we don't find any reason for them, we call them accidents. How we explain such events depends on how we see the world'. I personally would prefer neither of these deaths to have been murder but the evidence convinces me they are and their proximity makes me think they are connected."

"Good quote," Looney said nodding at her. "My favorite is from Erma Bombeck: ' Thanksgiving dinner takes eighteen hours to prepare and is eaten in eighteen minutes. Half-time of the football game is eighteen minutes. This is not a coincidence.' "

Gene added, "I don't think they are coincidences, either. I think he was killed to stop him from helping keep the girl alive."

They spent a few more minutes in quiet reflection and then agreed to keep open minds and each left the office with Tom sitting quietly behind the desk.

Chapter Fifty-Eight

Tuesday, March 16

After the detectives and Monique left his office, Tom found it very difficult to get back to work. None of the papers on the desk rose to the level of importance of what he was contending with in his mind. Murder, whether first degree or second degree didn't seem really all that different to him right now, and involvement of someone in New City was almost inconceivable. But, he knew from reviewing scores of investigations in the Air Force, people were often capable of actions far beyond what members of their family or friends were aware. Spouses had poisoned their partner, children had allowed parents with disabilities to waste away. He remembered specific examples of each but the direct poisoning of a co-worker still seemed very far 'out of the box' for Tom. Which made him consider the possibility that maybe it's not a co-worker. Maybe this is another of the all-too-familiar cases where a spouse wants to be rid of a partner. Could Liz have been the one to administer the nitro? Wil was a creature of habit; he always had a cup of coffee at home and one in the car. Maybe the idea was he would pass out driving and have an accident. Liz certainly had the opportunity – but what could possibly be the motive? Did she blame Wil for her accident? Was she trying to get him to see what it was like to be crippled and without use of his hands for months?

Tom didn't want to keep thinking about his friends this way – but he couldn't stop. He began to put himself in Liz's shoes and to try to think like her, planning a serious accident for her husband. He guessed that she could have put the nitro in the travel cup at almost any time, that way no matter who poured the coffee it was already there. But what if Wil had picked up the cup and rinsed it out before filling it with coffee? Could that have happened? If so, how would she get around that? Distract him maybe, get him to take the garbage out before leaving or remind him to change his tie for some reason. If she was prepared she could that quickly and not be suspected. Damn! This was really possible he thought and leaned back in his chair and pulled up a mental image of Liz opening the little brown bottle, shaking out one or two tablets and screwing the top back on before dropping those tablets into the travel cup or, in the event that Wil had rinsed it out, popping the top on the cup to add the tablets while he was briefly out of the room. Yes, it certainly could be done, he thought. Only a very small doubt existed in his mind about this scenario. He knew he might never be privy to the motive, but there was something about that mental film track that seemed, well, wrong; not clear on what it was, Tom leaned further back in his chair, closed his eyes and began to play the mental film again.

When the phone rang, it broke his concentration and pulled him back into the moment. Automatically he reached for the receiver and answered, "Dr. Bolling. Can I help you?"

The voice on the other end of the line was a little scratchy, like someone that smoked too much. But the words were clear and jerked Tom's mind out of any possible doldrums.

"Dr. Bolling, This is Dan Edderman and I want to talk to you about the murder at New City."

Tom froze for a second, then answered in his best 'I'm just an old country doctor' voice, "Well now, Mr. Edderman, I don't rightly know of any murder here."

"C'mon Doc," Edderman said, "you were escorting those detectives around yesterday and they came back today and spent a lot of time in your office area."

Tom was casting about in his mind to recall what Beverly had told him that Edderman told her he already knew. He imagined that the reporter was guessing and trying to get him to tip something off by acting like he knew more than he did.

"You mean my old buddy from the Air Force?"

"So, are you saying you called an old friend to try to cover up a murder?"

"Son, I didn't say anything like that, and you know it. Why are you asking me about a visit from an old friend? What's that got to do with anything that might interest you?" Tom wanted Edderman to disclose the extent of his information, but the reporter was equally cagey.

"Well, for starters, I didn't know you and those detectives were friends, but I do know they don't travel in pairs like that except when they're working. And their work is homicide."

"Well," Tom said in the same voice as before, "they were here and now they're gone."

"And I want to know why they've made at least three trips in the last few days."

"And why is that of interest to you?"

"Because I smell a story. Something is off if you have the homicide team coming in and snooping around the hospital. Looks like something went badly wrong at New City and now the cops are in there snooping around."

"Hardly snooping, son, they dropped in for a talk."

"About what? Or who?"

Tom was beginning to feel a little pressed against the wall. Should he say that the police swore him to silence? That would certainly imply there was something big going on around New City. Maybe he could just stonewall the reporter and buy some time. That's what Ron said he needed – and maybe Ron could give him some tips on how to handle this guy.

"Well now, son, that's seems a little like gossip and I don't go in for that. I suggest that you try to find something important to report on."

"Oh, I think this is important. And I'll just keep on looking."

Tom knew he didn't want Edderman looking into anything around the hospital.

"How 'bout this," Tom said, still the good ole boy, "I can ask my buddy on the force to give you a call and tell you why he was here. You know, I just don't feel comfortable trying to explain why other folks do things they do. I have enough trouble explaining why I do certain things." Tom was hoping this ploy would re-direct the caller interest to the police and away from New City.

"You can do that, and that's all well and good, but insufficient," retorted Edderman. "Those homicide detectives won't give me the time of day. I'm more likely to get hung up on than to find out anything from those guys. There's something going on there in New City and I'm gonna find out what it is. And I'm not hanging around waiting for some homicide dick to feel friendly enough to give me a call. I'll just have to start nosing around on my own."

Tom knew this was not a threat but a reality. He couldn't ban the reporter from the hospital and if he started snooping around and asking questions, Wil's death would come up since everyone was talking about it and concerned. He decided to make a gamble.

"All righty then. How 'bout if I were to call him and then let you know what he says."

"Didn't he talk to you when he was there?" Edderman persisted.

"Well, yeah. Yes he did. But not about whatever you're talking about."

"Really?" The sarcasm was obvious.

"Well, nothing he'd want me talkin' about behind his back, anyways."

"So, you'd call him now and ask what you can tell me? Why would you do that?"

"Sure I'd do that. I think you're barking up the wrong tree. But I'd also rather you just let us do our work here and not get all wrapped up in some idea you got about wrong-doing."

After a short pause, Edderman responded, "All right. When will you talk to him?"

"Probably tomorrow, afternoon maybe. Evening at the latest."

"And you'll call me right away?"

"I'll call you after I talk with him," Tom said, leaving himself some wiggle room on the timing of any such call.

There was another short pause and Tom began to feel hopeful he had bought the time for Looney.

Then Edderman said, "I'm not waiting forever. Here's my cell number. I know something's going on in there and if you don't call me soon, I'm going to start some real investigating."

"Uh huh. Well, you have a nice day." Tom remained the 'good ole boy' to the end. He wrote down the cell phone number he was given and hung up and sat back in the chair realizing that his heart rate was elevated and that his armpits were wet with sweat. And there was the very real beginning of a headache right behind his eyes.

Chapter Fifty-Nine

Tuesday, March 16

Meg fixed her fried chicken for supper that night. Looney loved fried chicken – the home made kind, not the 'extra crispy' commercial stuff. In his opinion, 'fried chicken' was shorthand for "deep fried chicken parts" with lots of rich fried crust and skin covering the moist and meaty parts of leg, breast and thigh. His mother had always fried chicken that way and Meg learned that the technique and results were the only way Looney was happy with fried chicken. So, Meg had 'gone to school' on Looney's mother's techniques in the kitchen and learned the deep fry technique. It wasn't as simple as it looked, after all. One had to be careful about dropping chicken parts into the frying grease – things that splashed out were painful and dangerous. Plus there was the necessity for reading the chicken just right; too long in the grease and the meat was tough and the outer crust would begin to flake away. And if the parts were not left long enough then crust was doughy and the meat not fully cooked. Even so, the actual frying time should be rather short because the cooking time is brief seeing that the meat is enveloped in hot grease. Of course it had taken Meg several attempts before she got it even close to what Looney had experienced growing up. And every time she missed the mark, Ron simply said, "Well, this is an interesting way to fry chicken," or something like that – not opprobrium but hardly praise, either. When she finally got it right – and it was only a trial of three or four times – Ron got out of his chair and gave her a big kiss and said, "Better'n Momma's."

Meg had also learned the trick from Ron's mother of testing the frying oil before starting – sprinkle a little flour in to the liquid to see that it sizzles but doesn't burn. She also learned to judge the temperature of the oil by whether the first piece into the cooking pot sank and properly rose back to the top; pieces that didn't sink indicated oil too hot for cooking and pieces that sank and never rose were in oil that was too cool for proper cooking. Who knew there was this much science to dinner? Or to just frying up some chicken. Meg was especially glad she could just hike down to the SuperMart and buy the chicken parts – she knew that Ron's mother usually killed one of their own hens for dinner and Meg was definitely not interested in the gutting and skinning part of fried chicken meal preparation.

The reason Meg spent this much time and effort on this particular meal came after she learned that fried chicken was one of Looney's comfort foods. When he was sick or just troubled about something, fried chicken seemed to settle him down and help him repair. And, she also discovered that in addition to properly cooked chicken parts, the fried chicken entrée simply had to be served with the appropriate sides: mashed potatoes, green beans and cornbread. Without the sides the whole function of the meal is disrupted. Over their years Meg had learned when best to prepare this meal by being attuned to her husband's moods.

Meg had spent the afternoon preparing the meal and when Looney opened the door and smelled the food his spirits rose measurably. He went in the kitchen and walked up behind his wife. He encircled her in his arms and kissed the back of her neck. No words were spoken; they just leaned against each other in recognition of the moment. Looney went and changed into jeans and his spirits continued to rise throughout the meal, probably peaking about the time Meg set in front of him a piece of hot apple pie covered with a thick slice of cheddar cheese and a fresh cup of coffee.

"How'd you know?" Looney asked.

"Last couple of days you have been too quiet and kinda moody, honey. And I know you get that way when you have a case that's bothering you. I know what's coming. I went out to the library today and got me a couple of books to read so you can have all the room you need."

"And a man asked me today if I was married," Looney said, smiling at his wife.

"I hope you told him 'Happily'," she said, picking up on the joke.

"Told him I couldn't remember not being married . . . happily, of course," Looney responded as he turned to the pie.

Later they stood side by side washing and drying the dishes in one of their little rituals. Meg understood that Ron was about to sink into a reverie about the case and profoundly ignore her, hence the trip to the library and so they would eschew the fancy electric dishwasher and stand side-by-side, actually touching at the hips and shoulders while cleaning every last dish and pan from the 'comfort' meal. Their pattern, developed over several years, allowed him slowly to withdraw from her and the world for some time and ponder various inscrutables while allowing her to feel loved and not neglected. They would signal the end of the ritual with a second cup of coffee at the table sitting across from each other and making inane small talk until the coffee was gone. Then she would take the cups, rinse them in the sink and go upstairs to read and sleep and leave him to his own devices.

Looney's devices were simple. He would get still another cup of coffee, walk into the living room and spend several minutes going through his record collection. A thoroughly old-fashioned guy, Looney had a collection of vinyl going back three decades. Several years ago, his old turntable died and he went searching for another only to find that hardly anyone carried turntables anymore – they tried to sell him various kinds of CD systems but he would have none of it. After almost four months of searching he found exactly what he wanted, a plain turntable on EBay, so plain it came with both 78 and 33 rpm settings. But it had a new Denon DP-300F cartridge and was a reasonable price. The fact that it was old and had no pre-amp was unimportant; Looney's home system had a built-in pre-amp and two JBL EON615 15 inch speakers that he had placed in the corners of the living room.

This night he selected a Kai Winding album from 1963 and Charlie Parker's platter "Night and Day" from 1957 for starters. He set the volume low enough to keep from bothering Meg and started sorting papers on the coffee table while the music rolled over him. He carefully re-read the folders on each person involved in the case, including Tom Bolling and Monique Song. After reading each folder, he would consult his notebook, flipping back and forth to find every instance of a note concerning the individual he had just reviewed. Then he would stare at the wall over the fireplace conjuring up a timeline and trying to fit things into place.

An hour later, he found his coffee to have gotten cold; he took the cup to the sink and rinsed it out and then opened the refrigerator and took out a bottle of beer, opened it and resumed his seat on the couch and picked up the next file.

Somewhere around two in the morning, Looney had read all the files and all his notes and had a twisting timeline in his head but no real answers. He was still stumped about "why?" and couldn't even begin to get close to "who?" And now, after three beers, his eyes were dry and burning and his head was aching and he felt hungry and sleepy at the same time. Without really planning to do so, he lay down on the couch and rested his head on the arm and closed his eyes "just to help me think a little" and then he was asleep.

Just after four in the morning, Looney felt a call of nature and got up to pee. Coming back from the bathroom he circled by the refrigerator and got a piece of fried chicken to eat. After carefully cleaning his hands he picked two other records for the turntable; he had made a couple of changes earlier in the night and now he chose some Coltrane and Brubeck. Pushing himself not to lie back down he sat on the edge of the sofa and recalled why he had ever developed the habit of trying to piece together a case while listening to jazz.

It had happened almost by accident while he was stationed at Sembach AFB in Germany in the late 1970s. It was before he met Meg and as a bachelor he spent many nights after work in the town of Kaiserslautern where he and another AP rented a room. Looney found a small bar around the corner from his lodging where U.S. Airmen frequented and the band played mostly blues and jazz. On more than one occasion he realized he had spent the hours between supper and closing nursing one or two beers, listening to fair renditions of trombone duets of Kai Winding and J.J. Johnson or Miles Davis wannabes wailing on their trumpet into the wee hours. And, he also realized, that the next morning he seemed to have unusual clarity about his case, often being able to synthesize facts into a tenable theory that had seemed impossible the day before.

Looney also remembered how Meg had resented his going to jazz bars to work on difficult cases and how they had developed the current methodology with a high quality sound system and quiet dinner at home before he took over the living room. He decided, for about the hundredth time that year, that he had definitely married up.

Now awake, he began sorting through his notes to identify the key elements that he did not yet understand and when Joe Morello began his drum solo in "Take Five", Looney just leaned back and let the staccato sounds aid him in conceptually putting pieces of the puzzle together and rearrange them on a large mental whiteboard.

Even with the rapid tattooing of the drums echoing in his head, the whiteboard suddenly began to fill in an orderly fashion with the individual pieces floating into their place not requiring even virtual hands. The process was initially what only seemed to be a repeat of his scrutiny for the past several hours. Then as he was about to open his eyes some of the pieces landed out of order, or at least Looney thought they were out of order but he didn't want to move them . . . just yet. Eyes closed, and with sleep lapping at the edge of his consciousness he noted that the pieces that had seemed out of order actually were in order – just not in the order he had previously considered and, most astonishing of all, in a way that was very different from the way he had been looking at things before. Before he could sit up, the darkness at the edge of his mind became a closing circle around the whiteboard. As the darkness inched forward the center of Looney's vision was focused on a couple of key pieces of his puzzle . . . and they almost made sense . . .

Then, he slept.

Chapter Sixty

Wednesday, March 17

"Rick Harrelson?" asked Looney as he slid on to the bar stool next to man eating breakfast at Betty's Diner.

"That would be me," the man said with barely a sideways glance as he picked up his cup and sipped his coffee.

"Detective Ron Looney, CPD. And this is my partner Detective Novalchek."

"Detectives," Rick said nodding at each and then turning back to his food. "And how can I be of service to Cincinnati's finest?"

"We would like to talk to you about a car accident," said Looney, signaling the waitress for a couple of cups of coffee.

"Uh hunh? Must be a specific one since you guys have your own motor pool and mechanics downtown, right?"

"You are correct, sir," said Gene. "A very specific one."

"And, I'm just guessing here, one that I had in my shop."

"Again, you are spot on," said Looney semi-saluting him with his cup.

"Look guys, I'd be happy to help if you'll just let me finish my breakfast."

"Sure. Sure. Tell you what, we'll get us a booth and you join us when you're ready, OK?"

"Fine," Rick said and then spoke to the waitress, "Sally, can you get my friends a booth?"

"Sure thing, honey" she said and motioned the detectives to follow her toward the back of Betty's to an empty booth. They took their coffee cups with them. They sat on the same side of the booth and sipped at their coffee.

About ten minutes later Rick Harrelson strolled back to the booth and sat opposite the detectives. Rick was about six feet, mid to late forties, square jawed with dark hair streaked with gray worn long but shorter than pony-tail length. His eyes were grayish-green and his tanned face was crinkled with more smile lines than frown ones. As he took a seat he smiled at each of the detectives and said, "OK, what's up guys?"

Looney took this open approach to be exactly what it seemed and was very open and frank in his questioning thereafter.

"First," he said, "do you remember fixing Dr. Wilford Adamson's car after a wreck in January?"

"Sure do."

"Do you remember all the wrecks you take care of?" asked Gene, a little surprised that Rick didn't want to refer to some records somewhere before answering.

"Nope, not all of them. But certain ones I do."

"What makes the difference?" asked Looney.

"Well, in this instance there were a couple of things. But the biggest was that I've been taking care of Wil's car for a long time. Cars, actually. He's lived just over there" indicating behind the diner, "for a long time and he's always brought his cars down for me to maintain and fix. So I've known Wil a long time and I've known his cars even more intimately."

"So you knew this car before the wreck?"

"Absolutely. That 911 was his baby. Fortunately, the wreck was actually pretty light on the car – hurt his wife more, I've heard."

"Do you know what caused the wreck?"

"You guys aren't doing the insurance investigation are you? 'Cause I already told them what happened."

"Would you mind telling us again?"

"Not at all. Appeared that the right front tie rod broke and she went into a ditch – luckily at a rather slow speed. Ran into the bridge abutment."

"OK. That's what you told the insurance investigators. Did they ask you if you were the regular mechanic on the car, or whether you had failed to do due diligence in your maintenance checks? Or anything like that?"

"Nope. They wanted to know what caused the accident and I told 'em what I found. That's all. Two guys looked like they didn't want to get their suits dirty out in the bay and they left pretty quickly."

A slight pause. Then Looney said, "Anything else, Rick?"

Rick stared at the ceiling for a few seconds then took a deep breath and said, "Well, I told you there was something else that made me remember that wreck, right?"

"Yes, I heard that," said Looney, nodding slightly and encouraging Rick to fill in the rest of the story.

"Well, when I was pulling the front end for the repairs I noticed that the front tires were not worn unevenly." He stopped and looked directly at each man. "Do you have any idea what that means?"

"No," said Looney waiting for enlightenment.

Gene said, "That means the tie rod wasn't loose or anything and just broke without warning, I think."

"That's exactly right, Detective," Said Rick. And that's not what the 911 does. It may get loose on either end and the front end gets out of alignment and the tires begin to wear unevenly. I think I woulda seen that. But, even more, the tie rod wearing loose like that will cause problems driving."

"Like what?" asked Looney.

"For one, the front end would feel loose. And I think Wil would of noticed that and brought the car in. But the other thing is, the steering would tend to wobble at the extremes like when you're parallel parking the car and I know he would have noticed that."

"He has a parking slot at the hospital," said Gene.

"And he parks front-in in the driveway at home," noted Looney.

"Well then, maybe might not have noticed the looseness," Rick said, his face showing some doubt about his previous semi-certainty that something was funny about the wreck. "But, anyway, that tie rod didn't break – it came loose."

"How likely is that?" asked Looney.

"Not very damn likely" said Rick. "Couple that with the tires not being uneven and I really think someone did a job on that car."

"Why didn't you tell the investigators about that?" "First off, they weren't looking for opinions, they just wanted the facts and to get out of my bay. Second, I hadn't pulled the front end when they came around so I didn't have a reason to be suspicious of nothing."

"You really think, now, that somebody tampered with the car?" asked Looney, making notes in his little book.

"Yeah, I do."

"How hard would that be?"

"Not hard at all for someone who knows what they're doing. Doesn't need a pit or a lift. The parts are right there at the wheel housing. A couple of wrenches and five-six minutes and the tie is off. Or you could leave it with a little connection and it would come off while driving."

"What kind of driving?"

"Well, almost anything but certainly going through a lot of turns or over a bumpy road and that thing will pop off. Then it's Katy bar the door."

'Tell me again why you think this was tampering," asked Looney.

"Tie rod was unscrewed, not broken, and I have never heard of that happening by itself. And the tires were worn evenly so it hadn't been there a long time."

"And what would it take for someone to do this?"

"About ten minutes, tops."

"I mean in terms of materials," pushed Looney

"Oh. Let's see . . . two end wrenches. Maybe a little WD-40 to get it started but probably not."

"And some foreknowledge of what to do," added Gene.

"Well, yeah, I guess. But you can find all this out on the Internet, you know. I'm actually using the Internet more every day and relying on the manuals less. You-tube has almost everything."

"Including giving us more headaches," said Looney. "Thanks for your time."

"You betcha," said Rick, sliding out of the booth and leaving the diner.

Gene turned to his partner and said, "Now that's not at all what I was expecting to hear."

"Me either, partner," said Looney, "and I gotta go think this through a little more."

“Gonna go partner with J.J. and John?” Gene was familiar with his partner’s habit of working out problematic issues through ‘immersion therapy’ in 1950s and 1960s jazz.

“Actually, I did that last night and that’s why we came out here today. Now I need to talk to Brookhalter.”

“Norm Brookhalter? He retired three years ago.”

“But he’s the one that can help us now,” Looney said as he threw some money on the table and headed for his car.

Chapter Sixty-One

Wednesday, March 17

Looney and Gene drove back to the station. They parked and took the elevator to their floor without much chatter or discussion between them. Looney clearly was not ready to share his insight with Gene and Gene was thinking about the implications of tampering with the Porsche that injured Mrs. Adamson. He was actually considering listening to some jazz to help him get this straight but he was more of a country and western music listener. He was quite sure that for every difficult situation in life there was a country song title that perfectly described the situation or, better still, the solution. What immediately came to his mind was "I can't love you back," but that was not a good fit. He thought, "I gotta stop this or I'll spend the whole day just running song titles through my head instead of working on this case."

Meanwhile Looney found his desk, sat down and started searching through his computer for the Human Resource office number. When he found it he called and asked for someone who could tell him how to contact a retired policeman – and, yes, it was a specific policeman he was looking for.

After a brief wait, someone answered, "This is Melanie."

"Melanie, this is Detective Looney in Homicide. I wonder if you can help me find one of our retired officers?"

"Probably so, Detective, who are you looking for?"

"Norm Brookhalter, and I actually know where he is, I just don't have a contact number for him."

"Brookhalter, Norman. Let me see . . .," her voice dropped off and Looney could hear some clicking of her computer keyboard keys. After his long night, Looney was looking around for another cup of coffee. The stuff at the diner had seemed weak and wasn't helping him stay alert. He wondered if he had time to lay the phone down and go to the coffee pot in the back room for a cup before Melanie could find Norm's retirement papers and follow-up information. The longer he sat there and didn't get up and try for the coffee, the more he was sure that he should have gone some time before. He began thinking about how to have a secure coffee maker of his own at his desk when Melanie came back on the line.

"I have him living in Bowling Green with a contact number," she said without preamble.

"Yeah, that's right. I thought that's where he went."

"That was three years ago," Melanie added.

"Right. Can you give me the number?" Looney asked.

"Sure," she said and did so. Looney was impressed that this HR person was so cheerful and happy to be of assistance. That had not been his overall impression of those in the department that he had had dealings with in the past. But this was clearly different. He thanked Melanie and hung up. There had been something in one of the in-house bulletins recently about remembering internal 'customers' of the services in the department. Seemed like someone took that to heart.

He decided to go get that cup of coffee before calling Norm. He went first to the break room but looking at the thick liquid in the bottom of the pot and remembering that it was the responsibility of the one taking the last cup to make a new pot, he opted for a little walk down the block to the nearby coffee shop. He waved at Gene who appeared distracted but who waved briefly back. Looney took the stairs.

One floor down he met the Captain coming up.

"Looney," said Thor.

"Captain," responded Looney, carefully not making prolonged eye contact to reduce the likelihood of a prolonged conversation.

"Pot low?" asked the Captain as they passed.

"Yep."

" Get me one, too, then," Thor said without stopping. "I'm not gonna make a new pot either."

"Right," said Looney, also not pausing in his descent. This was a little unusual for the Captain to ask one of his detectives to run a personal errand but the circumstances – including that viscous remnant in the pot in the break room – made this completely understandable. And, anyway, Looney was in the mood for treating his 'internal customer' properly.

At the street he turned right and crossed at the corner entering the coffee shop in the middle of the next block. There was a short line to order and he took the time to review the deli options available in the glass case. It was creeping up toward noon and Looney was aware that he might end up sitting at his desk waiting for Norm to call back. He ended up grabbing a ham and cheese sandwich before stepping up to the counter and ordering two black coffees.

After paying, he grabbed the small tray holding the cups and the bag containing his lunch and headed back out the door.

Sitting back at his desk, Looney decided to eat the sandwich before making his call. Gene had left the office but came back just as Looney finished the last bite of his food. Gene had also gone for food – three burritos with ample hot sauce. "Hey," he said taking his seat at the desk next to Looney's.

"Yeah?" asked Looney.

"Made that call yet?"

"Nope. But I found him. He's up in Bowling Green."

"Oh yeah, I remember about that. He had some kind of part-time job up there. I think his wife is from there, too," Gene allowed.

Downing the last of the coffee, Looney said, " No time like the present." He picked up the phone, waited for dial tone and dialed. And someone answered on the second ring. "Hello?"

"Norm?"

"This is Norm."

"Storming Norman, this your old buddy, Ron Looney. How you doing, pal?"

"Walker? I haven't heard from you, old buddy, since I been up here. You must be wanting something."

"Well, you're right about that but can't I chat a bit first?"

"Sure. And how's the department treating you, Walker? You running things down there now, or are you calling me to see about getting a job up here?"

"No, none of that. Things are fine. Since you left Thor is three years closer to retirement. That's all. And he's still taking the stairs," Looney said, hearing Gene at the next desk almost snorting part of a burrito out his nose at the remark.

"Well, old buddy, it's pretty good up here, too. Fish are biting almost anytime you can get a hook in the water, neighborhood kids want to mow my lawn to make a little money – and that's all I pay 'em, too. A little. We bought a boat and get out in it several times in the summer. Are you looking to retire?

"Nope. I called because I need a little information and I thought you might be willing to help," Looney was putting on his 'this is important' voice tone.

"Oh sure, it's not a question about me helping out. I'm just the old retired guy with nothing to do. You'd be surprised what you gotta do every day when you're retired to just stay in the same place, none of it actually getting you ahead or anything.

"Hey," Looney said, "How'd we go from "It's great up here" to "Man, I'm working my butt off" in less than two minutes?"

"Whadda you need, old buddy," came the satisfied reply. Norm knew he had needled Looney sufficiently.

"As I recall you're doing some kind of deputy sheriff work in the county, right?"

"That's right," said Norm. "It's not a deputy, though. I'm a member of the Sheriff's Auxiliary."

"Auxiliary? Have you joined some woman's club up there, Norm?"

"Cut that out, Walker. The Auxiliary is a bunch of us that help the Sheriff on special occasions like all the festivals we have. Most of us are certified peace officers and many are retired police."

"You got a gun and a badge?"

"Damn straight."

"Then you're a deputy, man. And that's what I need," Looney was tickled to find that his contact actually had an official role in the county.

"What is it?" asked Norm

And Looney gave Norm a little background on the New City cases with Gene looking around the barrier between their desks and nodding his agreement with Looney's presentation. Norm got the story in the way Looney and Gene had gotten it, chronologically and with each step included its contemporary medical explanation. After setting the story and giving a little background on several of the major people of interest, Looney came to his point. He wanted Norm to visit one of the High Schools in the county, peruse the yearbooks of certain years and see what people remember about one particular student. Oh yeah, and do it right away.

Norm agreed and with a final couple of insults, both men signed off.

"So, what got you thinking in that direction, partner?" asked Gene after Looney had ended the conversation.

"You know all the trouble we've had trying to find some kind of motive?" Looney asked.

"Yeah, sure. But I still don't see . . ."

"Well, Gene Krupa couldn't have drummed it into my head any better than Joe Morello did last night. We've been stuck looking at these events in the order we learned them. We needed to look at them in the order in which they occurred."

Chapter Sixty-Two

Thursday, March 18

Thursday was a fairly usual day at New City. Ambulances arrived with sirens screaming and lights flashing as early as 0530. Doctors and nurses scurried from one area to another, trying not to run which might frighten patients. Others, carrying the ubiquitous cup of coffee moved deliberately on their rounds, checking what had happened in the previous 24 hours, noting new laboratory and radiographic results and ordering follow-up testing where needed. Patients were wheeled into the Operating Room and, later, back out. Some patients were examined and determined ready for discharge and another pile of forms was prepared to document their status, medication lists, knowledge about their condition and terms of their care after going home. Women were admitted to the Obstetric floor and created the most wonderful of hospital stays: one admission and two discharges.

Activity was pitched in some areas and dolorous in others and all in all, very ordinary. And the progression of the day was perceived differently by almost everyone involved. For some, it was tedium and boredom personified and for others the day raced by with their tasks pulling them in all directions without enough time to complete them.

Tom Bolling was one of those who thought the day would never get to noon, let alone end. He started that morning, as always, standing in his kitchen finishing his breakfast when Sandra came in.

"You didn't sleep very well last night, honey. Something up?" she greeted him as she went to get her orange juice.

"Yeah. I'm still thinking about Wil and the fact that Ron is pushing the murder angle."

"You agreed to give him a couple of days."

"That'll only get me to the weekend. What if that reporter guy starts snooping around? Sam will hear of it and all hell will break loose. I've got to tell him before that happens. But I can't do it just yet."

"I know you think he will over-react and get somebody running to the newspaper before Ron gets his chance. Can't you get Sam to understand the importance of giving Ron the time he's asked for?"

"The chances of Sam not wanting to take complete control of the situation are slim, none and no chance at all." Tom kissed his wife and went out the door headed for his car and a gloomy ride to New City.

At about the same time, Liz Adamson was having a cup of coffee with Virginia. She had regained her mental balance and was no longer crying at the slightest memory. But she wasn't her usual happy, smiling person, either. After the silence stretched out to four minutes, Virginia spoke, "It's been a week, Liz. Let's do something about cleaning out things."

"I don't really feel like it."

"I doubt you will ever think that cleaning up all of Wil's things is an enjoyable task or look forward to it. But it still needs to be done."

"Why now? I just want to sit and drink my coffee. I can always do it later."

"You mean after I leave? I don't see that happening. You need a push. I'm a pusher."

"That's been your role in the family all right," Betty said with a slight upturn of the sides of her mouth.

"And we don't have to do it all today," Virginia said, grabbing on the little bit of encouragement. "Let's just do one room – the bedroom."

"You know that's going to be the hardest!"

"Then it will all be downhill after we get that one done."

They agreed to take frequent breaks for more coffee and went down the hall to the bedroom.

Less than a half hour later they had boxed up the items that belonged to Wil from the bedside table and the small bookcase next to the overstuffed chair where he liked to sit and read before retiring. They agreed not to discard the books but everything else had to go. He had saved bottles of eye drops in the top drawer of the bedside table, along with some nasal spray for allergies, a couple pair of old reading glasses and some ticket stubs from previous airline trips.

"What in the world did he want these for?" asked Virginia. "Was he planning a collage of his tickets?"

"Those aren't ticket stubs once they go in that drawer," said Betty. "Those are bookmarks. He kept them so he would always have a way to mark his place when he read in bed."

"What about the clock radio, leave it?"

"Yes. I can see it from my side and it orients me in the middle of the night. Just leave it there on the bookcase."

"OK. Do you want me to start in the bathroom?"

"No. Much as I will hate it, I know what's his and what's mine." In spite of this bravado, Liz's shoulders slumped when she opened the medicine chest and saw various items that brought back a memory of Wil so forceful she had to sit on the commode.

"You going to be alright?" Virginia asked from the doorway.

"In a second. I just had a vision of him standing there shaving. I'll be OK in a minute."

Virginia left her there and went back in the bedroom and in a minute she heard the clinking of items being tossed in the small wastebasket. Liz took a short time to get the razors, nail clippers, shaving cream, brushes, whitening toothpaste, styptic pencil and assorted medications out of the cabinet. When she had removed all the items belonging to her late husband she looked at the bare shelves and realized Wil had taken a much larger share of the cabinet than she had and that she had never noticed it. The bareness of the shelves and the now seemingly insignificant space taken up by her items seemed to mirror her new life. The big emptiness of the bathroom medicine cabinet mocked her and once again the emptiness of her life caused the emptiness in her to feel like a vacuum that would collapse inside her into nothingness. She sat back down on the commode and quietly started crying again.

Looney was sitting at his desk, moving various pieces of paper around before placing them in the order he wanted them in the Murder Book. The Book was filled with clear plastic envelopes and the detectives kept all their pertinent evidence in these folders. Pictures of crime scenes, affidavits from witnesses, transcripts of interviews, references to evidence in bags kept in storage, it was all there. Looney had entered all the material into the plastic sleeves as he went along but now he was re-organizing the envelopes in a new order. He knew all these items by heart so he didn't spend much time looking at them or reading their content.

When he finished, he looked at his empty cup of coffee and started to get up when his partner, who had been watching the envelope shuffling said, "Let's go down the street. The pot here is close to empty."

Looney put the Murder Book on the back of his desk, pushed his chair back and stood, grabbed his coat off the hook on the divider between their desks and said, "Your idea. You buying?"

"Hell, no. I've been waiting for you to get through with all that shuffling nonsense. I'm the injured party here, you buy."

"Let's go Dutch. I'm gonna have a bun," Looney said leading the way to the back stairs.

Heading down, one behind the other, they met the Captain coming up when they hit the second floor.

"Cap'n."

"Looney."

"Captain."

"Novalchek."

When the Captain was almost ten steps beyond them he hollered back down the staircase, "You guys got anything you need to tell me, yet?"

Looney answered, "Nope. We're just sluffing off."

"I know you're waiting on a warrant. Got to be something there, right?" Now they were all stopped, standing about a half staircase apart and talking more loudly than normal.

"We'll see. After we get the warrant. Have a good day, Cap'n," Looney said turning and hurrying down the rest of the stairs.

At the coffee shop they sat at a corner table where both could see the door and drank their coffee. Looney, true to his word, got a morning bun and slowly ate it by unwrapping it down to the center, one bite at a time.

"You sure about this warrant?" Gene asked.

"Sure as I can be without having the evidence in my hand. In fact, I'm so sure I'm gonna tell you that you just might make that basketball game anyway.""

Looney had asked one of the Assistant District Attorneys to present his findings to the judge to request the warrant. He preferred, just on principle, to not have unnecessary contact with the judiciary. Once, in the past, when a judge questioned his reasoning for a warrant, Looney had been personally offended and let it show. Looney was certain that his reaction resulted in the judge deciding against the request and denying the warrant. Looney was also certain that the resulting delay had almost allowed their suspect to escape jurisdiction. Almost. But the possibility had remained in his head whenever a case demanded a warrant. Now he was better off - content one almost could say - to let one of the ADAs handle the personal aspect with the judge. Besides he found it useful to articulate his reasoning to the ADA who also would challenge any weaknesses in the request. Slow to admit that he had actually learned something from these encounters, he had pondered these situations and discussed ramifications with Meg. Somehow, largely through the rationalizations of his wife, Looney took such challenges as attempts to help him strengthen his petition for a warrant rather than as an attack on his analysis of the case.

Now they were just down to waiting, waiting to see if Looney's case and the ADA's presentation was enough to get the warrant. Looney and Gene had laid out a plan for implementing the warrant earlier that morning. Part of that plan involved Looney getting some interviews set up at New City. But he would wait on those until the warrant was in their hands. For now it was hot coffee and sweet bread . . . and musing with his partner.

Beverly had forgotten the call from Dan Edderman and was busy working on a credentialing and privileging package for a plastic surgeon applying for access to New City. She was rightly impressed with the man's training and his recommendations from a previous worksite in Memphis. His credentials all seemed in order and Bev was simply checking all the boxes in the New City format before sending the package to the Surgical Credentialing Group. At mid-morning she made a run out to the coffee kiosk in the lobby and brought back a latte for herself and one for Mary. They were past the 'hump' day but in a hospital where only a small amount of the day-to-day activity can be scheduled, both women were quite busy rounding up paperwork from earlier in the week and setting meeting schedules and prioritizing time and effort to get things done. Both of them bought into Tom's adage of 'get today's work done today' even if sometimes that meant they weren't able to end their 'day' at five o'clock. Bev had spoken briefly to Tom before the morning meeting but not afterward. He had stayed in the room with Sam and she assumed they had discussed something that needed privacy. Since then she had been in her office working on the C&P package. As she sipped on her latte and selected the next bit of paperwork there was a knock on her door and she looked up to see Angela Pirini leaning around the doorframe.

"Dr. Pirini, come in. How can I help you?"

"Good morning, Bev. I have a funny little request. Sheila told me this morning that Wil was planning to attend the American College of Cardiology meeting next month. He was on one of their Guideline Committees. Is that right?"

"That's right. I had forgotten about that trip. He and Dr. Bolling discussed the workload of the Committee and decided the outcome was worth us supporting him. Baltimore, I think," Bev said thinking about where she might have filed that information.

"Well, the Guideline he was to work on involves repeat placement of coronary stents – and that's really my specialty," Angela said, coming completely into the office.

"Oh, I see," said Beverly, wondering where this conversation was going.

"And so I thought maybe I could make that trip instead of Wil. If the funding is all set anyway, I mean."

"Uh huh," said Beverly. "I think that would be up to Tom – Dr. Bolling – at least," said Beverly. "What about the College?"

"I actually called them when I found out about Wil's involvement and all. The chair of the Committee knows me and said he would think it perfectly appropriate for me to replace Wil. He hadn't heard about Wil's death and was pretty taken aback by it."

Beverly nodded, remembering where she had filed the paperwork on Wilford's trip. "I'm pretty sure that the Education Committee would agree with you taking his place. Could you get the chair of that committee to write a letter asking for you to attend?"

"No problem. He already offered."

"Get that to me and I'll talk to Dr. Bolling and we'll send it back to the Committee. I doubt there'll be a problem."

"Thanks," Angela said waving as she slid back around the doorframe and out the door.

Dan Edderman stood in the lobby at New City, sipping on a tall Americano, watching to see who entered the hallway where he had seen the two detectives earlier. He had already figured out that the two hallways on either side of the elevator bank led to the offices of clinical and administrative staff. By his rough count over the past hour he had seen more than a dozen individuals come and go from each hallway. Each hallway was closed off with a single glassed door of frosted glass. Across the elevator lobby was the door to the Director's office; it was larger and was of solid clear glass. Edderman had asked the lobby guard and discovered that door led to the office not only of the Director but also the Chief of Staff, the Associate Director and the Chief Nurse. The 'Head Shed' someone called it and Dan recognized the military connotation and ascribed that to what he had found out about Tom Bolling, MD, retired Brigadier General USAF. He had scoped out that location and spent some time researching Tom Bolling in preparation for calling him on Tuesday. The person he talked to did not sound like a Brigadier General but Dan was accustomed to people trying to be something they were not when they talked with him. Usually, however, most of those he interviewed wanted to appear more important than they actually were and as if they had far better insight and information than they actually did. It was unusual, but not without precedent, that the General would deny knowledge and act like he was uninformed. But now Dan knew where to catch him when he needed to. But first, he wanted some further information about why the detectives had gone into the West hallway next to the elevators.

The East hallway door, closest to the front door, opened into a plain paneled area that Dan could see from his vantage point. There were no doorways near to the opening so he couldn't see any titles on doors. But, over the time he had been watching, every person who entered that door was wearing dress clothes, a suit and tie or a dress. He decided that the East hallway led to a series of administrative offices. It didn't matter to him what those offices were or what they dealt with because the detectives had entered the West door when he had seen their hurried approach and, shortly thereafter, their slower walk back into the Head Shed hallway.

The West doorway opened into a similarly paneled area like on the east, also without any titled doorways visible behind. Many, but not all, of those entering the west doorway were wearing white coats and carrying stethoscopes and Dan concluded this doorway led to some sort of clinical area. After several hours of careful watching he realized he had not seen anyone resembling a patient – street clothes, on a cane or in a wheelchair or even needing assistance from another person. He decided this was not a clinical area for seeing outpatients. This was most likely the office area for certain clinical specialties. That's where the Chief of Staff and the detectives had gone – to someone's office. Someone on the clinical staff was involved in some way with the visit of two homicide detectives to New City.

Sam Mastone stepped out of his office to speak with his secretary, Diane Ruttiger. Diane had been the secretary to the Director of New City for nearly twenty years, the last seven working for Sam. She considered him the second-best director she had worked for; bright and energetic but somewhat impetuous and impatient. Her gray hair gave her, as she explained it, experience to know how to deal with different Directors and Sam was not really that big a challenge to her. She quickly assessed what his needs were and made sure that every day she supplied those needs as soon as he asked for them – and occasionally beforehand. In that frame of mind she knew when he stepped out that he was going to confirm that a scheduled conference call with a small subcommittee of the ACHE was going to occur and that there had been no change. Sam had been elevated to Fellowship in the American College of Healthcare Executives just three years before and was proud to have been asked to serve on this subcommittee. Diane had dealt directly with the office of the chair of the committee and arranged the call at a time that would not conflict with other events on Sam's schedule. There really weren't many items on his schedule and the task was not all that difficult but Sam acted as if it was very hard to find time for such tasks. But, he accepted the arrangement she had made and had asked every day to ensure no change had occurred.

"Diane, the ACHE call is in 15 minutes, isn't it?" Sam said, looking not at her but at his watch.

"Yes, sir. Have you decided whether to have anyone else on the call?" A couple of times in the past Sam had decided at the very last moment to have one or more people join him on such a call and she had sometimes had difficulty in finding them in time.

"No. I don't think so. How long is it going to last again?"

"Mr. Hudgens said to block off an hour but it wouldn't likely go that long."

"Right. Right. OK. I'll be in here," he said, ducking back into his office.

"I wonder if he thought I believed he would be anywhere else," Diane said to herself and then looked around to make sure she hadn't said that out loud.

Monique Song was in the Autopsy Room reviewing some findings with a group of house staff. The resident, an eager guy from Texas, had both interns and the three students from his team there to observe the pathological findings so as to compare them to the clinical findings they had made prior to death. The patient was a 66-year-old man with poorly controlled diabetes and who had come to the hospital two days previously with fever, cough and a dense infiltrate in both lungs. All members of the team had examined him and the resident had each of them draw a picture of their findings on chest exam; now he wanted them to compare their original findings and the changes that occurred over the last two days with what they could see at autopsy. The chest cavity was open and Monique was poking on the lungs.

"Very congested, almost hard in some of the lower lobes," she said directing each of the students to feel the lung tissue. "How much effusion did you think was in there?"

The answers varied from 100 milliliters to 2 liters and drew some wry smiles from both Monique and the resident. She said, " it takes a minimum of 300 milliliters of pleural effusion to even blunt the angles on the chest x-ray, so if you see evidence of an effusion, its got to be more than that."

The resident spoke up, "remember how we percussed out the top of the effusion?" Everyone nodded. "That would indicate about 1-2 liters"

"But it was really hard to do that because he couldn't sit up," said one of the female students.

Monique spoke again, "Did you try using the tuning fork?"

"How does that work?" one of them asked.

"I should have thought of that," said the resident. "If you put the tuning fork on the sternum and snap the tongs, and listen with your stethoscope, the vibration sound changes at the top of the effusion. You can hear it through the stethoscope very clearly and it's actually more accurate than percussion. And you don't need the patient to make a sound."

Monique remembered that she had taught that concept to that resident two years before and smiled to herself. She really enjoyed teaching. Much more than she had enjoyed her time in the medical examiner's office. She wanted so much to forget what was going on upstairs about Wilford's death.

"Now let's measure the amount of effusion after I take these lungs out," she said to the group.

Dan Edderman had a directory of medical staff at New City. He had looked up the office numbers for each of them and quickly noted that only the cardiologists had room numbers in the one hundreds. That meant that the western hallway opened into a suite of offices that held only cardiologists. Another quick look through the list confirmed that all the cardiologists were down that hallway. Further, the directory gave titles for the various physicians: Director of Non-invasive Cardiology, Director of Intensive Care, etc. Dan decided that Monday morning he would begin his investigation by interviewing the Director of Cardiology, Wilford Adamson, MD.

Tom was standing at Mary Brighthouse's desk as Sam walked through the common area. Tom glanced at Sam carrying his overcoat and cocked his head inquiringly.

"I'm having lunch with the Mayor. At the Club." Sam said by way of explanation, but actually making certain that those within hearing knew he was on important business.

"Have the sweet potato fries," Tom said. "They're much better than the others." This was Tom's way of letting the Director know that he, too, had eaten at 'the Club'.

"If you say so," Sam said sliding into his coat and heading out the door.

"And I'm going to have a working lunch with Roslyn," he said *sotto voce.* Mary smiled and said, "want me to page you at a particular time?"

"Sure," he said. "We can't spend more than an hour together without getting into the 'handmaiden' thing. I've had a long career in surgery and have never seen a nurse treated like a handmaiden. That urban legend just won't die."

Tom left the office area and headed for the canteen to get a sandwich and a drink to have for lunch in his office. Roslyn would join him there with her lunch shortly.

"Does anyone ever make a new pot of coffee," asked Gene. He and Looney had been sitting in their chairs for three hours waiting for a call. And nothing was happening. Looney had called his friend in the DA's office but got no answer. So the two detectives sat and re-talked their understanding of the case to that point, searching for weaknesses.

"It's all gonna come down to the warrant," Looney opined. "We are never gonna get a confession without something turning up from the warrant."

"Yeah," said Gene, "and I remember a couple of times when we thought that and never could get a warrant because the case was so thin."

"Won't happen this time," Looney said looking heavenward as if imploring a Higher Power to convince the judge. "This ADA knows her business. She understands these weak points and has all my arguments to make them stronger."

"Yeah, well it's almost four o'clock. I thought she was going over this morning to get the damn thing signed."

"Yeah, well, who knows? Schedules are tough right now."

"Don't I know it? Especially tight when it comes to making a new pot of coffee. If it wasn't so late in the day, I might just have to go make one."

They both shrugged and stood up. They were clearly committed to going back to the coffee shop. But their good intentions fell short for a common reason – something more important intervened. They didn't get their coffee right then because the phone rang.

Beverly stuck her head in the door of Tom's office and said, "Hey, it's almost four thirty. I'm going to leave a little early to stop by the garden shop on the way home. It's planting time, you know."

"I know it's too early to be planting tomatoes, yet."

"I'm planting some impatiens and border liriope around the front porch."

"Can you eat that stuff?" Tom asked jokingly.

"Sure, if you're hungry enough." Beverly waved and left. She heard the phone ringing in Tom's office as she walked out.

Chapter Sixty-Three

Friday, March 19

Looney drove alone to New City that Friday morning. He had called the day before to set up some additional interviews and he arrived early to be certain that everything else was set up. After parking in the Visitors' Lot he walked around to the front of the building in order to enter the main lobby. He paused just inside the door and glanced around at the various people there. The usual gathering of employees and an occasional visitor were clustered around the coffee kiosk. Others were seated on some of the chairs scattered about the lobby into small seating areas, each with its own central rug and coffee table. Looney paid particular attention to these individuals without really seeming to do so. The expected adult with a child, an elderly couple quietly huddled together, two separate bored teens with ear buds thumbing through a magazine. None of these looked like a newspaper reporter hanging around waiting for a break. But you never could be certain.

After a bit, Looney joined the clutch of coffee seekers and ordered himself a medium sized Americano. Shunning the milk and sweetener bar, he then ambled across the lobby and stopped just outside the door to the Director's Suite and turned back to scan the lobby. Still, there was no suggestion of a reporter skulking. Looney didn't really care if Edderman saw him today or not. He thought, 'If ever you were going to be lurking around, today's the day it you should be'. He pulled the door open and entered.

Tom was waiting for him just outside his own office. Looney greeted Tom and Mary and waved his coffee at them. "Already got mine and I'm ready to go."

"You're clearly ahead in the game," said Tom. "We've got things set up for you in the conference room." He led the way across the common area of the suite and into the conference room. There, he gave Looney his choice about where to sit. He chose the end of the table, the chair that Sam Mastone usually sat in for the morning meetings. Tom sat next to him on the left side of the table after closing the door. "What's the deal here, Ron?" he asked. "We've got the interviews all set up and Mary is getting them settled in the outer suite. You've been rather secretive about this and we're getting down to the end of the 'couple of days' we agreed on. I really am going to have to talk to Sam – the Director – today."

"The deal is, I'm pretty sure I know what happened and who is responsible for Adamson's death. And I think I'm right about the young girl, too."

"Patricia Harding?"

"Yes. And I think the two are related. The cases, I mean."

"And they have something to do with the two interviews we have set up?"

"If I'm right, when I walk out of here we will have the answers."

'Where's Gene?" Tom asked, suddenly off topic. "Why don't you have your partner with you?"

Looney leaned back in his chair with a tight grin on his face and said, "Gene's getting the proof. Likely pretty soon if it's there at all. That's why I asked you to not mention these interviews to anyone until this morning."

"I didn't. Are you going to tell me why?"

"Of course I am, Tom. But not till after the interviews. Think we can get started now?"

The first interview was with Sheila Hester, Dr. Adamson's long-time secretary. Tom allowed Looney to step to the door and call Sheila into the conference room. As Looney stood in the open doorway he noticed that Angela Pirini was also in the suite. He nodded at her and ushered Sheila into the conference room.

"Please have a seat, Ms Hester."

She did so, at the same time asking, "What's this all about, detective?"

"I just have a few questions about the day that Dr. Adamson died. Do you mind?"

"No. Not at all. Anything I can do."

"Well, last time we talked, I was rather rushed and all I have are some little notes," Looney said as he laid his battered notebook on the table. "I really would like to have a better record of the events that morning, if you don't mind."

"I'll do anything I can."

"Fine, I'd just like to have you walk through the events that morning again with me and I'll record the conversation." As he said this he took a small pocket recorder out of his coat pocket and set it on the table. Sheila looked at it warily, but nodded her assent.

"Now, for this recording to be useful to me, I need to make sure that you acknowledge the recording. I'll ask your name and if you know you are being recorded."

"Are you going to read me my rights?" she asked.

"No, why do you ask that?" Looney was a little taken aback.

"Well, I watch those television shows and the police always tell people their rights before they start questioning them," she answered somewhat more sure of herself.

"Ms Hester, we only read people their rights after we arrest them. You are not going to be arrested."

"Oh. All right, then."

Looney started the tape and identified himself and gave the date and location and the circumstances and then asked Sheila to give her full name and assent to be recorded. Then he asked her to think back to the morning of Wilford Adamson's death and to tell him everything she remembered about what happened in the office that day. She told him about arriving just before 8:00 AM, hanging her coat on the hook behind the door and sitting at her desk to examine her email for urgent messages. She remembered that Wilford entered a little after 8:00AM with Don Horvath, a first year Fellow in Cardiology. They were arguing about Dr. Horvath having to leave the program in the summer and how he wanted to stay and thought he should be allowed to stay. She remembered that Wilford opened the door to his office and entered with Dr. Horvath right behind him but they both came back out shortly and Wilford had walked Dr. Horvath back out to the hallway.

Sheila said she had left the office area right after that to deliver some schedules to other members of the division. She thought she was gone for less than five minutes and when she returned Dr. Adamson was sitting at his desk and Angela Pirini was sitting in front of him and they were talking something about the upcoming Match. Sheila said she asked if they needed anything and they said no and she went to her desk. A few minutes later Angela came out and fixed each of them another shot of espresso from the office machine and took them back into Wilford's office. Shortly after that he got a page and left the office without speaking.

Looney asked her to repeat what she had told him earlier about the tradition of Angela meeting with Wilford and 'topping up' their coffee. She recounted that Angela brought both their cups out into the secretarial office area where he espresso machine was located and opened drawers to get the coffee pods while still talking to Wilford. She, Angela, put the pods in the machine, pressed the button and repeated this for the second cup. Then she stirred each of the cups and carried them back into Wilford's office.

On direct questioning, Sheila noted that this process of morning discussion and topping up cups was a tradition between the two doctors. She said Dr. Pirini sometimes called it 'getting her Wilford fix'.

She said no one else came into the office that morning before Adamson left to answer the page. She again told how Angela left Wilford's office and said to her, "Better him than me."

Looney was letting her tell the story for the most part and only occasionally having to ask a follow-up question or remind her of something she had said before. He was impressed that Sheila was observant and had a good memory.

As he was about to ask a couple of follow-up questions at the end, his cell phone buzzed and he excused himself from the conversation, turned off the recorder and answered the call. He moved to the far end of the conference room and spoke sparingly on his end of the conversation which lasted a little over three minutes and ended with Looney saying, "That's it, then. I'll take care of my end."

He returned to the head of the table and said, "Ms Hester, I appreciate your taking the time to repeat all this for me. I think that's all I need to know right now." He pulled her chair out for her and opened the door to the conference room for her to exit. He closed the door and sat down next to Tom who asked, "Now what was all that about? Recording her answers? Do you think she had something to do with Wil's death?"

"No, I don't," Looney answered. "But she has some very good testimony to support my case against the one who did. Let's talk to Dr. Pirini and maybe this will all become more clear."

Looney went back to the door and indicated to Angela that he was ready for her to come in. Again, he offered her a chair and held it for her then sat down and went through the business of getting her permission to record the conversation. She also seemed a little uneasy about the taping of the session but finally agreed. And once again

Looney started off by giving his name and the date and circumstances and asking her to spell her name and indicate she knew she was being recorded.

Then he asked, conversationally, "Could you again tell me about the morning when Dr. Adamson died? I mean what went on in the office and what you and he talked about and what you did?"

Angela shifted around a little in the chair and smiled at Looney and said, "Sure. Where do you want me to start?"

"At the beginning," he smiled.

"Well, I got to the hospital about 7:30 that morning. I got my coffee and went to the office. No one was there and I went to my desk to check on emails and stuff."

"Was Ms Hester at her desk?"

"Not when I got there. But I heard her come in a little before eight."

"Go on."

"Wil . . .Dr. Adamson came in shortly after that and I heard him arguing with Don Horvath."

"What about?"

"Same thing Don's been after everybody about in the last week or so. His fellowship was terminated."

"Why was that? Bad performance?"

"No. No, no. He was in a one-year slot. There's not any funding for that position after one year. We put residents into that slot to give them a chance to fill one of the three-year slots if someone drops out. No one did this year and Don doesn't have job for next year."

"Do you do that a lot?"

"Every other year or so. More often than not we know someone is going to drop out of the three-year track and we set this up for insurance."

"So, it's sort of like a redshirt year?"

"Well, a little. Except there's no guarantee they'll make the team the next year. And Don didn't and he was mad."

"How mad?" Looney leaned forward as he asked this question, putting pen to a page in his notebook.

"Well, he was more like begging for continuation."

"Are you saying he wasn't really angry? What did you hear them say?"

"Don was asking was it something he did and Wil was saying it doesn't matter, the issue is closed. Let it go."

"Was Don about to let it go? Or was he the type to make something of this. Take some action to get back at Dr. Adamson?" Looney was giving Angela an opening to create doubt about Don, maybe even to get him identified as a suspect in Wilford's death.

She didn't bite. "No. Don is a very introspective person. He was feeling that the decision to not keep him in the program was all his fault – and it sorta was. I mean, Don's a funny guy. Keeps to himself. Studies a lot but he can't be relied on to remember a patient's history or medication list. Someone had to go behind him and make sure all the stuff got done. I really don't think he would think of hurting anyone."

"What happened after that?"

"After Don left I went over to see Wi . . .Dr. Adamson. We usually start off days sharing a cup and getting our schedules straight."

"What does that mean?"

"We'd just talk about what we had to do that day. It wasn't any arranging of things to do. We just shared that time and those events. We did that almost from the time I got here. Started doing that when it was just the two of us. It was just a little habit of ours."

"What did you talk about that day?"

"The Match, like I told you before. And the patients that were admitted over the weekend. Just stuff."

"Did you tell him about Patricia Harding?"

A slight pause. "Who is that?"

"One of the admissions over the weekend. Funny heart rhythm of some sort."

"Oh, yes. I remember her. I'm sure I did. But she died. Why are you asking about her?"

"I wondered if you remembered her." Looney leaned back nonchalantly in his chair. Angela relaxed after initially tensing with the change in direction of the line of questioning.

With a little shrug, Looney went on, "And at one point you went out and got some coffee for each of you."

"Yes," she said, relaxing again. "We both get an extra shot of espresso and add it to the morning cup."

"Did you add anything else?" asked Looney seemingly off-handedly.

Another short pause. Then Angela cocked her head to one side and asked, "What are you asking, Detective? Are you asking if I tried to poison Dr. Adamson?"

"Did you?"

"Certainly not! Why are you asking that?"

"I'm just asking whether you added anything else to his cup than just 'another shot of espresso'."

"Why would you ask that?"

"Because Sheila told me she saw you stirring Wilford Adamson's cup just before you took it back and gave it to him to drink. And because the reason he died was from an overdose of nitrates he would not have knowingly taken because he was also taking Cialis. And because the nitrates caused him to go into shock shortly after they were administered and no one else had the opportunity to do it other than you. And because I know he doesn't put anything in his coffee that needs stirring. That's why I'm asking." Looney's voice had become harder throughout this brief discourse. He was again leaning forward and speaking harshly to Dr. Pirini said, "Now what's the answer? Did you put nitrates in Wilford Adamson's coffee on the morning of his death?"

Tom Bolling sat speechless at the table, transfixed in his chair and staring alternately at Angela and then at Looney. He knew better than to interrupt Looney's interrogation at this point but his mind was racing over all the possibilities. In spite of his own misgivings about one of the staff being responsible for Wil's death, Tom instinctively knew that Looney was right about the time line.

Angela sat in her chair, bolt upright as all the color drained from her face. Her nostrils flared and she took several deep breaths before answering.

"No, I didn't put anything in his coffee, then or ever. Sheila was just wrong!" Her voice started out strong but broke before she finished her statement. Then she looked down in her lap and folded her hands.

Looney responded, "What I do have is confidence that Sheila was right in her description. And I also have confidence I can pin the attempt on the good doctor's life back in January when you tampered with his car."

Tom Bolling snapped back in his chair so abruptly that Looney looked over at him quickly to ensure he would not interrupt. Angela's head also snapped up with bewilderment in her eyes. "What . . . what are you talking about?" she cried, hesitatingly.

"You tampered with his front end on that little Porsche and caused the wreck that could've killed his wife. But you were aiming at getting him weren't you?" Looney was no longer the laid back cop; he was an aggressive interrogator, pushing the moment and his advantage over a suspect.

"I . . I . . I don't know what you mean. I don't know anything about cars and all. Where'd you get that idea?"

"Well, I got that idea from your high school yearbook where you said your goal was to be the first woman working in the pit for an Indy 500 race car winner. And the fact that you took the mechanics course in your senior year and that you worked in your father's garage during summers. I got that idea from the fact that you are a very accomplished mechanic."

Andrea and Tom were both open-mouthed in astonishment. She finally struggled to say, 'You . . . you can't prove any of that!" but she sounded more hopeful than certain.

Looney stood and said, "If I had a nickel for every time someone said that . . . I just got a call from Gene – he's at your house right now, executing a warrant to search for evidence of your involvement. He found the wrenches you used on the Porsche in your garage toolbox; right on top, still got grease on them we can match to the Porsche. And the kicker was he found the veterinarian glucose solution and the insulin syringes in the cabinet in the garage, too. Only thing missing would be a selfie of you doing the deed!"

"I . . Well I don't think I have to say anything. I want a lawyer."

"And you shall have one. Please stand up." She sat immobile for a moment and then slowly stood up. Looney moved behind her, placed handcuffs on her and said, "Angela Pirini, you are under arrest for the murder of Wilford Adamson. Anything you say can and will be used against you in a court of law. If you cannot afford a lawyer, one will be provided for you. Do you understand what I just said?"

Angela stood quietly with her head down, not speaking. "Do you understand what I just said?" Looney asked again. This time she nodded, dispiritedly, and said "Yes," in a whisper. He took her by the arm and led her out of the room. In the director's ante suite two uniformed policemen met them. They took control and led her out toward the lobby and a waiting car just outside the front door.

Looney remained in the suite for a moment and then walked back to the conference room where Tom was still sitting, somewhat stunned, in his chair.

"Sorry, I couldn't tell you what was going on, Tom," Looney said leaning against the conference table. "We were waiting until we were sure she was here before executing the search warrant on her house. Gene found the wrench she used on Dr. Adamson's car as well as the box the veterinarian sugar water came in. This is all pretty tight. She doped the Patricia girl to set up some kind of catastrophe with Dr. Adamson."

Tom shook his head and said, "I never would have expected this. Why in the hell would she try to kill the guy who was mentoring her?"

"We may never get to the bottom of it all. But I gotta go. I'm going to have a long session with her down at the station and I'll let you know whatever I find out."

"Ron?"

"Yeah?"

"What if she'd tried to run when I called her about coming down here this morning?"

A small smile. "Wouldn't have worked. I had her car booted."

And Looney walked out leaving Tom open-mouthed in the conference room. Then he stood up, shook his head and walked out of the room and over to Diane's desk. "Sam available?" he asked.

Diane had watched the parade of Angela in handcuffs out the door and now looked at Tom with wide eyes and nodded. Tom took a deep breath, knocked once on the director's door and, without waiting for an answer, opened the door and went in.

"We need to talk," he said as he closed the door behind him.

Chapter Sixty-Four

Friday, March 19

That afternoon, Tom pulled into his driveway thinking, "TGIF". He turned off the ignition and sat for a moment, relishing the quiet. There had been precious little quiet at New City that day with all sorts of disruptions to schedules and at least 43 different staff members whispering to him, "You can tell me . . . certainly you can let me know the details!"

But he had only spoken to Sam and to Bev. Sam had been sufficiently shocked by the possibility of a misstatement that he agreed to let Tom, Bev and Johnny Taliaferro handle all the press details. Tom had personally called Daniel Edderman with the Reader's Digest story and promised him more details after Looney finished his investigation and Angela had been arraigned.

Now as he tried to enjoy the quiet in the truck, Tom was aware of a persistent echo in his ears of all the shouting and hubbub from the day's activities. And he hadn't gotten his second cup of coffee – afraid to go in the lobby for all the attention. But he knew he owed Sandra a fuller explanation than what he gave her on the phone right after talking to Sam. Surely she would have seen all the newscasts that afternoon with their speculation and attempted fabrications of the 'truth at New City'.

He left the truck and walked to the front door to find her there, waiting.

"Hey," she said pushing the door open for him.

"Hey back," he said. "Can we lock all the doors and go hide in the basement?"

"Sure. It's our house. We can even leave and go spend the weekend somewhere in Kentucky. But I want to hear the whole story while we do it."

Right then Looney's car turned in the drive and stopped right behind Tom's truck. Ron got out and looked around. Tom called from the doorway, "You looking for a hideout?"

"Nope. I was wondering why the press hasn't descended on you like chickens on a June bug."

"I told them you would have them arrested for witness tampering if they came to my house."

"That's a good one. I'm gonna use that myself next time. Can I come in?"

A few minutes later they were seated in the den, each with a drink and Tom with his shoes off and feet propped up. He started off asking Looney what he considered the key question, "What made you think it was Angela?"

"It fell together after I realized I was looking at things in the order they came to my attention and the secret was to see them in their own chronology."

"What do you mean?"

"For a while I thought of the car accident as something that happened to Mrs. Adamson and I learned of it after the other two deaths. Then one night I was re-examining the facts and the timeline jumped up in front of me. Mrs. Adamson's 'accident' was actually the first attempt on Dr. Adamson."

"Really?" asked Sandra.

"So, then it was a relatively simple task to reshuffle the ideas we had about motive, means and opportunity – after the mechanic confirmed that the Doctor's Porsche had been tampered with, I just had to determine who would benefit from the Doctor's death."

"And you settled on Angela because . . .?" asked Tom.

"Proximity, and the timing of when the Doctor dropped. You and the good Doctor Song told me it would be fast and she was the last to see him. I had a friend check her hometown and it turned out she was a first rate mechanic before going to college and med school."

"And she admitted all these things?" Tom asked, still uncertain.

Looney explained he had not had much trouble at all getting the whole story out of Andrea. She had been rather sullen and close-mouthed at first but when Looney started questioning why she would do something so drastic to someone who was looking out for her career she came undone and spilled a year's worth of venom. Things had been so straightforward that he had waved Gene off to Dayton for the basketball tournament.

According to Angela Pirini, she did not see Wilford Adamson as a mentor or a helper in her career or even, lately, as a friend. According to her, his referral of her for a position at Tulane was what had opened her eyes to how Wilford viewed her. She thought he was recommending her for a position in the Tulane department that would be a step upward in her career. And she visited the campus and interviewed with the chairman thinking of that type of career move. But, she was quite mistaken about the position and was told quite frankly by the chairman that what they were recruiting was someone to do exactly what she had already done and was even then still doing for New City and South West Ohio Medical School Department of Cardiology – set up, develop and run an academic CCU. The position was not any sort of advancement; in fact it was a parallel move, same academic appointment and same job title and the very same day-to-day job activities and expectations. Tulane wanted her to do exactly what she was doing – and had exhibited skill and acumen in so doing – that she was doing at New City – except that Tulane was several years behind where she was in New City and she would be expected to build the program all over again.

Initially she tried to see the value of the referral. She was being recognized as having built something really good and others wanted to get on the bandwagon. Clearly she would be the right person to make that program run at Tulane and she might even get additional recognition and funding for expansions. But the more she thought about why Wilford had recommended her it came down to him thinking that's all she had to offer. She thought he was giving up on her upward mobility in national cardiology as someone who had already reached her potential. Then she began to consider that the recommendation was more self-serving even than she had thought. She became convinced that Wilford was trying to get rid of her. Offering her a lateral arabesque, of sorts. She was pretty locked in at New City and at the University but she wasn't getting any grants and the last teaching award was over five years ago. Maybe he saw her as plateauing in her career and maybe he wanted to find someone else who would carry the department forward.

Then she became angry that Wilford wouldn't talk with her about the recommendation or explain his decision to mention her to the Tulane search committee. All this had gone through her mind and thoughts during the plane trip back from New Orleans. By the time she arrived back in Cincinnati she was persuaded that Wilford was trying to get her out of New City, that he didn't appreciate her organizational skills and how she had turned the CCU into a prime teaching experience for staff, faculty and students in the system. Further, she decided, Wilford was not going to help her move upward and she would have to make those steps and opportunities come through her won efforts.

After returning to work and seeing that Wilford didn't show any interest in discussing her visit she decided that her next steps might best be to show New City and the University that Wilford Adamson wasn't necessary in the Chief's chair at New City – in fact, it would be good to show everyone that the department could get along very well without him.

Her initial plans, she claimed, never included killing him. Even though she was upset with him for many reasons, she said she was never trying to kill him. Her initial plan was to loosen the tie rods on his Porsche to cause Wilford to have an accident that would take him out of the Chair for several weeks or months – during which time she would (naturally) take over and run the department. Her approach to recruiting both residents and faculty would convince others, possibly including the Chief of Staff, to help her get on a fast track for upward mobility.

That thought led her to tamper with the Porsche while Wilford and Elizabeth were out in Colorado visiting family. She thought Wilford would take the car the morning after their return and have trouble getting on the Interstate; she imagined a car in the ditch scenario with Wilford having one or two broken legs and being out of commission for 6-8 weeks. Angela never considered that Liz would take the Porsche and run out for eggs and milk. The Adamson's had taken a cab to the airport and back home. The car that Liz usually drove was in the garage and Wilford's Porsche was parked behind it; Liz just hopped in and took off while Wilford was moving the suitcases and clothes bags into the house. Angela was really very sorry that Liz had gotten hurt – she sent her flowers and cards during the convalescence.

But that failure led to another plan. She, like many of the faculty, was not pleased about the extra work created by the Chief of Staff's After Action Report following every Code in the hospital. As she thought about that program it occurred to her that maybe she could take advantage of the AAR by involving Wilford.

According to Angela the plan was simple: arrange for Wilford to attend a Code and pass out while there. The ready availability of the Code Team would insure that Wilford's incident would not be fatal and yet serious enough for him to be sidelined for some time for evaluation. That's how she laid it out and planned it. She then checked the AAR schedule to highlight those days when Wilford was the responding faculty member and realized that she would have to take specific action to assure that a Code occurred and that he responded. To that end she developed a plan to watch the cardiac admissions for someone likely to develop a Code while hospitalized and to create a clinical situation where that Code would happen when Wilford had the AAR pager. Of course, she was in perfect position to do this since the admitting resident discussed all the cardiac admissions after hours with her.

The admission of Patricia Harding gave her the perfect chance as she saw it. First, Patricia's clinical course had already involved a Code. Second, Patricia had an underlying condition that would easily explain another Code. Third, that condition was one that she, Angela, could precipitate easily enough. The admitting resident had called her about Patricia and Angela had been able to convince the resident to put her on the ward rather than in the CCU. When she learned of Patricia's admission, Angela talked with the nurses who were there over the weekend and learned that Patricia's husband would not be around on Sunday night. She then ordered the veterinarian's glucose for a next-day delivery and slipped a bottle of insulin out of the medicine cabinet in the CCU.

Angela calculated how long it would take for the insulin to lower Patricia's potassium and cause the arrest and prepared the dose at home. She used the entrance of others into the ED to cover her arrival and used the little known back staircase from the ED to cross over to the hospital and enter Patricia's room from the end of the hallway away from the nurse's station.

The next morning she planned her discussion with Wilford so that the usual addition of a second jolt of coffee would not be suspicious and she added the nitro to his cup during that refill. She anticipated the effect would take place after he arrived at the Code.

"He was never supposed to die!" she said repeatedly during the interrogation. "I never meant for that to happen. I planned this so he would be at the Code and the Team would be right there to help him." Looney repeated this to Tom and Sandra who just shook their heads.

Looney told them that Angela was adamant that she did not intend to kill him – or Patricia, either. She explained that she told Wilford about the low potassium and how Patricia responded to intravenous potassium and magnesium during her discussion with Wilford about the weekend admissions. Looney said, "Angela said she definitely wanted him to know what to do when he walked into the Code on Patricia that morning. She was completely taken aback when he died on the stairs."

According to Looney, Angela said to him, "How was I supposed to know he was taking Cialis? I mean, come on, that's not a discussion we would ever have!"

Looney had asked her about the bottle of nitro in Dr. Adamson's desk. She admitted that she was in the crowd waiting to get coffee that Friday and overheard Monique tell Tom about the nitro that turned up on the toxicology test and she knew there would end up being a search for nitro he might have taken. So she slipped in to his office and put a bottle in his top drawer.

When the story was finished, the three of them sat quietly for a minute and then Tom said, "I guess the unfinished business here is deciding who is going to tell Dan Edderman the complete story. But it seems it was a series of decisive and introspective detective maneuvers that led to the apprehension of the killer – so you do it."

Looney immediately responded, "Oh, no. This was a medical mystery all the way and only you could unwrap it for Edderman in a way that reflects well on New City."

Sandra grabbed the empty glasses and started toward the kitchen saying, "You two could always decide this like adults – you know: Rock, Paper, Scissors."

The men looked at each other and immediately began hitting their closed fists into their other hand. And, as the swinging door into the kitchen swung behind Sandra, the last thing she heard was someone saying, "Damn . . . Let's make it two out of three."

ACKNOWLEDGEMENTS

I want to thank my wife and children for their encouragement during this writing process. Their feedback, support, and encouragement were positive factors in me finishing the original manuscript.

I also want to recognize Elle Murray for her faithful and frequent efforts to clean up the manuscript and to assist me in getting to the right place in decisions about format, artistry, and pagination.

Any errors that escaped these screening activities are mine alone.

Galen Barbour
Alexandria, Virginia
January 2023

Want more medical murder mystery?
Turn the page for an excerpt from the next book in the Ron Looney series

Ben Nealy is a third-year medicine resident at New City Hospital. He becomes involved in the treatment of a homeless man whom he suspects is the victim of attempted murder. Ben engages Tom Bolling, the chief of Staff who brings Ron Looney, homicide detective into the case to help establish the identity of the homeless man.

Looney throws the whole case into turmoil when he discovers he has no way to learn the homeless man's identity.

EXCERPT

The old man was clearly uncomfortable. He lay in the middle of a large bed in an even larger room, an intravenous line in his right arm. The high headboard behind him was carved in an ornate pattern that matched the richness of the room. There was a sitting area to one side of the bed and a fireplace on the other; rich heavy drapes fell beside the two windows that flanked the bed. The old man looked small in the bed and even smaller in the room.

He was having obvious trouble breathing; his breaths came quick and short and did not seem to move very much air. He clutched at the covers and coughed with a rattling sound; this movement stirred the nurse sitting beside the bed.

"Having trouble again?" she asked soothingly.

He nodded jerkily.

"Do you want me to call the doctor?"

Head shake.

"If you want I can put in the tube," as she said this she indicated the ventilator machine at the head of the bed. "Just like the doctor said, a little relaxation and you can get deep breaths again. I have all the medicines to do it right here."

"No. He promised me," the old man croaked at her.

"Yes. I know. But if you change your mind . . ."

"No damn . . . tubes. Morphine!"

"Of course. He left that for you, too." She turned to a small table nearby and opened the simple black case sitting there. She drew up some medication from a vial and slowly injected it into the intravenous line. As the medication took effect, the old man began to relax. His face sagged and he slumped back against his pillows. His breathing was no better but it no longer bothered him.

Later, as the waning afternoon sun sent its last rays through the windows, the doctor came into the room.

"I've given him the morphine several times. He's really running down." the nurse explained.

"Thank you, Elana. I'll stay for a while."

The next time the old man woke he had a spasm of coughing that caused a bubbling in his throat and panic in his eyes. The doctor stepped up to the side of the bed with morphine ready.

"No . . .tube . . ." came a faint plea.

"I know, friend. I promised. I'll help you be comfortable." As he was saying this the doctor injected the morphine. And a little later the shallow breathing became irregular and then stopped. The doctor felt for a pulse, listened to the absent heart beat and said, "I'll go notify the family."

The nurse turned to the job of cleaning up the body and said, "I haven't seen them today."

www.ingramcontent.com/pod-product-compliance
Lightning Source LLC
Chambersburg PA
CBHW070640310726
48982CB00001B/357

* 9 7 9 8 8 9 3 5 6 5 1 3 3 *